Julia
Evans
11-12-12

# A BANNER IS UNFURLED

## NO GREATER LOVE

### 5

OTHER BOOKS AND AUDIO BOOKS
BY MARCIE GALLACHER AND
KERRI ROBINSON

A BANNER IS UNFURLED SERIES:

*A Banner Is Unfurled: Volume 1*

*Be Still My Soul: Volume 2*

*Glory from on High: Volume 3*

*Abide with Me: Volume 4*

## NO GREATER LOVE

### 5

# MARCIE GALLACHER
# KERRI ROBINSON

Covenant Communications, Inc.

Cover background image: *Nauvoo the Beautiful* © Al Rounds for more information, visit www.alrounds.com; model reference photo by McKenzie Deakins. For photographer information, visit www.photography-bymckenzie.com.

Cover design copyright © 2012 by Covenant Communications, Inc.

Published by Covenant Communications, Inc.
American Fork, Utah

Copyright © 2012 by Marcie Gallacher and Kerri Robinson
All rights reserved. No part of this book may be reproduced in any format or in any medium without the written permission of the publisher, Covenant Communications, Inc., P.O. Box 416, American Fork, UT 84003. This work is not an official publication of The Church of Jesus Christ of Latter-day Saints. The views expressed within this work are the sole responsibility of the author and do not necessarily reflect the position of The Church of Jesus Christ of Latter-day Saints, Covenant Communications, Inc., or any other entity.

This is a work of fiction. The characters, names, incidents, places, and dialogue are either products of the author's imagination, and are not to be construed as real, or are used fictitiously.

Printed in the United States of America
First Printing: September 2012

18 17 16 15 14 13 12    10 9 8 7 6 5 4 3 2 1

ISBN 978-1-62108-194-4

In memory of Ezekiel Johnson, our third great-grandfather, whose legacy is one of struggle, honor, and sacrifice.

We would also like to dedicate this last volume to all who have personally shared in the story of Julia and Ezekiel Johnson. We have journeyed together.

# EZEKIEL AND JULIA JOHNSON FAMILY
## November 1838

Joel Hills [b. 1802] [m. Annie Pixley Johnson, 1826]
    Julianne [b. 1827–d. 1829]
    Sixtus [b. 1829]
    Sariah [b. 1832]
    Nephi [b. 1833]
    Susan Ellen [b. 1836]
Nancy Maria [b. 1803–d. 1836]
Seth Guernsey [b. 1805–d. 1835]
Delcena Diadamia [b. 1806] [m. Lyman Sherman, 1829]
    Alvira [b. 1830]
    Baby son [b. 1830-d. before 1831]
    Mary [b. 1831]
    Albey [b. 1832]
    Seth [b. 1836]
    Daniel [b. 1837]
    Susan Maria [b. 1838]
Julia Ann (Julianne) [b. 1808] [m. Almon Whiting Babbitt, 1834]
    David Homer [b. 1835–d. 1836]
David [b. 1810–d. 1833]
Almera Woodward [b. 1812 ] [m. Samuel Prescott, 1836]
Susan Ellen [b. 1814–d. 1836]
Joseph Ellis [b. 1817]
Benjamin Franklin [b. 1818]
Mary Ellen [b. 1820]
Elmer Wood [b. 1822–d. 1823]
George Washington [b. 1823]
William Derby [b. 1824]
Esther Melita [ b. 1827]
Amos Partridge [b. 1829]
Mary Ann Hale [b. 1827, adopted 1838]

# ACKNOWLEDGMENTS

As we finish this final volume, we express overwhelming appreciation to all who have encouraged and supported us. We can't even begin to name you.

However, we do need to thank our husbands, children, and parents, who have walked the past eight years with us as the idea for this series was conceived, developed, and completed. Thank you for reading, listening, and sharing your thoughts and ideas. Thank you for exploring New York, Ohio, and Illinois with us—trekking through fields, graveyards, and jails. Thank you for allowing us to share our passion for this project and for giving us feedback.

We are also grateful to the talented staff at Covenant Communications who made this dream a reality.

And, finally, thank you to our readers, who have buoyed us up time and time again.

# 1

*With thee, his Seer, I've found at last . . .*
*My lot and all with thee I cast, . . .*
*Thy holy cause I will defend, . . .*
*Shall be my own, till life shall end, . . .*

Joel Hills Johnson

*Early November 1838. Kirtland, Ohio*

THE AFTERNOON SUN SHONE BRIGHT, and the wind blew briskly. Ezekiel halted the wagon at a small house on the grounds of the Kirtland Temple. Drawing in a deep breath, he stared at the temple's gleaming walls, its reddish roof, and the carved wooden door. He climbed out of the wagon seat. The images of those he loved flooded his mind: Joel cutting shingles; David laboring in a brickyard; Seth hefting rock from a quarry; Nancy holding Ezekiel's hand, leading him to the entryway; and Susan reaching her arms out to him, her black eyes full of softness. And finally Julia, his beautiful Julia, hanging the curtains that stretched from ceiling to floor, like the veil of a bride.

"Father Johnson."

Ezekiel turned at the sound of the voice. Rebecca Winters stepped out of the groundkeeper's house. Strands of hair blew from the knot at the base of her neck as she walked over and peered into the wagon bed. "The table is lovely! Is this Sister Holman's cradle?"

Ezekiel nodded. "'Tis. I'm obliged to you for the Holmans' business."

Rebecca smiled brightly. "You're most welcome. Hiram's at the temple fixing some things. He'll be back shortly to heft the table."

"I'll bring it in," Ezekiel offered.

With a grunt, he lifted the round table out of the wagon. He might be old, but carpentry kept him strong. Muscles straining, he walked to the doorway and tilted the table through, as keenly aware of its dimensions as a mother is of the fingers and toes of her newborn.

After placing it in the kitchen, he turned to Rebecca. "So you and Hiram are caretakers of the temple. That was a surprise."

Rebecca nodded cheerfully. "The apostates' hearts have softened. They're even allowing us to hold our worship services in the temple!"

An involuntary light flickered in Ezekiel's mind. He spoke without thinking. "Will the rest come back?"

Rebecca's smile lessened. "I don't think so. The apostates are outwardly friendly, but they gloat about the tragedy in Missouri. No one knows where the next gathering place will be, but it won't be here—no matter how much we wish it."

Ezekiel's features hardened despite the look of empathy in Rebecca's eyes. False hopes tormented him. Facts were that his family was gone—all except for Almera, who lived nearby. Julia, his younger children, and his eldest son, Joel, were living temporarily in Springfield, Illinois. At least they were safe. But the others—Delcena, Julianne, and Benjamin—were in Missouri, smack dab in the middle of the Mormon war. Were his daughters and grandchildren all right? Were his son and sons-in-law imprisoned? Did they live? Only one thing was certain—no matter what happened, Julia would not leave her religion and return to him. She would go wherever the imprisoned Joseph Smith directed.

Ezekiel took the money Rebecca handed him, thanked her, and left the house. With the wind at his back, he drove on to the Holmans, another Latter-day Saint family. He thought it strange, the amount of business he received from the Mormons who lingered in Kirtland. He arrived at the large frame house, the white paint bright in the sunlight. Ezekiel carried the cradle to the doorstep and shined the black lacquer finish with the edge of his coat. He had taken pride in this order. It was fine work, smooth as glass.

Ezekiel knocked on the door. Naomi Holman answered it. She was short, small-featured, and round with child. Her furrowed brow created a deep crease between her eyes. "Come in, Mr. Johnson, before we all catch cold."

She examined the cradle, running her hand over the smooth edges.

"Does it please you?" Ezekiel questioned.

She looked up at him, her brow still creased. "Yes."

Ezekiel wondered if she was telling the truth. Yet he didn't blame her for looking worried. Her husband, James, had left months ago to buy land in Missouri and had not yet returned. She had two young children and a baby on the way, as well as three orphaned siblings under her care—a heavy load. He cleared his throat. "Where would you like me to put it?"

"The parlor would be fine."

Ezekiel followed Naomi into the parlor, where a stately young woman with light brown hair piled high on her head was reading with a group of five younger girls. The young woman instructed the others to continue then stood and joined Naomi and Ezekiel.

After Ezekiel set the cradle down, Naomi addressed him. "Mr. Johnson, this is my sister, Melissa LeBaron."

"Miss LeBaron." Ezekiel bowed slightly to the young woman. She seemed familiar. Her skin was smooth and the color of cream—much like his Delcena's. When she spoke, her voice, level as a planed board, was very formal. At times, Almera talked that way.

He focused on her words. "Mr. Johnson, I've been wanting to speak with you. The Kirtland Academy will soon offer classes for girls. We would like Sister Almera to be one of the teachers. The academy meets in the schoolhouse in Kirtland. We begin Monday morning at nine o'clock."

A job for Almera. Women to work with and girls to teach. This would be manna to his daughter. With little happiness in her marriage, she was even more alone than Ezekiel. He nodded at Miss LeBaron. "I reckon she'll be delighted. I'll give her the message."

Naomi interrupted, speaking directly to her sister. "Melissa, you know Almera's husband does not allow her to associate with Mormons."

Melissa's lips pursed. Though the younger sister, she clearly had a mind of her own. "Mr. Johnson said she would be delighted. Shouldn't Sister Almera be allowed to do what she wants?"

Naomi continued. "We don't want trouble. Mr. Prescott is her husband."

Ezekiel's jaw hardened, and his voice was louder than he'd intended. "And I am her father. Miss LeBaron, I will bring Almera on Monday morning."

A grin lit Melissa's features. Her willful spunkiness reminded Ezekiel of his little Esther. Would he see all of his girls in this young lady?

Ezekiel bid the women good day and turned to leave. Melissa called after him, "Thank you, Mr. Johnson. I'm anxious to see Sister Almera."

Ezekiel turned back around. "What time is your meeting in the temple on Sunday?"

"Ten o'clock," Melissa returned.

"I'll bring Almera there too."

"God willing," Melissa said with a bright smile.

"God willing," Ezekiel repeated as he left. He climbed onto the wagon seat and lifted the reins. Energetic from the wind, the horses trotted on the way home. Ezekiel drew in a sharp breath. *God willing!* He scarcely believed in God. What was wrong with him—offering to take Almera to the meeting? There was a day when he had wanted to separate Julia from Mormons as much as Sam was trying to isolate Almera now.

But Almera tugged at his heart. She was his child. Last week when Sam was out of town, she had spent a night with him. He had come home from the tavern late, but she'd still been up, praying out loud in the bedroom. She had prayed for her family's safety. She had prayed for her father's health and happiness. Then she had prayed that she might someday be free to worship as she chose.

Ezekiel passed the temple and headed on to Mentor, the wind full in his face. He had not forgotten the day Joseph Smith had taken him through that temple, had told him of a vision of heaven, had promised him that Seth and David still lived. Joseph had almost convinced him to hope that day. Then Joseph's God took Susan and Nancy.

His heart pumped with bitter determination. What good was Joseph's God—a God who snatched away sons and daughters, a God who allowed women and children to suffer, a God who gave him Julia then took her away? He had no illusions! He was born an illegitimate child who had grown into a flawed, intemperate man. But one gem was still within his reach. Almera. He still had the will and muscle to help her. He turned the wagon onto his property.

If there was a God, then He wasn't much of a father. A father . . . a father ought to answer His child's prayer. On Sunday, Ezekiel would bring his precious Almera to the temple that haunted him. He would answer his daughter's prayer.

\* \* \*

*Richmond, Missouri*

Lyman Sherman halted and watched his traveling companion, John Babbitt, swing down from the sorrel gelding. At early candlelight, the tavern windows glowed. The wind was stiff and chill. After tying his horse, John whistled cheerfully as the two approached the door. Doffing his hat at a slave girl who was scraping ice off the porch, John took a penny out of his coat pocket and handed it to her. "I'm looking for my brother Almon."

The girl pocketed the penny. "What's your name?"

"Johnny Babbitt."

The girl nodded. "Go through the dining hall then up the stairs. Second room on the left." The girl turned to go as snow began to flurry.

As Lyman and John entered the tavern, a wave of warm, smoky air greeted them. An enormous fire blazed in the hearth, and they smelled beef stew, tobacco, and brandy. John glanced hungrily at the stew, but Lyman's stomach knotted. Over fifty soldiers sat at long tables with muskets propped next to them. Lyman had seen enough of the Missouri militia to last a lifetime. Recognizing General Clark at the head of a table, Lyman swallowed hard. Clark had told the men of Far West that they would never see their leaders again. Clark had the Prophet under his thumb and wanted him dead.

Lyman moved quickly through the dining hall. At the staircase, he took the steps three at a time. He knocked on the second door on the left while John, whistling again, sauntered up the steps.

Almon opened the door, pale in the candlelight. "Lyman, why are you here? I thought you might have been arrested. Where's Julianne?"

"She's fine. With my family."

Almon lowered his voice. "A Missourian's walking this way. Let's get inside."

"The Missourian is your brother."

John waved. "Hello, Manny!"

"Johnny!" Almon lurched forward and wrapped his arms around his brother. After the embrace, he looked carefully at John. "You haven't changed a whit. You got my letter! You came!"

John nodded and grinned. "Your wife's as pretty as you described."

Almon pulled both men into the room and closed the door behind them. His eyes glinted with new life as he turned to Lyman. "What happened in Far West after I left?"

Lyman took a deep breath, remembering the horror of the army-mob moving through the city. "Lucas herded the men into the square and kept us under guard while he sent the mob in. We couldn't protect our families. Terrible things happened, unthinkable things. But God shielded Delcena, Julianne, and my children. Now it is my duty to protect His Prophet. That's why I'm here."

Almon's green eyes suddenly became moist. "Thank God they are all right. But my friend, I fear that no one can protect Joseph right now. But you and I, we will try."

"With God, anything is possible. Do you know where he is?"

Almon nodded. "In a log cabin near the courthouse, with Hyrum and the others who were also arrested that night. Clark put a mean fellow named Colonel Price in charge. The windows are nailed down, and our men are chained to each other by the ankle. I counted sixteen guards, most with their finger on the trigger. About fifty other brethren are jailed close by in a half-finished brick courthouse. There're no doors or windows. They're freezing. Over a hundred guards are stationed inside and around the building. I guess I'd be a prisoner too if I had stayed in Far West."

Lyman shook his head. "Your name wasn't on Clark's list. The names on the list—they didn't make any sense. Most of the men weren't anywhere near Crooked River."

Almon's voice was low, incredulous. "Who gave them those names? Why?"

"I don't know."

John interrupted. "We have plenty to discuss, but first let's go downstairs and get supper. I'm starved."

\* \* \*

The three sat at an empty table on the periphery of the room. The slave girl brought them bowls of beef stew. John requested brandy. Almon and Lyman ate quickly, feeling the warmth of the meal move through them.

Suddenly General Clark stood, his voice rising over the tavern buzz. "Gentlemen," Clark pointed to the group of twelve men sitting with him, "these soldiers will have the privilege of shooting Joe Smith at eight o'clock Monday morning, after we court-martial him for mutiny. Make sure your rifles are handy."

The chosen men hurrahed then examined their guns. They loaded two balls apiece, bragging about how they would save those balls for old Joe until Monday morning . . . after they had rested and worshipped on the Lord's Sabbath. Almon's heart pounded. He felt Lyman tighten like a spring-loaded gun.

"General, sir, I have information." A young man stood up on the other side of the room. Almon's eyes widened in recognition. Why hadn't he noticed him before? It was Jedediah Grant, a member of the Church and the brother-in-law of William Smith. What was he up to? Jedediah continued. "I've heard that General Lucas tried to pursue a similar course at Far West. General Doniphan refused to carry out the orders, saying they were illegal, and if carried out by others, he would hold General Lucas accountable before the law. Sir, perhaps you should reconsider for your own protection."

General Clark stared momentarily at Jedediah. He then turned to a soldier sitting near him. "Stevens, ride to Fort Leavenworth and find out the military law. Come back as quickly as you can so we can put Smith to rest."

\* \* \*

Back in Almon's room, John was the first to speak. "The general at Leavenworth is a fair man. He won't give Clark permission to shoot them."

Lyman's fists clenched, every muscle taut and ready. Almon sat down on a chair, tapping his foot.

"We can't depend on that," Lyman exclaimed. "I won't stand by and see them shot."

Almon stood up. "The law is on our side. Governor Boggs did not declare martial law. Thus, this is a matter for civil, not military, courts. Joseph cannot legally be tried for mutiny in a military court. Legally, he can't be shot."

"Boggs' code of law allows women and children to be exterminated!" Lyman snapped.

Almon kept talking. "Alexander Doniphan is in Liberty. We need to make sure he knows what Clark is planning."

Lyman let out a breath of air. "You and Johnny go. I'll stay here to try to protect Joseph."

\* \* \*

*Monday, November 12, 1838*

In the wee hours of the morning, when the wind abated and a few stars shone through the clouds, John found Lyman wrapped in a blanket with his back against the log prison. John squatted beside him, put a hand on Lyman's shoulder, and whispered stringently, "Go back to the tavern. No one's coming to shoot your Prophet this morning. Almon will explain. I'll stay here and pretend I'm a guard."

Lyman nodded and stood, too numb to speak. Yet he forced his limbs to move, and crouching, he made his way to the line of trees. When he was well past the courthouse, he ran, stretching his frozen limbs, the blanket flapping against his back and the stars lighting a path through the darkness around him.

When Lyman entered the tavern room, a candle burned at the desk where Almon sat and a fire glowed in the hearth. Almon gave Lyman a long look. "Where were you last night?"

"Outside the jail. What's the news?"

"There won't be a military court. Word came from Fort Leavenworth that shooting the Mormon prisoners would be murder."

Lyman took a deep breath. "Did you see Doniphan?"

Almon nodded. "Yes. He's on his way. The Civil Court of Inquiry will open later this morning."

"Is there a chance that Joseph will be released?"

Almon shook his head. "No. Not with Austin King as judge."

"What are the charges?"

"No surprises. Treason, murder, arson, burglary, larceny. But this is only a court of inquiry to determine if there is sufficient evidence to bring the men to trial in the spring."

"There is not sufficient evidence."

"Evidence will be invented. I spoke with Sampson Avard. He's been told that if he swears hard against the heads of the Church, he will not be arrested. He intends to do it to save himself."

"The snake." Lyman's voice was bitter.

"I could not convince him not to strike," Almon said. There were dark circles under his eyes, the product of nearly two sleepless nights. "One more thing before I fall over. Doniphan wrote a note asking Colonel Price to allow me to visit the prisoners and carry letters to their families. Let's sleep for a couple of hours. Then we'll go see Joseph."

The men knelt in prayer, and Lyman pled with God to protect their Prophet and brethren. Afterward, Almon fell asleep immediately. Lyman lay awake. Would tomorrow be the last time he saw Joseph in this life? Tears pricked his eyes. Then a deeper knowledge filled him. God was at the helm. Whatever happened, it would be all right. Lyman closed his eyes.

\* \* \*

Two hours later, Lyman and Almon walked out of the tavern, combed and shaved. The sun shone, and the streets buzzed with life. People streamed into Richmond on horseback and on foot.

"You would think today was a circus, not the opening of a trial," Lyman commented under his breath.

"Joseph is a curiosity, a notorious man," Almon responded. The two men strode quickly toward the log prison, their shoulders squared. Almon carried a satchel filled with paper, ink, and quills. When they arrived, they found John drinking rum with Colonel Price and another guard.

Almon stepped up and spoke confidently. "Colonel, I have an order from General Doniphan permitting me to visit the prisoners and carry letters to their families."

Price cocked his head. "Doniphan's words hold weight, but how do I know you are telling the truth? Are you boys Mormon?"

"Yes, sir," Lyman said.

The other guard chuckled derisively and clapped John on the back, saying, "I haven't killed *my* Mormon yet. Have you killed *yours*?"

John grinned at the guard as he shouldered his musket. "Nope. And both these fellows are *my* Mormons. I'd be happy to kill any man who tries to kill them."

The guard stared at John, trying to absorb what he had said. Then John turned to Price. "Colonel, may I introduce to you to Mr. Almon Babbitt and Mr. Lyman Sherman. Though I don't agree with his religion, Mr. Babbitt is my brother. Yesterday, he and I were in Liberty discussing this situation with General Doniphan."

Price took Doniphan's note from Almon's hand and quickly read it. He ordered Almon to open his satchel for examination. Almon obeyed. Then Price nodded curtly. "Go in. Tell the prisoners I will examine the letters before you take them."

Lyman followed Almon into the log prison, blinking as his eyes adjusted to the dimness. His brethren sat on the floor in chains. Lyman passed out the paper, ink, and quills, while Almon spoke quickly, giving the men all the information he had, explaining that the civil court would open that day, and promising that he would carry the letters to their families.

When Almon finished speaking, Lyman squatted down next to Joseph. "My friend," Lyman whispered, "though you may not see me, know that I am close by. With God's help, I will stand between you and harms way."

Joseph clasped Lyman's hand. "Thank you, my dear friend. When you see Emma, tell her to be of good cheer." Lyman nodded. The tears in Joseph's blue eyes shone like a torch that even the depths of hell could not extinguish.

Almon and Lyman were told to wait outside while the prisoners wrote their letters. Joseph quickly instructed Almon, "When you can, go to Kirtland as my agent. Try to legally regain the Church's properties. Oversee the Saints who remain there. They are in my thoughts."

"I will."

A few minutes later, in the cold winter sunlight, Colonel Price inspected the prisoner's letters. He searched for treason in the letter Joseph Smith had written to his wife.

> *My Dear Emma,*
>
> *We are prisoners and in chains and under strong guards for Christ's sake. I have this consolation that I am an innocent man, let what will befall me. Oh, God, grant that I may have the privilege of seeing once more my lovely family. To press them to my bosom and kiss their lovely cheeks would fill my heart with unspeakable gratitude. Tell the children that I am alive and trust I shall come and see them before long. Comfort their hearts all you can, and try to be comforted yourself, all you can. There is no possible danger but what we shall be set at liberty if justice can be done. Tell little Joseph, he must be a good boy, Father loves him with a perfect love. He is the eldest and must not hurt those that are smaller than him but comfort them. Tell little Frederick that Father loves him with all his heart. Julia is a lovely little girl; I love her also. She is a promising child. Tell her Father wants her to remember him and be a good girl. Tell all the rest that I think of them and pray for them all. Brother Babbitt is waiting to carry our letters for us. Colonel Price is inspecting them therefore my time is short. Little Alexander is on my mind continually. Oh, my affectionate Emma, forever my heart is entwined around yours, forever and ever. Oh may God bless you all. I am your husband and am in bonds and tribulation.*
>
> *Joseph Smith Jr*

Colonel Price folded the letter and handed it to Almon.

\* \* \*

Back in the tavern, Almon and John waited long enough for Lyman to write a quick note to his family explaining that he was staying in Richmond until the trial was over. Then they mounted their horses and rode toward Far West. Almon planned to deliver the letters and then go home to Julianne.

When they arrived at Far West, it was the silence that shook Almon, the emptiness of the streets, the lack of horses neighing and cows mooing—a silence filled with pain and shadows, an inhabited city already forsaken. The few people on the streets were wrapped tightly in whatever they had for warmth and went about their business. One man wore only a woman's shawl to protect him; a child with fear in his eyes clutched his mother's hand.

Almon went first to the Prophet's house. Emma wept when he handed her the letter from Joseph. The Prophet's children clamored around. While Emma read, Almon lifted the children in his arms one by one, hugging and kissing them, explaining that the hugs and kisses were not really from Brother Babbitt but from their father.

Next, he delivered the letter to Mary, Hyrum's wife, who had just given birth to a baby boy. "His name is Joseph," Mary explained. "Joseph Fielding Smith." Almon held the infant while Mary read the letter from her husband. She too wept, and Almon felt tears come to his eyes. He was glad Johnny was waiting outside and did not see him crying. Almon had buried his own baby son. He wondered if this little Joseph Fielding would live through the winter.

After they left Mary's house and continued down the skeletal streets of Far West under a bleak sky, John turned to him. "You sure you want to be a Mormon? For the life of me, I don't understand it. You are smart. You could be anything."

Almon did not answer immediately. He was thinking of the Danites, of the mistakes made in Adam-ondi-Ahman. At times, even Joseph had listened to the vigilantes. If the leading brethren had made other choices, would things have been different?

"You sure you want this?" John repeated, louder this time.

Almon's thoughts flew for a moment then settled upon one image. How could he explain it to Johnny? How could he describe the feel of Julianne laughing in his arms and the sound of her singing? Years ago, when her brother David lay dying, she had asked with tears in her eyes, "Will you be there in the winter as well? I can't marry a man who is with me only in the summer season." He had promised her. And where else was there for them to go? This was the gospel of Jesus Christ. "I'm sure, Johnny," he said quietly.

"Babbitt!"

Almon and John turned abruptly at the sound of their name. A horseman galloped up then wheeled his mount to a stop. It was young Erastus Snow.

He spoke to Almon. "The mobber Bogart and his men just arrived from Richmond. They're getting witnesses for the court. They have a list of names and aim to force men to testify against the Prophet. They mean to lock up or whip any man who declares he'll stand up for Joseph. They are on the way to your house. May be there already. You need to get out of Far West now."

"I have more letters to deliver. Then I'm going to see my wife."

Erastus shook his head. "Didn't you hear what I said? They are hunting you!"

Almon's jaw was set, his green eyes defiant. "You said they are going to my house? My wife is there."

"They haven't harmed any women or children. They aren't after her; they're after you."

"Manny, you're out of money and out of luck," John said sternly. "It's time to run." Almon looked away. John continued, speaking to Erastus. "Tell Mrs. Babbitt that her husband is with his brother, Johnny. We'll be laying low for a spell then going to Fort Leavenworth, where there's work. As soon as it's safe, we'll come for her."

Almon handed Erastus the letters. He looked into his eyes. "Tell my wife to hold on. Tell her that Zion is not lost, that Zion is wherever she is."

*O how my heart yearns for a mother's caresses,*
*As when in childhood by sickness laid low,*
*When she swept my wan face with her dark silver tresses,*
*And printed a kiss on my feverish brow.*

George Washington Johnson

*November 18, 1838. Springfield, Illinois*

JULIA JOHNSON PUT DOWN THE stockings she was darning and stretched her stiff, pained fingers. She breathed deeply. Through God's mercy, she and her children had survived the fever. Convalescence heightened her senses—the soothing smell of the fire, the hum of the flames, and the rhythmic sound of her daughter, eighteen-year-old Mary, grinding corn into meal.

During the months of fever, her faith, like the hearth fire, had flickered and surged. For a time, it had seemed that she would not live. She had not been afraid to die, to join her children and parents beyond the veil. Yet, at the same time, her devotion to her living children had kept her struggling for life. Then, as she had improved, her son George had worsened. When his fever had finally broken, when his long bangs had been drenched with cooling sweat, she had known that her prayers had been answered.

Julia swallowed, wondering if George had been spared to strengthen her for news to come. She did not know the fate of her loved ones in Missouri—Delcena and her family; Julianne and Almon; and her twenty-year-old Benjamin, who had longed to be at the Prophet's side. But now the Prophet was in chains. Tears filled Julia's eyes. She breathed deeply.

Her faith was deep, and she willed her heart to trust in God, leaving her beloved children and Prophet to His keeping. Even in tribulation, her life was blessed. Her eldest, Joel, lived close by with his wife, Annie, and their children. Her twenty-one-year-old Joe sustained the family by teaching at a local school of sixty pupils. Her youngest two, Esther and Amos, and Mary Ann Hale, an orphan in her care, were at school today. George had gone too, feeling well enough to help Joe by tutoring the younger pupils.

But fourteen-year-old Will had not gone. He had laughed this morning and grinned at her with a glint in his eye when he announced he wasn't going to school anymore but would find work instead. Then he had combed his thick, wavy hair and said that he aimed to ask the rich widow who donated books to Joe's school for work. He'd bring home meat for supper—that might put some muscle back on George's bones. George, so thin from the fever, had looked at Will grimly. "You ought to go to school," he had muttered, looking so much older than fifteen, so much like Ezekiel.

"Mother, I thought I heard something." Mary's voice interrupted Julia's stream of thought. Setting down the pestle, Mary walked over to Julia. Mary's lips were pale and chapped; a single, long blonde braid snaked down her back. Julia sighed. Mary ought to have beaus and friends, rosy cheeks, and a light step.

There was a knock at the door. Julia stood to open it, and Mary joined her. On the doorstep, they found a young woman in a black, well-tailored dress and a wool cloak. Her gloves and hat were of fine silk. Her face vividly contrasted with the black of her outfit, shining white as the full moon, as flawless as china.

The woman held out a package wrapped in coarse butcher paper. "Mrs. Johnson, I'm Mrs. Forquer. I'm acquainted with your son, Joseph, the schoolmaster. Today, your William is chopping wood for me. In payment, here's pork for your supper."

Julia smiled and took the package. "Thank you, Mrs. Forquer."

"You're welcome."

Julia studied her for a moment. Joe had told her of Mrs. Forquer's wealth. Her deceased husband had been the secretary of state. She had a little boy.

Suddenly, Mary gasped. Julia glanced at her daughter and saw that Mary was looking down the road. A man in tattered clothing walked toward them. Julia recognized George Wilson, the thirty-year-old son of

Deliverance and Lovina. Like Benjamin, he had gone on to Missouri. He was back with news.

Struggling to maintain her composure, Julia looked back at Mrs. Forquer. She reached out and briefly touched the young widow's gloved hand. "Thank you again."

"My pleasure." The lady curtsied, and after glancing at the tramp-like man approaching, she walked slowly to her carriage.

"Sister Johnson, Miss Johnson." George Wilson took off his hat and shook Julia's hand first then Mary's. He had no gloves on, and his hand was cold and callused.

\* \* \*

A gust of wind blew into the house. Mary felt like a slender tree in a storm as her hand trembled in Mr. Wilson's. His face was rectangular, his square jaw solemn, and his eyes the color of honey, so much like her brother David's.

Letting go of Mary's hand, Mr. Wilson turned to Julia. "Could we sit down and talk near the fire?"

Julia nodded. "How are your parents?" Julia asked as they approached the benches flanking the hearth. Mary could not fathom how her mother could think of another family at a time like this.

Mr. Wilson sighed. "My mother is well, but my father is gravely ill."

"I'm sorry," Julia said, her voice quavering. "We too have battled the fever."

Mary interrupted with a whisper. "My brother and sisters. Do they live?"

"I pray so," George Wilson said, his voice direct and calm. "Dear ladies, the news I bring is dire but not without hope."

Mary listened as he told them that Delcena and Julianne were all right. Their husbands were alive and their children unharmed. However, Benjamin was a lone prisoner in Adam-ondi-Ahman. Mary's jaw shook. She tried but failed to stop herself from losing control. Her chest convulsed in dry, soundless sobs.

"Mary, darling," Julia implored as she put her arm around Mary's shoulders. "They are alive. We can, we must be strong."

"But Ben." Tears blurred Mary's vision. Benjamin—who she competed with, fought with, and teased—her brother, so annoying and so beloved. Had they tortured him? Was he freezing, surrounded by angry Missourians with guns aimed at his heart?

"That was eight days ago," George Wilson added. "Surely the general has come to realize that he is a boy, not a leader. Perhaps now he is safe and on his way to you."

Strange moans came from the depths of Mary's soul. She doubled over, shaking uncontrollably.

"Mary, child. Please."

She heard her mother's fragile voice as through a haze. Then strong hands rested on Mary's shoulders, gently lifting her and turning her to face him, willing her to stop shaking, to look and listen. But his eyes, his honey-colored eyes, yet again reminded her of David's.

"Miss Johnson, your brother needs your faith and prayers, not despair. When I was in the last stages of consumption, I joined the Church. Doctors said I would not live to be thirty, but I speedily recovered my health. Have faith—I promise you that it begets miracles."

His words struck her. How she had prayed for her brothers and sisters to live. But David was gone. And Seth had died five days after his thirtieth birthday. Then Susan and Nancy. No wonder her father doubted God's existence. Did God draw cards like a gambler? This one will live. This one will die.

"Have courage, Miss Johnson. For your mother's sake and your own."

Mary covered her face. She could not bear to think of her mother's pain. She could not bear the fact that Ben was a prisoner, if he was still alive. She turned and ran from the sitting room, the door slamming behind her. She crumbled onto the straw tick mattress.

*　*　*

As George Wilson headed for his parent's cabin, he couldn't stop thinking about Mary Johnson. Months ago, when traveling with the Kirtland camp, he had noticed her. She had been tall and slender, graceful and spry, despite poverty and hardship. She had seemed strong and willing, nursing the sick and helping with the children.

Yet when she had run from the room just now, she had seemed young and volatile, a weak woman who hadn't the faith in God to bear her up. Then Sister Johnson had explained that four of Mary's older siblings had died from consumption in Kirtland between 1833 and 1836. She had said that it was not like Mary to break down, but a limb can only bear so much weight.

How strange that he had come to Kirtland in the fall of 1836, in the final stages of the same disease, with nothing but death to look forward to. Then Joseph Smith had given him a Book of Mormon and told him to read it; and if he were not satisfied, to read it again. With his clothes draping from his emaciated frame and little hope of life, he had read the book and been baptized. Then God's grace changed his world. He had found new life. He had been healed.

Today he had hoped that this story would give Mary faith. But instead it had been salt in her wounds, vinegar when she had needed water. George Wilson hoped that somehow, someday, he could make it up to her. For now, he would pray for her brother Benjamin and find out what had become of him.

\* \* \*

*Saturday, November 17, 1838. Mentor, Ohio*

Almera sat reading by the fire. Her black-and-white cat lay nestled at her feet. The wind shook the house so violently that the flame wavered in the hearth. Closing the Bible, Almera stood up and placed a log on the fire. The cat followed her, looking up at her with an arched back and mewing.

"Oh, Coattails, it's just the wind," she crooned, picking him up and holding him close. His purring warmed her, and she felt thankful for his company. Many times, Sam didn't come home until morning. Sometimes he was drunk. But the evenings with him were worse, with silence welling up between them until he began shouting or demanding intimacy.

She sat back down, and the cat jumped from her lap. The clock on the mantel told her that it was past ten at night. She ought to go to bed, but she did not feel tired. She thought about the past few weeks, of the thrill of teaching the girls at the academy. When her father had told her and Sam of the position, she had been certain Sam would forbid it, but he had not; instead, he had listened silently before leaving the room.

Since then, life had been bearable, even though Sam demanded that she give him her earnings. She handed them over willingly, a small price to pay for her days of freedom. She knew that with most of the Mormons gone, Sam's business was failing. How he ranted against those who followed the Prophet! She prayed that Sam would never find out that when her father picked her up on Sundays they no longer went for a ride in the countryside. He took her to the temple, never coming in, just waiting in the wagon until she finished worshipping and rejoicing with the Saints.

A knock at the door interrupted the sound of the wind. "Who's there?" Almera called out.

"David LeBaron. Melissa's brother."

Almera opened the door. The sixteen-year-old's words tumbled out. "Naomi's in labor. Can you come? Melissa doesn't know what to do."

"What about Sister Winters or Sister Burdick?"

"Their children are sick with colds. Naomi won't have them. Please, Sister Almera!"

"Of course." As she wrapped her cloak around her shoulders, Almera thought about writing Sam a note. But if she told him where she was, it would anger him. She prayed that she would get home before he did.

\* \* \*

Naomi's body fell limp following the contraction. Melissa blinked back tears, frustrated because she did not know what to do. She was eighteen years old. She had been given much privilege and opportunity. She ought to know how to deliver a child. But she had been busy with the academy, busy reading, studying, and writing lesson plans.

Sweat poured from Naomi. Melissa bathed her head with a cool rag. Naomi gasped. Melissa could tell she was trying not to scream.

Was Naomi remembering Melissa's reaction when little Harriet was born four years ago? When Naomi had screamed, Melissa had run out of the room sobbing, terrified that Naomi would die. Their mother had died when Melissa was very young, and their father nine years ago. The four LeBaron children had been alone in the world until Naomi had married James Holman. Then James learned of Mormonism, and they were all converted to the new faith. With that blessing, they would never be alone again.

Another contraction gripped Naomi, and she gasped with the urge to push. The baby was coming. Then there were footsteps in the room, and Almera was beside Melissa. Naomi screamed.

"Tell me what to do," Melissa begged.

"Guide the head," Almera said calmly.

Naomi screamed again. Melissa listened to Almera's directions. With Almera's sweet voice instructing, Melissa's hands only trembled slightly as she helped her sister's baby into the world.

\*\*\*

At six the following morning, Almera's work was finished. Naomi had delivered a bonny baby girl: average weight, a bit short from head to toe but filled out for a newborn, with a shock of black hair and a lusty cry. Melissa placed her in Naomi's arms.

"What will you call her?" Almera asked.

"Sarah Melissa. Sarah after Abraham's wife, and Melissa after my sister. Sarah Melissa Holman. Little Lizzy."

Melissa straightened the bedcovers and said with joy in her eyes, "Little Lizzy, oh so pretty, keeping Auntie in a tizzy!"

Almera smiled, thinking about how Melissa, who was usually impeccably groomed, looked as if she'd been through a whirlwind.

A tear ran down Naomi's cheek. "I only wish James were here, safe with us."

"He'll come home from Missouri soon," Melissa assured. "I know it."

Almera glanced at Melissa. How could she know? Was this confidence born of faith and the Holy Spirit? Or was it wishful thinking? "Rest now," she said to Naomi.

Once outside the room, near the top of the stairs, Melissa hugged Almera. "Thank you for coming!"

"You are most welcome."

Two-year-old Jimmy, Naomi's little boy, darted up the stairs with Melissa's brother David in close pursuit. Melissa caught Jimmy and scooped him into her arms.

"Want Mama!" Jimmy struggled and shouted.

"She's sleeping with baby Lizzy," Melissa said. "You can see her when she wakes up."

"Another girl, Jimboy! What bad luck." David grinned. Then he turned to Melissa. "How's Naomi?"

"Fine. The baby's name is Sarah Melissa—after me," Melissa announced.

"Too bad yours is the middle name, not the first," David teased.

"Naomi calls her Lizzy," Melissa retorted then turned to Almera. "Stay and have breakfast with us. If you want, David can give you a ride to the meeting."

"I-I'd better not," Almera said. With the work of the birth complete, her worries had returned. Had Sam come home in the night to find her away? If he knew where she was, he would never allow her to step foot in the academy again.

Melissa seemed to understand. "David, please take Sister Almera home right now."

"All right."

Almera turned to David. "It would be best if you took me to my father's. I'd be in your debt."

David suddenly laughed. "What do you mean, Sister Prescott? We are all in your debt!"

\* \* \*

"Where is my wife?" Sam burst through the doorway of Ezekiel's house. Then he saw her. Almera sat at the table in the same brown dress she'd worn at supper last night. Her hair was down, and her hands folded. Her lips and cheeks were red from the cold, and there were shadows under her long-lashed eyes.

"I'm here, Sam. Papa's asleep. I'm making his breakfast."

"Where were you last night?" Sam hissed. "You did not sleep in our bed."

"When did you come home?"

"How dare you question me?" He moved toward her with fists clenched. Almera stood up and backed away, shaking. Sam's thoughts whirled. Why did she do this to him? Drive him to anger—and worse? He could not force her to love him. But she was his wife, and she would obey him. A door opened. Sam froze.

Ezekiel came out of the bedroom. "Morning, Sam. Somethin' the matter?"

Sam looked coldly at Almera. "Your daughter did not sleep in our bed last night."

"'Course she didn't. She was here with me."

Sam's light eyes narrowed. "You were at the tavern."

"I left before you did. Stopped by to check on Almera. Sure enough, she was scared of the wind and came home with me."

Sam eyed Almera, incredulous. "You were scared of the wind?"

Almera barely nodded. Then she walked over to the hearth and hoisted the kettle of mush away from the fire. She turned to Sam. "Should I set a bowl out for you too?"

"I'm not hungry," Sam growled. "But make sure my lunch is ready." Then he turned abruptly and left.

\* \* \*

Ezekiel sat across the table from Almera. "Where were you?" he asked.

"Delivering Naomi Holman's baby," Almera explained.

"You came here after. Instead of going home."

Almera nodded.

Ezekiel was quiet for a moment. He took no pleasure in lying to Sam. He had always tried to be honest with other men, to keep his word. He had taught his children to do the same.

Almera seemed to read his thoughts. Her eyes filled with tears as she dropped her spoon to the table. "Papa, forgive me for lying."

"You didn't lie. I did."

"Because of me," Almera said. She stood to clear the table.

Ezekiel shrugged and changed the subject. "How's Mrs. Holman? Did she have a boy or girl?"

"A girl. They are fine. The baby's name is Sarah Melissa."

Ezekiel pushed his chair back and looked at Almera. "You've been up all night. Go on in my room and sleep. I'll finish clearing up, then I'll be out for a while. I'll be back in time to get you home to make lunch for your husband."

After Almera lay down, Ezekiel hitched up Leo and headed to the Kirtland Temple. The Sunday meeting would be getting out when he arrived. He wanted to ask around, to see if anyone had word about his children in Missouri. Did Benjamin survive the fighting? And what of Delcena and Julianne? Last he'd heard, Delcena was going to deliver her sixth baby this month. He thought of how Julianne had been born on a November day like this, two years after Delcena, thirty years ago. Now they were suffering and in danger. Their husbands could have been injured or killed in the fighting. His head ached.

Suddenly, he wished he could tell Julia that he had been wrong all along. For whatever Delcena and Julianne suffered as Mormons, they were not in greater danger than Almera. They were safe with their husbands.

# 3

*When the hour of death shall come,*
*Cold will be my mortal clay;*
*Then, my Father, take me home;*
*Be my light along the way.*

Joel Hills Johnson

*Saturday, December 1, 1838. Liberty, Missouri*

THE AFTERNOON SUN HUNG COLD in the sky as the horse-drawn wagon approached from the east. The wagon box rose high from the bed and cast a long, awkward shadow. From the side of the wagon, the erect heads and broad shoulders of the Mormon prisoners were visible to the curious crowd. Lyman pushed through the crowd to the edge of the road. He glanced up and down the street. No one appeared aggressive. Yet, it would be so easy for a Missourian to shoot the Prophet.

The wagon progressed through the center of town and passed the courthouse. It turned north and went up Main Street. Lyman followed with the surging crowd. The horses jangled to a stop outside of Liberty Jail. One pawed impatiently. Lyman studied the structure: thick walls of rough-cut limestone, front doors facing east, steps rising on the north and south sides to a platform without banisters, and two small, grated windows at the base. A dungeon in every sense of the word.

The crowd hushed as the tall prisoners climbed out of the wagon and ascended the south steps. A guard opened the heavy door, and one by one, the prisoners stepped inside. Joseph, the last, paused for a moment. He turned around slowly, taking in the lingering sunlight and the spectators.

The Prophet took off his hat. "Good afternoon, gentlemen," he said. Then he turned and disappeared from their sight, the heavy iron doors screeching behind him.

"He looks nice, Pa," a young boy near Lyman whispered to his father.

"He is a deceiver, like Satan."

"What if he gets out?"

"He won't."

\* \* \*

Low clouds occluded the moon, blackening the night. Lyman sat cross-legged against a log near the Kingsleys' barn with his pistol in his lap. The Kingsleys, who were members of the Church, lived across the street from Liberty Jail. Lyman had spent a week there. Like in Richmond, each night he had been ready every moment to intercede if the Prophet were in danger—a minuteman like his father before him.

But this was his final night to stand guard over Joseph. Earlier today, Emma had arrived with little Joseph. Lyman had helped them from the wagon, embracing them both. Though her dark hair was neatly coiffed, Emma had visibly aged, sorrow and worry etching lines around her mouth and under her eyes. While Erastus Snow had gone to speak to the jailer about Emma visiting, little Joseph had pulled away from his mother's hand and announced that he was going to search for a stick to take home to Frederick—one that looked like a sword.

"Have you seen Joseph?" Emma had asked Lyman as she wrapped her cloak more tightly around her shoulders and watched her son.

Lyman had nodded, telling her that the night before he had slipped some of Sister Kingsley's biscuits through the window grates into Joseph's hands.

Then little Joseph had skipped back over to them, chattering, "We brought blankets for the prisoners, even though Mama's worried the babies will be cold. Mama says I might get to sleep with Papa in the jail tonight."

At the sound of the bright young voice, Lyman had turned back to Emma. "How are my wife and children?"

She had swallowed hard and told him his family needed him. Brigham Young wanted him to return to Far West and help remove the Saints from Missouri.

For the rest of the day, Emma's words had haunted Lyman. His family needed him. Lyman shivered, and a sharp pain sliced through his head.

It felt so much colder tonight, and he was very weary. Was he becoming feverish? A coughing fit gripped him as a thought came to him almost like a commandment: *Go home before you are too ill to travel.*

Lyman stood to warm and awaken himself. He crept across the street. All was dark, the prisoners and guards asleep. He crawled to the grated window. Was there a chance Joseph was still awake? Lyman longed to speak with Joseph one more time, to explain that he needed to leave before dawn, that he would come back if he was needed.

Lyman squatted next to the window, his face against the cold iron bars. He could not see inside, yet he heard the deep breathing of men and the light snoring of little Joseph lying cuddled next to his father. Perhaps the men slept so deeply because they finally had blankets to warm them. Tears gathered in Lyman's eyes, and he whispered a song.

*Lord, keep him safe each night,*
*Secure from any fear;*
*May angels guard him while he sleeps*
*Till morning light appears.*

*And when our days are past,*
*And we from time remove,*
*O may we in thy kingdom rest,*
*Where all is peace and love.*

\* \* \*

*December 13, 1838*

Delcena heard Lyman cough as he shaved in preparation for a high council meeting. He had coughed most of the night—a ragged, coarse sound that chilled her.

"Lyman, please stay home. You're not well," Delcena implored as she sat on a bench near the fire, braiding Alvira's hair. He coughed again. With legs tucked under her skirt, Alvira grimaced when Delcena divided the strands and began the second braid.

"I can't miss this one," Lyman said. "I'll be all right."

Delcena glanced at him, and he smiled reassuringly, his brown eyes large and soft behind the lenses of his glasses. Delcena looked away.

"Stop pulling," Alvira whined.

"I'm finished now," Delcena said.

Alvira turned to Lyman. "Papa, you promised to play shadows with us."

Lyman reached out and tugged lightly on Alvira's braid. "When I get home tonight."

"You'll be too tired," she whined again.

"Not too tired for shadows," Lyman said then coughed again.

"I'm glad you're not busy like you used to be . . . that you have time," Alvira said.

"Always remember that this time together is a precious gift from God," Lyman said to Alvira.

Delcena swallowed. Last night she had felt the fever in Lyman's body when she lay next to him. She quickly busied herself unhooking the pot at the hearth. Then she scooped a handful of cold ashes into it and carried it to the board.

\* \* \*

Lyman watched Delcena as she busied herself, scrubbing the pot with ashes. Without looking at either of them, she kept scrubbing. Eventually she turned to Alvira. "If Papa is too tired to play shadows tonight, you will need to understand."

"Papa never breaks a promise," Alvira said with a smile at Lyman. He winked at her, thinking that her eyes were so blue. How had God managed that with two brown-eyed parents?

"You must insist Papa break his promise if he is too tired," Delcena repeated.

Alvira glared at her mother then sidled up to her father, looking coy, demanding, and skeptical all at once. Lyman chuckled and coughed. He put his arm around her. Nine going on five one moment, nine going on fifteen the next, caught in that moment between the babe she had been and the woman she would become. "A promise is a promise. When I get home, we shall play a game of shadows, such that has never been played before!"

Alvira ducked out of his arm, ran to the door, and unlatched it. She shouted to Mary and Albey, who were sliding on a patch of ice. "Papa's going to play shadows with us tonight!"

Lyman stood and approached the door. Mary and Albey tumbled into the house, cheering.

"Shh," he said as they shed their coats. "The babies are napping."

He sat down and gathered Mary and Albey into his arms. He still had a few minutes before he had to leave.

"Sing us a song, Papa," Mary said as she cupped her hands around his chin and looked up at him. There were pink circles on each of her pale cheeks.

"Sing the 'Mobbers of Missouri'!" Albey chimed. "Joseph heard Brother Snow sing it to his papa in jail."

"Did he really?" Lyman asked. His chest felt tight, but he did not cough. He grinned at the sheer audacity of it—Erastus singing the parody to the prisoners with their jailers about. He could almost hear Joseph chuckle.

"Papa's hoarse. Let's sing it to him instead," Alvira chimed. Then the children shouted the chorus—Mary and Albey perched on his knees, with Alvira directing.

> *Go spread the news to small and great. Let truth to all be given*
> *In eighteen hundred thirty eight. The Church of Christ was driven*
> *Away from houses, homes, and land in this the land of freedom,*
> *Because a savage mob commands; Accusing the Prophet of treason.*
> *Oh Missouri, the Mobbers of Missouri! The Mobbers of Missouri!*

Lyman hugged his children close. They were his jewels, his beautiful ones. Would they be all right if his premonitions became reality? Susan cried out in the cradle. Lyman watched as Delcena lifted the baby to her shoulder.

He wondered if he should tell Delcena of his dream last night. He had been harnessed like a horse to a wagon, a wagon that expanded and contracted like things do in dreams. The wagon held all things precious to him: Delcena in her wedding dress, the Prophet preaching a sermon, his newborn crying. Then a voice instructed him to take off the harness and to lay his burden down. *The wagon will roll forward on its own accord. The field is white and ready to harvest.*

"Will you be busy tomorrow?" Alvira's voice broke into his thoughts as she eyed Mary and Albey on his lap.

"No, I won't be." Lyman winked at her. "You should write out a schedule of the things we will do. But leave an hour for Mama and me."

"But, Lyman," Delcena interrupted, her voice trembling, "you can't just play with the children. We have so much to do. We have to leave Missouri soon. We have to find a place to go."

Lyman's eyes met hers. He swallowed. "God will prepare a place for us."

Delcena balanced Susan on one hip and walked over to Lyman. She laid a hand on his forehead. "You're warm. Don't go today."

Albey wiggled off of Lyman's knee. Lyman took Delcena's hand and kissed it. It felt cold against his warm lips. "I've been asked to stand in for Newell Knight on the council until his return. I think this is the last meeting I will attend."

Delcena pulled her hand away and stared at him, her eyes frightened. He saw her struggle to keep her voice steady. "Why won't you rest and get well?"

Lyman held her eyes with his, and it seemed that the whole world receded around them—the baby on her hip, the prattle of the children. It was just Lyman and Delcena, suspended in a moment of time. He willed her to understand. "While a man lives, he needs his boots on."

"And Papa promised to play shadows with us after dark," Alvira chimed.

\* \* \*

Lyman sat slightly apart from the other brethren. Heber C. Kimball opened the high council meeting with a prayer.

Then President Brigham Young stood and spoke. "I feel it is all-important to have this council reorganized and prepare to do business. The faith of the Saints has been sorely tried. But as for my faith, it remains the same as ever. Even in prison, Joseph is God's Prophet. I join in fellowship today with all who love the gospel of the Lord and Savior Jesus Christ in act as well as word."

Lyman watched as each man with a desire expressed his feelings. He knew that today was not a day to stand and speak but to watch the wagon roll forth.

Heber stood. "I have endeavored to keep a straightforward course; but wherein I have been out of the way in any manner, I will mend in that thing. My faith is now as good as ever, and I am in fellowship with all who want to do right."

Had Heber struggled? Had his faith needed mending? But in the past year, whose had not?

Simeon Carter, whose brother Gideon had been brutally killed at Crooked River, remained sitting when he spoke. There were tears in his eyes. "As to my faith, it is the same. I don't think Joseph is a fallen prophet. I believe in every revelation that has come through him. Yet perhaps Joseph has not acted in all things according to the best wisdom. I don't know. Yet I don't think Joseph will be removed and another planted in his stead, for I believe he still has work to perform. I am determined to persevere that I . . . that I might at last gain a crown of glory in the kingdom of God."

Simeon's brother Jared, who had been studying his hands, looked up. "I agree with President Young's feelings and wish to remain with the brethren."

Lyman listened as other men spoke. Levi Jackman expressed confidence in Brother Joseph. Solomon Hancock bore testimony of the Book of Mormon. Samuel Bent said that he felt to praise God in prisons and in dungeons and in all circumstances.

Lyman felt peace. All was well. The work would roll forth, a stone cut without hands.

\* \* \*

Later that evening, a single candle glowed in the house; even the hearth fire had been doused. Julianne helped Delcena hang a white linen sheet near one end of the room. Lyman sat on a stool facing the linen sheet, knowing that his strength tonight was heaven sent.

The table had been moved and was two yards directly behind Lyman. In the center of the table, the candle shone. The rest of the furniture had been pushed against the opposite wall, where Julianne, Delcena, and the younger children waited. It was dark and chill as the children wiggled with anticipation.

"I will choose who goes first," Alvira bossed. "When it's your turn, you have to walk between the table and the back of Papa. Like this." She strutted in front of the candle, hands on her waist, her slim hips swinging in tandem with her words. Her shadow moved on the linen sheet, large and distorted. Alvira walked back to her siblings. "When you go, Papa cannot turn around and look at you. He will try to guess who it is from the shadow. If he guesses right, he gets a point. If wrong, we get a point."

Lyman pivoted around on the stool to face his family. "Ha! I will win at this game! I know all of you like the back of my own hand!"

The children noisily protested.

Alvira put a finger to her lips. "Shhh! Turn back around, Papa!" She waited a long moment until all was silent. Then she glanced at her father, making sure he had obeyed and was not peeking. Satisfied, she stretched out her index finger and pointed to Albey. Deftly, Julianne wrapped a tablecloth around Albey's waist like a skirt. Then he swaggered past the candle, swinging his hips in imitation of Alvira.

Lyman laughed and coughed. "Allie, why'd you give yourself the first turn?"

"It was me!" Albey shouted as he jumped and danced around the room, creating imp-like shadows. "I won!"

Alvira shook her head. "Papa, I have braids! Watch for details."

After Albey quieted, Alvira pointed to Mary. Julianne whispered in her ear. Mary tottered by the candle and sucked her thumb. Lyman guessed Danny. Mary ran and hugged him, her face merry with laughter. Next, Seth hopped across, and Lyman guessed Albey. Both boys hooted. Danny toddled by, and Lyman guessed Seth.

"Poor, poor, Papa," Mary moaned. "You're losing badly."

Julianne called the children together in a huddle. After muffled whispers, they broke apart. Julianne did a drumroll on the table. Alvira shouted above the ruckus. "Because Papa is losing, we will show mercy! This is the final turn, and it's worth a million points! If Papa guesses right, he wins the shadow game!"

All became silent as Lyman watched the linen sheet. Behind him, Alvira donned a bonnet and tucked her braids up in it. Then she walked daintily in front of the candle, rubbing her eyes like she was crying.

"Ah." Lyman rubbed his chin. "Is it Mama crying because her children aren't behaving or Aunt Julianne missing Uncle Almon?"

Alvira took off the bonnet. "Papa, you only get one guess. But it doesn't matter because you are wrong on both counts. It was me!"

Lyman turned around on the stool, facing his children. "Was it really?" Then he stifled a cough and knelt on the floor, holding his arms out to his little ones. Mary, Albey, Seth, and Daniel ran to him, laughing. They knocked down the forsaken stool, and it tumbled against the white sheet, causing it to fall. Alvira caught it and swung it like a banner as she joined the fray.

Delcena turned away from them and busied herself at the hearth. Baby Susan hung in a sling at her chest. She poked at the ashes with a stick. Julianne bent over to help rekindle the flame. In the light from the first blaze, she saw the tears on Delcena's cheeks.

"Oh, Delcie, go to them," Julianne whispered as she took the stick from her sister.

Lyman stood as Delcena approached. The white sheet hung from his shoulders, and five of her six children hugged his legs. Delcena smiled despite her tears. Lyman wrapped his arms around his wife and infant.

Julianne turned from the fire and looked at the Sherman family. Tears gathered in her eyes as she sang to them:

*Glorious things of thee are spoken,*
*Zion, city of our God!*
*He whose word cannot be broken,*
*Chose thee for His own abode.*
*See the stream of living waters,*
*Springing from celestial love,*
*Well supply His sons and daughters,*
*And all fear of death remove.*
*Bless'd inhabitants of Zion,*
*Purchas'd with the Savior's blood.*
*Jesus whom their souls rely on,*
*Makes them kings and queens to God.*
*Fading are all worldly treasures,*
*With their boasted pomp and show,*
*Heavenly joys and lasting pleasures*
*None but Zion's children know.*

\* \* \*

In a dark corner of the Liberty Jail dungeon, Joseph Smith, Sidney Rigdon, and Hyrum Smith knelt in prayer before responding to a letter of inquiry from Brigham and Heber, who were asking about the management of the Church and the vacancies in the Quorum of the Twelve Apostles. After they arose, they discussed which men should be called to replace Orson Hyde and Thomas B. Marsh. They decided on George A. Smith and Lyman Sherman.

\* \* \*

It was near sunset, and the house was still. Delcena swallowed back her grief. This moment would not come again. A half hour ago, Julianne and Louisa Beeman, a single woman in her midtwenties, had bundled up the children and taken them somewhere. Delcena could not remember where. They had done this so she would have some time with Lyman. There was so little of it left.

Delcena bathed his forehead with cool rags. She made a hot poultice and peeled down the quilt, placing the poultice on his bare chest. After ten minutes, she removed it, and his body shook. She lay down by him, wrapping her arms around him, her ear against his chest. The grating sound in his lungs was louder than the beat of his heart.

"I love you," she whispered.

She heard his whisper. "I love you."

She lay by him until his eyes closed, the fever making his breath hot, yet it seemed that his body had somehow grown accustomed to it. There were no more violent dreams, no more writhing as he slept. Then she heard a knock at the door.

She stood up and covered Lyman with the quilt then smoothed her blue linen dress. As she crossed the room, it seemed a hundred thoughts passed through her mind of the nights she had wept and pled with God not to take Lyman and the mornings when she had no tears left, when she simply prayed that his suffering would soon end.

She knew she had to go on—the never-ending needs of six little ones demanding what shreds of strength she had left, pushing and pulling at the depths of her grief, fear, and hope. Delcena opened the door. Brigham Young and Heber Kimball stood before her. They took off their hats.

Brigham spoke. "Sister Delcena, how is Brother Lyman?"

Delcena swallowed. "He is much worse than when you left for Liberty. It is pneumonia. How is Brother Joseph?"

"As well as can be expected," Heber said. "We rejoiced to be able to speak with him and hear his counsel. But now we have received news that Brigham's life is in peril. He and his family must leave soon for Quincy."

Brigham spoke up. "Could we speak with your husband for a moment?"

"Of course," Delcena said as she led them to Lyman's bed.

When the men saw the extent of Lyman's illness, they spoke privately in whispers. Then they laid their hands upon his head and prayed for God's will to be done.

When the blessing ended, Lyman whispered, "Thank you, brethren." He coughed weakly.

Heber spoke. "Rest, my friend. Truly you have been Joseph's right-hand man."

Delcena walked the men to the door. Heber turned to her with tears in his eyes. "The Prophet has asked that Lyman fill one of the vacancies in the Twelve. If Lyman does not live to be ordained, know that his calling will be sure in the spirit world. He will preach the gospel as an apostle of Jesus Christ. He is a good man, a noble man."

\* \* \*

A few days later, Delcena felt the light in the room change when Lyman took his final breath. Though tears fell from her eyes, she knew that Lyman was right, that their lives had been blessed beyond imagination. She took the spectacles from his face and laid them on the table, then she gently removed the boots from Lyman's feet.

A moment passed. Baby Susan awakened, crying out in hunger. Delcena picked her up and fed her, the baby's eyes wide open, watching Delcena as she nursed. Delcena wept, thanking her Heavenly Father that her infant daughter had Lyman's eyes.

# 4

*He whispered in his partner's ear,*
*That he was going home,*
*To labor in another sphere,*
*Where she must shortly come.*
*With grief I heard his partner sigh,*
*Then raised my heart in prayer,*
*That God would hear the orphan's cry,*
*And soothe the widow's care.*

Joel Hills Johnson

*Fort Leavenworth, Kansas*

THE OXEN PAWED AND BAWLED. Benjamin threw a pitchfork of hay into the corral. The sun hung low in the gray sky. Soon it would be time for supper.

Benjamin's mind roved. Two weeks ago he and Arthur Millican had escaped Missouri and made their way to Fort Leavenworth. After Benjamin had told General Kearney his plight, the general had hired him as a teamster and put him in charge of six yoke of oxen to haul supplies around the fort and reservation. The officers and soldiers treated him with respect and often kindness—his food was good, his wages were fair, and his bed was warm. Yet he was lonely, for he rarely saw Arthur, his friend and fellow fugitive. Also, the lifestyle of most of the soldiers troubled Benjamin. Gambling, drunkenness, and prostitution were all open-faced.

"Young Johnson!" Orkey, a large, good-natured German soldier rounded the corner of the new barracks. Orkey's term of enlistment was almost over, but he wanted to stay on as a hired man. Benjamin liked Orkey—a braggart, with a heart as large as his boasts.

"Have the oxen broken your thin arms in two?" Orkey yelled.

Benjamin straightened his shoulders and shouted back. "Steel bands never break! Has General Kearney decided to keep the likes of you around?"

"Yes. The general needs a German's strength after hiring a half-starved Mormon mite."

Benjamin snorted. "The widow's mite was worth more than the rich man's fortune. Watch out—the Mormon mite just might bring down the German giant."

Orkey laughed loudly. "I will give you the advantage of a good supper, then I will throw you around like a bandy ball." Then Orkey's voice became serious. "Two men are asking for you at the mess hall. One of them used to work here. He left a few weeks ago—something to do with the Mormon trouble."

Benjamin's eyes darkened. When he and Arthur had first arrived, General Kearney had offered them employment and protection. But would the general be able to follow through with his promise? The horrible days of being held prisoner in Adam-ondi-Ahman gripped Benjamin as his chest tightened and his palms began to sweat. "I'd better clear out."

Orkey shook his head. "No need to. John Babbitt and his dandy friend won't have any business with you while old Orkey is around."

"Did you say *John Babbitt*?" Benjamin's face broke into a grin. He threw the pitchfork to Orkey and sprinted toward the mess hall.

\* \* \*

Almon opened his arms wide when he saw Benjamin running toward him. The men locked in an embrace. Afterward, Benjamin wiped away an errant tear. Almon grinned. "You look hearty. Fort Leavenworth agrees with you."

Benjamin laughed. "I guess so. It's good to see you."

"Let's get some supper and talk. My brother's already off with a girl on his arm."

In the spacious mess hall, they piled beef and bread on their plates. A table long enough to seat seventy-five men stretched down its length. Bunks lined the perimeter. Men sprawled about the room, gambling and entertaining women.

Almon led Ben to the far corner of the table, where there was a bit of privacy. They sat down. "Ben, I want to know what happened to you. Every detail."

Benjamin washed a swallow of bread down with hard cider. Then he began. He described the terrors of being held prisoner, the torturous corn cutter that had swung about his head, and the man who had tried to shoot him but died when the gun backfired. He told of how General Wilson mercifully set him free and of his grueling journey to his sisters in Far West.

Almon stopped eating, and tears softened his eyes. "Ben, you are now a man by anyone's measuring stick. Tell me more about my wife. I want to know exactly how she looked and everything she did as near as you can remember."

"Julianne was in good health and pretty and sweet as ever. She and Delcie cried over me and rubbed my hands and feet until they were warm again. Juli gave me a quilt. The night we left, she packed Arthur and me cornbread and a little boiled beef. Then she found the last pint of honey. 'It's for you, Benja,' she said, hugging me and crying. 'Be far away by morning. Take my love and prayers with you.'"

Benjamin swallowed and stopped talking. He did not tell Almon everything. He didn't mention how he had thought of the honey as he and Arthur had plodded the trackless prairie by moonlight. Then the sun had come up. As the morning had worn on, the snow had melted into mud. They had come to a timber on the bank of a small creek. As they sat down to rest and eat, he had opened his pack, anticipating the pleasure of sharing the honey with Arthur. But it had not been in the pack. Somehow, he had forgotten it. A sense of disappointment and forlornness had swept over him. Sitting upon the log, he had sobbed like a little boy. Arthur had waited and had never spoken of it since.

Almon was uncharacteristically quiet for a moment. Benjamin shrugged his shoulders and continued the conversation. "Now tell me where you've been."

Almon took a deep breath. "Lyman and I were in Richmond, trying to help the Prophet. Then I carried letters to Far West but had to go into hiding before I made it home. Lyman might be in Liberty with Joseph or in Far West. I don't know. I need to make some money and get Julianne out of Missouri."

Benjamin and Almon's conversation abruptly ended at the sound of Orkey's voice. The German stood ten feet away, pointing at Benjamin.

"Young Johnson has challenged me. The Mormon mite against the German giant. Now, boy. Try me on."

Benjamin's heart pounded with a strange sense of excitement and power. He was no longer the boy weeping over honey; he was the man Almon spoke of. Benjamin sprang up and ran at Orkey. He grasped one arm around the German's legs and the other around his shoulder, then with a rush of adrenaline, he lifted the man up, carried him to his bunk, and dropped him down upon the bed. The bunk crashed to the floor.

There was a smattering of laughter in the mess hall and some clapping, but mostly the men gaped at Benjamin. Orkey stood up, dumbfounded. "How could you do that?"

Benjamin's face grew hot. He smiled sheepishly. "I-I'll go get some tools and help you fix the bed."

When Benjamin returned, Orkey grinned and shouted, "You men had better let Young Johnson have his way, for he is a darn good fellow anyhow, and no one in this room has any business with him."

Almon threw his head back and hooted.

\* \* \*

*Early February, 1839*

Lying in bed at dawn, Joel moved his hand over Annie's swollen abdomen until he found the place where the baby kicked. Annie smiled. "You found him. Or her."

Joel nodded and sat up. He looked down into Annie's wide-set hazel eyes that crinkled in the corners when she was happy. Her slightly square jaw held the breadth of her smile, and her untamed auburn hair flew in all directions over the pillow. He hoped he could move her out of this drafty storehouse before the baby was born.

"You look so serious," Annie said. "Has there been word from Far West?"

Joel shook his head. "No."

Annie took a deep breath. She closed her eyes for a moment then asked, "Are you glad we moved to Carthage? Are you happy here?"

Joel's brow furrowed slightly, and he shrugged. He had grown restless in Springfield, where he had organized and presided over a branch of about forty members. He had tried to preach, but the prejudice in that area was great, and few would listen to his message. After Christmas, he had traveled to Carthage in Hancock County, where he had found numerous families eager to listen. In mid-January, he had rented this old storehouse and moved his family to it. In truth, he rarely thought about whether or not he was happy, just whether or not his family had enough to eat, whether the Prophet would be released from prison, and whether he was useful to the Lord. But Annie was waiting for an answer. "I would be happy if this were Zion."

"Then we will do our best to make this place Zion," Annie commented.

"You can't make a place Zion that is not Zion."

"Oh, my Joel, you are a literalist. If we strive to be the pure in heart, our Heavenly Father won't mind if we call Carthage our Zion. The people are kind here, and it is a place of refuge." Then she smiled ruefully. "Yet, with five children, is any place a place of refuge?"

Joel smiled.

"Now I have made you happy!" Annie said triumphantly. "Do you know what I like best about Carthage?"

"I do not. But I suppose you are going to tell me."

"I like that there are enough rooms in this house to separate quarreling children. What about you?"

Joel dressed quickly in the cold room. Then he answered Annie as he stoked the fire. "I like that some are accepting the gospel. I like that a new jail is being built and that I shall be hired to shingle the roof. I like that there is ample land for sale. By the way, yesterday I met a Mr. Galland. He and other men own large tracts for sale in Commerce. It's swampland but could be drained. I sent word to the brethren in Quincy. And I like that I've found a parcel on Crooked Creek in the Perkins settlement with a sawmill already on it. I'm going to buy the land and the mill and build a large brick house for you and the children."

He bent down and kissed Annie. She closed her eyes for a moment and sighed deeply. Then she opened her eyes. "We need to get word to your family in Far West. Perhaps they could find land in the Perkins Settlement as well. How I would like to be with Julianne and Delcena again. And dear Benjamin."

Joel swallowed but did not speak.

Annie sat up. "Ben must have been released, Joel. I think we would feel amiss if he were not all right. I wonder about Susan Bryant too. I would like her with me when the baby comes. She is so good with the children. Perhaps she needs a home."

"Right now, all the Saints need a home."

Annie nodded and carefully swung her legs to the side of the bed. She slowly stood up, her nightdress falling to her ankles. "And ours is big enough to share."

\* \* \*

It was dusk a week later, and snow flurried outside. Annie felt big and awkward as she stirred the stew over the hearth. Joel was outside feeding the animals with the boys.

"Mumma, I hungry," three-year-old Susie whined.

"Soon, baby, soon," Annie soothed.

There was a knock at the door. "Sariah, please answer it," Annie directed her six-year-old.

"But, Mama, who is it?"

"We'll know as soon as you open the door."

Sariah skipped to the door while Annie took Susie's hand and steered her away from the hearth. Together they walked toward the door while Sariah pulled it open.

Annie gasped when she saw Sidney Rigdon and Edward Partridge. She quickly invited them in out of the cold. "Oh, President Rigdon, you're free!" Annie exclaimed as tears sprang to her eyes. "Is Brother Joseph released?"

President Rigdon took Annie's hands in both of his. Annie noticed that his face was gaunt, with a gray pallor. "Joseph is still a prisoner. There was a hearing on January twenty-fifth. I was the only man set at liberty." Sidney let go of Annie's hands and shook his head in irony. "Yet my brethren continue to suffer in Liberty's dungeon. I pray that through the grace of God I can ease the burdens of the suffering Saints. Is Brother Joel here?"

"Yes." Annie turned to Sariah. "Put a shawl on, and run get Papa."

Annie invited the men to sit at the table. She did not ask any questions but quickly fed them warm soup and bread. Joel came in, and the men stood, exchanging greetings and embraces.

They sat back down, and President Rigdon immediately cleared his throat and looked intently at Joel. "At Quincy, I received word that there is a large tract of land in this county. I should like to go see the land and visit Mr. Galland."

Joel nodded and gave the men all the information he had, promising to take them to Mr. Galland in the morning. Annie knew she should go make up beds for the men but felt rooted to the spot. When would Joel ask for news of their family? As if he read her thoughts, Joel turned to

Edward Partridge. "Bishop, is there any news of young Benjamin Johnson, my brother? We heard he was taken prisoner at Diahman."

"He escaped and is safe, working in Fort Leavenworth."

"And what of my sisters' families—the Babbitts and the Shermans?"

"Brother Babbitt is also in Fort Leavenworth. Brother Sherman fulfilled a mission to aid the Prophet in Richmond but became ill through exposure and died a martyr's death. Last week, he was buried in Far West."

Annie began to weep. Sixtus, tall and tenderhearted, guided her to the bedroom. Nephi and Sariah followed, lying down by her and hugging her as she cried. Sixtus picked up Susie, who asked over and over again what was wrong with Mama.

"Uncle Lyman is dead," Sixtus explained.

"What is dead?" Susie asked.

A few moments later, Joel brought the children's pillows and blankets into the room. "You'll sleep in here tonight, on the floor," he said. "Our guests will sleep in your rooms."

Joel knelt with the children and said a prayer. He bedded them on the floor, tucked their blankets around them, and blew out the candle. Then he climbed into bed and put his arms around Annie. "Heber sent a runner to Fort Leavenworth to tell Ben and Almon of Lyman's death. It is now safe for them to return to Far West. Ben has written the family, and Ben and Almon are on their way to help Delcena."

"Poor, dear Delcie and her children," Annie moaned. Then Annie felt Joel's tears in her hair.

\* \* \*

*Early March, 1839*

Benjamin stood on the dock with six other men. To their backs, the sun sank tremulously close to the horizon as sundown fast approached. The group stared at the river, half a mile wide with large masses of mush ice running with the current. The breeze was stiff and the sky gray. A single canoe approached.

"That canoe don't look big enough to hold all of us," a man called out to the middle-aged, thick-armed ferryman as he docked the canoe.

"It ain't. But this is the last trip tonight," the ferryman answered. "Is one of you Ben Johnson?"

Benjamin stepped to the front. "I am."

"Get in, son."

Benjamin climbed into the canoe, relieved that things were going according to Almon's plan. The Babbitt brothers had left at dawn, leaving Benjamin behind to train another teamster. Almon had secured Benjamin's passage and waited with a horse on the other side.

The six other men quickly crowded into the canoe. The ferryman suddenly laughed. "With you all in it, the rim of this canoe's barely an inch above the water. Two of you better git out." No one moved. "Ain't you fellows afeard of death?" Each man had a story, a reason why he had to get across the river tonight—a sick child, a message to deliver, a debt to pay. One asked if the ferryman would consider making one more trip.

"Cain't. After dark, the ice ain't seeable. It's nearly too late now. Two of you get out quick." No one budged.

"You fellows are stubborn as sin, but we cain't wait no longer," the ferryman exclaimed. Then he shoved off. "I'll either get you to the other side, or we'll all join Old Scratch tonight."

Benjamin gritted his teeth as they sculled across the river, dodging masses of ice. The setting sun colored the river red as cold water splashed over the side of the canoe. Benjamin wondered if he would live to fulfill his promise to Lyman—the promise he had made the night the printing press burned—that if Lyman died, he would take care of his wife and children. Benjamin pushed his wages deeper into his coat pocket. If he drowned on the river tonight, he knew Almon would retrieve his body and give the money to Delcena. Miraculously, the canoe stayed upright. Ten minutes later, they approached the shore. Benjamin saw Almon and John standing close by with horses.

When they had safely landed, Almon strode up, handed Benjamin the horse's reins, and whirled around on the ferryman, his eyes as fiery as the setting sun. "What do you think you're doing filling your vessel like that? Putting these men's lives in danger."

The ferryman shrugged. "I warned 'em."

Almon shot back, "I'd have killed you if my friend lost his life crossing the river."

"You wouldn't of had to. I'd already be dead. You got any more threats?"

"No, he don't." John put his hand on Almon's shoulder. "Let's go."

Benjamin stared at Almon as they mounted. The old Almon would have grinned at Benjamin's adventure on the river. But maybe Lyman's death was getting to them all.

*\*\**

## Far West, Missouri

*Almon will be here today. Today.* The thought registered again and again in Julianne's mind as she diced potatoes and put them in the pot. *He sent word. He is on his way.* Then tears clouded her eyes. Her life was so entwined with Delcena's. Their sisterhood had become a partnership cemented by surviving together while the world was falling apart around them. Just five months ago, Julianne had been envious of Delcena's pregnancy, had longed for a baby so intently that she had not been able to contain her tears when Delcena had given birth to Susan. Now that day seemed a lifetime ago. Almon was coming home, but Lyman never would.

Julianne glanced at Delcena, who was nursing. Silently, she begged Heavenly Father to keep the baby safe, to help her thrive. There had been days when Baby Susan had held them both together—no matter what, they had to smile at the baby and teach her to smile back. And she did smile back, her brown Lyman eyes sparkling, her infant smile lopsided. And in that brand-new smile, who could help but feel a ray of hope?

Five minutes later, Alvira came into the house and slammed the door. "They're almost here," she said curtly.

Julianne's heart pounded. "Who? Uncle Almon and Uncle Ben?"

Alvira nodded and tossed her head. "And that other man—Uncle Almon's brother. Albey and Mary couldn't even wait but went running down the street."

"What about Danny and Seth?" Delcena questioned.

"Following them. They will probably get trampled. They don't listen to me." Alvira squatted down near the fire and wrapped her arms around her knees. She looked over at her mother. "I'm not going back out to get the boys."

"You don't need to. Aunt Juli will make sure they are all right. Come rock Susan while I finish the potatoes," Delcena said gently.

Already at the door, Julianne glanced back at Delcena, who was settling the baby in Alvira's arms. She couldn't find any words. "Delcie," she whispered.

Delcena looked at her and swallowed. "Go."

Julianne went outside, closing the door behind her. She saw Almon almost immediately, spurring his gray horse toward her then reining back so abruptly when he reached her that his mount almost reared.

She looked up at him; he looked so vibrant and alive against the gray winter sky—handsome and strong, his hair dark, his eyes so green, his jaw quivering. As he slid from the horse, it was as if the strength that had held her up for the past four months left her, and she doubled over weeping. Then she was upright again in Almon's arms, feeling his kisses and tears on her forehead, cheeks, and lips. She clasped her arms around him. "I love you. I love you. Forever and ever."

\* \* \*

*A week later. Kirtland, Ohio*

Ezekiel held the letter from Benjamin in his hands. He read of how his son had been a prisoner in Missouri. Benjamin believed that his life had been miraculously spared. He wrote that he was now in Far West with Delcena and the children—that Lyman was dead. He and Almon were getting teams and provisions together. They would soon take the women and children to safety in Illinois. He hoped to travel to Kirtland to visit his father—as soon as he had time.

*Time.* Ezekiel took another drink of brandy. Why was he getting drunk when he knew his son and his daughters were alive? *Time*—time had run out for Lyman, time was running out for Ezekiel, each day another day closer to the grave. The years he and Julia spent together had already run out. How was his precious Delcena? There was no letter from her, just a quick scrawl from Julianne. *Papa, Delcena and I send our love. We are busy with the children. Will write more as soon as we can. We love you, Papa.*

*As soon as we can,* his sweet girl had said. Didn't his children understand how fast time could end—there might not be any *as soon as we cans.* They had lost four siblings. Their Zion was finished. Lyman was dead. His Julia was gone. Then Ezekiel was laughing, laughing at the terrible absurdity of it all, and wondering at the same time if that bitter laughter turning into sobs was actually his own.

\* \* \*

*Richmond, Missouri*

It was late morning, and the sun shone bright on the snowy countryside as Benjamin and Almon rode from Liberty to Richmond. In Liberty, they had gone to the jail and requested to see the Prophet. The jailer had refused and would not even let them approach the window grate, stating that the prisoners had already tried to escape with tools their Mormon friends had slipped to them. "I, too, am under the eye of the mob," the jailer had added, almost apologetically. "If anything happens to these prisoners, I'm a dead man."

As they rode farther and farther away from the Prophet, Benjamin forced himself to think of the rest of the day's mission. They were on their way to Richmond to inquire about the goods his mother and other members of the poor camp had sent there months ago. Then they would go to the quartermaster to try to get their guns back.

"Do you think there's a chance we'll get them?" Benjamin asked. He knew the militia had been ordered to return the Mormons' firearms, but he couldn't imagine a Missourian giving him back his father's gun. Straight shooting and inlaid with silver, it had been the finest piece in upper Missouri.

"They have to," Almon said. "Boggs feels the pressure of bad publicity. The Quincy newspaper calls us 'a mild, inoffensive people who could not have given cause for the persecution they have met with.'"

Benjamin snorted softly. "Mild and inoffensive. I guess they've never met you!"

Almon smiled. "No. But I hope to meet them soon. I'm done with Missouri."

They rode silently through Richmond until they came to the shipyard. "Let's inquire about the goods and furniture first. Then we'll find the quartermaster and ask about our firearms," Almon suggested.

Ten minutes later, the massive Missourian's eyes were not friendly. "When did you say those shipments were sent?"

"Last July from Kirtland, Ohio," Almon repeated. The Missourian opened up a record book then closed it before Almon could peer at the writing. "Looks like you're out of luck. The last of those shipments was sold earlier this morning at auction to pay freight charges."

Almon's jaw tightened as he turned away from the Missourian. His voice was cold and crisp. "Ben, let's go talk to the quartermaster and get our guns."

As they walked away, Benjamin stepped up beside Almon. "I s'pose we're off to another battle we can't win."

"We'll win the next one," Almon said, his jaw set.

The quartermaster directed Benjamin and Almon to a low brick building where a young soldier stood outside. Almon explained that they had come to claim their weapons. The soldier nodded briskly, opened a door, and led them into a room where guns were piled around the perimeter. Benjamin and Almon looked through the piles of weapons and found Almon's and Lyman's guns.

"Mine's not here," Benjamin said.

"Then I guess you better describe it to this gentleman," Almon said. He glanced hard at the soldier. "Maybe he's seen it."

"It's a fine piece. Double-barreled. Inlaid with silver," Benjamin said, his voice a bit louder than he intended it to be.

"I haven't seen a gun like that," the soldier responded quickly. But Benjamin saw the soldier's eyes dart, for a fraction of a second, to the door at the end of the room. The soldier picked up a decent shotgun and handed it to Benjamin. "Take this one."

"It's not mine. I won't leave here with any gun but my own."

The soldier's face reddened. "You men had better leave, or I'll get my superior."

"I believe that's a good idea," Almon said as he cradled his own rifle like it was a long lost child. Then he put it to his shoulder to check the aim. He spoke once more to the soldier. "I wasn't referring to the bit about leaving. I meant the part about you getting your superior."

"If you men move a muscle, I'll have you arrested," the soldier said as he stalked out of the building.

Without speaking, Almon raised his eyebrows toward the door that led into the other room. Benjamin nodded. Momentarily, the soldier returned with the quartermaster.

"What's the problem?" the quartermaster questioned.

"Sir, my gun isn't in this room. I would like permission to continue to look for it in the adjoining room." Benjamin then described the gun his father had given him.

The quartermaster turned to the soldier. "Are there any other guns in the building?"

"No, sir. We have all the confiscated weapons in here."

"Then there is no harm in satisfying these gentlemen," the quartermaster replied as he walked to the door and opened it.

Benjamin quickly followed. Inside the room, he saw his gun leaning against the wall near a desk in the corner. Benjamin immediately walked to the gun and picked it up. "This is it."

"That belongs to one of the officers. It is not your gun!" the soldier blurted angrily.

"No, it is not my gun," Benjamin returned. "It is my father's gun. And by heaven, I will return it to him! If you don't believe me, ask General Robert Wilson."

"Perhaps there has been some mistake." The quartermaster scratched his chin.

"No, there is no mistake," Benjamin responded, his dark eyes flashing. He spun around and left the room and building with Ezekiel's gun, Old Betsy, under his arm and Almon following.

As they rode back to Far West, Almon turned to Benjamin and smiled. "Now that was a battle worth fighting."

"And winning," Benjamin added.

\* \* \*

*Wednesday, March 6, 1839. Crooked Creek, eight miles from Carthage, Illinois*

Annie took her apron off the nail and tied it around her waist. Her breath stopped for a moment as another contraction gripped her abdomen. She sat down on the bench that flanked the kitchen table and stared at the log wall. Though it was cold outside, beads of sweat shone on her temple. With a finger, she moved her long auburn bangs behind her ear.

Two weeks ago, she and Joel had moved from the drafty storehouse in Carthage to this log house near the sawmill on Crooked Creek. The log house was warmer than the storehouse but much smaller. Her three oldest slept together in the loft upstairs. The downstairs had only two rooms—a good-sized kitchen/sitting room and the bedroom she and Joel shared with little Susie. It reminded her of the cabin in Amhearst that Joel and David had built her long ago. She had given birth to Sariah there. Would this baby too be a girl?

She listened to the wind outside. Snow flurried today, even though spring was on its way. Joel would be back soon. He had taken the children into Carthage for school and had promised to bring back a midwife. Annie stood up to put more wood on the fire.

Another pain, hard and steady, tore through Annie as her water broke.

"Joel, hurry," she involuntarily cried out.

She scarcely made it into the bedroom before the baby came. She didn't even have time to lie down. After the birth, she lay on her bed, her legs shaking. She pulled the baby to her body for warmth and saw that he was a boy. Somehow, she was able to pull a string from her dress to tie off the cord.

Exhausted and alone, she wiped the baby clean and wrapped him in a blanket. She held the baby close and pulled a quilt over them both. Then, as she lay with her brand-new infant in her arms, light broke through the snow flurries and filtered through the small window. She looked at her baby. He had a shock of wet auburn hair. He breathed evenly. So quiet. So gentle. So new. And then, miraculously, her mind opened to see her son as a grown man. He had a wide smile and gentle hazel eyes. He was a happy man with a warm, open laugh. His name was Seth Johnson, after Joel's brother.

Annie heard the wagon outside. As Joel and the midwife hurried into the log house, calling out to her, she knew she had never been alone. God had given her a gift—a vision of who her son was and would become.

*　*　*

*March 10, 1839. Far West, Missouri*

Delcena watched as Benjamin was asked to go to the front of the meetinghouse and sit down in a high-backed chair. He walked forward, tall, slender, and strong, his hair black as night and his color healthy and ruddy from exposure to wind and sun. The younger brother she loved was now a man in his own right. He was about to receive the Melchizedek Priesthood and be ordained an elder. Others had stayed after sacrament meeting to witness the ordination. The Huntingtons were there and Julianne and Almon.

With a hand on Benjamin's shoulder, Heber C. Kimball told the group of Benjamin's worthiness and of the Prophet Joseph's love for him. As Apostle Kimball continued, giving a short discourse on the sacred responsibilities associated with the priesthood, Delcena's thoughts turned to the past ten days since Benjamin's arrival. He had done all a priesthood holder or brother could—working hard to fix a broken-down wagon the Committee for Removal had given them, mending harnesses, securing a team of oxen, purchasing supplies, and reaching out to the children. Mary, Albey, Seth, and Daniel clung to him. But Alvira kept a cool distance, as if her uncle's very presence hurt her. Delcena understood; she felt the same way each time she saw Almon take Julianne in his arms.

On the bench diagonal to Delcena, Zina Huntington sat with a small smile on her lips, her eyes warm and earnest. She was a pleasant, attractive girl, and Benjamin spent most of his evenings with her family. Delcena thought of her own courtship with Lyman—their rosy cheeks, beating hearts, and wreaths of smiles; all they saw in the world was each other. Delcena swallowed. Julianne sat next to her with Almon's palm in hers, and she was tracing the tendons on the back of his hand with her thumb.

Delcena closed her eyes and listened to the words Heber C. Kimball spoke, the same words Elder Brackenbury had used when he'd ordained Lyman eight years ago. "By the authority of the holy priesthood and in the name of Jesus Christ, I ordain you to the office of elder in the Melchizedek Priesthood." The shadows of those who lived and died filled her—men with the high priesthood ordaining others to that high and holy calling. How Lyman had treasured that power of God given to man on earth to act in His name! Her brother David had yearned for this priesthood but had died before receiving it. Seth had magnified his priesthood until his death. Were their spirits in the room today? Did they watch Benjamin with pride? Were they unaware of her tears? No, they would see her too. And beyond the veil, Lyman would love and bless her with his priesthood. Yet she needed him here.

Julianne let go of Almon's hand to take hers. But Delcena's tears came anyway. *Oh, Lyman, what shall I do these long years without you? Father in Heaven, help me.*

# 5

*When each can feel the sigh
That heaves a brother's heart
And in afflictions will draw nigh
And share with him a part.*

Joel Hills Johnson

*Springfield, Illinois*

CLOUDS LOOMED THICK IN THE sky as Mary walked home from school with Joe, Amos, and Esther. She held a letter from George Wilson tightly in her hand. Brother Snider, who had recently moved his family to Springfield, had delivered it to her this morning when he brought his children to school for the first time. Brother Snider had mentioned that, although the letter was to the entire Johnson family, Brother Wilson had specifically expressed his desire that Miss Mary receive it.

The words in the letter echoed in Mary's mind.

> *Dear Sister Johnson, Miss Mary, and family,*
> *After I last saw you, I determined to find your son and brother Benjamin. I inquired after him in Far West and was told that he was delivered from prison, had spent some time in Fort Leavenworth, and is currently back in Far West with Sister Sherman. I had planned to bring you word myself but was detained in Quincy, where the brethren asked me to return to Far West to help the Saints leaving Missouri.*
> *Your Humble Servant, George D. Wilson.*

"Mary!" Joe's voice, louder than usual, rang in her ears.

"Joe, there's no need to shout."

"I'm not shouting. I've been trying to talk to you, but you haven't heard a word." Joe glanced at the letter. "You're thinking about George Wilson, aren't you?"

Mary tossed her head dismissively. "It's nothing. He didn't know that we received a letter from Ben two weeks ago—that we already knew he was all right."

Joe cocked an eyebrow. "Nothing? A man rides all the way to Far West, Missouri, to find out news of your brother and then starts back to Springfield, Illinois, just to tell you, and that is nothing?"

Mary's color heightened. "He just felt sorry for me. Because I ran out sobbing the day he told Mother and me that Ben was a prisoner."

"Pity was not his only motivation," Joe commented.

Mary's brown eyes flashed. "We know very little about Mr. Wilson's motivations."

Amos laughed. "Do you mean *dear George's* motivation?"

"She can't call him that," Joe teased. "We have a brother named George. *Dear Wilson* works better."

"Enough." Mary picked up her skirt and marched ahead. Was he interested in her, or was he just a kind man helping a single mother whose daughter was falling apart? Mary very clearly remembered his brown-gold eyes looking intently at her and the feel of his callused hand reaching out to calm her. For the past two months, she had thought of that moment, and of her outburst, a thousand times. *Dear Wilson* did not sound so terrible after all.

"Joe is horrible!" Esther suddenly exclaimed as she stepped up next to Mary. She tossed her head back toward her brothers. "And Amos is getting to be just like him!"

"Are you sure you aren't mad at Joe because you didn't win the spelling bee?" Mary asked, changing the subject.

"I spelled *committee* right, and he said I spelled it wrong," Esther said loudly.

"You forgot one of the *m*'s," Joe called out from behind them.

Esther spun around to yell at her brother. "You think you are such a grand schoolmaster!"

"I am a grand schoolmaster," Joe responded, pointing at Esther good-naturedly. "I am *your* grand schoolmaster!"

"You are my belligerent older brother!"

"Spell *belligerent* for me."

"I won't. And you're being mean to Mary!"

Joe threw his hands up. "Is it my fault that Mr. Wilson has his eye on Mary?"

Mary stopped in her tracks and turned around. The wind tousled her long, loose, blonde hair. "You don't know that, Joe. Please stop teasing me."

Joe's brown eyes became serious. "Amos, you and Esther run on home. I want to talk with Mary privately."

Esther put her arm protectively around Mary. "I'm not leaving Mary! School's over, and you're not my master right now."

Joe's face became stern. "School might be over, but I am your elder brother and the provider in our family."

"Joe's right, Esther. We need to respect him, even when he's annoying," Mary said, handing the letter to her sister. "Besides, I don't want you to get in trouble on my account. Take the letter home to Mother. Don't worry; I'll keep Joe in line."

With a glare at Joe, Esther relented but kept her distance from Amos as the two walked home. Joe watched his younger siblings and remarked, "Esther's angry with me. Why?"

Mary's voice was thoughtful. "When she was little, you praised her lavishly and spoiled her with treats. You don't do that anymore."

"I can't do that with a class full of students. And she's not a small child anymore."

"I know. But she is jealous."

"Jealous of what?"

"Of the attention you give other students. And of Mary Ann, her new sister."

"Come now. She and Mary Ann are the best of friends."

"And you and Mother spend many hours tutoring and praising Mary Ann."

Joe shrugged. "Mary Ann is a member of our family now."

"And Esther feels like she's losing her place in the family."

"That's ridiculous," Joe scoffed.

Mary glanced at him. "You obviously don't know how complex a young lady's sensibilities are. Esther told Mother that she wants to go back to Kirtland to be with Papa. But she doesn't know how hard it is living with him."

Joe took a deep breath as he and Mary walked along the road paved with split logs, flat side up. After a long moment, he commented, "I'll talk to Mother about Esther. I want to talk to you about George Wilson. Surely you know he's paying his respects to you."

"I don't know that. He could have come if he really wanted to."

"Didn't you hear what Brother Snider said? When Wilson got to Quincy, he was asked by the Committee for Removal to take a wagon back to Far West to help a widow and her babies leave Missouri. He did what the brethren asked him to do. He helped someone like Delcena. That's the sign of a good man."

"Or maybe the sign of a man who is thinking about a widow rather than a weeping girl. He's thirty, Joe."

Joe grinned. "That is old. But trust me, Mary, we men are not as complex as young ladies. I know what Wilson is up to."

Mary could not help but smile. Joe continued. "Wilson will come here soon enough. You need to examine your heart and decide what you'll do. I think he's a good man . . . but perhaps too old."

Mary walked more quickly. When she finally turned to Joe, her brown eyes sparkled while the wind blew her hair to one side of her face. "Since we are talking about the complexities of young ladies and gentlemen, have you noticed that you have an abundance of students who are young ladies? And have you noticed that a new young lady tends to join your class each week? They all have such pretty names—Miss Nancy Carroll, Miss Ann Vance, Miss Sylvia Carter. And have you noticed how they all seem to vie for their schoolmaster's attention? Another reason for Esther to be annoyed."

Joe laughed. "I have noticed. But I have also noticed their fathers. What would they do to a Yankee Mormon upstart schoolmaster who courted one of their daughters?"

Mary hooked her arm into her brother's. "Perish that thought! But a new young lady, Miss Harriet Snider, has joined the class. Her father likes you well enough."

Joe shrugged. "I have enough to think about with the family to feed and a large class of students to educate."

"And I have enough to think about as well. Let's forget Miss Snider and Mr. Wilson. Let's think about Ben coming home. That will be the happiest day!"

But Joe was quiet instead of enthusiastic.

"What's wrong?" Mary asked.

"Some things are best not to anticipate. For if they don't happen, it would be too horrible."

"But it will. The Lord has protected Ben. He will come home. I'm certain of it."

Then Joe smiled again. Mary saw that it was kind and troubled, forced and genuine, all at once. Was he thinking about the terrible things—the fever, Lyman's death, and Ben's imprisonment?

"You're right," Joe said as he stretched an arm around her shoulder. "The happiest day is just around the corner."

\* \* \*

*Mid-March 1839. Far West, Missouri*

"I'm not going tomorrow," Alvira said as she held Delcena's hand tightly. The two stood by Lyman's grave. The air was brisk and cold.

"Darling, we have to," Delcena said stoically. The thought of the mob's demand that the Mormons be out of the state of Missouri by the first of April terrified her.

"I won't leave Papa."

Delcena swallowed; she was determined to be strong. "Sister Emma is in Quincy with Julia. You girls will be able to play together again. Brother Joseph will send word of where we should go from there."

Alvira jerked her hand out of Delcena's. "Didn't you hear me? I'm not going! I'm not following Brother Joseph anywhere ever again. I don't care if he is Julia's papa!" Alvira doubled over, sobbing.

Delcena tried to touch her, but she shrank away. "Darling, darling, try to understand. Governor Boggs has decided that the Mormons will be killed if they stay."

"I don't care! Papa is already killed. I want Papa."

Delcena knelt down in the snow and wrapped her arms around Alvira's rigid, sobbing body. She began praying aloud, not knowing if the words would reach her daughter. She thanked her Father in Heaven for Jesus and His sacrifice. She begged Him for help and to give them wisdom and strength. She asked Heavenly Father to comfort Alvira, to help her know that her papa lived in heaven and loved his little girl. Then she pleaded with Heavenly Father to let Alvira know what Papa wanted her to do.

When the prayer was over, Alvira reached for Delcena. "Does Papa want me to go?" She clung to her mother.

Delcena nodded. Then she picked Alvira up and carried her through the lingering snow, back toward the cabin Lyman had built for them, where they would spend their last night in Far West. She was surprised at the strength in her arms.

\* \* \*

*Two weeks later*

Benjamin led the horses as they walked with bent heads through the storm. Julianne and Almon walked near him, Almon's arm wrapped around Julianne's shoulders, helping her keep her footing. Delcena, her children, and their few remaining belongings were in the wagon. They wouldn't even make ten miles today. Above the howl of the wind, Benjamin heard Delcena's babies crying.

A moment later, Benjamin saw the outline of a cabin up ahead. Almon shouted to him. "Stop there. The women and children are freezing."

When they arrived at the cabin, Almon and Julianne helped Delcena and the children out of the wagon while Benjamin knocked. A middle-aged woman opened the door. A child ran into a back room.

"We are on our way to Quincy, Illinois," Benjamin said as the rest of the group made their way to the doorstep. The woman did not speak but stared at Delcena and Julianne, who were ill-dressed and carrying crying babies. Albey and Mary, clutching at Delcena's skirt, had no shoes. Their bare feet were wrapped in rags.

"Ma'am, could we come in to warm and dry ourselves?" Benjamin asked.

The woman's jaw was set, and she did not answer. She didn't close the door, but she turned around and moved to the far end of the room. Almon pushed the door wide open and hustled the group inside. The children gathered around the fire, their faces red and chapped, their noses running, and the warmth of the flames drying their tears. Julianne stood near them, drying her cloak.

Delcena spoke to the woman. "Thank you for allowing my children to warm themselves at your hearth. Could we sleep in your barn tonight? The weather does not permit us to set up camp."

"Stay in the barn, but don't get near my family!" the woman snapped. "If you steal anything, my husband will come after you."

"Thank you for your hospitality," Almon said, looking directly at her, his voice hiding the bitter sarcasm of his words. "Certainly you are a Christian woman who follows the Lord's injunction to *do unto others as you would have them do to you.*"

The woman turned abruptly and left the room. Almon told the group to stay near the fire until they were warm and their clothes were completely dry.

\* \* \*

That night, in the barn, the children slept close together for warmth. Almon held up the candle while Julianne tucked a quilt around Delcena's three oldest, then she piled hay over the quilt to insulate the children as much as possible. The wind howled, and sleet battered the sides of the structure. Albey coughed and shivered.

"I know you're cold," Julianne said as she stiffly bent down and tucked the quilt more tightly around Albey. Every muscle in Julianne's body was sore, and she too was chilled. "In a few days, we'll cross the Mississippi River. Then we'll be in Quincy, Illinois. I've heard that the people are kind there and let the Saints sleep in houses and there's more food than you can imagine."

"But tonight we sleep in the Wicked Witch's barn," Almon exclaimed. "Like Hansel and Gretel."

The candlelight heightened the thinness of Albey's face and the shadows under his wide eyes. He looked up at Almon. "If that lady is a witch, why did you say thank you and call her *Christian?*"

Alvira rolled over, disrupting the hay. "Cause it's April first, and she didn't shoot us like Boggs says she can. Isn't that true, Uncle Almon?"

"You bet that's true," Almon said, reaching down and tickling the children. "Let's hope the witch doesn't eat you in your sleep."

"At least we'd be warm while she cooked us," Alvira added.

After Julianne retucked the children in, Almon took her hand and led her away into a corner of the barn where he had made a bed out of clean hay. "Of all the luck in the world, mine is the worst," he whispered. "Here I am in a barn with a beautiful woman while the wind howls outside. But I have to share it with eight other people, six of whom are children."

Julianne could hardly fathom the fact that he was joking when they were freezing, exhausted, and fodder for any Missourian who might want to kill them. "Just get me warm," she whispered as she blew out the candle. They lay down in the hay, and she wrapped her cloak around them both. Lying in Almon's arms, she closed her eyes, knowing that she had been dead wrong so many years ago when she had doubted if she should marry him. She had feared that he might not have the inner strength to help her through the horrible times. What was it that she had said to him—*I can't marry a man who will only be with me during the summer season.* But it turned out that he wasn't only with her in the bitter cold, but his beating heart was now her hearth fire.

\* \* \*

Delcena lay awake in the dark barn, smelling dank manure and listening to the wind howl. She and her three sleeping babies were wrapped in her wedding quilt. She remembered how Lyman had chosen the quilt's palm leaf pattern because it represented protection and an oasis, the Savior's love. Her mother, sisters, and neighbors had pieced and sewn the quilt. On that day, ten years ago, she would have never imagined that she would be here, in this barn, using the quilt to protect her against the cold and filth as she nursed her babies.

Danny cried in his sleep. Delcena gently pulled him to her. He wasn't even two yet, but he had lived through so much. She would nurse him first, then tiny Susan, and last of all Seth, who was nearly three but still desperately needed the nourishment. How strange that her body had plenty of milk when her soul felt so used up. But only one thing really mattered now, and that was Lyman's children. She would find a safe place for them, a place where she could teach them the gospel and tell them stories of their father. And someday Jesus and the righteous who had died would come to earth again. And they would be a family forever. Her heartbeat slowed, and her eyes closed. There was enough warmth under the palm leaf quilt for Delcena and her little ones to survive the night.

\* \* \*

*Early April, Quincy, Illinois*

The cold wind tugged at Delcena as she stepped off the ferry in Quincy. She held Baby Susan in a sling fastened around her shoulders so her arms were free to help Albey. Last night, camped in the mud near the bank of the river, Albey's fever and cough had worsened. This morning, they had been required to stand on the crowded ferry during the river crossing. Albey had leaned against her, warm to the touch, close to collapsing. She had left the men and Julianne to get the wagon, team, and the rest of her children off the ferry. She had to get Albey out of the wind and find a place for him to lie down. She had to get him a drink of water. If only they had quinine.

As her eyes darted, searching for a place to rest, a woman in her early thirties with blue eyes and prominent cheekbones strode quickly up to her. "Ma'am, do you need help?"

Delcena swallowed. "Is there a well close by? My son is ill and needs a drink of water."

Albey's teeth chattered, and he began coughing and crying.

"I'm Jane Eells. My husband is a physician here in Quincy. We would like to help you. I can take him to my husband's office."

Delcena stared at the woman. Why did she feel frightened? The lady was well-dressed, and her manner open and friendly. Surely this was a blessing. But the terrible words used to justify killing Mormon children echoed in her mind—*lice make nits*. "He-he would be scared without his mother."

"Of course you shall come with him. Would you like me to wait with your children while you tell your husband to meet you at Dr. Eells' office? Near the corner of Main and Fourth Streets, four doors east of the Quincy House."

Delcena blinked back tears. She carefully took Susan out of the sling and handed her to the woman. The baby did not cry but looked around with wide, dark, trusting eyes as the woman held her close. Then Delcena reached her other hand out to Albey. His teeth still chattered, but the woman's kindness had quieted his crying.

\* \* \*

Doctor Eells, with his black hair just starting to gray around the edges and his green eyes direct and warm, spoke confidently. "It appears that the infection has not reached his lungs. With this medicine and good nursing, I would wager that Albey will be well soon. And your baby girl seems hearty and strong. Still, I would like to come check on Albey in a few days. Do you know where you and your husband will be staying?"

"She don't have a husband no more," Albey said suddenly.

The doctor glanced at Albey, who was lying on the bench, then looked carefully at Delcena, as if waiting for an explanation. Delcena looked down at her baby girl, fast asleep in her arms. "My husband died two months ago. My brother will be here shortly with my other children. He'll help me find a place. How much do I owe you?"

"Not a penny, ma'am. How did your husband die?"

"He became ill from exposure."

"Exposure? How so? Was your home burned?"

Delcena shook her head. How long would this interrogation continue? "He was traveling on foot, trying to help and protect our leader, Joseph Smith."

"How many children do you have, besides Albey and the baby?"

Delcena's cheeks felt hot as she answered the question. "Four more, sir."

"Could you excuse me for just a moment?" The doctor bowed and left the room. He returned a few moments later with the young clerk from the office. "This is Mr. Jones. If it is agreeable to you, he will take you, Albey, and the baby to my house, where my wife is fixing supper. I would like you to stay with us so I can keep an eye on Albey. When your brother comes, I will send him and the rest of your children to the Quincy House. That way your other children will not be exposed further to Albey's illness. Of course, their rooms and meals will be provided for."

Delcena had seen the beautiful Quincy House on the way to the office. It was a famous hotel, four stories high and very grand. She began to weep.

Dr. Eells stood up and paced across the room. "Mrs. Johnson, forgive me for upsetting you. Of course, this is only a suggestion."

"Forgive you?" Delcena managed. "How will I ever repay you?"

"You must not. You see, charity is the only medicine that heals the wounds of inhumanity."

\*\*\*

*A week later*

"It will be good to see Mama and everyone again," Julianne said as she and Delcena sat on a bench outside the wholesale store near the boat landing. The sun would soon burn through the mist that had risen over the river the previous night. It promised to be a bright afternoon. Delcena's little ones were among the children congregated near the shoreline who were making a village with gathered stones. Julianne continued. "Almon is going to buy supplies this afternoon. Is there anything you need for the trip to Springfield?"

Delcena gazed out at the water. Instead of answering Julianne's question, she asked one of her own. "Did you notice the ten little houses on the riverfront east of here?"

Julianne nodded. "Yes. Some of the Saints live there."

Delcena turned and looked at her sister. Her voice sounded soft and hesitant. "Juli, I'm not going to Springfield. The Porters recently moved out of one of those little houses. I'm going to move in tomorrow. It's arranged."

Julianne tried to keep her voice even to not betray the shock she felt. "When did you decide this?"

"Two days ago, I was talking with Jane Eells. She told me that if I would rather stay here, she and Dr. Eells would help me arrange it."

"You would rather rely on the charity of strangers than be with your family?" Julianne could not keep the note of confused hurt out of her voice.

Delcena's eyes burned, but she blinked hard, refusing to allow tears to dim her resolve. She shifted the sleeping Susan back into her arms and took a deep breath. "I don't want to further burden Mother. And I can't bear to continue as a stone around you and Almon's necks. He wants to travel, to preach the gospel, to go to Cincinnati and get his license to practice law. He wants you to go with him. And Benja should not have to support my family. He needs to be free to live his own life, to go on missions or marry."

Julianne turned to Delcena with tears in her eyes. "You don't need to do this. Your family is a precious burden."

Delcena swallowed. "I am resolved."

"But how will you and the children survive alone?"

"Next month the Eells will be adopting two children, a niece and a nephew who have lost their parents. I'm going to teach the children their lessons in exchange for provisions and medicine. And Mr. Bagwell has offered to give me meat from his butchery."

"But Almon tells me that Dr. Eells has been elected president of the antislavery society. They are abolitionists—and certainly part of the underground railroad."

Delcena interrupted Julianne. "That's true. They are saintly people—unafraid to help the oppressed wherever they find them."

"I know that. And slavery is abhorrent. But the Missourians hate abolitionists as much as they hate us. This river might not be wide enough to protect Dr. Eells. If something happened to him, what would you do?"

"I would be with friends. Emma is here. Lyman's mother and sister will arrive soon. When the time comes, we will find a way to gather with the Saints."

"But, Delcie, after all we've been through, how can I leave you?" Tears gathered in Julianne's eyes. Her emotions were a complete jumble—love, compassion, and commitment to Delcena and her children but also a conflicting longing to move on in her life with Almon. Julianne's shoulders curved inward, and she began to cry.

"Don't cry, Juli. Please."

Julianne took a handkerchief out of her apron pocket and wiped her eyes. "I'm so sorry that you feel like you have to go on alone. That I'm not enough."

Delcena stared at the river as tears trickled down her cheeks. "You mean so much to me. But with Lyman gone, I guess no one is enough. But I have to try to go on, Juli. On my own. I have to try. I will miss you. More than words can express."

Julianne reached out and put her hand over Delcena's. The sisters sat together while the April sun melted the lingering mist.

*Remember, love, our reason*
*Is given for a purpose great,*
*Our lives on earth to elevate,*
*That we may know that happier state.*

Joseph Ellis Johnson

*Springfield, Illinois*

"'Let reverence for the laws be breathed by every American mother to the lisping babe that prattles on her lap; let it be taught in schools, in seminaries, and in colleges; let it be written in Primmers, spelling books, and in Almanacs. And, in short, let it become the political religion of the nation.'"

Joe looked up from his notes at the forty children in his charge. All were attentive except his sister Esther, who was tapping her fingers as though infinitely bored. Joe paused for a moment then went on. "This is a quote from our state legislator, a tall fellow named Mr. Lincoln, who lives here in Springfield. He said this at the Young Men's Lyceum. Do you agree? How important is law?"

A boy in his early teens raised his hand. "Our founding fathers built a nation of law. God is first. Law is second."

"Well said," Joe responded. "But have you considered that our founding fathers rebelled against the laws of England when they rose up against King George?"

Seventeen-year-old Nancy Carroll raised her hand to her shoulder, almost as if she were waving.

Joe nodded to her. "Yes, Miss Carroll."

"Master Johnson, those laws were unjust," she said with a sweet smile.

"But the English crown thought them just," Joe challenged.

His sister Mary spoke out before Joe could call on her. "The laws were unjust in the eyes of all who believed in the unalienable rights of man."

Joe grinned. "Excellent point, Miss Johnson. The rights of life, liberty, and the pursuit of happiness. Who gives those rights?"

"God," Mary Ann Hale responded.

"I agree," Joe said as he smiled at his adopted sister. Then he turned back to the class. "But who wrote of those rights?"

With her elbow on the desk and her head resting against her palm, Esther rolled her eyes and flipped up a finger—as if the answer were infinitesimally simple. "Thomas Jefferson."

"And whose writings influenced Jefferson?" Joe pushed, his eyes not leaving his youngest sister. Three students in the room raised their hands. Joe shook his head. "Miss Esther, can you answer this question?"

Esther glared at Joe. "No, I cannot."

"Perhaps if you had not been talking during history lesson," Joe chided gently.

"Perhaps if you were a better teacher," Esther responded, her eyes angry as her cheeks reddened.

The room was silent, all eyes on Joe. Disrespect of a schoolmaster was never tolerated. Joe knew he could lose control of his school if he did nothing. He ought to call her in front of the class and punish her. But he could not even imagine striking her hands with the ruler.

Joe swallowed. "Miss Esther Johnson, I regret that I must suspend you from this school. Leave immediately."

Esther wrapped her shawl around her shoulders and ran from the room with tears running down her cheeks. Joe could not look at Mary or Amos. He remembered how he had loved attending Seth's school when he was Esther's age, how he had been devastated when Seth was dismissed because of his conversion to Mormonism. Now he had dismissed Esther—Esther, who used to be his adoring baby sister. How had this happened?

"I believe it was John Locke who influenced Mr. Jefferson," Nancy Carroll remarked.

Joe forced his mind back to the subject and continued the lesson. "Yes. He was the thinker who wrote of the rights of man, who influenced Jefferson and our other founding fathers. In our nation, do these rights extend to all men?"

Sylvia Carter raised her hand. "All men have these rights, except for Negroes."

Then Harriet Snider's slim, pale hand went up. Joe suddenly remembered the first time he had seen that hand, had noticed the blue vein branching down from the ring finger. She was a pretty girl but so quiet. He did not know what her mind was like. "Yes, Miss Snider?"

Harriet blushed. "The Mormons in Missouri were denied these rights."

Joe took a deep breath. This was a day he would not forget. He had dismissed his sister, and now he would be required to discuss his religion in front of his class. His students knew he was a Yankee, but not all of them knew he was a Mormon. The shock and sorrow of Seth's expulsion so many years ago ran through him. But they had not been dependent on Seth's income for sustenance. His family would starve if he lost his employment.

Did Harriet know that he was treading on dangerous ground? He looked into her blue eyes. *What had she suffered in Missouri? What had Ben suffered?* "Go on, Miss Snider," he said gently.

He saw her fingers shake and that blue vein bulge slightly. Yet her voice was quiet and clear. "The Mormons' rights were taken from them. They were not allowed to vote. They were driven from their homes."

"There must be more to it," Sylvia Carter spoke out. "I have heard that the Mormons as a group were undesirable citizens." She flashed a smile at Joe. "Although, Master Johnson, I am certain that isn't true of many individual Mormons. But the Missouri Mormons must have broken laws. Otherwise this could not have happened."

"But it did happen," Joe said, his heart pounding—to deny it would be to cheapen the sacrifice of his people. He continued. "I know that as surely as I know that I breathe. A state in a nation ruled by law disregarded the very laws by which that state ought to be governed. The question is not whether or not it happened, but how do men justify disregarding law and doing such things to their fellow men?"

Mary spoke. "Perhaps in a state like Missouri, which already justifies slavery, it is easier to justify taking the rights of other groups of people away."

"Perhaps," Joe said.

Jacob Vance raised his hand. "My uncle owns slaves in Kentucky. And he's an honest, God-fearing man."

"Interesting point, Mr. Vance. But we shall save a discussion of slavery for another time and place. Let us go back to the Missouri situation. If reverence for law should be the political religion of our nation, as Mr. Lincoln recommends, what should the Mormons do now?"

"Get guns and drive the Missourians out of the country," Johnny Snider spoke up.

"No," Harriet responded, still blushing. "They should seek redress with the federal government."

Joe looked at Harriet and smiled. "Excellent deduction, Miss Snider." Joe took out his pocket watch and glanced at the time. He looked back at his students, hating the fact that Esther's desk was empty. "Now, scholars, we will move on to mathematics."

\* \* \*

Julia stared at the stationery in front of her. One piece of paper was full and the other empty. She hadn't much more time. The elders would be leaving soon and taking her letters east with them.

The first letter was to her younger sister, Diadamia. It had been six years since she'd heard from her baby sister—six years. *Oh, my dear sister,* she had written. *How shall I use words to express my feelings when I look back on the time we last saw each other, the last change in our situation and circumstances in life.* Then she had written of her children's deaths, of seeing Nancy and Rhoda in Cincinnati. She had borne her testimony. She had ended the letter begging Diadamia to study the gospel, to ask the Lord in sincerity to show her the right way. Would Diadamia listen, or would the circumstances of her life cause her to look another direction as Rhoda and Nancy had?

Julia sighed and took off the glasses she wore for close-up work. They didn't seem quite strong enough of late. She rubbed her eyes and repositioned the spectacles. The letter had not been easy to write. Revisiting the deaths of Nancy, Seth, David, and Susan pained her, regardless of how many times she wrote or spoke of them. But the next letter was even more difficult. It was to Ezekiel. How should she address the once-treasured husband whom she missed every day but could not bear the thought of living with?

Julia's thoughts reverted back to yesterday when Esther had come home in the middle of the school day, her face stained with tears. Esther had choked out the story, telling her of how Joe had expelled her for rudeness. The schoolmaster/brother Esther had painted a picture of was nothing like the son Julia knew so well. She had tried to suggest that perhaps Esther was unfair to Joe, and it might be wise to rein in her words and emotions. But at the gentle chide, Esther had erupted.

"No one understands. Not you! Not Mary! I want to go home, Mama. I want Papa. Please! Please! I miss Papa!" Esther had wept and shaken so violently. But worse, each time Julia had reached out to hold her, Esther had recoiled. The words of Mary Magdalene when she had reached out to the resurrected Lord entered Julia's mind. *Hold me not, for I have not yet ascended to my father.* Had this been a direction from the Lord? Did Esther too need to go to her father?

Julia picked up the pen and dipped it in the ink.

> *Ezekiel,*
> *We were previously ill but are now well in body and hope that you, Almera, and Sam are well too. Joel and Annie have moved about 100 miles west of here to Carthage, Illinois. I have recently received word that Annie has delivered a healthy baby boy, Seth Johnson, the namesake of our beloved son. I expect Julianne, Delcena, and Benjamin here shortly. Then Julianne and Almon will go on to Kirtland to visit you and Almera. I plan to send Esther with them.*
> *Esther has expressed a great desire for you. Perhaps it will comfort you to have her near for a time. See that she attends the Young Lady's Academy where Almera is teaching. The classes will be beneficial to her. If you are not at home in the evenings, have her stay with Almera. When I know where we will settle, I will send for Esther. Give Almera my love, and tell her that I will write her at the first opportunity. Elder Conley waits at the door for this letter. May the Lord bless and keep you and our children.*
> *Julia Johnson*

\* \* \*

*Two weeks later. Mentor, Ohio*

Almera glanced out the academy's window and saw Sam pull up with the wagon. She reached for her cloak and fastened it around her shoulders. Then she turned to Melissa LeBaron, who was tidying the tables. "My husband's here."

"I wish he would be late just one day so that we could visit," Melissa commented.

Almera sighed. "Me too." But Sam was never late picking her up. Sometimes she wondered if he waited around the corner for the first young lady to leave so he could come claim her, reminding her that she was his property.

Almera bid Melissa good-bye and walked outside. Sam sat like a statue in the wagon. The sunlight filtered through the fog that had lingered into the afternoon. Almera lifted her blue dress as she descended the porch stairs. The flash of her ankle seemed to awaken Sam. He swung out of the seat and was by her side when she reached the wagon. His eyes were bloodshot, and he didn't smile at her, but he extended one hand to her and put the other on the small of her back. Almera took his hand and climbed up onto the seat, feeling the pressure on her back. She was glad when he let go of her. She folded her hands in her lap while he climbed in. He was hatless, despite the cool weather. It was strange how his hair remained so blond throughout the winter and into the early spring. When summer approached, it would be platinum, whiter than winter wheat.

"Did you get a letter from your mother?" Sam questioned when they were on their way.

"No," Almera answered truthfully. "Why?"

"Because your father did. Some Mormon stopped by the shop today."

Almera spoke more to herself than to Sam. "Why would Mother write him and not me?"

"Why indeed?" Sam stared straight ahead. "When she up and left him."

Almera did not respond for a moment, knowing that anything she said could make things so much worse. Yet she wanted to know, she needed to know why her mother had written. "Would you stop by the shop, and I'll ask Papa about it?" Almera suggested carefully.

Sam nodded curtly. "Yes. But if you read that letter, I'm reading it too."

Almera nodded, knowing that Sam suspected the truth—that she planned to someday rejoin her mother and the Saints. With Sam, there was no hope for happiness, for freedom. If she could only survive living with Sam a little longer, if she could get away with her father before Sam hurt either of them, then there was hope.

"Do you hear me, Almera?" Sam shouted and gripped her arm.

"Yes, Sam, I hear you."

\* \* \*

"Papa," Almera said as she and Sam entered the shop.

Ezekiel put the hammer down and stood up. He stretched his shoulders, stiff from long hours at the bench. Then he embraced her and kissed her cheek. "Hello, darlin'. Those girls become ladies yet?"

Almera noticed that her father seemed happier than usual. Had he been drinking? Yet there was no alcohol on his breath. She smiled back at him. "An inch at a time, Papa, an inch at a time. Sam said you received a letter from Mama."

"Yes. She sends you her love. Julianne and Almon will be visiting soon. And Esther will be coming to live with me for a while. Your mama wants her to attend the academy."

"Really?" Almera said, her brow creasing in near disbelief.

"Surprised me too. Here's the letter. Go ahead and read it." Ezekiel took the letter from his pocket and handed it to her.

Almera opened the letter, feeling Sam's breath hot on her neck, his arm tightening around her waist as he read over her shoulder. After she handed the letter back to Ezekiel, Sam pivoted her around, saying it was time to leave. She knew he was remembering the letter Julianne had written her, which Sam had intercepted, offering to take her away. As they walked out of the shop, she felt her father's eyes on her, the light in them fading as Sam led her away. Yet Almera knew that Sam would not strike her, not when he knew Ezekiel's eyes were on him as well.

On the way home, Sam's voice was cold. "Don't think for a moment about running off with Babbitt and his wife. Not over my dead body."

A chill ran through Almera. "I'm only thinking about Esther coming."

Sam stared ahead as the horses plodded through the mud. The horizon grew crimson from the setting sun. Almera's thoughts moved quickly. What had caused her mother to decide to send Esther back to Kirtland? Something must have happened. And how many times had she imagined Almon and Julianne coming back? How many times had she dreamed of slipping out on a moonlit night and climbing into a buggy with Julianne, with Almon's quick whip flashing as his fast horses pounded the ground, running far away from Sam and sorrow. But now she would have to stay. Esther would need her. But when the Saints were settled and her mother sent for Esther once more, her chance would come.

*How glorious is the sight*
*When saints with one accord*
*Shall in each other's peace delight*
*In deed as well as word.*

Joel Hills Johnson

*Springfield, Illinois*

JULIA'S BREATH CAUGHT IN HER throat as the door flung open. The day had come! It was her children. She wept as she embraced Julianne and Benjamin. Julianne, who had endured so much, a woman so beautiful and good. And she had feared that she would never see Benjamin again. But here he was, standing before her, straight and strong. Julia looked beyond them for Delcena but found only Almon—dear, spirited Almon. But where were Delcena and the grandchildren?

"Mama, they're in Quincy." Julianne answered the question before she asked. "Delcena decided to stay. She and the children are well and provided for."

A pang of sadness and worry tugged at Julia's heart. Did Delcena somehow realize that Julia had lain awake at night wondering how she would feed them? But didn't her beloved and bereaved daughter realize that they would always make room?

Julia's thoughts were interrupted when Benjamin picked Esther up and swung her around. Afterward Julianne hugged Esther, exclaiming, "You've grown so tall. I thought you'd be in school with the rest. Did Mama make you stay home to help?"

Esther's exuberance evaporated as she passionately exclaimed, "I can't go back to school. Joe has kicked me out. Now you and Almon must take me to Pa in Kirtland."

Julianne looked at her mother, her eyes questioning. Julia smiled reassuringly. Then she turned to Esther, her voice firm. "We'll discuss this later. Right now, it's time to celebrate. Let's help carry things in before we get supper on the table."

As they walked outside, Esther moped. Julianne put her arm around her. Almon tugged lightly on Esther's braid and said under his breath, "Sounds like Joe has turned bad. Do his students call him Mean Old Joe behind his back?"

Esther grimaced, but beneath it was a small smile.

Benjamin cut in. "Mean or not, I can scarcely wait to see Old Joe."

"They should be home soon," Julia remarked.

Twenty minutes later, Julia was in the kitchen when she heard a shout outside. She hurried to the front door and saw Benjamin and Julianne running down the road. In the distance, Amos sprinted toward them. Will quickly outdistanced him. Mary, her blonde hair flowing behind her in the March wind, clasped Mary Ann Hale's hand, and the two ran together. George and Joe ran too, their satchels full of school supplies, bouncing against their sides.

Julia watched her children as they mingled. She saw Mary sob for joy. She watched the rapture on Joe and Benjamin's faces when they shook hands then embraced, weeping. Julianne moved from one sibling to the next, hugging them ecstatically.

Almon turned to Julia and grinned. "I never could figure out why your children like each other so much."

"Except for me," Esther said.

"That's right. Except for you," Almon laughed. "But you like all of them except for Joe. That's good odds. Let's join them."

Esther suddenly giggled and followed Almon.

The words of King David's psalm rang through Julia's soul: *Thou hast turned my mourning into dancing: thou hast girded me with gladness.*

\* \* \*

*Wednesday, April 22, 1839*

Albey awakened before the sun rose. The black night was easing, the darkness thinning. The sky would turn pink soon then blue. As light stole into the window, Albey thought about his day. He wanted to play with Joseph but couldn't. Yesterday, when Albey had asked to go over, his mother had told him that Joseph wouldn't have any free time for a while. Sister Emma had caught him shooting a rifle with the Huntington boys without permission. He wished Joseph lived by him instead of the Huntingtons. Albey sighed as other ideas gathered in his mind.

He could watch a ferry come in before breakfast. Maybe he'd find the stray he'd seen yesterday and had immediately named Old Coop. His mother had told him to leave the dog alone, that a stray could hurt him or even kill him if it had rabies. But anyone could tell from the way Old Coop's tail thumped that he was fine. Albey slipped out of the trundle, squeezing past Seth and Danny, who were snoring. He pulled on the boots Dr. Eells had given him and headed for the front door.

"Where are you going?" Mary whispered from a nearby straw-tick mattress.

"To the landing. I'll be back soon. I want to see the first ferry come in. Maybe Dr. Eells will be there helping an escaped slave."

"You better ask, or I'll tell Mama."

Alvira suddenly awakened, her voice crabby. "Mary, Mama needs her sleep, and nobody likes tattletales. Albey, be careful, and don't bother anybody at the landing."

"I'll be good, Allie. I don't want to get shot by a stinkin' Missouri slave catcher."

Alvira rolled her eyes and pulled the blanket snugly under her chin. Then she went back to sleep. Mary pulled the covers up over her head and whimpered.

"What's wrong?" Albey asked.

Mary's eyes peeked out. "I am not a tattletale. You like Allie better than me."

"If you don't wake up Mama, I'll like you best," Albey said. Mary nodded, wiped her eyes, and disappeared under the quilt.

A few moments later, as Albey walked near the riverbank, the breeze blew cool and the damp grass smelled fresh. When he neared the landing, he spied the dog lying near the end of the dock. Albey whistled for him. The dog's tail thumped when he saw Albey.

"Kids ain't supposed to go out there so you gotta come to me," Albey explained to him. The dog's tail thumped more wildly, but he didn't move. "All right, I'll come."

Albey walked out on the landing and sat down on the edge, putting his arm over the dog's back. Old Coop's hair was matted and dirty. Albey's legs dangled as he peered down into the dark, mysterious water. Maybe when they got to a new gathering place, Mama would get him a puppy. Then Albey startled at the sound of a man's voice.

"Git away from there; the boat's coming in!" Dimmick Huntington shouted as he stood with his horse near the other end of the dock.

Albey walked back off the dock, his heart pounding. "I didn't mean no harm. I was just petting the stray."

"*Stray* children aren't allowed on the landing. You could fall in the water or get in the way with people and animals unloading. Do you even know how to swim?"

Albey shook his head.

"Well you ought to have your pa teach ya before you drown."

"My pa's dead."

Dimmick looked more closely at Albey as recognition dawned in his eyes. "Are you Lyman Sherman's boy?"

Albey nodded. Dimmick's voice softened. "You favor your ma more than your pa."

Albey bit his lip. "No. I look like him."

Dimmick's brow furrowed as he bent down and peered at Albey. "My mistake. You look a good deal like your father." Dimmick reached into his pocket and held out two pennies. "If you go tie up my horse by that post near the store, you can have these."

The ferry whistled as it slowed and headed for the landing. The experienced captain eased the craft into the dock. Men with ropes jumped out and guided it. Albey stared first at the pennies then at the boat.

"Go on," Dimmick put the pennies in Albey's hand.

Albey walked back to the store. He tied the horse then watched the ferry unload. Not seeing any escaped slaves, he focused on a ragged beggar man who disembarked and walked down the landing. The man's torn pants were tucked into a pair of tattered boots. He wore an old blue cloak with the collar turned up. Even from that distance, Albey could tell the man was thin and worn. His beard was scruffy, and he wore a wide-brimmed black hat with the lip flipped down so it shadowed his features.

Suddenly, Brother Huntington saw the man. His hands flew up like he was surprised, and he reached out. But the bedraggled man raised a finger to his lips, just like Albey's mother had done when the Missourians came to their house and she had said, "Hush, hush."

Brother Huntington turned and walked away as if nothing had happened. The man followed at a distance. Albey shrugged and went into the store. With his pennies, he bought a pocketful of candy shaped like tiny fish and three peppermint sticks. He decided to give one of the sticks to the beggar man. But when he came out, the beggar man was gone. Brother Huntington and his horse were gone too. However, Old Coop was waiting for him with his tail thumping. Albey went behind the store, where he squatted down and shared a peppermint stick with the dog. Then he stood up and decided to walk to the Smith's house, no matter how long it took. Maybe Sister Emma would let him see Joseph long enough to show him Old Coop.

An hour later, when Albey arrived at the Smith's house, he was in a bad mood. He was extremely thirsty, and Old Coop had run off. He went straight to the well and got a drink. A moment later, Joseph came out of the house and ran up to him, grinning.

"What are you so happy about?" Albey questioned.

"I can't tell you yet," Joseph said. "Want to play ball?"

"I thought you were in trouble and your mama is making you stay in."

"Well my papa said I can play outside today."

"Fibber. Your papa is in prison."

"He escaped."

"Go get him."

Joseph's features clouded. "I can't. I'll get in trouble. Mama and Papa said not to tell anybody until they know what the sheriff will do. Want to play ball?"

"I don't play with fibbers," Albey said. Then he turned around and stalked away, figuring that Joseph would run after him and admit he was lying. But Joseph shrugged and ran back into the house.

Albey started for home, so mad that he started to cry. Then he heard the rhythm of horse's hoofs. He stopped and looked up. Dimmick Huntington reined in the horse and grinned down at Albey. He looked as happy as Christmas and didn't seem to notice Albey's tears.

"Why Albey Sherman, our paths cross again," Brother Huntington exclaimed cheerfully. "Sister Emma sent a doughnut for you. Now climb on, and I'll take you home."

Albey allowed Brother Huntington to lift him up and put him in front of the saddle, just like his Papa used to do. Albey ate the doughnut with one hand and gripped the horse's mane with the other. He was glad Brother Huntington didn't put his arm around him to hold him in the saddle. Albey was big now.

\*\*\*

At ten that night, Delcena sat working near the fire. The children were asleep, and her fingers grew raw from weaving rushes into palm leaf hats. The dry river rushes were rougher than the rye grass her mother and sisters had used. But it was all she had. Delcena planned to sell them to young men who needed good shade hats for working the fields. She desperately needed the money.

Delcena labored wearily, feeling lonely and overwhelmed as she thought of Alvira's moodiness, Mary's tears, Albey's willfulness, and the babies' incessant needs. There was no relief in sight. Tears threatened, and she prayed for the strength to continue. In two more hours, it would be time to put her work away and nurse Susan. Then, if the children permitted her, she would sleep until dawn.

Suddenly there was a knock. Delcena set down her work and stood. She walked toward the door, wondering who it could be so late at night. She remembered just fifteen months ago when Lyman was in hiding, when he had come home to her in the dead of night. But now Lyman was gone. No one would be bringing good news at such an hour.

"Delcena, it's me. Are you home?" She heard Emma's voice. Swallowing, Delcena wiped her eyes and opened the door. Joseph stood behind Emma, pale and clean-shaven, his blue eyes large in his gaunt face. Overcome, Delcena's shoulders bowed and she wept.

Emma took Delcena into her arms. "My dear friend, don't weep so," Emma begged. "Heavenly Father has delivered Joseph from prison. He came home to me this morning. We—we wanted you to know."

Delcena struggled to compose herself. "I'm so glad. If only Lyman were here to share this moment with us." They walked together and sat on the benches by the fire.

"Sister Delcena," Joseph began. His voice was tender and strong. "When Heber brought me word of Lyman's death, I grieved for you and for me. I wept, knowing that I would not hear my friend's voice again in this life. My prayers have been with you and your children. I made a promise to God and to Lyman. As long as I live, you will be cared for and your children will not be fatherless."

Silent tears fell from Delcena's eyes as Emma held her hand. Joseph stood and laid his hands upon her head.

"Sister Delcena, beloved of the Lord, your husband has sealed his testimony with his blood and has died a martyr to the cause of truth. Do not sorrow as those without hope. The time will come when you shall see him again and you shall rejoice together, without the fear of wicked men. Your heart and your children's hearts shall be comforted, and every tear shall be wiped from your faces. The trials you have passed through shall work together for your good and prepare you for the society of those who have come up out of great tribulation and have washed their robes and made them white in the blood of the Lamb. The Lord shall bless you exceedingly."

The Prophet's eyes shone with unshed tears. Emma wept, holding fast to Delcena's hand. Strengthened, Delcena felt a measure of peace and the promise of hope.

They talked for ten more minutes. Joseph and Emma told Delcena of the kindness of the local authorities whom they had called upon that afternoon. They had assured Joseph that he need not worry about arrest while he remained in Quincy.

Before they left, Joseph asked about each of the children, then the Prophet added, "Brother Dimmick tells me that Albey cannot swim. When the weather is warm enough, I will teach him."

# 8

*While sitting by him, day or night*
*The words of life to hear,*
*My heart was filled with love and light,*
*Devoid of doubt and fear*

Joel Hills Johnson

*Springfield, Illinois*

ALMON SAT WITH JOHN IN the Sniders' kitchen. It was midmorning, and the maple table was scrubbed clean. Sunlight spilled in through the windows. "You're well situated, with room to spare," Almon mentioned cheerfully. "If I didn't know better, I wouldn't have guessed you were among the driven Mormons."

John smiled. "I just received the final payment for my farm in Canada. Mary insisted we rent a house large enough for guests. Bring your wife for supper, and stay with us."

Almon grinned, thinking of the additional privacy and comfort. His mother-in-law's home was full to the brim. "We'll be here."

"Good! A gentleman named Judge James Adams is dining with us as well. I want you to meet him. He's read the Book of Mormon but hasn't been baptized yet."

"Really? Tell me more."

John went on. "He's an older gentleman, a probate judge and a veteran of 1812—and a staunch Democrat, like you. He believes the Book of Mormon to be the word of God but has questions. And he has noticed that there are problems among the members of the Church here."

Almon frowned slightly. "My mother-in-law mentioned that the branch is disorganized."

John let out a deep breath. "That's the tip of the iceberg. The brethren debate doctrine rather than explain it. One brother thinks the gift of tongues paramount to salvation. He regularly shakes and quakes. It's like a flock that keeps increasing with no shepherd to tend it. And the Laws will be here soon with more Canadian Saints."

"So William is finally leaving Canada. He will be a capable shepherd. What about Wilson? Did that rascal ever join the Church?"

John shook his head. "No, but he's coming too. We expect them in October or November."

"And you, John? Have you tried to shepherd the Springfield flock?"

"I've tried, but my voice isn't loud enough to be heard over the quaking and shaking. The moment I found out that you'd arrived, I knew it was an answer to prayers."

"My wife *has* accused me of a loud voice."

John smiled. "Precisely. Among other gifts, you have volume to spare."

Almon chuckled then became serious. "But, John, my call isn't here."

"Are you sure? Julianne's family is here, and the field is white. There's Judge Adams and the widow of the former secretary of state, young Mrs. Forquer. She's related to a wealthy man by the name of Lamb, who's a wholesale merchant and banker. He's impressed with the Church."

"I've heard of Lamb. Benjamin hopes to work for him." Almon scratched his sideburn and tried to explain his dilemma to John. "Last fall in Richmond, the Prophet made me his agent in Kirtland. If it is possible, I want to build Kirtland up again. The apostates have softened. Perhaps we can return to our temple."

Almon and John continued their discussion. Mrs. Snider joined them, bringing in slices of fresh bread and butter. The front door suddenly flung open, and their adolescent son Eddie burst into the kitchen, his cheeks ruddy with excitement. "Brother Almon," he exclaimed. "Master Johnson said you were back and I'd find you here!"

Almon stood and heartily embraced the boy. "Hello, Eddie. Has Master Johnson suspended you? I hear he has been doing that lately."

Mrs. Snider eyed her son sternly. "I should hope not."

Eddie grinned and put out his hands. "I'm just an innocent messenger boy."

"Innocent?" Almon raised an eyebrow.

Eddie laughed. "I'll prove it. Brother Wilson just arrived with news. The Prophet and the others have escaped. They're safe in Quincy. There's going to be a conference on May fourth and fifth. Brother Almon, the Prophet has sent word for you to attend."

John jumped to his feet and embraced his wife. Whooping with joy, Almon vigorously shook Eddie's hand then joyfully hugged the entire Snider family.

\* \* \*

Mary could not concentrate with George Wilson's eyes on her as she set the bowl of grape preserves on the table. Joe had invited him for dinner. The only place left for her to sit was next to him on the end of the bench flanking the side of the table. Joe winked at her. Had her brother arranged the seating?

With a graceful swish of her skirt, Mary sat down, wishing they had a roast or a chicken to serve rather than corn mush and biscuits. But at least her mother had told her to fill a plate with cheese and get out a precious pint of preserves.

After Benjamin said the blessing, Amos spoke up. "Mother, you told me we couldn't open the preserves until Joe's birthday."

"I give permission," Joe said. "This is a special occasion."

Amos glanced directly at Mary. "It sure is a special occasion, isn't it Mary? Having a guest and all."

Mary's face reddened, and she kicked Amos under the table. He yelped and tried to kick her back, but she had tucked her feet away.

Julia cleared her throat. "We're also celebrating because God has answered our prayers. The Prophet is free and home with his family."

"Do you think Delcena is happy?" Esther suddenly asked. "Or is she sad because Lyman won't ever come home?"

Julia swallowed and explained, "I'm sure she rejoices because the Prophet is safe. People can rejoice and grieve at the same time."

"Not me," Esther said.

"Someday you'll understand," Julia added as she passed the biscuits.

As the family began eating, Mary knew she ought to be thinking of the Prophet's liberation and of Delcena. But it was difficult with Brother Wilson sitting next to her.

"I have more good news," Benjamin said. "I've been hired by Mrs. Lamb! I'll be driving her and her sister, the Widow Forquer, in their carriage."

"Have you met the widow?" Will grinned. Ben shook his head, so Will continued. "That carriage is the finest equipment in the city besides the widow herself."

At Ben's confused look, Will laughed. "The Widow Forquer might wear black and have a child, but she's pretty as a picture."

"They're good people," Julia redirected the conversation. "And Ben is fortunate to have employment." She looked to her guest. "Brother Wilson, could you tell us the details of the Prophet's escape and arrival in Quincy?"

The family sat in rapt silence as he told of the guards who allowed the Prophet to escape. He described the arduous journey to Quincy and the warm reception by both the Saints and city officials. As the meal wound down, Benjamin suggested that he and Brother Wilson walk together to the Sniders' to make sure Almon had received the message about the coming conference. Brother Wilson did not answer immediately. Joe glanced at Mary. She stood up and began to clear the table. In the side room with the washboard, she was unable to hear Brother Wilson's reply. She started scrubbing the trenchers.

A moment later, Brother Wilson was beside her with another pile of trenchers in his arms. He placed them on the board. "Miss Mary, I'd like a word with you."

She stopped and looked at him, her hair stretching down her back, her brown eyes sparkling in the candlelight. His eyes, though honey-colored, were not young like David's had been, but were so much older. "Yes, Brother Wilson," she said.

"I've told Benjamin I can't go with him to the Sniders'. As you know, my father passed away this winter, and my mother is waiting at home for me. Your mother asked if you would prepare a plate of food for me to take to her."

"Of course," Mary said.

"There's another thing I want to speak with you about." Brother Wilson paused. Mary waited, her heart pounding, wondering if he would now tell her that he admired her. He continued. "I-I must apologize to you for the words I said last time I was here."

Mary swallowed. "You needn't apologize."

He went on earnestly. "Regardless of circumstances, a gentleman ought never to treat a lady as if she is faithless and weak."

Mary stared at him. "Did you treat me that way? I don't recall."

"I cannot forget my rudeness."

"Your apology is accepted," she said quickly.

He looked away and was silent.

*Faithless and weak.* The words stung in Mary's mind. She tried to remember the moment when Brother Wilson had put his hands on her shoulders. "Your brother needs your faith," he had said. "Have courage." But all the time he was thinking *faithless* and *weak.* If he admired her now, why didn't he say that he was mistaken in thinking that of her? It must be because he still thought it. Mary turned quickly, took a clean trencher, and filled it with food. After covering it with a cloth, she handed it to him, careful not to let her hand brush against his.

"Thank you," he said. "My mother will be grateful."

"You're welcome," she said shortly, feeling her face flush. Then she turned from him and started scrubbing the trenchers again. When he said farewell, she mumbled a response. After he was gone, she realized she had not asked about his mother. Angry tears stung her eyes. Now he would think that she was thoughtless as well as faithless and weak.

A moment later, Joe walked into the room and sidled up to her. Esther stood at the door. "I told you he would be back," Joe said. "What did he say?"

Mary pivoted toward Joe. "That he thinks I am weak and faithless."

"He said that?"

"He apologized for treating me like I was weak and faithless."

"Because he knows it is not true."

"He did not say that. Don't tell me again what a man thinks." In tears, Mary threw down the cloth and left the kitchen.

Esther glared at Joe, her hands on her hips. "See, now you've made Mary cry too." Frustrated and defensive, Joe grabbed his coat from the hook. "Where do you think you are going?" Esther demanded.

"To catch up with my brother."

\* \* \*

By the time Joe caught up with Benjamin, he was nearly out of breath.

Benjamin grinned. "I'm glad to have your company! I thought you were going to stay and find out Brother Wilson's intentions."

"I think he offended her without meaning to. And she probably offended him in defense."

"What happened?" Benjamin asked, and Joe explained.

"That's all right," Benjamin responded. "Wilson's too old for Mary anyway."

As they continued to walk, they talked of other things. Joe told Benjamin of the family's financial situation and of the sickness they had endured that winter. Benjamin opened up about his experience as a prisoner in Missouri.

Joe listened intently. His brother seemed much older now, and stronger. Joe marveled at the look in Benjamin's eyes, the sheer determination, and the hard-won confidence. It seemed that Benjamin had suffered terribly and had grown up completely. Joe no longer felt like the older brother who could advise and comfort.

"You've changed, Ben," Joe remarked.

"How so?" Benjamin asked.

"There's none of the boy in you. Not anymore."

Benjamin smiled. "Maybe it was scared out of me in Missouri."

Joe nodded. "I suppose that would do it."

Benjamin chuckled and cuffed Joe lightly on the shoulder. "You might be wrong though."

Joe felt his heart lighten. "I've been wrong before."

They continued to walk together. Joe watched the waxing moon rise in the sky, with clouds weaving around and across its brightness. How often had he watched the waning and waxing moon, hoping that his brother lived, praying that somewhere, somehow, Benjamin beheld the same moon? Then Joe realized something. Now that Benjamin was home, it was time for Joe to move on with his life. It was time to leave.

\* \* \*

*May 4, 1839. Quincy, Illinois*

Almon shook hands with those around him and sat down on a bench in the back of the Presbyterian campground before the meeting started. The morning was cool and bright. He had arrived in town late the previous night and had not had the opportunity to speak with any of the brethren. President Rigdon went to the stand and announced the opening hymn. Almon's voice rose in song:

> *Know this that every man is free,*
> *To choose his life and what he'll be;*
> *For this eternal truth is given,*
> *That God will force no man to heaven.*

After the opening prayer, the Prophet stood and expressed his love for the brethren and his feelings about being separated from them for so long. Tears pricked Almon's eyes as he thought about the last time he had seen Joseph—in chains in Richmond. Joseph prayed aloud, thanking Heavenly Father for safety and deliverance and pleading for the welfare of the Saints and for the gospel to spread to the ends of the earth.

Next, Elder Greene and President Rigdon spoke briefly about the purchase of land in the Iowa Territory. Then Joseph stood up again to read a series of resolutions that he hoped the brethren would unanimously adopt. "First, we propose that Almon Babbitt, Erastus Snow, and Robert B. Thompson be appointed a traveling committee to gather up and obtain all the libelous reports and publications that have been circulated against the Church of Jesus Christ of Latter-day Saints, as well as other historical matters concerning the Church." Joseph went on to explain that the material would be used to let leaders of nations and the world at large know about the unfair publicity and horrific treatment the Saints had received in a free republic.

Almon swallowed, wishing he had been here to talk with Joseph about this before the conference. Was it a mandate from the Lord? For the past two days, Almon had felt strongly that he should stay awhile in Springfield to set the Church at rights and to answer Judge Adams' doctrinal questions. And what of Kirtland? His heart was in Kirtland. Yet, perhaps returning to Kirtland was part of this assignment. After all, many of the libelous reports originated in Kirtland. He could do great good there. He knew it.

The Prophet continued. The second and third resolutions were about Vinson Knight's appointment to the bishopric and the purchase of land. But the fourth and fifth resolutions took the breath out of Almon. "Fourth, that Elder Granger be appointed to go to Kirtland to take charge and oversight of the House of the Lord and preside over the general affairs of the Church in that place. Fifth, that the advice of this conference to the brethren living in the Eastern states is for them to move to Kirtland and the vicinity thereof and again settle that place as a stake of Zion, provided they feel so inclined, in preference to their moving father west."

Almon's thoughts spun. Kirtland was to be a stake of Zion! Families from the east would come. Families who had lingered in Canada and needed a place to go would find a home there—perhaps William and

Wilson Law among them. Kirtland was joy, growth, prosperity, and faith. Kirtland was home. This resolution was an answer to prayers. He would see that Kirtland became even more than what it had been. It was where he and Julianne were married, where the temple was built, where David and Seth lost their lives, where his son was buried. If only he had been called in the place of Brother Granger.

As the brethren raised their hands, Almon's joined the rest. He looked up and saw Joseph's eyes upon him. After the meeting, Joseph found Almon and embraced him warmly. "We meet again, my good friend, and under happier circumstances. I will never forget your visit while I was in prison. Come home with me, and let us have lunch together."

A short time later, as they ate the chicken and dumplings Emma had prepared, Almon looked carefully at the Prophet. There were lines where his face had been smooth, and he was thin. Yet he seemed to be regaining his natural vigor.

Joseph opened the conversation. "Brother Almon, four days ago, Hyrum, Sidney, and I rode to a place about fifty miles north of here called Commerce. It's largely swampland but has potential, if drained. We purchased nearly two hundred acres. There's a log house on my land. I plan to move Emma and the children there next week. This might be the next gathering place."

"Are you sure?"

"Not yet. For now, I hope that my friends and I will find a resting place there—at least for a little season. It's on the banks of the Mississippi and not far from where your brother-in-law Joel lives. Perhaps you would like to come take a look."

"Perhaps," Almon said before taking another bite of chicken. He didn't know what to think. Kirtland beckoned to him like a magnet. "Brother Joseph, I would like to talk with you about today's resolutions and my place in them."

"So would I," Joseph said with a smile.

Almon swallowed his food then began talking as Joseph listened. Almon described the difficulties of the Church in Springfield. He told the Prophet of Judge Adams' growing testimony. Could it be the will of the Lord that he go back to Springfield to set the Church to rights? And what of his assignment as agent in Kirtland? He had not yet filled that calling and longed to return there. His wife's father and sister were in Kirtland as well. Yet he had been called to gather libelous reports. And what of his legal aspirations? He had been studying the law but had not yet traveled to Cincinnati to obtain the licenses.

Joseph gazed for a moment out the window then turned back to Almon. "Converts from the east and from the British Isles need a place to rest before they gather with the main body of Saints. Many will be penniless and will need to be strengthened spiritually and temporally. Kirtland is that place. I believe that you will aid the Church in building it up once again. But first, I feel that it is the will of the Lord that you return to Springfield. We should not lose one soul if that soul can be saved by our efforts. Then continue east as a missionary in Indiana, preaching the gospel on the way. Make your way to Kirtland and settle there. Study the law as you continue to serve the Lord. When the opportunity comes, go to Cincinnati to obtain licenses to practice law in Ohio, Missouri, Illinois, and any additional states you deem needful."

"What about the appointment to gather libelous reports and publications that have been circulated against the Church?"

"I trust that you will do that as well. Beloved Brother Almon, I know that you are a man of many talents."

Almon grinned. "And Brother Joseph, I know that you are a prophet of God."

Joseph smiled warmly. "Yes, and you shall soon be a prophet's attorney."

The next morning, on the second day of the conference, the Prophet stood up and declared, "Almon W. Babbitt will be sent to Springfield, Illinois, clothed with authority and required to set to rights the Church in that place in every way which may become necessary according to the order of the Church of Jesus Christ."

\* \* \*

*Mentor, Ohio*

Almera sat in the rocking chair with her cat Coattails on her lap. Sam answered the knock on the door.

"Hello, I'm Elder Roundy." The man wore a traveling cloak. "I have a letter for Mrs. Almera Prescott. It's from Springfield, Illinois."

Before Almera had time to stand up and walk over, Sam took the letter and dismissed the elder, closing the door hard behind him. Almera saw her name on the sealed envelope.

"Stay put," Sam said firmly. Almera obeyed. Sam walked over and stood between Almera and the fire.

"Please read it to me," Almera said softly, praying that Sam would not burn the letter.

Sam looked at her, nodded, and tore the letter open. He began reading aloud. She stared at the fire, stroking Coattails' beautiful black-and-white fur and listening to her mother's sweet words through the cold voice of her husband.

*Dearest, we are all well in body and spirit and pray that this letter finds you well. I regret to tell you that your sisters will not be able to come as soon as we had planned. It will be at least another season. I pray that this news does not make your heart too heavy. Julianne is disappointed. She longs for your companionship. We all do. But Almon has been asked by the Prophet to remain in Springfield for a season to set the Church aright. Then Almon will preach the gospel in Indiana. Eventually, he and Julianne will go on to Kirtland unless missionary work delays him. Esther is unhappy. She had hoped to see her father soon and begin studying with you and Miss LeBaron. She will have to wait until the fall or early winter. Then you can expect all of them.*

*We rejoice that the Prophet is free. He has purchased land in a place north of here called Commerce. Perhaps this will be the new gathering place. Joe will leave soon with a man named Micham. They plan to claim land in Iowa, across the river from Commerce.*

*It's good to have Benjamin and Julianne here in Springfield. Delcena and the children stayed in Quincy. Joel and Annie are well.*

*My darling daughter, continue in the knowledge that Jesus is our Savior and will one day put all things to right. My heart yearns for you, and I look forward to the day when we will be together again, when I can hold you close.*

Sam stopped reading. "What does she mean by that?"

"She misses me."

Sam's voice rose. "You mother doesn't say a word about your husband! Only that she anticipates being with you and holding you close." Almera saw Sam's eyes redden. Was it sorrow or anger? His voice rose. "When I hold you close, you cringe at my touch."

Almera stared up at Sam. "I-I never meant for it to end up like this."

"Like what?" Sam wadded the letter, pivoted, and threw it into the fire. When he turned back to her, his face was contorted with rage. Almera buried her head into Coattails' fur, crying. Sam tore the cat from her, his arm cocked, preparing to toss the shrieking animal into the flames.

"Don't, Sam! Please!" Almera screamed as she dropped to her knees, wrapping her arms around his waist. "Please don't."

"Promise you won't leave me!"

The cat shrieked. Almera imagined the innocent animal burning. "I promise," Almera sobbed.

Sam stood still for a moment; then he put the cat down. "You have promised." There were sudden tears in his ice-blue eyes. He bent over the sobbing Almera. "Please don't make me hurt you," he moaned. "Burn your church and your mother from your soul as I have burned the letter. Turn back to me. I love you." Then he wrapped his iron-muscled arms around her.

*How sweet the spirit's voice
That whispers life and peace,
It makes the sorrowful rejoice
And all their mourning cease.*

Joel Hills Johnson

*Kirtland, Ohio*

It was midmorning, and the day was bright and growing warmer. With a pounding head, Ezekiel forced himself out of bed. He had stayed at the tavern late the previous night, his drinking binge triggered by the news that the Mormons were buying land in Commerce, Illinois, along the Mississippi River. He recalled the stinging words of Jerold Clapp: *I've been up that way. There's a reason the land's cheap. It's swamp. Half of the people die each summer when the river scourge hits. Malaria will finish off what the Missourians started.* Bill Leonard, a local doctor and drinking companion, had read Ezekiel's mind and said under his breath, "I s'pose your wife's on her way. Just got a big shipment of quinine in the form of Sappington pills. You can have half of it."

Ignoring his aching head, Ezekiel gulped down some water, ate a biscuit, and filled his purse with money. Then he took his gun off the mantel. He walked outside to the stable, blinking in the sunlight. After saddling Old Leo, he rode to Dr. Leonard's house. The doctor answered the door with bloodshot eyes.

"Mornin', Bill. I'm here for the quinine," Ezekiel said.

"You don't look sick," the doctor responded. "I'm going back to bed."

Ezekiel stuck his foot in the door. "Last night you said you'd give me half of it."

"What?"

"I aim to send it to my family in Illinois."

The doctor's brow furrowed as the memory flitted across his eyes. "I was drunk last night."

"In my book, a man's word means something, drunk or not. You said you'd give it to me, but I won't take advantage of you. I came prepared to pay."

"I don't have enough to sell."

"I'm not leaving without it."

Dr. Leonard stared at Ezekiel for a moment then reluctantly suggested a price. After a few minutes of haggling, Ezekiel paid the money and was handed the quinine.

"You better hope I have enough left for my patients here," Dr. Leonard snapped.

"I do hope that," Ezekiel said, offering his hand to the doctor. Leonard hesitated for a moment then shook it.

With the medicine in his saddlebag, Ezekiel rode south toward Pittsburg. It would cost him a pretty penny, but he would send the pills by water, first west on the Ohio River then north up the Mississippi. The package might get lost on the way or stolen. But it might make its way to Commerce, Illinois, about the time his wife and children arrived.

\* \* \*

*Early June. Hancock County, Illinois*

Micham, though not a Mormon, was a strong rogue of a fellow, ambitious and boisterous. When Joe met him, he was an uneducated hired hand, hoping to one day have land of his own. Joe suggested they join forces—claim and develop land in Iowa, directly across the Mississippi River from Commerce, Illinois, where the Mormons were settling. Micham agreed—he needed Joe's mind, and Joe needed Micham's muscle.

Joe left Mary and George to finish up the term as teachers in his Springfield school, and he and Micham headed west on a blithe June day. If things went well, Joe would send word to his mother and claim land for her as well.

On the final leg of the journey, as darkness fell, the two men arrived at Joel and Annie's home near Carthage. Later that night, Joe and Joel talked under a sky full of stars, discussing crops, poetry, religion, politics, and family. Joe took a deep breath; it felt good to be with his eldest brother, to be men on equal terms.

The following morning, Joe and Micham rode to Commerce. The Prophet warmly greeted them. As Joe surveyed the tents lining the Mississippi, the scattering of huts surrounded by bogs, he hoped prospects were brighter on the other side of the river. While the Prophet talked to Micham about the Church, Joe sought out the Huntingtons for news to give Benjamin.

He found them in a tent near the river. Sister Huntington was extremely ill with the fever. Joe opened his medicine bag and gave her his last bit of quinine. Zina carefully gave her mother a drink of water and helped her take the pill. Joe noticed Zina was thin and tired. "Have you had the fever?" he asked.

Zina nodded.

"Ben will be sorry to hear it," Joe said.

Zina's cheeks colored. "Please send Ben a message from me," Zina began uncomfortably. "Tell him . . ." She did not finish her sentence because a dark-haired, handsome young man ducked into the tent. He moved over to Zina and put his arm around her shoulders. Her face colored as she stretched her arm around his waist. "Henry, this is our friend Joseph Johnson," she introduced. "Joe, this is Henry Jacobs."

While still holding Zina close, Henry Jacobs reached out his right hand to shake Joe's. "Any friend of Zina's is a friend of mine." Joe shook his hand but left shortly after, not relishing the thought of giving Benjamin this message.

That afternoon, Joe and Micham crossed the river into Montrose. During the next twelve days, they claimed land, prepared it for planting, and plotted out a spot for a store. Then on a Monday afternoon, William Huntington came, bringing word that his mother had died and that the fever ran rampant. He begged Joe to come to Commerce to help nurse the sick.

Ignoring Micham's protests, Joe began preparing medicines. Day after day, he crossed the river to help those suffering. Joe knew Micham was growing bitter from working the land alone, but what could he do? His people were sick and dying.

\* \* \*

It was midafternoon. Joe slapped at a mosquito as he searched the wooded area for lobelia. He had spent the morning across the river in Commerce. Each day the sickness spread. The lobelia couldn't cure the fever like quinine, but the Saints were out of quinine. Lobelia would ease the shaking and help the sufferers retain their broth. Joe sighed wearily. He moved deeper into the moist woods. Mosquitoes swarmed him. His pack felt heavy, though it only contained a few branches of alder.

Then Joe saw them—purple lobelias in the midst of the weeds. He squatted down and picked the bell-like flowers, carefully placing them at the top of his pack. His mind went back to the faraway gulf in Pomfret, New York, where he had searched for lobelia with Rachel Risley. He recalled her willow-long braid, but he couldn't visualize her features. Instead, the face of Harriet Snider rose in his mind. But she was so young and quiet. He needed someone who shone brighter, someone as vivacious as Rachel.

Joe felt a mosquito sting and noticed numerous welts that had sprung up on his forearms. He would itch tonight, but a salve from the alder bark would help that. He placed more lobelia flowers into his pack. Why did his legs suddenly feel so heavy and his head so light? He turned and headed out of the mossy woodland.

As he trudged back to the cabin, he broke into a sweat. He forced his thoughts away from the possibility that he was getting the fever. Facing the setting sun, Joe thought of how lovely this country was—green trees spiraling upward, moss and grasses—it was tragic that the river scourge and malaria blighted its wonder. What in heaven's name caused the disease? Was it the humidity, the air so thick that you were dripping with sweat by midmorning? Or was it the swamp water seeping into your skin? And should he bring his family here?

Back in the cabin, Joe began making tea with the lobelia. By the time he finished, he was shaking so violently that he couldn't hold the cup of tea still enough to drink it.

* * *

*Springfield, Illinois*

Benjamin thanked the postmaster as he took the letter with his name on it. Three-year-old Henry Forquer tugged on his pant leg. "Where Mommy?"

Benjamin smiled and took the hand of the curly-haired, blue-eyed little boy. "She's getting a new hat with Auntie. Let's go."

They walked outside. It was noon, and the sun, high in the sky, was momentarily shadowed by a stray cloud. Benjamin only had a few moments before he had to pick up Mrs. Lamb and Mrs. Forquer at the milliner's. He helped little Henry into the velvet-seated carriage. Then he opened the letter and saw that it was from Heber C. Kimball. As he read, excitement and anxiety spread through him. The letter informed him that he had been called in the June conference to accompany the apostles on their mission to Europe. It was a joy and a challenge beyond his dreams.

With a pounding heart, Benjamin put the letter in his pocket and stroked the horses. They were bright chestnuts with stars on their foreheads, the finest animals Benjamin had ever driven. He climbed into the driver's seat. As the horses trotted down the street, the clouds moved on and the full sun beat upon him. When Benjamin arrived at the milliner's, he found Mrs. Lamb and Mrs. Forquer waiting outside. They were sisters, both wealthy and attractive. Mrs. Lamb, the older of the two, wore a new yellow hat perched on her highly coifed hair. She acknowledged Benjamin with an impersonal nod as he reached out a hand to help her into the carriage.

In contrast, Mrs. Forquer smiled warmly. Today she was not in black but wore a lavender dress with a white lace collar. Her new hat was lavender and white and set off the rich darkness of her hair and the fairness of her skin. Coyly, she took Benjamin's offered hand and smiled up at him, her petite features perfect even in the noon light. "How was Henry?" she asked, still holding Benjamin's hand but not moving her feet to get into the carriage.

"As good as gold," Benjamin said, his smile reflecting hers.

"I'm glad. He is attached to you."

"And I to him," Benjamin added honestly. In the past month, while working for Charles Lamb, he had often attended the ladies and had become captivated by Henry, who was just learning to talk.

Mrs. Forquer continued. "And this hat? Do you think it becoming?"

"Very becoming."

"I have worn black for so long. Do you think it is the right time to put behind my widow's weeds?"

"High time, Mrs. Forquer," Benjamin agreed. Her palm felt so soft and warm in his hand. He forced himself to think of his mission and of Zina.

"Then you mustn't call me Mrs. Forquer anymore. Let me be *Anne* to you."

Benjamin felt his face color.

"Anne, stop dawdling. It's time to go," Mrs. Lamb said from within the carriage.

"Up you go." Benjamin helped the lovely young widow into the carriage. Then he mounted the outside driver's seat. As he drove, Benjamin turned her name over in his mind. Anne Forquer, the relict of the secretary of state. Anne, lovely Anne. Certainly her little boy needed a father. Ought he to try to woo her? But wouldn't she just laugh at a poor Mormon boy? Yet she did not act as if she would laugh.

He directed the horses into the countryside. The grass quieted the clomping of the hooves and the whirring of the wheels, allowing Benjamin to hear within the carriage. Little Henry chattered and then was silent. He must have fallen asleep. Then Mrs. Lamb began a conversation, seemingly unaware that Benjamin was listening.

"Anne, you must stop favoring him."

"Am I not allowed to favor whom I please with my friendship? Ben is earnest and kind. Henry adores him."

"He is a handsome young man, and you are a beautiful woman."

"Is it a crime to befriend a handsome man?"

"This ought to be. He is uneducated, penniless, and a Mormon! Are you thinking of becoming a Mormon?"

"Don't be ridiculous. Of course not."

"Anne, you were married to the secretary of state. You have a son. George Forquer would turn over in his grave if he saw you now."

"I grieve for my husband, and Benjamin Johnson's friendship eases my heart."

"He is not a friend, Anne, but a hired man."

"Beatrice, this is my choice. He is as a breath of fresh air."

An uncomfortable silence followed. When they came to the stream, Benjamin stopped the carriage. After climbing down, he helped the ladies out, avoiding their eyes.

"We'll eat under the maple tree. Ben, will you join us for lunch?" Mrs. Forquer invited. Benjamin declined with a quick shake of his head. He felt Mrs. Lamb's eyes studying him as he said, "I'll wait with the carriage until Henry awakens."

Benjamin sat in the silken carriage. He gazed at the sleeping child, so innocent and lovely. If he won Anne Forquer, he would have a life of wealth and ease. Benjamin took the letter from his pocket and read his mission call once more. Silently, he prayed. Memories of Missouri entered his mind like a dark labyrinth of pain and terror. But the Lord was a light in the darkness, guiding and preserving his life. He had a mission to fulfill, both his own and Seth's. The Prophet had trusted him enough to call him to go to Europe with the apostles. He had a calling with new and bright hopes as a servant of God. Would he measure up?

As he closed his prayer, Benjamin knew what he must do. This month he would earn as much money as he could. Then, in July, he would go to Hancock County to see the Prophet, Zina, William, and Delcena. From there, he would leave for his mission.

He would erase Anne Forquer from his mind. She was not a member of the Church and had no inclination to become one. The price of a lovely wife and an inheritance of wealth was just too high.

\* \* \*

*Tuesday, July 2, 1839. Crooked Creek, Illinois (near Carthage)*

Annie opened the door with Baby Seth on her hip. "Susan, come in!" she exclaimed joyously when she saw the tall, somewhat stiff woman standing before her.

Susan Bryant stepped into the log house. "I had hoped to come sooner and offer my help with the baby. But it wasn't possible. He is a beautiful boy."

"We named him Seth, after Joel's brother. I just put together a picnic lunch for Joel and the children. They will be happy to see you. Would you like to hold Seth?"

Susan nodded and extended her arms. Annie noticed the way Susan's stiff frame softened at the touch of the infant, her shoulders curving down as she held him close.

Annie went on. "Joel told me you've moved in with the Kimballs. I've wanted to come see you, but I've been so busy with the baby."

Susan's deep-set eyes became very serious. "There's been much illness in Commerce. That's partly why I came."

Annie's cheer evaporated, and she bit her lip, sensing bad news. She put the cloth over the food in the basket. "Is there any relief in sight?"

Susan shrugged slightly. "Blessings and prayers relieve some of the suffering. There's very little quinine left, and in many cases it doesn't help. Your brother-in-law, Joseph, has done all he can to nurse the sick.

We received word last night that he has come down with the fever. He's across the river in Montrose."

Annie shuddered and lifted the lunch basket. "We need to hurry and tell Joel."

\* \* \*

Susan carried Seth as she walked with Annie toward the mill creek. The baby was as lovely as Annie's other children, with his auburn hair and bright eyes.

Annie walked quickly, carrying the lunch basket and quilt. "I pray that Joel gets there in time to help. I have a bit of quinine that I can send," Annie said. Her face was flushed from the heat, and worry lined her brow.

"General Robison's daughters were sent for to nurse him," Susan added. "God willing, he will be all right."

"Joel has already lost two brothers and two sisters. I don't think my mother-in-law would survive the loss of her Joseph. Surely God will not take him."

"I pray not," Susan added, wishing she had other words of comfort. But she had seen much sickness and death in Commerce. Up ahead, Annie's four other children played near the creek. With a stick in his hand, five-year-old Nephi turned and saw them. He whooped to the others. Bright warmth flooded Susan when the children ran to them, calling her name. Why were they so happy to see her? Did they know she loved them? Is that why they came running, effervescent, with smiles as warm and wide as their mother's?

Eight-year-old Sariah hugged Susan first then reached up to take Seth from her. Tall, tender Sixtus smiled with boyish self-consciousness and shook her hand. Five-year-old Nephi wrapped his arms tightly around her skirt. Susan blinked back tears. Only three-year-old Susie stood back shyly, gripping her mother's hand.

"What have you brought for us?" Nephi exclaimed.

Annie interrupted. "Sister Bryant's coming is a great gift. Nephi, only selfish children ask for things. Children, help Sister Bryant set out lunch while I go speak with Father."

Sariah, bouncing Seth in her arms, sidled up to Susan as soon as her mother was out of earshot. "Sister Bryant, Nephi didn't mean to be rude. He remembers when we last saw you. Do you recall saying that you would bring us something if we were very good?"

"Now *you're* being selfish," Sixtus said as he examined the food in the basket.

"I didn't ask for anything," Sariah humphed.

"Of course you didn't. You were explaining," Susan commented as she raised the quilt into a billow and laid it smooth. Straightening her skirt, she sat down on the quilt and called the children to her. "I did say I would bring you something if you were good children. And I have brought new quills." Susan reached into the deep pocket around her waist and took out four lovely peacock feathers.

"Thank you," Sixtus exclaimed as he and Sariah each took a quill. But Nephi's eyes filled with tears.

"Why, Nephi, what's wrong?" Susan inquired.

Nephi began to howl. "I want one. But Mama said I'm selfish."

Susan invited the little boy onto her lap. "Nephi, everyone is selfish sometimes. But you shall have one, for you are a good boy most of the time."

\* \* \*

Joel rode hard to Commerce in hopes of crossing over to Montrose before nightfall. However, when he arrived, the sky was already turning crimson, and he was told the ferry would not be making any more trips that day. He would have to wait until morning.

As the sun began to sink, Joel walked to the Prophet's log house to inquire about a place to spend the night. He found Joseph outside near a grove of trees with the Twelve Apostles and some of the Seventy. They sat on makeshift benches, with the Prophet standing in their midst, instructing them. Upon seeing Joel, the Prophet stopped and welcomed him.

Joel found a seat at the end of one of the benches then listened attentively as the Prophet's voice described the last days. "The hearts of the children of men will have to be turned to the fathers, and the fathers to the children, living or dead, to prepare them for the coming of the Son of Man. If Elijah did not come, the whole earth would be smitten.

"There will be here and there a stake of Zion for the gathering of the Saints. Some may have cried peace, but the Saints and the world will have little peace from henceforth. Let this not hinder us from going to the stakes; for God has told us to flee, not dallying, or we shall be scattered, one here and another there. In the stakes of Zion, your children shall be blessed. We ought to have the building up of Zion as our greatest object."

The moon rose as Joseph continued to speak. Joel remembered the pang of envy he had felt at Benjamin's call to go to Europe with the Twelve. Yet tonight, Joel envisioned a new stake of Zion growing up around Crooked Creek, another place of refuge for the Saints. As the Prophet closed his remarks, Joel said a silent prayer that the Lord would spare the life of his brother across the river and that together they might build up Zion.

\* \* \*

Friday morning was cooler than usual, with clouds covering the sun. Julia wondered if they would have a summer shower today. It was baking day, and she took the first loaves out of the brick oven that adjoined the hearth. Mary Ann was churning the butter, but Esther and Amos were still asleep and should have awakened a half hour ago to milk. If they didn't hurry, they would be late for school. Mary and George had already left to prepare the lessons.

Julia put another loaf into the oven as she thought of her children. It was more difficult to motivate the younger children to work than it had been with her older ones. Was it because the older ones had been required to help with so many little ones underfoot? How did one keep from spoiling the babies in a large family? Julia went to the girls' room. At the sound of her name, Esther pulled the quilt over her head. "Just one more minute."

"The early bird gets the worm," Julia said. "If you don't hurry, you will have to milk rather than eat breakfast. It is almost time to go."

"But Amos isn't up," Esther groaned.

"Then go get him up," Julia said. "I need to get back to the bread."

A few minutes later, Esther came barreling into the kitchen. "Mother, something's wrong with Amos. He can't get up."

Julia hurried into the boys' room to find Amos half sitting on the edge of the bed. He was sweating and crying. The bed smelled of urine. Now sobbing, Amos cried out, "I can't walk. Mama, help me."

\* \* \*

Fifteen-year-old Will stood outside of the bedroom while the doctor examined Amos. Will had spent the morning chopping and loading wood to keep the baking fire going. It was hot work, and sweat dripped from his face, mirroring the heat inside him. Something was wrong with Amos.

His mother had brought them here, and they were dirt poor and living on bread and milk. Now Amos was sick. She should have known better.

A few moments later, the doctor came out with his mother.

"Will, go in and wait with Amos while I speak with Dr. Thomas," Julia suggested.

Will didn't move. Fully aware of his mother's searching look, Will's jaw tightened. "I want to hear for myself what the doctor has to say."

The doctor cleared his throat and glanced at his pocket watch. Julia turned to Doctor Thomas. "Go on, Doctor," she said.

The doctor's white mustache bounced rhythmically as he talked. "Amos suffers from sciatic rheumatism. I don't know what caused it. It could be an infection or a growth on the hip joint. Sometimes it goes away on its own—other times it doesn't. The worst cases end in paralysis. I don't think this will happen to Amos."

Julia swallowed. "What can I do to help him?"

"Keep him moving as much as his pain permits."

"How much do I owe you?"

Will's face reddened. He grimaced, knowing they couldn't pay much.

"Not a penny, ma'am," Dr. Thomas said. "Judge Adams has taken care of the cost. He was with Mr. Babbitt when word came to me that your boy needed a doctor. I'll come again in three days. If Amos worsens, send for me immediately."

After the doctor left, Julia reached out to Will, but he felt cold inside and took a step backward. Julia swallowed and dropped her hand. "William, what is it?" He did not respond. Julia continued. "I need to check the bread before I go back in to Amos. Could you tell him that everything is fine and I'll be back in a few minutes?"

Will nodded tersely. His mother turned and walked toward the kitchen. However, Will didn't go straight into Amos's room; he went into the girls' room and found Nancy's old cherrywood crutches under the bed. He took them to Amos.

"Why do you have those?" Amos whimpered. "Aren't I going to get better?"

"Of course you're going to get better," Will snapped. "But if you think I'm going to do all of your work until then, you're wrong. I'm going to fix these so you can get around until you're well. Hold still while I measure you."

Laying the crutches next to Amos, Will marked with his knife where the ends needed to be cut off. Then he went outside and sawed and sanded until the ends were smooth and rounded. When he was finished he looked up and saw his mother watching him from the porch. He wiped the sweat off his forehead with his sleeve.

"Thank you," she said.

"I did it for Amos, not you," Will said.

\* \* \*

Later that evening, Will stood in the corner of the room while Benjamin and Almon gave Amos a priesthood blessing. After the blessing, his mother hugged Amos then glanced at Will with tears in her eyes. Will looked away from her and went outside.

It wasn't quite dark, but the moon already hung bright in the sky. He heard the door open and close. Almon came and stood next to him. "Why are you hurting your mother's feelings? What's she done to make you mad?"

"I don't know what you're talking about."

"It would take an idiot not to notice. Things have changed in this family. Esther couldn't stand the sight of Joe when he was here. And you can't stand the sight of your mother. It's madness all right. Joe's about the kindest man who ever walked this earth. And Julia Johnson's about the best mother. I've been around enough to know."

"You haven't been around here. We've been sick and starving. She ought to have done something. She ought to have known better."

"What do you think she should have done? Taken you on to Missouri smack dab in the middle of a war?"

"Maybe we should have stayed in Kirtland for a while longer. We wouldn't have starved with Pa around."

"Come on, Will. She couldn't have known that war would break out."

"Maybe she could have. If she had prayed hard enough."

"Tell me something. Do you still believe that Brother Joseph is a prophet?"

Will was quiet for a moment. Then he nodded. "Yes."

"A lot of people think he should have known better. They think it's his fault that the Kirtland bank failed, that the war in Missouri happened, and that he ended up in prison. They blame him for starvation, death, and disease. They think he should have known because he's the Prophet. The problem is that we put people up on a pedestal. We expect them to be bigger than life. And when things are bad, we want to lay blame. I had to change the way I thought. I had to remember that Joseph Smith's intent is to obey God and help His people. We're blessed to have a leader like that. Your mother is the same way. She gives everything for her family and for God. You can blame her when life is hard, or you can thank God for her."

Will stared straight ahead. Did Almon understand how anger cut into him like a knife? How Amos's illness terrified him? How he would rather be dead than not be able to walk? For if you couldn't walk, you couldn't change things, you couldn't make your life better by working harder and smarter than the next man.

"I want to go back to Kirtland," Will said.

Almon put his hand on Will's shoulder. "I'll go back there first. I'll make it a place worth coming to. Who knows, maybe your mother will go back there after all."

Almon went back into the house. Will swallowed. Maybe it wasn't his mother's fault. But he couldn't tell her he was sorry, not yet. If Almon could fix things, if they could go back to Kirtland, then maybe things would be all right.

# 10

*How sweet was her smile and how fervent her prayer
... How patient her toiling how watchfull her care*

George Washington Johnson

*Springfield, Illinois*

JOE AWAKENED IN THE PREDAWN darkness and realized his mind no longer swam with fever. He felt strangely alive again, almost exhilarated—so different from the thick, feverish fog that had melded the past three weeks into one: Joel ferrying him across the river, Joel explaining that the land was gone but that he had salvaged the outfit and made things square with Micham, Annie nursing him until he could travel. Then the trip to Springfield, where he lay in the wagon in the heat of the day shivering under blankets, and a jolting arrival, with Esther sobbing, telling him she was sorry he was sick, sorry that she had been mad at him, that she loved him.

And the most vivid memory of all: his mother embracing him with tears of joy and worry, his own emotions spilling over at the sight of her dear face. How deeply he had missed her! She would be in the room soon, checking his fever at dawn then seeing if Amos needed help dressing. Joe's exhilaration faded. Amos, who used to run and skip, now walked stiffly with pain in his hips. And Joe, who had been his mother's rock, had become another burden for her to carry. That would end today.

Benjamin, who was sleeping on a rug next to the bed, stirred, stretched, and sat up.

"Hello, Ben," Joe said.

Benjamin startled and turned toward his brother, a large shape in the dark room. "Are you all right?"

"I'm better. You can have your bed back."

"Really? You, Joseph Johnson, are offering to sleep on the floor? Has the fever addled your brain?"

Joe laughed softly. "No. Yesterday, John Snider came and offered me a room at his house with a feather bed. Fever or not."

Benjamin's voice became serious as he lit a lamp. "You don't need to go. I'm leaving in two weeks."

Joe sighed. "It's not right for me to come back and burden Mother. I was supposed to go build up a place for us."

"It doesn't matter. Mother has decided to stay here until the swampland around Commerce is drained. But I'm going now. Joel said that the Prophet will call his city Nauvoo. It means 'beautiful' in Hebrew."

"It's not a city yet. And it's hardly beautiful with malaria and typhus running rampant. Are you sure you want to go?"

Benjamin nodded. "Are you sure you want to move in with the Sniders?"

Joe shrugged. "I think so. I can teach their children in exchange for room and board. They live close to the schoolhouse, where I can finish teaching the summer session for Mary."

Benjamin chuckled. "You mean the *girls'* session. All the boys are gone doing field work. I've seen some of the older girls. No wonder you're feeling better."

Joe grinned in the darkness, feeling a bit like a youth in cahoots with his brother. "Mary says she's sick and tired of teaching a bunch of silly, giggly females nearly her own age who don't see her as the mistress. I'll relieve our sister's suffering."

Benjamin laughed. "You're a charitable man, indeed!"

Benjamin got up to shave. Joe joined him in front of the mirror. The lamplight emphasized the hollow shadows of Joe's face. Benjamin must have noticed because he commented, "Take it easy. The fever comes and goes."

"It's gone this morning," Joe said, speaking to his brother's reflection. "And, Ben, I really think you should stay here until you leave on your mission. You could save money." Joe's smile faded. "There's another thing I must tell you. Sister Huntington died of the fever."

"I know. William wrote to me."

"That's not all. Zina has another beau. A man named Henry Jacobs."

Benjamin took a deep breath and set the razor down. He turned and looked directly at Joe. "You're sure?"

Joe nodded. "I saw them together."

Benjamin was quiet for a moment as he put his razor into its box. "That's why she hasn't written."

"That's why you should stay."

Benjamin shook his head. "Zina isn't the only reason to go back to Nauvoo. The Prophet and Saints are there."

The rooster crowed. Dawn light spread through the windows and into the room. Joe and Benjamin heard their mother's footsteps in the hall.

\* \* \*

*July 1839. Commerce (Nauvoo), Illinois*

Benjamin arrived in Commerce on a dark bay mare that he had purchased in Springfield. Joe was right—although situated on a lovely knoll of the Mississippi, the town was anything but beautiful. It was a bog that reeked of swamp odors. Here and there on firmer ground were a few cabins and shabby houses. The area sweltered with humidity, and mosquitoes teemed thicker than flies. Men, women, and children lay in huts and tents, their faces bright with fever.

With anxiety rising in his chest, Benjamin followed Joe's directions to the Prophet's log house, where Joseph and Emma made their way through the sick, ministering to those who lay in the yard under makeshift tents. Sweating, in trousers, with his sleeves rolled up, the Prophet immediately left what he was doing and walked over to greet Benjamin.

Benjamin dismounted, and the Prophet embraced him. Joseph's blue eyes shone bright with purpose. "Bennie, you have joined me again! Many are sick. President Rigdon thinks Nauvoo may never be a place of beautiful rest. But we will survive this scourge as we survived the expulsion, war, and prison. And you are here. This cheers my heart!"

"Brother Joseph, what can I do?"

"You have a good horse. Go to the sick who are spread out on both sides of the river. Administer their medicines, prepare gruel and other food, bring water, make beds. Bless and pray for them."

Emma looked up after giving an elderly man a drink of water. "Some of the sick need watchers. They can't be left alone through the night.

Girls have agreed to alternate coming whenever we need them. But some of them live in the country. Doctors Wiley and Pendleton just returned and are in the house resting. They can tell you where you are most needed. There's soup in a kettle if you're hungry."

"If you're weary, rest first," the Prophet added. "The house is quiet. The children are with Lucy today."

"Thank you," Benjamin said.

"Thank you, Bennie," the Prophet said warmly. "We are glad you're here."

As Benjamin walked into the house, the Prophet's energy and love infused him. Joseph's vision became his own, and Benjamin knew Nauvoo would become beautiful.

*  *  *

*Springfield, Illinois*

On the second Monday in July, Joe's ague returned with such force that he couldn't get up when the rooster crowed. He shook in the Sniders' feather bed as malaria blurred his vision. Joe closed his eyes. He had to get up. He had to fight this. The Snider children were waiting to walk to school with him. Would it be only sixteen-year-old Harriet today, or would Eddie and Johnny be coming?

He hoped it was only Harriet. He liked the days they walked to school alone: she the student, he the master. He would quiz her on points of science and literature. She would answer dutifully and respectfully, her deep blue eyes focused on the ground in front of them as she concentrated. He would throw in a riddle that would make her smile.

Another chill gripped Joe, hitting him like a wave that struck and receded. Joe felt a cool hand on his forehead. He opened his eyes, and the hand was gone. Had it been there at all? Then he saw Harriet in the room, her hair falling around her face in brown ringlets, her eyes edged by long, black lashes as she took a cloth and dampened it in the basin.

"I'll get up directly," Joe said. "Are the boys going today?"

"Please stay in bed," Harriet said, her voice soft and kind. She placed the damp cloth on Joe's head. "You're burning up, Master Johnson. I'll get mother."

"Wait." His voice detained her. "The school. I'm expected there."

"I'll tell them you are ill. Your sister Mary can teach us."

"But if she isn't there?"

Harriet swallowed. "Then I'll direct the class."

For a split second, Joe was so intrigued by this change in shy Harriet that he nearly forgot about his fever. "You will? How?"

"I'll quiz them."

Joe felt a chill coming, but he didn't take his eyes off of Harriet. "What questions will you ask?"

She smiled slightly. "I shall ask them to repeat all of the magical properties of the number nine."

Joe wanted to smile but began shaking violently instead. Harriet hurried over to the bureau. She took another cloth from the drawer and dipped it into the basin. She sat on the edge of the bed and bathed Joe's arms and neck with the cool water. When the shaking subsided, she arose again and poured him a cup of water. "You're burning up," she said worriedly. "Drink as much as you can." She placed a slender arm under his neck to support his head as she helped him take a sip.

"Thank you," Joe whispered. Her pursed lips were pink and pretty. He wondered if his own lips were as red as those whom he had nursed with fevers.

Harriet stood and checked the rag on his forehead. It must have grown warm from the heat of his body because she took it off and he heard her dip it into the basin. Then she was bending over him once more, placing the cool rag on his forehead a second time. He looked up at her. He had always thought her pretty, but she was more than pretty; she was exquisite. Impulsively, he reached up and took hold of her hand. Her soft fingers felt cool in his, like dipping his hand into the Mississippi. "Another quiz question," he said. "How do eyes resemble a schoolmaster disciplining unruly boys?"

Harriet looked down at their entwined hands. Her lashes were so long. Did he see a tear in them? "How?" she asked.

"They are pupils beneath lashes."

She lifted her head, suddenly emboldened. Her moist eyes now held a smile. "But you have never lashed your pupils."

"And your eyes cannot be described. Harriet, they are the loveliest I have ever seen. You are lovely."

She looked away and gently extricated her hand from his. "Master Johnson, I fear that you are in delirium."

"Not so." He shook his head.

She swallowed as she stood. "I'll get Mother now and go on to school."

"I wish you would stay," Joe said as he watched her walk toward the door.

She turned to him before leaving the room. "I'll be back as soon as I can."

\* \* \*

*Nauvoo, Illinois*

It was midmorning as Benjamin rode his horse back to the Prophet's home with sixteen-year-old Lucinda Morgan behind him. He felt her arms around his waist, her blonde head resting between his shoulder blades. With the reins in his left hand, he covered her loosely clasped hands with his right one. He let the horse walk slowly. He had gone to get Lucinda an hour ago from the Taylor's home, where she had been up all night caring for the sick. She was exhausted. Benjamin breathed deeply. He too was nearly worn out. During the past month, he had scarcely taken off his boots; he had been so busy riding from place to place to aid the sick and dying. But during this time, he had also fallen in love. Like Benjamin, Lucinda boarded at the Prophet's home when she was not tending to the sick. She was lovely—petite and blue-eyed, with a quick smile and a charming, eager willingness. She had promised to marry him after his mission.

When they arrived at the Prophet's house, Benjamin dismounted; then he gently lifted Lucinda off the horse. She sleepily smiled up at him as he cradled her in his arms like a man would carry his bride over the threshold. Benjamin was about to kiss her when he startled at the sound of Emma clearing her throat. The front door was open, and she stood in the entrance with a slight smile. "Is Lucinda too tired to walk?"

Benjamin grinned sheepishly and set Lucinda down. Emma continued. "We just received word that the Grangers are ill. Ben, please take Anne Robison to them."

\* \* \*

The wind blew, and a drenching rain soaked Benjamin as he rode with Anne Robison toward the Granger's house. Miss Robison wore a hooded cloak, but Benjamin had only a thin linen shirt. When he had left Lucinda that morning, it had been warm. But the weather had turned, and cold rain knifed through him.

When they arrived, Benjamin was shivering and felt utterly exhausted. Miss Robison tended to the couple while Benjamin stood by the fire and made the gruel. As night approached, the rain continued coming down in sheets. He could not ride back in this weather without a coat.

"Brother Johnson, you should sleep by the fire," Miss Robison suggested. "I'll stay up with the Grangers."

Benjamin thanked her and rolled up in a rug near the hearth. A few hours later, he began shaking and surrendered to the delirious visions of malarial fever.

\* \* \*

*Two days later*

"Brother Ben." Benjamin opened his eyes to find Sister Granger looking at him. On the table next to her was a bowl of gruel, a cup of water, and two pills. He wondered when he had gotten from the floor to this cot. He could feel the fever in his aching bones, but for the moment, he was not delirious and the chills were gone. He noticed how gaunt Sister Granger's face looked and how she shivered beneath her shawl.

"How long have I been here?" Benjamin questioned.

"Two days. I got word to Brother Hyrum, and he has sent you some gruel and Sappington pills. Try to sit up."

"Sappington pills?" Benjamin questioned. "That's quinine. Where did it come from?"

"They are yours. Brother Hyrum said that a boat recently brought them. Your family's name was on the box. Some of the pills were missing. I have taken two and given my husband two. Hyrum didn't think you would mind."

"Of course not," Benjamin whispered. He could feel another chill coming. Sister Granger helped Benjamin take the pills then spoon-fed him a few bites of gruel. "Hyrum said Brother Joseph wants you to go back to his house as soon as you can."

\* \* \*

Three days later, Benjamin came out of the bedroom for breakfast in the Smith's home. Lucinda was not there because she was spending the week nursing a sick family. The Prophet was also absent. The children waited patiently while Emma finished dishing up sweet mush. Benjamin thought about how Emma's properness and grace brought out decorum in others, even her own children. Around her, Benjamin felt that he should always be at his best. Emma sat down and asked her oldest son to bless the food. During the prayer, young Joseph asked that his father be healed.

As soon as the boy said amen, Benjamin looked searchingly at Emma. But before he spoke, she answered his question. "Joseph came down with the fever last night."

Benjamin swallowed. Since his return, Joseph had attended to Benjamin's needs and insisted he rest and take care of himself. Now the Prophet, their pillar of strength, had been stricken. For the first time, Benjamin noticed the dark circles under Emma's eyes.

"What can I do to help?" Benjamin asked.

Emma took a deep breath. "Joseph knows how busy I am with the children. He asked that you be his companion and nurse. Will you do this for us, Ben?"

"With the Lord's help, I'll not leave his side until he is well again."

\* \* \*

*Monday, July 22, 1839*

Seven days passed as Benjamin nursed the Prophet day and night. On Monday morning, Benjamin was at the hearth dishing up the Prophet's gruel when he saw Sidney Rigdon standing at the door talking to Emma. Sidney's face was gaunt and his eyes bright with intense emotion. "You must convince him. It's time to leave this place."

Emma's back was to Benjamin. She stood very erect. "I won't try to convince him. He is God's Prophet."

"Great fear is prevailing among the people. We could not even hold a meeting yesterday because of the sickness and death. Your voice is the one he listens to above all others."

"After all you have been through with him, don't you know him better than that? Though he listens to me and loves me, it is God's voice that is above all else. If we abandon Nauvoo, it will be due to God's voice and not mine."

"I hear God's voice in this scourge, telling us to leave before it is too late."

There was the sound of footsteps. Benjamin turned. Joseph stood in the doorway, straight and tall. He did not look like a man who had shaken with the fever most of the night. There was majesty and strength within him. "The Lord wants you to repent, Sidney. He asks that you fear not. That you complain not. Come with me." Then Joseph turned to Benjamin. "And you too, Bennie. For today we will behold the power and will of God."

Joseph walked along the bank of the river toward the Rigdons' stone house. Many lay sick in tents along the bank. The Prophet stopped by each one and healed all that were in his path. At the door of Brother Henry Sherwood's tent, Joseph commanded Brother Sherwood in the name of Jesus Christ to arise and come out. Brother Sherwood, who was close to death, obeyed and was healed. Joseph called for a skiff and asked Elder Kimball to come with them across the river to Montrose, where several of the Twelve and many other Saints were living in an old army barracks.

A cool breeze blew in Benjamin's face as the craft skimmed across the Mississippi. The Prophet's features were still as he stared across the water, his blond hair pushed back by the wind, his blue eyes focused on the power within him, the priesthood of God. In Montrose, the Prophet first visited Brigham Young, the president of the Quorum of Twelve, who lay sick. Joseph laid his hands on Brigham's head, and in the name of the Lord, Brigham was healed. Brigham arose and followed Joseph. They then visited Wilford Woodruff, Orson Pratt, and John Taylor, all of whom were blessed and healed. They too followed the Prophet.

With tears in his eyes, Benjamin accompanied the men to Elijah Fordham's hut. Once inside, Joseph immediately walked over to Brother Fordham's bed, knelt beside him, and took hold of his right hand. Joseph called him by name, but Brother Fordham did not respond. Benjamin swallowed and blinked back his sorrow. It was too late. Brother Fordham's eyes were set in his head like glass, and he was unconscious. Grief welled up in Benjamin as he remembered the deaths of his siblings, David, Seth, Nancy, and Susan. Sometimes it was just too late.

Joseph continued to hold Brother Fordham's hand and to look into his eyes. Tangible silence filled the room as moments passed. Then Brother Fordham stirred. His countenance changed as his eyes focused on Joseph.

"Elijah, do you know me?" Joseph asked in a low whisper.

"Yes," Brother Fordham said.

"Do you have the faith to be healed?"

"I fear it's too late," Brother Fordham whispered feebly. "If you had come earlier."

"Do you believe in Jesus Christ?"

A scarcely perceptible whisper. "I do."

The Prophet stood erect, still holding Elijah's hand in silence for several minutes. Then the Prophet spoke, his voice loud. To Benjamin, it did not sound like the voice of his dear friend; it sounded like the voice of a flame, the power of God. Benjamin's heart beat wildly as the Prophet cried out, "Brother Fordham, I command you in the name of Jesus Christ to arise from this bed and be made whole."

Elijah sat up and kicked off the poultices that bound his feet. He put on his clothes while his wife brought him a bowl of bread and milk. After eating, he followed the Prophet of God into the street.

# 11

*Hear your Heav'nley Father call you,*
*Rise, repent, and be baptized . . .*
*Then, the Holy Spirit's sealing,*
*You will share, when hands are laid*
*On your head, with pow'r of healing,*
*Through the peaceful Spirit's aid.*

Joel Hills Johnson

*Springfield, Illinois*

With the sun a fiery sphere on the eastern horizon, Joe purposely did not hold Harriet's hand as they walked to school together on the final day of the summer session. A month ago his fever had been high on the day he had confessed that he found her lovely. After that, she had spent hours tending to his needs and reading to him. As he had grown stronger, they had grown closer. Often he had held her hand on the way to school, and twice he had kissed her. However, inside the schoolroom, he had always hidden his feelings, acting as if she were just another pupil. Then five days ago, on Sunday afternoon, his sister Mary had pulled him aside, her brow furrowed. "Harriet has fallen in love with you. If you aren't serious about her, don't trifle with her."

Joe had not been able to get Mary's words out of his mind. Did he want to marry Harriet someday? If not, he had to change things, for it wasn't fair to her. But marriage was a staggering commitment. All week Joe had avoided being alone with Harriet. There was hurt in her eyes, and it troubled him. He wanted so much to reach out and touch her. But was it right for either of them?

"Harriet," Joe said.

She turned, inclining her head toward him. "Yes?"

He suddenly realized that she didn't know what to call him. *Joe, Joseph, Master Johnson?* What was he to her? And she to him? How did he tell her that he needed to figure it out and that he didn't want to hurt her in the interim? He cleared his throat. "I-I have decided to move back in with my mother since the summer session is ending. Do you think that's best?"

"If you think so," she said, looking away. She walked silently the remainder of the way. Joe felt like kicking the road planks. What was wrong with him? He wanted to stop and kiss her. Why did he quail at the thought of marriage?

Once in the schoolroom, Joe forced Harriet to the back of his mind. He had to focus on being schoolmaster. It was the last day of the session—a day for riddles, contests, games, and fun. After lunch, Joe announced that it was time to pass autograph albums around to use their writer's wit and poet's skill as they left notes to one another. Pretty, plump Nancy Carroll raised her hand. Earlier that morning she had told Joe that she wouldn't be coming back to the fall session. She'd had the misfortune of turning sixteen, and her father deemed her too old to continue her education. Joe knew she was disappointed. He smiled and called on her.

"Master Johnson, might I borrow your autograph album first?"

"Of course," Joe said as he handed it to her.

Nancy opened the album to a page decorated with flowers and scrolls. She suddenly stood up. "Let's have one more contest. We will all write farewell poems in Master Johnson's album. He will read them aloud, and we will vote by secret ballot. The winner will get a reward."

"And what should the reward be?" someone asked.

"A friendly kiss," Nancy Carroll replied with a coy smile. "All in favor?"

There was a resounding "aye" as laughter skipped through the schoolroom. Nancy sat back down and tilted her head attractively as she began writing. Harriet looked down. Mary, Joe's sister, shot Joe a withering look.

Joe cleared his throat. "Let's think of a different reward."

Nancy Carroll looked up with a bat of her eyelashes. "But you have taught us that in a free republic the will of the majority rules."

"Ah, but I have the power of the veto," Joe countered.

"Then I shall hope that you will not use it."

The girls in the class whispered and giggled as they began passing Joe's and other albums around.

An hour later, Nancy Carroll bounced up to Joe and handed him the autograph book. "Master Johnson, we have all signed it. Now it's time for you to read the entries aloud so we can choose a winner."

"Hmm." Joe opened the book. He read the first poem in Nancy's handwriting. "*If on these lines perchance thine eyes / May wander in some future year, / Let memory breathe a passing sigh / For thy true friend who traced them here.*" Joe smiled warmly. "It is signed *Amicus*. Miss Carroll, you have used my favorite nom de plume. I shall not forget you."

"And I will not forget you, sir," Nancy said. Her face started to crumple as if she might cry any minute.

Joe quickly turned to the next poem. "This one is by Miss Vance: *True, sir, our acquaintance has been short / Yet loath I feel to leave / A school that is so well devised / To do young ladies good. / 'Tis education I desire / 'Tis what will do me good / And if possible I should acquire / A part of it from you.*"

"Here, here," Joe said and clapped. Then he read Sylvia Carter's, hoping that Sylvia was joking. Mary rolled her eyes and buried her head in her arms. "*Blest be the dear uniting tie / That will not let us part, / Our bodies may far off remove / We still are one in heart. / But let us hasten to that day / Which shall our flesh restore / When death shall all be done away / And our bodies part no more.*"

Joe rushed to the next entry. The "bodies parting no more" was too much for him. A few minutes later, he came to the last page. There were two poems written in a neat hand with Harriet's signature at the bottom. Joe swallowed.

"Go on, Master Johnson, finish reading," Nancy Carroll encouraged.

Joe cleared his throat. "These two poems are by Miss Snider. The first is called *Where Is She?* and the second *Forgive and Forget*. *Where is she? / The one with a smile on her face / Where is she? / Has she left without a trace? / No. She lingers just beyond the summer glade / Holding fast to a moment that will never fade.*"

Joe looked at Harriet. Her deep blue eyes were fastened on him. He continued. "*Forgive and forget—good advice indeed / Yet it can be difficult to heed / Forgive? I'll try. And in time I will. / But forget? Though years pass, I'll remember still. / He brought the sun when by my side. / I'll forgive, but not forget at this turn of the tide.*"

Emotions welled within Joe. He smiled into Harriet's eyes, realizing that a frightening commitment would be easier to endure than separation from someone as dear as Harriet.

"Master Johnson," Nancy Carroll said. "We all know who the winner is. Most of us have suspected for some time. Go on and kiss her."

Joe walked over and reached his hand down to Harriet. She took it and stood. Joe pulled her close and kissed her tenderly, feeling her tears on his cheek. The young ladies in the room clapped and wiped their eyes. Mary sighed as she watched her brother, a small smile turning up the corners of her mouth.

\* \* \*

*September 1839*

Benjamin lay on the couch in the Prophet's home. The quinine pills had run out, and he was once again stricken with malaria. After the shaking subsided, Benjamin reached for the letter that Emma had given him. It was from Springfield. After breaking the seal, he could almost hear his sister Mary's voice as he read.

*Ben, will you come home before your mission? Mother is anxious to see you. The day after the summer school session ended, I came down with the fever. I'm coughing still. It frightens me when I think about our brothers and sisters who died at our age. And now Mother is very sick too. Amos is walking but painfully. Julianne and Almon have gone on a mission to Indiana. Esther wants to be in Kirtland, not here. Will is also dissatisfied.*

*Oh, Ben, Mother needs you and longs to see you again. So do I. Please come home. The thought of not seeing you before your mission is more than we can bear. What if something happens, and we don't see you again in this life? Please come home. Mary*

Benjamin folded the letter and put it in his pocket. His sister Mary was sick and frightened—Mary, who used to try so hard to boss him around, Mary who could not endure the thought of him suffering as a prisoner in Missouri. And his dear mother was ill and asking for him.

Benjamin stood up, his legs shaking. Before he could travel, he needed quinine. He'd heard a rumor that a fellow named Jim Jones across the river had the medicine but charged a pretty penny for it. Most of the Saints hadn't the money to pay. Benjamin put his last three bank notes in his pocket. He had to get the quinine, no matter how much it cost. He would take double doses so he could get home.

\* \* \*

Two days later, Benjamin prepared to leave. After procuring the quinine, the fever and chills had subsided, but he still felt weak. Discouragement plagued him. He had ruined his best clothes and spent most of the money he had saved for his mission. To make matters worse, he wouldn't be able to tell Lucinda good-bye. A week ago, she had gone with her mother to visit a cousin in Van Buren County. Yesterday, Benjamin had received a note from Lucinda saying her mother had insisted she remain because of the sickness in Nauvoo. The letter had continued with Lucinda expressing her love and promising to be true regardless of the advice of others. Benjamin wondered if Lucinda's mother was trying to keep her away from him as much as from the malaria.

After saddling his mare, Benjamin went into the house and gathered his few possessions. He opened his small purse. Only a single ten-dollar note was left. Benjamin fingered the money. There was one more thing to do. He walked over to the Prophet, who sat at his desk.

Joseph turned to Benjamin and smiled, his clear blue eyes cheerful. "Bennie, are you ready to go? We will miss you. How I would like to see you smile before you leave us."

Benjamin swallowed. He felt almost too sad to speak. He handed the ten-dollar note to Joseph. "Please take out the tithing."

Joseph nodded and took the money. He put it in his desk and retrieved nine dollars in coin. Joseph placed the money in Benjamin's outstretched hand, and then with sudden mirth, playfully hit the bottom of Benjamin's hand, spilling the coins on the floor.

With a burst of emotion, Benjamin went for Joseph—part desperation, part a grab at happiness, a moment to pretend they were boys in a wrestling match, unshackled by poverty and disease. But instead of wrestling Joseph to the ground, Benjamin fell into the Prophet's arms, almost fainting. With his arms around Benjamin, Joseph half carried him over to the couch. He brought him a drink of water, his blue eyes full of concern. "I'm sorry, Bennie. I didn't realize how weak you are. Are you certain you must go today?"

Benjamin nodded. "I have to." His eyes burned with unshed tears. The Prophet bent down, picked up the coins, and gave them to Benjamin.

When Benjamin started to stand, Joseph put his arm around Benjamin to support him. He kept his arm around him as they walked outside together to the gate where the horse waited. Then before Benjamin put his foot into the stirrup, Joseph laid his hands on Benjamin's head and blessed him in the name of the Lord, telling him that an angel would go with him and protect him on his journey.

\* \* \*

*Monday, September 9, 1839. Kirtland, Ohio*

Restless, Ezekiel shifted uncomfortably on the bench as he sat next to Almera in the main hall of the Kirtland Temple. Almera smiled at him and whispered, "Papa, thank you for coming in with me. I can hardly believe it."

Ezekiel nodded a response. Midmorning sunlight blazed in through the side windows. He didn't tell her that he had come inside this haunting structure for only two reasons: first, that it would make her smile; second, that Oliver Granger was the speaker. Granger had recently arrived from Nauvoo, and Ezekiel craved news.

A few minutes later, Granger walked up to the pulpit. He had aged since Ezekiel had last seen him. There was a marked puffiness in his features—like a man who had taken to drinking. Perhaps malarial fever had taken its toll.

Granger began speaking. Ezekiel listened skeptically as he described a personal revelation that caused him to join the Church. Ezekiel shook his head slightly, thinking about how people constantly claimed to know things that no man could know. He thought of Joseph Smith, who claimed to know these things from firsthand experience, from open visions.

With earnest eloquence, Granger bore testimony of the restoration of the priesthood and exhorted the people to embrace the truth, that they might be saved in the kingdom of God. Almera watched the speaker intently with tears in her eyes.

Ezekiel sighed. How strange that his children were deeply religious. What would it be like to truly believe in a benevolent God? Almera rested her head on Ezekiel's shoulder. He put his arm around her. Was some of her faith and love seeping into him, sanding off the hard edges of his skepticism? He was growing old. Someday in the not-distant future he would know if this was true. In his mind, either Joseph Smith was right or there was nothing. The trouble was that it seemed far more likely that there was nothing after death, just a decaying body in the ground. Yet if he were wrong, if Joseph's visions were actual fact, then Seth, David, Nancy, and Susan lived. And if God were as loving as Joseph claimed, surely Jesus would allow him to hold Julia close after death. He would tell her that she was the best part of his life—and then willingly be consigned to the eternal punishment reserved for unbelievers. That would be enough.

Ezekiel shook himself to attention. What was it about this temple that made his thoughts run wild? Almera lifted her head from his shoulder.

Granger continued. "In closing, I will share with you the resolution concerning Kirtland that was adopted during the May fourth general conference of the Church. 'We advise the brethren living in the Eastern states to move to Kirtland and the vicinity thereof and again settle that place as a stake of Zion, provided they feel so inclined, in preference to their moving farther west.' Brothers and sisters, Kirtland will once again grow and flourish. Let us follow our prophet. It is good to be back among you in this hallowed place."

Ezekiel glanced around the room. Hiram Winters put his arm around his wife, Rebecca, who wiped away a tear. The Burdick family listened attentively. Naomi Holman blew her nose into a handkerchief while holding her chubby baby girl. Melissa LeBaron sat tall, with tears streaming down her cheeks. He knew what they were thinking. Kirtland was their home, and they would be allowed to stay. His eyes burned. Would Julia come back? Now she could do so without turning away from her prophet. But would she even consider it?

\* \* \*

*Springfield, Illinois*

The smell of fall was in the air as Joe drove the wagon carrying his brothers and sisters home. His eyes took in a man on horseback, but the lowering sun was so bright that it was hard to see. It looked like the horseman was slumped over in the saddle. "There's a rider up ahead," Joe said. "Things don't look right."

Amos, who was sitting at the front of the wagon next to Joe, shaded his eyes with his hand. "It's Ben! That's his horse!" he screamed.

The rider tried to lift his head then fell unconscious from the horse. Joe pulled hard on the reins, stopping the wagon. George and Will swung out and sprinted to Benjamin. Joe followed, his heart pounding.

Will was the first to reach Benjamin's crumpled form. He rolled Benjamin over. Then George was there. Joe was with them in an instant, bending over his brother, taking his pulse and listening for his breath. "Ben's alive but bad off. Let's get him in the wagon."

Will ran back to the wagon and jumped into the driver's seat. In the bed, Esther sobbed hysterically. Mary Ann put her arm around Esther, saying over and over, "It will be all right."

Regardless of the comfort, Esther kept crying. "Ben might be dead."

"Be quiet, Esther. He's not dead," Will shouted as he jiggled the reins and drove the wagon closer to Benjamin. "He's fainted from the fever. We need to get him home."

Together, the brothers lifted Benjamin into the wagon. Joe folded his vest and tucked it under Benjamin's neck to ease his breathing. George sat next to Benjamin, and Joe climbed into the driver's seat.

Will mounted Benjamin's horse. "I'll ride ahead and tell Mother to get a bed ready."

Joe shook his head. "No. We're taking him to the Sniders'. It's closer. And Mother and Mary are too sick to nurse Ben." While driving the horse into a trot, Joe gave further instructions. "I'll stay at the Sniders' with Ben. The rest of you go home in the wagon. Tell Mother that Ben's back, that he's run down and is recovering at Sniders'. Don't tell her how bad off he is."

"I won't lie," Will shot back. His brothers and sisters stared at him in disbelief. "Mother asked Ben to come back. Because of that, he's near dead."

"You say anything against Mother, and you'll answer to me," Joe snapped.

"What will you do? Thrash me?"

"If he doesn't, I will!" George erupted. "What's the matter with you?"

"I'd like to see you try," Will flamed back. The horse jigged with tension.

"Stop it. It's Ben that matters right now," Joe yelled. He gritted his teeth as he focused on the road ahead.

Amos tapped Joe's shoulder and whispered, "Don't worry. Will's crazy right now. It'll pass."

\*\*\*

Benjamin opened his eyes to find himself in a strange bed. He looked up and saw Joe sitting on a couch nearby with a young lady. She snuggled against him. His arms were around her, his head resting on hers. Their eyes were closed. How long had they been sitting, waiting for him to wake up? Benjamin tried to sit up too, but his head pounded and he felt groggy and chilled.

Joe opened his eyes. He straightened, awakening the girl. "You're awake," Joe said, standing quickly and walking over to Benjamin with relief etched in his tired eyes.

"What happened?" Benjamin asked.

"Yesterday we found you unconscious by the roadside. I brought you to Sniders'."

The girl followed Joe. Her deep blue eyes rested on Benjamin. He remembered her now. Harriet Snider. Joe must have decided that she was not too young, nor too shy. Benjamin's head hurt, and his muscles ached. Seeing Harriet near Joe made Benjamin miss Lucinda terribly, even with the pain that clouded his mind.

Joe laid a hand on Benjamin's forehead. "How are you feeling?"

"Been better," Benjamin muttered. He looked at Joe's worn face. "How are Mother and Mary?"

"Not as sick as you. They're at home," Joe added.

Harriet left the room then came back with a cup of warm liquid. But as Joe bent down to put a pillow behind Benjamin's head and help him drink, Benjamin began shaking violently. In the clutches of the malarial chill, his stomach violently spasmed, causing hemorrhaging. As warm blood wet the bedclothes, Benjamin was conscious only of terrible pain and his brother's arms around him.

Joe cried out, "Harriet, send Eddie for the doctor."

\* \* \*

*Pleasant Garden, Putnam County, Indiana*

Julianne sat close to Almon in the carriage as he drove the horse. The night was dark, with a waning moon. Patches of light from the two lanterns dangling on each side of the vehicle bounced as the horse trotted. Feeling the light pressure of Almon's arm against hers, Julianne sighed happily. They were on their way back to the hotel after Almon's third night of preaching at Pleasant Garden, a city twenty-five miles east of the Wabash River. It was called the "seat of literature" in Indiana, and most of the people were educated. After his first sermon, Almon's reputation as a profound reasoner had spread like wildfire; the last two nights, he had attracted large congregations. Now, despite a few hecklers, he had more invitations to preach than he could manage.

"How long do you think we'll stay here?" Julianne asked.

"I'm not sure. William and Wilson Law and their group should arrive in a few days. I'd like to talk with William before they go on. I want to convince him to settle in Kirtland instead of Nauvoo."

"That might not be the best for the Laws. Right now, Kirtland is the home of those who lingered, not the faithful who went forward."

"Kirtland has great promise and needs strong Saints. I'll be so glad when we're back that I might even kiss the ground."

Julianne smiled. "I'm anxious to see Almera and Papa again."

"It won't be long." Almon jiggled the reins to get the horse to pick up its pace. "Last night I dreamt that I baptized six people here. We'll stay until that happens. I hope that two of the converts are Dr. Knights and his wife. I like Knights' hot Southern blood."

"Hmm," Julianne said, her mind reliving the moment that evening when the hecklers had interrupted Almon, shouting that he was hiding something, that the Mormons weren't driven out of Missouri due to the doctrines he was preaching. The next instant, Dr. Knights, a wealthy, eminent physician who was originally from Virginia, had stood tall, cracked his buggy whip at the hecklers, and shouted like a lion, "Pay this man proper respect, or I'll have you ridden out of town on a rail!"

Almon chuckled. "I think I'll introduce the Laws to the Knights. I wonder what you get when you mix hot Southern blood with stubborn Irish blood."

"Hopefully not a bloodbath. I wouldn't want to be on Dr. Knights' bad side."

"Come," Almon said with a twinkle in his eye. "Don't you like Dr. Knights? Or are you prejudiced because his wife is twenty-five years his junior? After all, my darling, you are older than me and such feelings would be natural."

Julianne elbowed Almon. "If a man wants to marry someone young enough to be his daughter, then it is his business. I'm just glad I married a boy. How else could I have molded him into the man I've always wanted?"

Almon chuckled and put his arm around her. He was about to say something more when, through the darkness, three men on horseback rode toward them. The horsemen broke into a gallop, their black shapes approaching fast. Almon's arm tightened around Julianne as her heart raced.

An instant later, the men were in front of the carriage, halting Almon's horse and nearly scaring it into a rear. The men stared at Almon with their shotguns by their sides. Their hats were tilted over their eyes, even though it was dark.

"Gentlemen, what can I do for you?" Almon's voice did not shake.

"We're taking your carriage," one of the men said as he raised his gun and pointed it at them. "Get out and uncollar your horse."

Almon hesitated. The other two men raised their guns. "We don't want to harm you or your wife, but you'd better get out of the carriage."

Almon climbed down then reached up with both hands to help Julianne. As he lifted Julianne out of the carriage, she felt his heart pound against hers, fast and strong. Almon kept Julianne next to him as he took off the horse's collar.

One of the men dismounted and took a lantern off the carriage. He handed it to Julianne. "Ma'am, we aren't horse thieves or murderers, but your husband has to be stopped. We're giving him a chance to quit preaching before something worse happens."

Before Julianne could respond, Almon said evenly, "You can take my carriage and threaten me, but there is nothing you can do to stop the truth."

\* \* \*

*Springfield, Illinois*

Through the fog, Benjamin heard the doctor talk with Joe. "If the chills come again and he hemorrhages, we'll lose him. I'm prescribing India Cholagogue in double doses. You can get it from Mr. Steed. It's expensive. I'm sorry about that."

"I'll take care if it," Joe said as the doctor handed him the prescription.

Benjamin lay still, the chills and hemorrhaging eroding his desire to live. He was conscious enough to know that the bottom had fallen out of his life. He was destitute and desperately ill. No mission was possible. No mother would allow her daughter to marry someone without prospects. He was a burden to his family and friends. He closed his eyes, too weak to even moan. It would be better to die.

The doctor left. Benjamin's eyelids fluttered, and he saw Joe and Harriet standing over him. Joe bent down. "Ben, Harriet will stay here with you while I get the medicine."

Benjamin shook his head, his chapped lips forming the words, "Costs too much."

Joe swallowed. The look in his eyes was sweet and sad. He forced a smile. "I'll get credit. Promise not to steal my girl while I'm gone."

Benjamin didn't answer. His eyes burned, but he hadn't the strength to cry. He felt Joe's hand cover his. "It'll be all right," Joe said softly.

The memory of the Prophet's hands on his head came back to Benjamin—the promised angel.

"I won't steal your girl, if you don't steal my horse," Benjamin managed.

"It's a deal," Joe said.

Benjamin jerked and gripped Joe's hand once more as a solution formed in his mind. "Sell my horse to pay for the medicine."

\* \* \*

*Pleasant Garden, Indiana*

Two evenings following the destruction of Almon and Julianne's carriage, Dr. Knights hosted a dinner for the Babbitts in his spacious home. Mrs. Knights, glowing in a flattering gown of pink lace and ruffles, welcomed her guests, her blue eyes shining bright and her cheeks and lips flushing from the excitement of the evening. Two dozen attended, and after dinner, Dr. Knights called for a collection. Almon and Julianne stood in awe, eyes wet with gratitude, as people they scarcely knew pressed money into Almon's hand—enough to pay for a new carriage.

Later, as the guests mingled, Mrs. Knights clasped Julianne's hand and drew her away from the crowd and out onto the porch. The hostess's hand was warm, and in her musical Southern accent, she invited Julianne to sit next to her on the bench.

"How can I thank you enough?" Julianne asked as they sat together.

Mrs. Knights turned to her with a voice full of tender emotion. "Sister Julianne, please don't thank me. I'm so glad you and your husband have come to Pleasant Garden." Mrs. Knights swallowed, and her eyes filled with tears. "My husband is studying the Book of Mormon. I hope he believes it, for I want desperately to be baptized. Can you tell me? Will baptism truly wash away my sins?"

"Yes," Julianne responded; then she explained the miracle of baptism. Tears slid down Mrs. Knights' cheeks. They sat in silence for a few moments. Julianne put her arm around her new friend's shoulders and watched the breeze bend the nearby forsythia branches.

At the sound of the door opening and shutting, Julianne pivoted, removing her arm from Mrs. Knights' shoulder. Young Dr. Shepherd, Dr. Knights' handsome protégé, walked over to them. Mrs. Knights immediately brushed away her tears and composed herself. She stood formally. "Thank you, Mrs. Babbitt, for answering my question. Now if you will be kind enough to excuse me, I will get back to my guests."

Shepherd's eyes followed Mrs. Knights as she went inside; then Shepherd turned his eyes to rest on Julianne. He smiled charmingly and sat down beside her. "Mrs. Babbitt, I'm delighted that you will have a new carriage. A few may even embrace Mormon doctrine. I must admit that your husband has a keen mind. Though no one will convince me that Joe Smith is a prophet, it is entertaining to see him try."

Julianne smiled uncomfortably. "Sir, though I cannot completely thank you for your sentiments, I do thank you for your generosity."

"And it is delightful being in the presence of a lovely lady." Dr. Shepherd took her hand and kissed it as Almon came outside and found them.

Almon took the hand Shepherd had kissed and helped Julianne stand. "My dear, join me. Mr. and Mrs. Allen would like to meet you." Almon put his arm around her possessively as they walked away and whispered, "What did Shepherd say to you?"

"That your preaching is entertaining."

"Hmm. I'll have to thank him for the compliment. However, I don't like the way he looked at you."

Julianne laughed softly. "Perhaps he isn't the only man here with an eye for older women."

"He had better watch himself when that older woman is mine."

\* \* \*

*Springfield, Illinois. October 5, 1839*

It was midafternoon when Benjamin sat on a couch in the parlor of the Sniders' home. He was finally able to walk unaided from one room to the next. Early that morning, Brigham Young and Heber C. Kimball had arrived on a conveyance. They had left Nauvoo a few days previous for their mission to Europe but were still too sick and weak to travel far. They planned to stay in Springfield for a few days to gain strength.

Benjamin reached out his hand as the apostles entered the room. They smiled, their faces thin and drawn, and shook Benjamin's hand before sitting down in nearby chairs. A moment later, Heber C. Kimball led them in prayer, asking that the Lord's Spirit guide and direct them.

Following the prayer, Brigham Young addressed Benjamin. "Elder Johnson, Brother Snider has informed us of your poverty. You are very sick and weak. You no longer have adequate clothing or a horse."

Benjamin swallowed, intensely aware of his losses. "That's correct."

Elder Kimball commented, "We understand your discouragement. We too left home sick and poor. Each day we trust in the tender mercy of our Savior."

"You have great faith," Benjamin said, unable to keep his jaw from quivering. "If I had such faith, perhaps I would be healed. But I am not."

Elder Kimball continued. "Brother Joseph taught us that many of the righteous will fall prey to disease and death. Do not blame yourself for your illness or circumstances."

Benjamin swallowed. "If you want me to go in this condition, I will try."

Elder Young looked into Benjamin's eyes. "Brother Ben, we have prayed earnestly about what is best. You are inexperienced as a missionary but have great promise. The Lord has whispered in our minds that this decision is in your hands. At times, circumstances change the direction of a call the Lord has extended. That may be the case with you. We leave your mission up to your own judgment, your own faith and desire."

For a moment, Benjamin did not speak. He focused on Elder Young as his eyes filled with tears. "I want to go, but I fear I will be a burden to you. I-I don't have the faith to start."

Elder Young stood and put a hand on Benjamin's shoulder. "The Lord does not judge your choice, nor do your brethren. The Lord would have you *fear not*. He has not rescinded your call as a missionary. You are to take a mission east as soon as you're able. May our Heavenly Father bless and guide you as you bring souls to Him."

Elders Young and Kimball laid their hands on Benjamin's head and gave him a blessing. As he listened, a scripture from the New Testament entered his mind: *By this shall all men know that ye are my disciples, if ye have love one to another.*

\* \* \*

*Pleasant Garden, Indiana. October 18, 1839*

During the three weeks while the carriage was being constructed, Almon preached thirty-three times. He baptized five people and organized a small branch.

A few days before the carriage was finished, the Laws arrived with a small company of Canadian Saints on their way to Springfield and then Nauvoo. Almon talked to William, trying to convince him to move to Kirtland instead.

William listened carefully then shook his head. "I want to meet the Prophet and see this city he is building. But Kirtland is tempting. I'm worried about malaria."

Almon took a deep breath. "It's been terrible, but with the change in the season, things are getting better."

William sat silently and thought. Almon reached out and placed a friendly hand on his shoulder. "Don't worry, my friend. When the river scourge returns next spring, come to Kirtland. A home will await you."

William grinned, stating that it was a good plan. They talked for a few more minutes about family and friends. When they were finished, William warmly embraced Almon, mentioning that the company planned to be on the road within the hour.

Almon walked into his hotel room, where Julianne sat writing letters to her family. He stepped behind her and kissed the top of her head. Julianne's pen stilled, and she leaned back into him.

Almon sighed. "The Laws will be leaving in an hour and will carry our letters. I couldn't convince William to go to Kirtland."

Julianne tilted her head to look up at him. "That doesn't surprise me. The whole company is looking forward to meeting Joseph."

"I know. I suppose if I'm going to write to the brethren, I'd better do it now." Almon sat down and picked up his pen. His mind turned to the people of Pleasant Garden—the hundreds he had preached to and the handful he had baptized. He couldn't stay here much longer, yet the field was still white. He decided to address his letter to Don Carlos Smith, who was working on the first edition of Nauvoo's newspaper.

Pausing, Almon thought about Don Carlos and the infancy of the Church. He remembered the day he had introduced Don Carlos to David—how the three of them had worked together, laughed together, and borne testimony together until David's death. Did Carlos still think of those times? Did images of Kirtland fill his mind as they did Almon's? Julianne's radiance on the day of their wedding. The first cry of their baby boy. The dedication of the Kirtland Temple, where he held his baby close, where he watched Julianne sing in the choir, where he felt and heard the sound of the angels surrounding the house, the shining glory of lives that would never end, of families that would always be. The endowment of faith and fire. Those who were left behind. He would return to Kirtland. He had to. He would bring all who would hearken back to the house of the Lord.

Almon picked up his pen and wrote a letter to the *Times and Seasons*, calling for another elder to come labor in Pleasant Garden, Indiana.

*Dear Brethren,*

*In great haste, I improve this opportunity of addressing a few lines to you to inform you where I am laboring, and the fruits that attend the same . . .*

*I have just begun to baptize here . . . among whom is Doctor Knights and his Lady. He is an eminent physician, who has practiced in this county for thirteen years. The prospect is that many of the first class of people in the county will be baptized . . . that never has a greater field opened than I am in now . . . I want an elder of experience sent here as soon as you receive this. I have had three attacks but have found that they could do nothing against the truth, but for it.*

*Yours in the bond of the everlasting covenant,*
*Almon Babbitt*

# 12

*Hear the Gospel word,*
*And all its truth believe;*
*Come, be baptized into the Lord,*
*And life for death receive.*

Joel Hills Johnson

*November 4, 1839*

WILL SAT NEXT TO JOE on the wagon seat as he drove the horse toward the Sniders' home. He thought about the past month. Although Benjamin continued to board at the Sniders', Joe had moved back home. In the evenings, Joe often invited Will on long walks, and they talked about the past and future. Joe told him stories of Pomfret—what it had been like when David and Seth were alive. They discussed ideas for succeeding in the world. The only thing they didn't discuss was their mother. Will knew Joe practically worshipped her. But hard as he tried, Will was still torn—a part of him loved her, but another part of him blamed her. He shook his head to quit thinking about it. He was glad Joe had asked him to go to the gathering at the Sniders' tonight. The Prophet was staying there on his way to Washington to seek redress for the Missouri persecutions.

A slender moon lay in the starlit sky. As they drew near, the dark shapes of eight covered wagons rose from the Sniders' yard.

"Whoa! Looks like the Prophet is taking a lot of people to Washington with him." Will whistled.

Joe shook his head thoughtfully. "I don't think so. Only President Rigdon, Brother Higbee, and Porter Rockwell were appointed to go with him. This might be the company of Canadian Saints Harriet told me about. The

Sniders have been expecting them for some time. Their leader is a man named William Law, a close friend of Harriet's father. It would be quite a coincidence if they arrived the same time as the Prophet."

Lantern light flickered as Will watched two families with young children leave the house and walk toward the wagons. He suddenly felt stupid. Of course the Prophet wouldn't be taking an entire company to Washington. He felt relieved that Joe was the only person who had heard.

When they were well into the yard, Will reined in the horse. The brothers climbed out of the wagon and then unhitched and tied the horse. As they approached the house, Joe stretched his arm around Will's shoulder. "Let's go find out exactly who's here. With this crowd, we might need to bring Ben home tonight."

Harriet answered their knock at the door. Smiling, she beckoned them inside. The house overflowed with light and voices. Will stepped out of the way as Joe kissed Harriet's cheek and took her hand. Harriet's deep blue eyes sparkled. "Brother Joseph's here with his committee, along with the Laws and their company. They ran into the Prophet's group a mile outside of town and all came together. Hurry! Right now, Brother Law is telling the Prophet about seeing Almon and Julianne in Pleasant Garden."

The three stepped quickly to the perimeter of the group and listened as William Law, with his Irish accent, spoke animatedly to the Prophet. "Almon told me that Kirtland is to be built up. He encouraged us to settle there. However, we decided to travel on to Nauvoo."

"God bless you," the Prophet responded, his blue eyes warm and direct. "Your decision was inspired. It's right that you go to Nauvoo." The Prophet then looked at the whole group, drawing them in with his hands as he continued. "All the faithful Saints who come to Nauvoo will be blessed. It is the gathering place sanctioned by the Lord. It's probable that a few, like Brother Babbitt, may be asked to go back to Kirtland to conduct business there, but that is the exception. Nauvoo is the headquarters of the Church and the destination of our scattered people."

As William Law nodded thoughtfully, the Prophet turned to Will and Joe. Shaking Joe's hand first, he explained that Benjamin was weak and resting in his room. Then he withdrew two letters from his vest pocket and handed them to Joe. "One is from your sister Delcena and the other from your brother Joel," he said with a twinkle. "I think Joel will try to convince you to move to a new town twenty miles from Nauvoo. It's a good idea."

As Joe took the letter, the Prophet reached out to Will. The clasp of the Prophet's hand felt electric with energy and purpose. As Joseph spoke, warmth such that Will had rarely experienced spread through him. "Dear Brother Will, I remember when I first met you, a sleepy lad when your mother's wagon rolled into Kirtland with Seth in the driver's seat. I told her that day that the Lord would bless her and her children for gathering with the Saints. And the Lord has blessed her. Look at the sons Sister Julia has raised. At Bennie whose life has been spared. At Joe, who tends to the sick and enlightens the minds of the young. There is faithful George reaching manhood. And look at you, a young man of such goodness and strength. May God continue to bless you all."

Will's eyes burned as he clung to the Prophet's hand. The question that never left him alone spilled out before he had time to stop it. "But what of the others?" *What of David, Seth, Susan, and Nancy? What of Lyman? What of poverty and death?*

"They too are blessed," the Prophet said softly to Will alone. "They are in the kingdom of heaven. We must all strive to be found worthy to join them. Never doubt that God's all-seeing eye is upon you and upon your dear family."

Porter Rockwell walked over and asked to speak privately with the Prophet. Will composed himself and moved closer to Joe and Harriet, who were mingling with the Laws.

William Law glanced at his brother and laughed. "Wilson here is a confirmed bachelor. Now that Miss Snider is spoken for, another pretty lass has escaped him."

Wilson, whose green eyes matched his brother's, though his jowl was markedly heavier, tilted his head toward Joe and Harriet. He looked both amused and aloof at the same time. "I suppose I am destined to be forever the groomsman but never the groom."

Joe grinned and pulled Harriet closer. "That may change, for I hear that there are many attractive ladies in Nauvoo. However, we hope you are single long enough to be our groomsman."

As the lively talk continued and Harriet's color heightened with joy, Will scarcely noticed. His mind was on the Prophet's words. The aching places in his soul had been touched by healing power.

\* \* \*

Later that night, Julia lay awake thinking of Delcena's and Joel's letters. Delcena had written that Lyman's mother, brother, and sister-in-law had come to Quincy to be with her. Soon they would help Delcena move to Nauvoo. This news brought Julia conflicted emotions. She was glad Delcena had family to help her, yet Delcena was her daughter, and another grandmother grew ever closer to Julia's beloved grandchildren. She remembered Asenath's blue eyes and quick wit. The children would adore her. She smiled at her own folly. How childish to want to be the favorite grandmother.

Then she thought of Joel's letter encouraging her to move close to him. However, there seemed to be two gathering places. Kirtland was being built back up. Almon and Julianne had encouraged her to settle there. Almera needed her. And Esther longed for her father. But what of Ezekiel? Leaving had been terribly hard. Would returning be even harder? What of the vivid memories of their life together, their children's deaths, and their painful separation?

An owl hooted. Julia arose and wrapped a shawl over her white nightdress. She walked out into the kitchen and lit a candle. Joel's letter lay on the table. Candlelight shone as Julia reread a portion of the words: *Mother, a city called Ramus will soon be built here. There is fertile land for you and the children. It is close to Nauvoo. I believe that in a short time a stake of Zion will be established. Talk to Joe and the others. I've been hired to shingle the roof for Carthage's new jail. It will bring in extra income. When you decide to come, I'll send money to help with your journey.*

Julia sighed and sat down at the table. She had already talked to Joe, Mary, and George. During the discussion, Joe had said that the Sniders would be moving to Nauvoo in the spring, and Harriet would go with them. He hoped to go to Ramus to establish a home and marry Harriet. George and Mary had been noncommittal, willing to go either place. The youngest three had not been with them.

Julia turned at the sound of footsteps as Will entered the kitchen. He looked so young and handsome, his hair tousled on top of his head. He had been so distant lately. Julia smiled at him. "William, I'm surprised to find you awake."

"The owl woke me up, and I saw the candlelight in the kitchen."

"Do you want to sit down with me?"

"All right." Will's voice wasn't eager, but it wasn't grudging either. He sat across from Julia, the candlelight reflected in his brown eyes.

Julia opened the conversation as she handed him the letter. "Joel suggests that we move to a town near Nauvoo called Ramus. How do you feel about going there in the spring?"

"Mother, does it matter how I feel?" Will asked as he scanned the letter.

"It matters to me. I'm not sure what to do. Julianne, Almon, Almera, and your father are in Kirtland. I've promised to send Esther there. Almon says that it will grow and that we should all go back. Joe wants to go to Ramus. George and Mary are willing to go wherever I think is best. But what about you, Will? What do you think? I'm torn between Kirtland and Ramus."

Will looked down for a moment. Then he lifted his head and looked directly at Julia. "Tonight Brother Joseph said that Nauvoo is the gathering place for faithful Saints. It's not Kirtland anymore. Ramus is where we should go. It's the right choice."

Julia swallowed, her heart swelling for the boy in front of her who was trying desperately hard to become a man. "We'll go to Ramus. Thank you, William, for your counsel."

Will nodded and stood. He walked toward the door but turned around before leaving the kitchen. "You're welcome," he added. "I'll give you advice anytime you want it." In the shadowy candlelight, Julia thought she saw him smile and wink. Her William Derby was back.

\* \* \*

*December, 1839. Kirtland, Ohio*

The blazing fire warmed the kitchen as Julianne sat at the sturdy white-beech table grating suet. A slab of beef crackled on the spit near the hearth. Her hands ached from grating, but she kept at it. They would need plenty of the hard fat when Almera arrived to make pies after lunch.

Suddenly, a loud click startled Julianne. The noise came from the roast as it made a quarter turn on the spit's clocklike apparatus. Julianne got up to check the meat and smiled to herself. She wasn't accustomed to such an elaborate kitchen with so many hooks, kettles, spits, and screens. This was the house Joseph Smith had built for his family. This had been Emma's kitchen. During those days, Julianne had never imagined that she would one day be mistress there. She paused and said a quick prayer, hoping Nauvoo would bring Emma an even more wonderful home. Then she checked the juices dripping into the pan beneath the roast. Hearing voices outside the front door, she straightened.

Almon strode into the kitchen, followed by Ezekiel. Julianne hurried into Almon's open arms.

"Smells good!" he exclaimed.

Snowflakes melted in his hair, his green eyes shone bright, his cheeks were red, and his grin was contagious. Whatever the weather outside, he brought sunshine. After kissing him, Julianne turned and hugged her father. "The roast is ready."

Almon took the roast off the spit while Julianne covered the suet with a linen cloth and brought bread and cider to the table.

"I'm the luckiest man!" Almon exclaimed as he sat down. "A wonderful wife, a good lunch, and a prosperous morning."

"A prosperous morning? Tell me about it," Julianne said as she cut two apples into pieces and set them in a dish on the table.

"We bought two hundred dollars in Kirtland Safety Society notes for ten dollars." Almon reached into his vest pocket and began pulling out bank notes.

"Two hundred dollars in worthless money?" Julianne tilted her head as she asked the question. "I know you're a radical Democrat who believes in specie, not paper money, but how does this prosper us?"

"Because they are now out of circulation! We can't build wealth as a Church until these are gone. Then when the Prophet's debts are paid, we'll get the deed to the temple back and open a printing press. What do you think of the name *The Olive Leaf*?"

Julianne's brow furrowed slightly. "I like it. But these are ambitious plans for a man who'll be in Cincinnati soon studying law."

Almon chuckled. "Your good father will continue buying up the bank notes for us while I'm in Cincinnati. People trust him and are delighted to get rid of them for almost any sum. While the foundation strengthens, I'll get my law license. One step at a time."

"Papa?" Julianne looked quizzically at her father. "Why are you spending your money and time helping the Church?"

Ezekiel swallowed a piece of meat and cleared his throat. He looked at Julianne, his voice slightly gruff as he spoke. "I'd do about anything to have the rest of my family back in Kirtland. If the Mormons prosper here, maybe Joseph will be smart enough to leave that malaria-ridden swamp."

A shadow fell across Julianne's face. She said little as the men continued their meal but glanced at the cupboard where she had placed a newspaper that Hiram Winters had brought over that morning. There was an article in it that would upset Almon. She had planned to talk with him about it later. She took a deep breath and exhaled slowly. The news would be an even bigger blow to her father. After a long five minutes, she walked over, retrieved the paper, and brought it back to the table. It would be better if the men found out now. It was often kinder to stop dreams before they grew too large, for the larger the dream, the greater the heartbreak when it shattered.

Almon's eyes followed Julianne. "What is that?"

She handed the paper to him. "This came while you were out."

Almon fingered through it with delight. "It's the first issue of Nauvoo's *Times and Seasons*! Why didn't you say something earlier? Carlos has been busy. And here's the letter I wrote from Pleasant Garden."

"There's another letter following yours," Julianne said softly. "It might not please you as much. It's from the First Presidency and high council. It's about Kirtland."

Almon glanced at her, his eyes perplexed. Then he read aloud: "To the Saints scattered abroad in the region westward from Kirtland, Ohio: Beloved brethren, we have heard it rumored that many are making calculations to move back to Kirtland next season. Now brethren, this being the case, we advise you to abandon such an idea; yea, we warn you in the name of the Lord not to remove back there unless you are counseled so to do by the First Presidency and the high council of Nauvoo. We do not wish by this to take your agency from you; but we feel to be plain and pointed in our advice, for we wish to do our duty . . . It may be considered wisdom for some of us to remove back to Kirtland to attend to important business there. But should any be so unwise as to move back there without being counseled to do so, their conduct will be highly disapprobated."

Almon closed the paper and put it down on the table. His green eyes darkened. "Joseph told me that Kirtland is to be built up. It was announced in the May conference. I don't understand this. Are the brethren concerned that there aren't enough resources for the European and Eastern converts as well as those who might want to come back from the west? I will assure them that I will change that."

Julianne's voice was gentle. "Almon, Kirtland is to be built up as a stopping place for the European and Eastern converts to rest for a season. But I think the Lord wants His people to gather in Nauvoo. We are counseled to stay here, but others are not."

Almon hesitated for a moment. Julianne could almost hear the wheels in his mind turning as he prepared a rebuttal. But before he spoke, Ezekiel stood up. "I'm going now."

Julianne's gaze followed her father. His shoulders were stooped. Was it possible that a man could age visibly in only a few minutes?

She followed him to the door and impetuously took his hand. "Oh, Papa, I'm sorry that Mama and the others won't be coming back. We both know they will follow the instructions in the letter. I miss them so much too. But Almon and I aren't going anywhere. You're stuck with us for a long time."

Ezekiel patted her hand. "It was too much to hope for. When you see Almera this afternoon, try to get her to smile." Then her father left. Julianne watched him slowly walk to his horse.

\* \* \*

Almera held on to the sidesaddle as the horse stepped forward down the snow-covered lane. She could scarcely control the sorrow that shook her, making it difficult to take a deep breath. Her neck and forearms hurt. She should not have told her husband the truth. The fight with Sam was seared into her mind.

He had come home from work, unexpected, to find Almera on her way out.

"Where are you going?"

"To Julianne's. Just this once. To make beef pies for Christmas dinner."

"Make them here—by yourself."

"I don't have suet or beef."

"I'll be lenient today because of Christmas, but don't go again. Ever."

"Please, Sam. She's my sister."

"Stop defying me!"

"But you are unfair."

"Me? Unfair?"

At those words, he had grabbed her shoulders and shaken her hard, her teeth knocking together and her neck snapping back. It was the first time he had laid a hand on her. When she screamed, he suddenly pushed her away, staring at her and shaking. Crying, she wrapped her cloak tightly around her shoulders and headed out the door.

"Promise you'll come back tonight!" he had shouted after her. "I love you. Don't make me follow with my gun."

"I promise," Almera had sobbed.

Almera continued to sob as she rode to Julianne's. In her panic to leave, she had forgotten the flour she'd promised to bring. So many broken promises.

Ten minutes later, she knocked on Julianne's door. "Dearest, what happened?" Julianne wrapped her arms around Almera and helped her inside.

"Sam found out," Almera wept, flinching at the pressure of Julianne's arm around her sore shoulders.

"Did he touch you?" Julianne asked.

Almera shook her head. Another lie. "He-he let me come because we don't have suet. But never again. I forgot the flour." Uncontrolled tears streamed down her face.

"I don't care about flour. Come sit down."

Almera trailed Julianne to the couch, following directions like a child, too powerless to know her own will. She sat down and waited while Julianne brought in two steaming cups of cider. Almera took a sip. A tear fell. It hit the warm liquid, making concentric circles like a pebble in a pool.

Julianne put her cup on the table. "You don't have to go back. We want you to live with us."

Almera's jaw quivered. Should she tell Julianne the truth—how Sam had shaken her, how he had threatened to come after her with his gun? Her imagination spun forward to a limp body in a pool of blood. Who would he shoot first? Her? Julianne? Almon? Could the man she once loved do something so horrible? But if she told Julianne, Sam might end up dead, with her father or Almon becoming murderers. She shivered, taking another sip, feeling the hot liquid warm her. "I-I have to go back. I promised."

Julianne shook her head. "No. You don't have to."

"I-I can't stay with you and Almon. Not with Sam in the same city. Watching us. Hating us. I don't know what he would do."

"Almon isn't afraid of him."

"Almon's leaving for Cincinnati."

"But Delcena and I were alone when the mobs came through Far West. God protected us, and He will aid us now. Papa will come if we want him to. We shouldn't be afraid."

"Of course we should be afraid!" Almera exclaimed, her chest convulsing. "Hatred changes people."

"I know," Julianne said, taking Almera's hand in hers. Julianne took a deep breath and closed her eyes for an instant. The cup shook in Almera's right hand, and she placed it on the table. When Julianne opened her eyes, her voice was low and determined. "I am afraid. But I love you more than I'm afraid."

Almera's tears increased. "Maybe someday, but not today," she whispered. "But today . . . today . . . in a little while, can we still make the pies?"

Julianne held both of her sister's hands. "Yes, dearest. Just tell me when you're ready."

\* \* \*

*Early March 1840. Pleasant Garden, Indiana*

Benjamin sat on the stand as he waited for the large congregation to gather. The hall was full, but his friend Dr. Knights was not there. Dr. Knights was at home caring for his wife, who was extremely ill. Benjamin's heart raced, which frustrated him. He had been a prisoner in Missouri, where men had threatened to murder him daily. Why on earth was he frightened now? He was an elder, a Mormon missionary. These people had requested that he preach to them. They certainly weren't going to kill him.

Benjamin stood and glanced at the dozens of people. Well fed and well groomed, with Bibles in hand, their attentive, intelligent eyes pierced him. Benjamin's face grew hot with anxiety. Almon's letter had requested an experienced elder. Why had Benjamin felt impressed to answer the call? He had headed out alone, inexperienced, too weak to walk more than a short distance, and with only the twelve dollars Joe had collected. Yet it had been as if the protecting angel promised by the Prophet had been with him. There had been kind people, both members and nonmembers, who had risen up to feed and house him every step of the journey.

Still too timid to speak, Benjamin closed his eyes and prayed silently. His prayer was answered as thoughts filled his mind. *You are not inexperienced in your knowledge and love of the gospel. It is not the vessel that matters but the contents of that vessel.* Benjamin began talking, his mind filling with words, with scriptures, and with testimony. He preached for an hour and a half, his eyes remaining tightly shut the entire time.

It wasn't until after Benjamin closed his sermon in Jesus' name and asked for those who desired to come forward for baptism that he opened his eyes. He looked into the faces of the five people walking up to him: an elderly gentleman, a young husband and wife, and a widow and her daughter. As they walked together to the millpond, Benjamin felt a joy that he had never before experienced, and he felt as if his brother Seth accompanied him. *How great shall be your joy in the kingdom of God if ye bring but one soul unto me. Seth, I'm here because of you,* Benjamin's heart whispered, *and so are they.*

\* \* \*

*Carthage Jail, Illinois*

Joel stood with his son Sixtus in the shade of the new Carthage jail. His son had filled out and would be as tall as him in a few years. Joel had just finished nailing the final shingles in place. The brisk wind was refreshing following his labor. Joel smiled. The money earned would make it possible to build a comfortable home in the newly plotted town of Ramus. He would move Annie and the children in after the summer, sometime during the fall. Taking a step back, he squinted up at the roof; the shingles, red from resin, held tightly in place. Not only was the job well done, but he had also made numerous friends in Carthage, largely dissipating the prejudice against the Mormons.

"Papa, a squall's on its way," Sixtus said, moving closer to his father as he pointed westward. Dark clouds threatened, a flash of lightning slicing through them. It was strange: a day could become clear or clouded in a matter of moments. Joel thought of the last two buildings he had roofed: the Kirtland Temple and the Carthage jail—the house of the Lord and a prison for thieves.

"Let the rain come, then. No one will get wet in this building," Joel commented, placing his hand on Sixtus' shoulder.

Sixtus grinned. "Who cares if prisoners get wet? It serves them right."

Joel glanced at his boy. "Brother Joseph was a prisoner in Liberty Jail, though he did not break the law."

Sixtus shifted his weight, chewing on the thought. "When's Brother Joseph coming home?"

"The Prophet sent a letter to Nauvoo. He's on his way," Joel said. He didn't elaborate. The brethren were coming home because there was nothing they could do in Washington. How do you explain to your eleven-year-old that the highest levels of government did not support the rights of the people? That the president of the United States closed his eyes to murder and plunder? The bitter taste of Van Buren's words to the Prophet echoed hollowly in Joel's mind: *Your cause is just, but I can do nothing for you. If I take up for you, I shall lose the vote of Missouri.*

Sixtus's bright voice interrupted his thoughts. "I hope Brother Joseph stops by on his way home like he did on his way to Washington."

"I hope so too."

Sixtus continued as Joel listened. His boy was a talker, like Annie. "When Brother Joseph came last time, I was outside chopping wood. Brother Joseph took the ax from me and split the log I was working on. Then he looked at two cocks fighting and said, 'Sixtus, my boy, I'd chop wood any day rather than fight. Never forget that.'"

"Really," Joel commented, his interest piqued. "You never told me about this."

"I guess I forgot to."

At the first smattering of rain, Joel cleared his throat. "Sixtus, my boy, I'd rather be dry any day than be wet. Never forget that." They hurried inside the Carthage jail to escape the downpour.

# 13

*No more let sin and darkness gain*
*Possession of your breast;*
*But walk with Christ, till you shall reign*
*In his eternal rest.*

Joel Hills Johnson

*Pleasant Garden, Indiana*

IT WAS EARLY EVENING WHEN Benjamin arrived at the Knights' home on Main Street. Mrs. Knights had been very ill, but Benjamin hoped she had improved following her priesthood blessing three days previous. The black housemaid answered his knock, her face wet with tears as she held the Knights' three-year-old son in her arms. "Brother Johnson, the missus died this afternoon. Doctor left on horseback. Said he's goin' to the plantation and not to disturb him. He's crazy with sorrow."

The sun sank, a fiery globe in a seamless sky as Benjamin galloped the roan mare toward Dr. Knights' plantation. The horse surged forward, sweat lathering her neck and flanks. Green fields and trees, some tipped with blossoms, sped by. Benjamin gave the mare her head. *Faster, go faster.* Ten days ago, Dr. Knights had presented Benjamin with a saddle and bridle. Then he had taken Benjamin to his plantation and had told him to pick any horse from his band. The mare knew the way home.

Upon arrival, Benjamin dismounted and quickly tied his horse to a hitching post. As he approached the country house, he heard a crash. He flung the front door open and ran down the arched hallway and into the parlor where Dr. Knights swung a club wildly, striking lamps and tables.

"Stop!" Benjamin shouted.

The doctor spun toward Benjamin, his club raised. Benjamin stumbled back, an arm flying up to ward off a blow. But the blow never fell as recognition flickered in the doctor's eyes. He lowered the club. Benjamin straightened and said, "Dear sir, I beg you to find comfort in God."

Dr. Knights' eye twitched. "You don't understand."

Benjamin wrapped his arms around the wealthy, hot-blooded man who was twenty years his senior. He held him for a few moments then whispered, "Have peace. God has taken her to Himself."

Dr. Knights stiffened and moved out of Benjamin's embrace. "No, there will be no peace until Dr. Shepherd is dead. You don't know what happened."

"What happened?"

Dr. Knights' hands shook with rage as he explained. "Shepherd was a poor young man, almost a boy, but I saw promise in him. I took him in and made him my protégé, like he was my own son. On her deathbed, my wife confessed that he had seduced her and betrayed me."

Benjamin's thoughts staggered under the magnitude of what he had just heard. It was no wonder that fury consumed Dr. Knights. But what would happen to Dr. Knights' soul if he killed a man? Benjamin tried to explain. "Your wife already answers to God. I beg you to leave Shepherd to the Almighty. They are not worth losing your soul."

Dr. Knights gripped Benjamin's hands like a man sinking in quicksand. "My wife, my lovely one, died innocent! Elder Babbitt baptized her. She was washed clean. But what if Elder Babbitt hadn't come? Shepherd would have destroyed her soul forever." Dr. Knights wept again. Benjamin did not know what to say, but he tightened his hold on the doctor, steadying him, not about to let go.

* * *

The next morning, Benjamin shaved and dressed quickly. It was eight o'clock, two hours past the time he usually arose. He had stayed with Dr. Knights until late last night and was anxious to check on him. He opened the door to a day that promised to grow hot. The sun beat against a thin layer of sultry clouds. Benjamin stepped on an envelope and heard dry paper rustle beneath his boot.

Squatting down, Benjamin picked it up and noticed Lucinda's handwriting. *Elder Benjamin Johnson.* He opened it.

*Elder Johnson,*

*I hope that my words do not grieve you. I sincerely pray for your welfare and happiness. Because you are gone and because I do not know when you shall return, I have followed my mother's advice and accepted the courtship of another suitor. My mother wishes me to marry him, and I have agreed to do so. I will be wed by the time this letter reaches your hands. Mother believes it will be best. I trust in her judgment.*

*Yours in memory,*
*Lucinda*

Tears filled Benjamin's eyes as he tore the letter to shreds. Lucinda had broken her promise. There was nothing he could do. Benjamin leaned against the clapboard to gain his bearings. He thought of Lucinda's mother and his hands knotted into fists. After going back into the room and closing the door, Benjamin forced himself to his knees. In his mind's eye, he saw Dr. Knights wielding the club. His vision shifted to Rogers, the Missourian who had tortured him with the corn cutter. Rage unchecked turned men against themselves, turned them into monsters. He prayed for strength. Then he stood, wiped his eyes, and left the hotel.

When Benjamin arrived at the doctor's home, he found his friend pacing. The agony and obsession were back in his eyes. Dr. Knights spoke quickly. "You are a good man but very young. And you are wrong. After I bury my wife, I'm going for Shepherd. Justice will only be served when Shepherd has paid for his crimes with his life. God wants him dead before he has the opportunity to destroy another life."

"No," Benjamin argued. "Think of your little son. He will never understand why his father murdered a man."

Dr. Knights jaw quivered. "How can I allow Shepherd to live, to continue his debauchery? I cannot rest while he breathes."

"What will happen to your boy if you hang for murder?"

"I don't know," Dr. Knights cried out in agony.

Benjamin placed his hand on Knights' arm. "Leave your boy here with your housemaid for a time. Go to Kirtland and talk with Brother Babbitt. He baptized you and your wife. He'll know what to do."

The doctor gazed out the window for a few moments. Then he turned back to Benjamin. "My mind is crazed. Come with me. I don't trust myself alone."

Benjamin nodded. He knew in part the doctor's pain. His mind was full of Lucinda and shattered hopes. He would go to Kirtland and leave Dr. Knights in Almon's care. He would also visit his father and sisters. There, he would find the strength to continue his mission.

\* \* \*

*Three weeks later. Kirtland, Ohio*

It was Friday afternoon, and school was over for the day. Melissa LeBaron looked out through the window of the academy building. Almera stood on the porch, her dark eyes soft and her smile warm, as she chatted with her missionary brother, Benjamin. Benjamin's brow was moist from the heat, and his weight was on one hip. He chuckled at something Almera said. Melissa moved closer to the window, hoping to hear their words. However, it was useless because a breeze blew and they talked softly. Feeling a sharp pang of guilt at her own nosiness, Melissa stepped away. It was just that Benjamin's tall leanness, his appealing, expressive features, and his affectionate concern for his sister drew her like a magnet.

Melissa sighed. She wished things were different, that she could really get to know Benjamin. But he only seemed interested in his mission and in his sister's welfare. With a shrug, she went back to tidying the schoolroom. *Besides,* she thought, trying to reason her way out of disappointment, *he would complicate things. I already have two men who want to court me. I just need to choose.* The difficulty was that neither of these suitors suited Melissa. One was so short that she towered over him, and the other, though an impeccable conversationalist, had a haughty, knowing smile that rubbed Melissa wrong. Furthermore, she was never sure if a man liked her for her inheritance or for herself.

Melissa put away the stack of slates then glanced at the window. Benjamin embraced Almera warmly then mounted a lovely roan. But before he rode away, he suddenly turned toward the window where she stood. He smiled and nodded. Melissa smiled back, her heart pounding. He turned away, spurred his mount, and was gone. Melissa took a deep, happy breath and began sweeping.

A moment later, her smile evaporated when she heard shouting on the porch. Melissa ran to the window. Almera's husband was next to her, his face red with heat and anger, contrasting starkly with his light hair. Enraged, he pounded his fist against the clapboard and yelled at Almera.

"You refuse to obey me! I said to stay away from Ben. From all of them. You aren't coming back here."

Embarrassed to be watching, Melissa turned for a split second. Then she heard a thud. In horror, she saw that Almera had fallen backward down the steep porch steps. She saw Sam Prescott's outstretched arm. Did he push her? Or did Almera step backward and trip? Did he try to catch her?

Melissa ran to the door and flung it open. She hurried down the steps. Almera lay on the ground. Her cheeks and lips were pale, and her eyes looked frightened. Bright red blood dripped down her temple. Sam squatted beside her. He took a handkerchief from his pocket and pressed it firmly against Almera's head to staunch the bleeding then reached the other arm around her back, stood, and lifted her in his arms. Almera allowed it, almost as if she had no life of her own—a rag doll, a fallen doe. But when Melissa looked into Almera's eyes, she saw a plea for help.

"Mr. Prescott, bring her inside," Melissa said. "She can rest in here while I fetch the doctor."

Sam's head turned, and he glared at Melissa, his light blue eyes hard with loathing. Melissa's legs shook. Would he strike her? Strangely, when he spoke, his voice sounded almost normal. "My wife accidentally fell down these steps. The cut isn't deep. She'll recover at home. Tell whoever is in charge that my wife won't be back."

Melissa watched him carry Almera around the corner, where he must have left the wagon. As soon as they were out of sight, she left the schoolroom, lifted her skirts, and ran to Brother Babbitt's house just a few blocks away.

When Melissa arrived, her cream cheeks were red, and she was hot and sweaty from exertion. Julianne answered the door. Directly behind her, in the parlor, Almon sat with Dr. Knights.

"Melissa." Julianne's smiled faded into concern. "What's happened?"

"Almera needs help," Melissa gasped. Almon and the doctor stood and joined them. Melissa blurted out the story.

"Almon, this has to end," Julianne cried.

Almon nodded. "I'll ride to Mentor to get your father and Ben. Then we'll go get Almera."

Julianne's eyes filled with tears, but she nodded stoically. "May God go with you."

Almon kissed her forehead before putting his pistol in his pocket and shouldering his rifle. Dr. Knights gave Melissa a glass of water and invited her to sit down. Then he turned to Almon. "I'm coming with you."

Almon nodded. "I'd be obliged."

As Dr. Knights went to get his gun, Almon looked at Melissa. "Miss LeBaron, would you be so kind as to wait here with my wife?"

"Of course," Melissa said. The glass of water trembled in her hand.

* * *

As the four men strode to the Prescott's, Ezekiel's jaw was tight, his blue eyes grim with purpose. He had seen this coming for a long time. The memory of his stepfather's abuse flamed in his mind. His gun, Betsy, which Benjamin had returned, hung at his side. The inlaid silver along the gun's shaft glinted in the waning sunlight. Fifty years ago Ezekiel had promised Isaac Chapel that he would never kill a man with this gun except in self-defense—self-defense extended to his children. He would do whatever it took to free Almera, even if he hanged for it. Upon arrival, they saw the wagon in the yard, packed with provisions and household goods. Almon's whistle was low. "Looks like Prescott plans on running."

"And taking Almera with him," Benjamin added. He was a missionary in his suit clothes—an elder with a gun.

Dr. Knights glanced at Almon and Benjamin. "If any killing needs to be done, stay out of harm's way. I'll do it."

"No," Ezekiel's voice was authoritative. "Ben and I are her family. We'll go in. Almon, stay outside by the door and back us up. Doctor, get Sam's horses hitched to his wagon. I'll give him one chance to leave."

No one argued. Ezekiel and Benjamin crouched below window level and approached the front door silently. Ezekiel put his hand on the latch—it was not locked. He nodded to Benjamin, who kicked the door open. The two burst into the house with their guns pointed. Sam, who was thirty feet away, carrying a load of firewood, whirled around. He dropped the wood and lunged for the rifle on the mantel. Benjamin got there first, grabbing the rifle and throwing it out the front door to Almon.

"Don't move!" Ezekiel shouted. "Hands in the air. Now."

Sam raised his hands, feigning innocence. "What's goin' on, Zeke?"

"You abused my daughter."

"Who's been telling you stories?"

"I'll ask the questions. Where's Almera?"

"She's in the bedroom sleeping. She had a hard day, so I'm taking her on a trip to Niagara Falls in the morning."

"Liar. Ben, go find Almera." Ezekiel did not take his eyes off of Sam. Benjamin glanced at Sam's powerful build then back at his father. He hesitated.

Almon poked his gun inside the door. "Get her, Ben. Sam knows he's outnumbered. He's not stupid."

\* \* \*

Almera huddled in the corner of her bedroom, shaking violently, her head in her hands. She had heard her father's voice. Her temple throbbed, and hot pain coursed through the hand she had fallen on. Sam's words on the way home resounded in her brain. *I reached for your arm! I didn't push you! Zeke will come for you. If we leave before he gets here, I won't have to kill him.* Immobilized by terror, she waited for the sound of gunshots.

The house was silent. Then she heard footsteps in the room. She turned, her eyes bloodshot and haunted. It was Benjamin. "Mera," he said gently. "It's time to go. Pa and I have come for you."

"I can't," she convulsed. "He'll kill you and Papa if I don't go with him."

Benjamin put his arm around her shoulders. His voice shook with bitter rage. "He'll never hurt you again. I'll thrash his bones to the earth first."

Almera buried her head in Benjamin's shoulder and wept dry, silent sobs.

\* \* \*

Ezekiel and Sam stood with their eyes locked on each other as they waited. After a few minutes Benjamin came out of the bedroom with Almera clinging to him, her face buried in Benjamin's side. Ezekiel's trigger finger twitched. He stared at Sam, his voice low and menacing. "Don't say a word. Don't move a muscle."

Benjamin and Almera walked past and out the front door. After she was gone, Ezekiel shook with rage. "I gave you my daughter, and you abused her. I ought to gun you down right now."

"I didn't push her down those steps!" Sam thundered back. His fists were clenched, and his face was bright red, but he dared not move his feet. "She fell on her own accord. I love my wife. If you shoot me, you kill an innocent man."

Ezekiel chewed on his lip—his gun pointed steadily at his son-in-law's heart. This was Sam—the man who had shared his carpenter's bench, the man who had built Seth's coffin. They had been friends. Ezekiel had rejoiced when he'd married Almera. But now he was destroying Almera's life—the gash on her forehead, the sorrow in her eyes.

"Finish this," Sam raged. "Shoot me now or leave my property."

"No, Sam," Ezekiel said grimly. "You are the man leaving. If you value your life, get in your wagon and drive away. Never come back."

Sam's face stained red with rage. "She's my wife. This is my home. I'll see you hanged!"

Ezekiel shook his head. "No court is gonna hang a man for protecting his child. A witness saw what you did to my daughter. Leave town! You could kill some of us, but there're too many Johnsons and too many Mormons. You'll never get her back. One way or another, you'll end up dead."

Sam cursed savagely at the Mormon Church. He threatened vengeance. Almon's face reddened, but Ezekiel did not bat an eyelash. He waited until Sam was done. Then Ezekiel spoke in a low voice. "I always swore I'd kill any man who laid a hand on one of my children. I haven't shot you, Sam. Why? Because I'm like you. I've spent the last ten years cursing the Mormons for tearing apart my family. But I'm different too. I left my wife because I couldn't stand hurting her anymore. Leave while you have a chance for another life. Leave and find a wife who is not a Mormon. In the name of heaven and earth, get out of here while I'm willing to let you go."

Sam stared at Ezekiel, his fists clenching and unclenching. Then his ice-blue eyes filled with tears. His hands stopped moving, and he walked past Almon and out the open door. Almon followed Sam, his rifle at his shoulder. Sam climbed onto his wagon and left without looking back.

When it was over, Ezekiel felt incredibly tired. He lowered Betsy and walked outside. "Do you think he'll be back?" Dr. Knights questioned.

Ezekiel shook his head. "I don't know."

"We better take turns watching for a few nights," Almon suggested.

Ezekiel nodded, longing for a drink to deaden the pain.

# 14

*She heard the Lord unto her say*
*Go daughter sleep in peace and rest*
*Until the morning of that day*
*When Michael's trumpet awakes the blest.*

Joel Hills Johnson

*Summer 1840. Ramus, Illinois*

OUTSIDE THE TENT, JULIA WATCHED the dawn emerge, edged with pink. It was a balmy, windless early morning, and a light mist rose from the trees bordering the banks of Crooked Creek. Last night they had arrived and set up camp on this stretch of cleared land near the Perkins' settlement. If all went according to Joel's plans, this would become the outer edge of the town of Ramus, a branch of the city of Nauvoo. Julia took a deep breath. Should she settle here as Joel had recommended or travel twenty more miles to Nauvoo, where her children could daily hear the words of the Prophet?

Julia turned at the sound of someone else coming out of the tent. Seventeen-year-old George walked over and stood near her. "Good morning, Mother."

"Good morning, son," Julia put her arm around his slim waist and gave him a hug. George sucked in a deep breath of the early morning air then coughed. He pivoted, his eyes taking in the countryside.

"How are you?" Julia asked.

George cleared his throat. "Tolerable."

Julia looked at her son carefully. In Springfield, she had nearly lost him to typhoid fever. She remembered how he had borne his suffering quietly, asking for paper and a pen and writing poems when he couldn't sleep. On the journey here, he and Joe had both struggled with bodies weakened by disease. Will, in contrast, had borne the brunt of the physical labor.

"Joe should be awake soon," Julia mentioned. "He plans to ride into Nauvoo today to see Harriet. I wonder if we ought to go with him and find a place there to rent. Your older brothers will be busy here building houses of their own. Also, Delcena is in Nauvoo."

"Mother, Will and I can help you here. Father was on his own at fourteen. He made it."

"His lot was hard," Julia said, her mind going back to Ezekiel when she first met him, so handsome and passionate, full of ambition and pain, without family or God. She had been very young, captured in the whirlwind of his manhood and held tightly in the arms of his glory and promise. That man was gone, stolen by intemperance, and she had moved on, her purpose to direct Ezekiel's children to God, to give them all that had slipped through their dear father's hands.

George stretched out his arm. "Look at this place, Mother, surrounded by prairie and timberland. There is space here, wild land to cultivate and farm. The soil is rich. Joel and Annie are building here, and Joe and Harriet. They'll tell Will and me how to do it. In the meantime, it's warm enough to camp." There was passion in George's voice. He had his father's profile, the set of his jaw.

"All right," Julia said with a nod and a wistful smile.

*\*\*\**

*Two weeks later. Crooked River, Illinois*

A smile wreathed Joel's angular face as he opened the door to his house and found his wife sitting in the rocking chair, holding their youngest son, Seth, who had fallen asleep in her arms. "Annie, it's done! The town of Ramus is surveyed and relinquished for use. The public square and lots are laid out. Joe and I purchased adjacent lots next to the public square, where we'll build a store and post office. Between Mother, Joe, and I, we have secured six other lots as well."

"I'm glad," Annie said softly. Her auburn hair was tucked beneath a crocheted cap, and she was still in her nightgown, though it was early afternoon.

"Hurry and get dressed," Joel said as he took Seth from her. "I want to show you our lot. Will and Sixtus will help me begin to clear it this afternoon."

Joel strode into the bedroom and laid the baby in the crib. Annie slowly followed him. He turned to her. "Where are the children?"

"Wading in the creek with Esther and Mary Ann," Annie answered weakly.

"I'll tell Sariah to come in until Seth wakes up," Joel continued.

"Joel, I don't feel well," Annie said.

Joel focused on Annie and saw that she was shivering, even in the afternoon heat. He touched her forehead. It left his hand warm. Joel's cheer evaporated. "You have a fever. You need to go to bed."

"I'm sorry," she managed, her hazel eyes filling with tears as she lay down and pulled the quilt over her. Joel knew it was beyond their control, but the feelings of disappointment and helplessness came nonetheless. He had hoped to share this day with his wife.

"Are you all right without me?" Joel asked.

Annie nodded. "Go and build our house."

\* \* \*

*Kirtland, Ohio*

Julianne turned when Almon stomped into the kitchen. She knew that look—his lips pursed together, his green eyes nearly bulging out of his face. Her husband was livid. "What is it?" she questioned.

"Is the doctor here?" Almon asked, his eyes darting around the room.

Julianne shook her head. "No. Ben rode out with him this morning."

"Good. I'd rather he not be burdened with Oliver Granger's stupidity."

Julianne swallowed. Almon and the elderly Oliver Granger were the appointed leaders of Kirtland, but they were at odds. Almon was the Prophet's agent, but Brother Granger had been called to be the spiritual leader and acted like he was agent as well. Once, Granger had come over and sternly asked Almon how he came to live in Emma and Joseph's home. Then, in front of the elders quorum, he had questioned Almon's motives in buying up the Safety Society notes. Almon had explained that he agreed with the radical Democrats, that paper money only caused trouble. He had bought the notes with coin to get them completely out of circulation. Then Granger demanded an immediate account of every penny. When Almon asked why, Granger stated that he intended to send a full report to the First Presidency. Angered by the obvious mistrust, Almon had quipped that Joseph and Sidney did not give an account for every gown and new suit they bought their wives and themselves in Washington, and neither would he give Granger a report. If the Prophet wished to question him, Joseph would have to come to Kirtland to do so himself.

Since that day, things had seemed to calm down. But obviously, the problems were stewing, not erased. Julianne said an inward prayer, asking God to help her know what to say to calm her husband. Almon paced the length of the room. Then he spun to face her. "Granger has accused me of not supporting the Prophet, of not upholding him in my prayers."

"On what basis does he imagine this?"

Almon shook his head briskly, incredulous. "It is probably because I don't always pray for Joseph when the former apostates come to the meetings."

"But shouldn't we always pray for the Prophet?"

"Of course. In our hearts," Almon said quickly. "But there are times when I know that praying specifically for Joseph will cause problems. Take Luke Johnson, for instance. He struggles with divided feelings. He was certain that Joseph had fallen. He now feels that he might have been mistaken. He needs to figure this out on his own. If I raise up my voice for Joseph in every prayer, it will push him away."

Julianne swallowed. "Brother Granger does not know your heart."

Almon raised his voice a notch. "Does not know my heart? That isn't all. Granger has taken the keys of the temple. He has accused me of holding secret meetings in the temple and of teaching false doctrine."

"Secret meetings?"

"Ben and I took Dr. Knights there last week when he was in a foul mood. You know how he gets. He's fine most of the time, then the rage returns. We went there to pray, to give him a blessing, and to describe the temple dedication and Joseph's visions."

"And you wouldn't let Brother Granger in?"

"That's right. I knew that man might follow! I locked the door behind us so we wouldn't be disturbed. We weren't there for ten minutes when there was banging on the door. We ignored it and went to the upper rooms. When we were finished, Granger and half the elders quorum were outside waiting. Hiram Winters asked me to give him back the key he had lent me."

"Did you do so?"

"Willingly. I explained that we were teaching Brother Knights the doctrine of the temple and desired privacy so the Spirit would be unrestrained. Granger had the gall to demand an explanation of what doctrine I was teaching. So I put my arm around his shoulder and told him that he needn't worry, I was only teaching the doctrine of the elect and infant baptism."

"You actually said that?"

Almon's anger lessened at the memory, and he couldn't help chuckling. "You should have seen Granger's face turn red. Ben immediately started explaining how I was only joking, and Dr. Knights laughed out loud. Thomas Burdick looked rather worried, while Hiram Winters tried not to smile. Then Granger started shouting, saying that the false doctrine I taught was for Saints to stay in Kirtland rather than gather in Nauvoo. I told him he was mistaken, that I most strongly suggest that Brother Granger and his family move to Nauvoo immediately."

Julianne put her hands to her head. "Almon, how will I convince anyone that you are good when you say such things! Now you are accused before the brethren."

Like the changing shape of mercury, Almon laughed, his anger gone. He took Julianne in his arms playfully. "Perhaps I'm actually bad and have been fooling you all this time."

She shrugged away from his mischievous green eyes and put her hands on her hips. "What am I going to do with you?"

Almon grinned. "I know what we should do. We'll go on a trip. With Sam gone, Ben's anxious to get back on his mission. He wants to go to Canada, where I served. And a trip would do Dr. Knights good. We'll take them both to see Niagara Falls then on to Toronto. While we're gone, all this will blow over."

Julianne eyed Almon, "And you think Brother Granger will just forgive and forget?"

Almon laughed. "One can only hope."

\* \* \*

*Crooked Creek, Illinois*

Annie writhed in bed, the torment of the fever unyielding. A moment later, Susan Bryant knelt beside her, her hands moving over Annie's body, bathing her with a wet towel. Annie shook—the cool water was like shards of ice scraping against her skin. "Stop. Please."

"Soon," Susan said gently. "The bath will lower the fever."

When it was over, Susan put a light sheet over Annie. Though still shivering, Annie's mind felt a bit clearer. "The children?" Annie managed.

"Joel took them to your mother-in-law, but he's back now. He said they already miss you."

"Keep them away," Annie begged. "The fever could take them too."

Susan took Annie's hand. "Don't give up. This too will pass." Susan's voice was firm. Yet Annie wasn't strong enough to explain anymore, to tell Susan how she had found the black spider in her bed, dead against her shaking leg. The fever and then the spider. The nightmares that came. But how could she leave her children? Annie shook uncontrollably. Pain seared through her head as she cried out in agony. Susan called for Joel.

Then Joel's hands were on Annie's head, calling down the powers of heaven, fighting darkness and terror. Night came. Joel was there. He lay down next to her, wrapping his arms around her to lessen the shaking. Sometime during the night, Joel slept and Annie stilled. Then a voice spoke to her aloud, a voice of love and light, that pierced dreams and evaporated fear. It was the voice of daybreak, of rushing wind and roaring water, a voice as small and still as the evening star. "Go, daughter. Sleep in peace and rest. Your children will be as well taken care of as they would be if you had the care of them yourself."

\* \* \*

*Kirtland, Ohio*

Almon's hand flew out in one swift movement as he caught the fly that had the misfortune of landing on top of his dinner. With the fly smashed in his fist, he stood up, went to the front door, and threw it outside. After rinsing his hand in the basin, he returned to the table and continued eating without a word.

Julianne's brow furrowed slightly as she dipped her biscuit in gravy. Flies were rampant this time of year, but Almon usually ignored them. However, this was the fifth he had captured and flung outside since they'd sat down to eat ten minutes ago. He was unusually quiet as well. Something was bothering him. Almon grabbed another fly out of midair.

"You're fighting a losing battle," Julianne commented. "Three more flies came in when you threw the other one out."

"Don't condemn a valiant effort," Almon responded as he sat back down at the table. Though his words were playful on the surface, there was an edge to his voice.

Dr. Knights swallowed a bit of chicken. "Sister Julianne, he's put out about what happened during the quorum meeting." Then he turned to Almon. "My friend, tell your wife. You'll feel a good deal better."

Almon shrugged dismissively. "Knights and I will be leaving for Nauvoo in a couple of days. If you want to come along, you're welcome."

Dr. Knights elaborated. "The Prophet has received some false reports about Almon. I will be a witness in his defense. And I look forward to meeting Brother Joseph."

Julianne took a deep breath. "Oh, Almon, I'm sorry. And you were planning on going to Cincinnati for your law licenses."

"It's no matter. I'll travel to Cincinnati from Nauvoo."

"What exactly happened?" Julianne questioned.

"Some time ago, Granger and two other brethren wrote letters to Joseph complaining about me. Granger recently received a letter back from Joseph. The high council in Nauvoo has unanimously agreed to withdraw fellowship from me. Joseph has told Granger to take away my license to preach. Now I suppose you will say that you told me so."

Julianne hesitated. How she wished Almon would learn to hold his tongue! Many others did not understand that his goodness far outweighed his pride. She would have expected this from Granger, but men from his own quorum had complained about him. And the decision from the high council had been unanimous. She felt the hurt beneath his self-confident façade. At this moment, he needed encouragement, not additional criticism.

"I'm going to go with you," Julianne began. "We ought to go without delay. We'll take Almera and invite Papa. I'll stay with Mother while you're in Cincinnati. In the spring, you can return to Nauvoo by water. We'll come back to Kirtland together and bring Esther home with us like we promised her long ago. This will be a blessing."

"A blessing?" Almon repeated dolefully as he grabbed another fly. "My license to preach has been suspended. I am disfellowshipped. Dishonored."

Julianne smiled kindly. "Cannot troubles yield blessings?"

Almon opened his fist, and the fly flew out of his hand. "My dear, you turn the world upside down. You equate troubles with blessings. You should be the lawyer rather than me."

\* \* \*

The next day Ezekiel was busy at the carpenter's bench sanding the leg of a table when he looked up and saw Almera come in.

"Papa," she said, the warm weather giving color to her cheeks. The bruises on her forehead had vanished, but she would always carry the scar. "Julianne and Almon are going to Nauvoo for a visit. I . . . I have decided to go with them. You could come, Papa. We could move there—like we talked about a long time ago."

Ezekiel cleared his throat. He knew Almera constantly bolted doors and looked over her shoulder—afraid that Sam would come back. Ezekiel felt a knot in his throat. "When are Almon and Julianne coming back?"

"In the spring. They'll bring Esther with them."

It was August. Nine months was a long time. "Darlin', you should go to Nauvoo and start a new life. Your mother will be glad. I'll stay here. I'm too old to start again."

"But things might be different between you and Mama. You've done so much for me. You've changed."

Ezekiel blinked his eyes, remembering his bitterness when Julia had moved to Kirtland without him. He had followed her there and no good came of it. "I am who I am. I'll stay put."

Almera's eyes filled with tears. "I don't want to leave you."

Ezekiel stood up and held her close. "But this time I want you to. For your own happiness. At least I've changed that much."

\* \* \*

*Sunday, September 6, 1840. Nauvoo, Illinois*

Mary walked with Julianne down the dusty road. Sacrament meeting had ended ten minutes ago, and they were headed in the direction of Delcena's cabin. Immediately after the meeting, Delcena had left because the children were restless. Mary had waited for Julianne, who had lingered to hug Almon and whisper a few words of encouragement. Yesterday he had met for two hours with the Prophet and the high council to answer the charges against him. They had adjourned without making a decision. They were meeting again, right now, to come to a final consensus.

The afternoon sun shone warm on Mary's hands. She loosened her bonnet so it fell to her shoulders. The feel of sunlight on her face and hair pleased her. It was far more pleasant than worrying about her complexion.

As they walked, Mary thought about the meeting. They had arrived ten minutes early and had sat on a front bench. Zina Huntington had hurried over to her and hugged her warmly. William Huntington had nodded and shaken her hand. He was rather handsome. Then she had seen George Wilson's form approaching the gathering. She had turned around quickly before their eyes could meet. Why did she care if he was around? He was too old for her anyway. How fortunate that she didn't live in Nauvoo, where she could run into him daily. She turned back to talk with William, but he was already smiling at another girl.

"Ladies, how is your mother? I didn't see her at the meeting this morning."

Mary startled at the voice. George was behind them, taking quick, long strides to catch up to them. His hand brushed against hers. Where had he come from? When the meeting ended, Mary had made sure she didn't leave her seat until he was gone.

"She's well," Julianne said while Mary remained tongue-tied. "However, our sister-in-law is gravely ill. Mother and our sister Almera remained in Ramus to tend her children."

"I hope your sister-in-law is well soon," George said. "Did you enjoy the Prophet's sermon?" He looked at Julianne while asking, not meeting Mary's eyes.

"It was wonderful," Julianne replied. "When Brother Joseph talked about the doctrine of baptism for the dead, my heart pounded within me."

"Mine too. However, new doctrine requires faith and can be difficult for some," George continued, his brown-gold eyes turning to Mary. "Sister Mary, what are your feelings on this new doctrine?"

Mary stared at him for a moment. Was he thinking that she might not have enough faith to accept this doctrine? Then she said pointedly, "Brother Wilson, I am surprised that you would call this new doctrine. Baptism for the dead was mentioned in the New Testament. If the Christian world and members of the Church would read the Bible as they ought, they would know that it is restored truth, not new doctrine."

"Forgive me for my error," George said. He bowed stiffly when they neared Delcena's cabin. "Sister Mary, I try not to make the same mistakes twice. I won't call *baptism for the dead* new doctrine again. Good day, ladies."

Then he was gone. Mary's face burned. She put her bonnet back on and tied it firmly under her chin. Now she had offended him. Why did she say the wrong thing every time he was around?

\* \* \*

Delcena, Mary, and Julianne were almost finished preparing dinner when Almon burst into the house. Danny was on his shoulders and Seth on his back. He galloped around the room, bucked like a horse, and discharged them on the floor. Then he kissed Julianne and laughed. "It's over! Joseph withdrew the charges, and we are completely reconciled. I'm going to stay here for a month to preach in the vicinity. Then off to Cincinnati with Joseph's blessing. During October conference, Joseph is going to announce that when we return to Kirtland, I will be the new stake president."

"What a change a day makes." Julianne smiled at her husband.

"It can make all the difference," Delcena said as she gathered her children around for the blessing on the food. Mary looked toward the door wistfully. When would a day change the course of her life? Certainly not today.

\* \* \*

*Friday, September 11, 1840*

In the afternoon, Joel sat alone in the cabin with a pen and paper in his hands. Annie's body lay near him in a pine coffin, dressed in a white shroud. Tears fell from Joel's eyes, wetting the paper. She had died peacefully in the early morning, as if falling asleep. He had called the children in, and they had embraced her, feeling the warmth of their mother's body one last time. Did they understand that she was gone?

Joel buried his face in his hands—the paper and pen untouched. Two days ago, she had clasped her arms around his neck and exclaimed, "I have been all night thinking about you and the children. I know you cannot take care of them alone when I am gone; you must marry another companion. I have been trying to think of one for you, but I know now that you must select one for yourself. The Lord has told me that the children will be as well taken care of as they would be if I could stay and care for them."

Another companion? Annie was his companion! Just five weeks ago their lives had held every hope. Then the fever struck. Tomorrow she would be buried in Ramus's burial ground. She would never live in the new house he had planned for her.

He thought of the terrible nights during the first weeks of her illness. Then one morning she had awakened with a smile on her countenance and told him that the Lord had spoken to her. *Go, daughter. Sleep in peace and rest.* He would inscribe those words on her tombstone. Joel stood, placing the pen and paper on the nearby table. He walked near the coffin. Annie's thick auburn hair was combed and arranged around her pale, lovely features. Her eyes were closed. He ran his fingers through her hair. Her brow was cool, empty of life's warmth. Yet her body was sacred to him—his Annie's mortal tabernacle.

Joel's thoughts encompassed the evening they had wed, the birth and death of their little daughter, the other children born to them, their move to Ohio. Annie was the first to accept the restored gospel. How she had blessed his life! Death could not erase what they had built together. He walked back to the table and picked up the pen and paper.

*The shrouded form before me*
*White as in that evening tide*
*When with the marriage vow upon thee*
*I took thee for my bride.*

*And now I must wander mournful*
*Round my loved and silent home*
*Ever listening for my loved one,*
*Which to me no more can come.*

*Still in those dear babes she left me,*
*I can see her smile and form.*
*Which shall bring to sweet remembrance*
*Her fond heart so kind and warm.*

*Short the time my Father gave me,*
*To be blessed with her sweet love*
*Yet the golden link that's severed*
*Shall unite again above.*

*Shine on thou lovely gem so dear*
*In your sweet world of light*
*I soon shall come to meet thee there*
*And claim thee as my right.*

# 15

*Altho trials now beset me*
*I have faith that God is just*
*And will bear me safely through them*
*If His promises I trust*

George Washington Johnson

*Tuesday, September 15, 1840. Nauvoo, Illinois*

JULIANNE SHIFTED HER WEIGHT ON the hard oak bench where she sat next to Almon. Her mother, younger siblings, Almera, Joel, Delcena's family, and Lyman's mother were on the same row. Harriet and Joe sat behind them with the Sniders. Surrounded by hundreds of Saints, they attended the funeral of the Prophet's father, the patriarch Joseph Smith Sr. He had died yesterday, three days after Annie's passing. The overhead sun shone bright. Hints of fall color edged the nearby trees.

Julianne's hands shook as Elder Robert Thompson began the address. "The occasion that has brought us together this day is one of no ordinary importance, for not only has a single family to mourn but a whole society. Yes, thousands will this day say, 'A Father in Israel is gone.'"

Tears filled Julianne's eyes. Father Smith had been elderly, but Annie had been a young mother. Then Elder Thompson looked at the Johnsons. He talked to the whole congregation while he spoke to their hearts. "The friends we have lost prior to our late Father were such as rendered life sweet. Their virtues and kindnesses will long be remembered by the sorrowing widow, the disconsolate husband, the weeping children, and the heartbroken parent. These, like the stars in yonder firmament, shone in their several spheres. We feel to mingle our tears with their surviving relatives."

Julianne looked at her siblings. Almera sat very still. Delcena stared straight ahead, beyond grief, her eyes a moist sheen. Joel's jaw trembled. Julianne's tears fell without control. All her siblings had lost their spouses. Almon took her hand and held it securely.

Julianne's mind went back two weeks to the day she had taken Joel's children to see Annie. They didn't go inside, for Annie feared to expose them to her illness. Julianne had led the children around the side of the cabin. They had reached to their mother, separated by the bedroom window. Annie's pale freckled hand had lifted up to meet theirs, palms matching, clear hard glass separating them. Sixtus's hand dwarfed Annie's and Sariah's, and Nephi's were about the same size. Susie had blown her mother a kiss. Seth's baby fingers stretched the width of Annie's palm. Then Julianne had lifted her hand to Annie's.

A week later, two days before Annie died, Joel had come to get his children, reasoning that neither he nor Miss Bryant had contracted Annie's disease. It was time for the children to come home and say good-bye to their mama.

Julianne had prepared to go as well, but Almon had begged her to stay. Then when she insisted, his entreaties became orders. She had obeyed because he had never ordered her before, because they both feared the nervous fever that had taken Annie's life in five short weeks.

\* \* \*

Following the funeral, the Sniders invited all of the Johnsons, including Almon and Julianne, over for lunch at their newly constructed hotel. During the meal, Joe, with his arm around Harriet, proposed a toast. "To our ever-dear family. We cherish each one of you and each day we have together." After everyone took a drink, Joe continued. "Harriet and I have an announcement. As all of you know, I haven't completely regained my strength. Nor is our house in Ramus finished. But regardless of my circumstances, Brother Snider has kindly consented to give me Harriet's hand. We plan to be married here three weeks from today."

Amos, George, and Will led the children in clapping and whistling. Harriet and Joe kissed. Julia wished them joy, and her eyes shone with unshed tears, reflecting that depth of sweetness borne of suffering and selfless love.

Julianne wondered how Joel and Delcena felt as others' lives went on. And how did Almera feel? At the moment, Delcena looked busy, quieting her exuberant children. Joel ate slowly, his expression unreadable. Almera sighed deeply.

Later that night as Julianne and Almon dressed for bed, Almon said matter-of-factly, "Tomorrow I'm taking a trip with Hyrum Smith. We're going to Lima, a town due south, to create a branch and then on to Quincy to organize a stake."

Julianne slipped into her nightdress. "How long will you be gone?"

"Eleven days. I'll be back for general conference and the wedding. I'm going to book passage for Cincinnati the last week of October. The term at the school of law begins in mid-November. I won't be able to return until the planting season."

Julianne shivered as she lay down in bed and pulled the covers close. Almon blew out the candle and lay down next to her. She snuggled against him as he reached his arm around her. "I'm thinking of going with you," Julianne said.

"I'd like that. Your aunts and cousins are there. You wouldn't lack for company."

"But what about Annie's children? And would Mother be hurt?"

"Almera, Mary, Susan Bryant, and Harriet are all here and very capable. Your mother will understand."

Julianne paused then said, "You're right."

"I'll book passage for two."

Julianne turned to face him. Although the night was dark, his feel and smell were familiar. He kissed her tenderly. Julianne's eyes were wet with tears as they held each other. She would go with Almon. Six months was too long to be separated. Much too long when five quick weeks could steal a life.

\* \* \*

*Monday, October 5, 1840. Nauvoo, Illinois*

Though the wind blew and the rain fell for the third day in a row, Almon felt as happy internally as if the sun were shining on a field of golden wheat. He sat on the outdoor stand with the First Presidency; clerk Robert Thompson; Lyman Wight; and a newcomer, John C. Bennett. It was Monday morning, the third and final day of general conference. The meeting would start in five minutes. The day's theme revolved around the priesthood, with Almon scheduled to preach. The benches filled with men, women, and children who braved the weather to hear the word of God.

As he waited, Almon smiled, thinking of how the past few weeks couldn't have been more satisfying. He had gone from a state of disfellowship to trusted leader. During Saturday morning's meeting, he had been appointed to preside over the Church in Kirtland, taking Oliver Granger's place. Joseph had also announced the construction of the Lord's house in Nauvoo. Sunday's meeting had been equally satisfying. Almon had offered the opening prayer. Afterward, the Prophet had given a discourse on baptism for the dead. Then John Bennett had thrilled the congregation by presenting an outline of the proposed Nauvoo Charter. If it went through, the city council could pass any laws that didn't conflict with the state and federal constitutions. For example, they could issue writs of habeas corpus, keeping the Prophet safe from extradition to Missouri. Immigrants to Nauvoo, even those from other nations, could vote after living only six months in the state and thirty days in Nauvoo. They would be protected from Missouri's disenfranchisement and extermination order forever.

Almon straightened in his chair. Following the opening prayer and business, Almon stood and walked to the stand. He spoke about the priesthood, the power of God on earth. He read from the Bible and Book of Mormon, giving anecdotes, explaining, cajoling, and testifying. He spoke for more than an hour with the attention of the entire congregation riveted on him. He spoke as if each person there were his closest friend. Following Almon's discourse, conference was adjourned for an hour. Despite the weather, a large number of people requested baptism during the intermission.

*　*　*

*Tuesday, October 6, 1840. Nauvoo, Illinois*

Two days later, Almon stood outside Sniders' Hotel with the Law brothers, William and Wilson, as they waited for the Prophet to arrive to perform Joe and Harriet's wedding ceremony. Following a week of rain, the wind was brisk, and the sun shone intermittently between billowed clouds. With good nature, Almon, a committed Democrat, attempted to sway William from his Whig leanings.

The two debated for five minutes while Wilson, broad shouldered and restless, looked distractedly down the street. Then he changed the topic of conversation. "Illinois politics bore me," he said, his words tinted with an Irish accent. "Where's Joseph Johnson? As groomsman, I'd like a word before he ties the knot."

Almon turned to him. "Last I saw him, he was helping Harriet pack her trunk. The newlyweds and my wife are going to Ramus first thing tomorrow morning. Joe's mother and siblings didn't make it here. The sloughs this preposterous weather has formed are too deep for their wagon. It's too dangerous."

William raised an eyebrow. "Won't it still be too dangerous to travel tomorrow?"

Almon grinned. "My carriage has wide, high wheels and can manage the sloughs. Thank goodness. Julianne is impatient to spend time with her mother, and Joe wants to get to Ramus as soon as possible. He's worried that his mother will sorrow because she missed the ceremony, but he couldn't postpone the wedding with the brethren and me leaving on our assignments."

"Poor fellow," Wilson snorted. "Bound to two masters—a wife and a mother."

William looked at Almon. "Forgive my brother. Wilson rides through the streets of Nauvoo bragging that he's the only free man left—fettered by neither woman nor baptism."

Almon chuckled and added, "I think Wilson ought to be bragging on the streets of Kirtland, rather than Nauvoo. I've not given up hope that the two of you will return with me next spring, even though you are a Whig."

William's brow furrowed in thought. "I do fear malaria returning to Nauvoo. But if adopted, the Charter will protect the Saints here. And the building of the Lord's house is planned. I've also heard the Prophet mention an eventual scourge in Kirtland."

Almon cocked his head and folded his arms. "The only certainty is that the river scourge will be back in Nauvoo next spring. More people will die from malaria. And Kirtland already has a house of the Lord—it's not a dream written down on paper. The wheels of prosperity are rolling in Kirtland. I'm not advocating that everyone come back. But it's the place for me and my family. And I hope for my friends as well."

Almon drew silent as two men rounded the corner. "Good morning, brethren," Joseph's voice rang out as he and John Bennett approached. Joseph warmly shook hands with Almon and the Laws. Bennett shook hands as well, his eyes dark and vibrant. Then the men followed Joseph into the house, and the Prophet jovially exclaimed that this was a great day and that a wedding was about to take place in the best city on earth.

\* \* \*

Harriet felt hot and cold at the same time—both joy and timidity as the Prophet pronounced Joe and her *man and wife*. Once, Joseph Johnson had seemed an untouchable dream, but now he was hers. And she was his. Her cheeks reddened as Joe kissed her in front of everyone who had come—her family, the Laws, the Babbitts, and John Bennett.

"How are you?" Joe whispered in her ear after the guests had congratulated them. "You're flushed."

"Just excited and happy to be married to you. I'm sorry your family couldn't get here."

"We'll have dinner with them tomorrow." Joe kissed her hair.

\* \* \*

The next morning, in the second seat of the buggy, Joe held Harriet close. He felt her warmth through the soft blue silk of her dress. The color matched her eyes. His heart beat happily—after so much sickness, this was what he had waited for.

Julianne, in the front seat, drove the dark bay gelding. The horse was an English draft, strong and powerful. They had been on the road two hours, and Julianne hadn't looked back once. Joe appreciated the privacy as he kissed his bride. They came to a large slough. Julianne stopped the horse and hesitated. "It looks too deep."

"The left side isn't any deeper than the others we've gone through," Joe remarked.

Julianne nodded and jiggled the reins. They were halfway through the slough when the wheel caught a boulder. The horse's powerful hindquarters churned. Feeling trapped, the animal panicked, pivoting toward the center of the pool and frantically trying to bolt. Off balance, the buggy tumbled forward as the harness broke, plunging the passengers headfirst into deep water as the horse, alone, escaped the slough and tore down the road.

Underwater, Julianne's ankle lay trapped beneath the axle. She clawed frantically at the mud with her hands, knowing she only had minutes. Joe and Harriet were pinned inside the carriage. They held their breath and tried to push the vehicle up and off of them. It was too heavy. Harriet's eyes were wide with horror, her long hair floating around them, her dress billowing around her petticoat. It was useless. Joe stopped struggling and put his arms around her. Death would come quickly.

Then, as instantly as the accident had happened, two men were in the water lifting the buggy up, their strong arms around the victims as they helped Julianne, Harriet, and Joe to safety. They sucked in deep gulps of air, clinging to each other and coughing as they stumbled out of the water. Joe recognized their rescuers, George Wilson and Anson Call.

"Thank you for saving our lives," Joe said as he shook the men's hands.

"The ladies are freezing," George remarked. "Anson, take Sister Babbitt on your horse. Brother Johnson and Miss Snider can ride mine."

Harriet spoke through chattering teeth. "I'm not Miss Snider. I'm Mrs. Johnson now."

Her boldness caught Joe off guard, and he wondered if his shy bride had hit her head in the fall. The men stared at her.

"We were married yesterday," Joe explained. Then the terrifying hilarity of the situation gripped him. What a thing to happen after their wedding! Joe put his arms around his wife and sister and laughed out loud. Harriet and Julianne clung to him laughing, crying, and shaking with cold.

"What are you waiting for, man?" Anson exclaimed, shaking his head. "Get your bride home! You've lost your senses." Joe mounted, and Anson helped Harriet on behind him. She wrapped her arms around Joe as he urged the horse into a trot.

When Anson and Julianne mounted the other horse, Anson turned to George. "Sister Johnson lives a few miles from here, along this road. When I get there, I'll send someone for you."

"Of course," George said.

\* \* \*

Mary went outside. The fire wasn't hot enough to finish the cake her mother was baking for supper. They were hoping that Julianne and the wedding couple would make it home today to celebrate. She bent down to lift the heavy bundle of firewood. If her brothers George and Will were home, this would be their job, but they were working for Brother Perkins, who lived a short distance away.

When Mary straightened with the wood in her arms, she heard a whinny. Turning her head, she saw Almon and Julianne's horse, soaking wet with the broken harness dragging behind him. Mary dropped the wood, her heart pounding with fear. "Mother, something has happened!" she shouted.

Julia, Almera, Esther, and Mary Ann ran outside, with Amos limping behind them. Julia wrung a dishtowel between her hands as she stared at the horse.

"The accident was probably near the big slough. I'll go find them," Mary said. She lifted her skirt and ran to the shed, where the bridle and sidesaddle were stored.

On the porch, Esther bit her lip, her eyes welling with tears. Mary Ann looked pale. Almera put her arm around the girls. "We mustn't panic. They're probably walking home right now."

Amos limped over to the grazing horse. "Hey, Jimbo," he said as he carefully removed the tattered harness. Amos stroked the gelding while Mary saddled him.

"Be careful," Julia told Mary. "I'll have the girls walk to the Perkins' to get George and Will."

Mary nodded. She stroked Jimbo's neck and mounted.

Less than half a mile down the road, Jimbo whinnied excitedly. Rounding a rim of oak trees, two horses trotted toward Mary, and she could make out four drenched riders. She stopped the horse, flooded with relief as tears burned her eyes. Within seconds, they were beside her. Joe told Mary everything that had happened—that he and Harriet had gotten married, that they had almost drowned, and that Anson Call and George Wilson had rescued them.

Before she could digest the information, Anson looked at her intently. "We need to get these ladies home before they catch their death of cold. Miss Johnson, would you go on and find Brother Wilson? He's soaked to the skin and as chilled as we are."

"Of course," Mary replied, swallowing. She could not meet Joe's eyes.

A moment later, Mary cantered Jimbo, her blonde braid flying behind her, her brown eyes focused on the road ahead. The large horse was well trained, his gait as smooth as a rocking chair. What would she say to George when she found him? She no longer cared what he thought of her. He had saved Julianne, Joe, and Harriet.

Thirty minutes elapsed before she saw him. Mary halted the horse and slid out of the saddle. A surge of emotion filled her as she stood in front of him. She smiled, trying to hold back her tears. He seemed tongue-tied, standing there soaking wet. His lips looked slightly blue from the cold. "Brother Wilson, thank you," Mary began earnestly. "Please ride this horse to my house where you can get dry and warm."

He shook his head. "Miss Johnson, what gentleman would leave a lady to walk?"

"The brave gentleman who saved the lives of my brother and sisters," Mary exclaimed. She blinked hard, not wanting to cry in front of him.

"I did nothing," he replied quickly. "I ran into Brother Call in the street today. He told me he is thinking about settling in Ramus. The idea occurred to us to leave immediately and see the town. It was Heavenly Father who inspired us and saved your loved ones. Had we come five minutes later . . . I can't think on it."

Now Mary's tears came. Four of her siblings were gone. Annie was dead, but Joe, Harriet, and Julianne had been miraculously spared. And here she was, crying once more in front of George. She stomped her foot and burst out, "Oh, you have always thought me weak. And I am sobbing again."

"No," he said emphatically. "If I ever thought you weak, it was the gross error of a foolish man. Your tears are due to love. I-I admire you very much . . . and would like to get to know you better." Then his words tumbled out. "I came to Ramus today in order to tell you this. But if you don't admire me, I understand and will never speak of it again."

Mary looked up at him as she quivered with emotion. His eyes still reminded her of David's—the brown flecked with gold. But he was different too. He was older than David had been, less talkative, less jovial. There was a manliness about him, and his eyes were kind. "Brother Wilson, I would like to get to know you better. I admire you too."

"Thank you, Mary."

He called her *Mary*. Should she call him *George*? Now she couldn't help but smile, thinking about how Amos had teased her long ago. *George* was their brother's name. Amos had said she should call him *Dear Wilson*. But right now, he was staring at her, probably wondering why she was smiling so stupidly. Mary composed herself. "Please don't thank me. I thank you a thousand times."

The next moment turned into an uncomfortable silence. Then George cleared his throat. "You should get back. Let me help you into the saddle."

"Only if you agree to ride with me."

George helped her mount. Then Mary took her foot out of the stirrup so he could swing up behind her.

\*\*\*

After cutting all the boards and shingles he would need for his house in Ramus, Joel sold his land and sawmill on Crooked Creek to another member of the Church. He had until the end of November to leave the cabin. Joel immersed himself in building his new house—the heavy labor giving him a brief respite from sorrow. He hired Susan Bryant to take care of his children and often stayed in Ramus, sleeping at his mother's. He worked from dawn until dark every day except for Sunday, when he functioned as the Ramus stake president.

Then on Saturday, October seventeenth, after staying in Ramus for the week, he went back to Crooked Creek after dark. He paused and watched through the window for a moment. The little house he had shared with Annie was in perfect order. Every dish was done, and the floor was swept. Miss Bryant sat in Annie's chair, rocking Seth to sleep. Sariah was reading to Susie, and Sixtus was teaching Nephi how to tie a shoe. Annie's words rang in his heart. *The Lord told me that my children would be as well cared for as if I were here with them.* Joel took a deep breath and opened the door.

Miss Bryant turned to him. "Hello, Brother Johnson. Have you had supper?"

"I ate at my mother's," Joel replied. She stood up with Seth in her arms. Joel walked to her and held out his arms for his baby. Miss Bryant handed him the drowsy child. Seth whined. Joel sat down and rocked him. The other children began talking at once, asking him questions and telling him stories. They chattered to him about little things, like Annie had.

"I'll get my things," Miss Bryant said, standing near, watching. Joel looked at her. He noticed that her eyes were bright blue, that her brown hair was parted in the middle and smoothed perfectly beneath her cap. She was different from Annie but hard working and stately. Annie's words echoed in his mind again. *You can't care for the children alone. I have thought about choosing a companion for you, but I know that you must choose for yourself.*

Joel's little boy Nephi reached up and pulled on Miss Bryant's skirt. "Why won't you stay and tuck me in bed?"

"Because your father is home, and the Pages have a room for me," Miss Bryant answered. "But I'll bring an apple pie on Monday morning."

Nephi grinned and hugged her legs.

A moment later, Miss Bryant went into the bedroom and came out with her satchel. She bid the children good night. Joel told his children that he would be back soon and followed her outside to the wagon.

As Joel drove her to the Pages', the moon was full and the stars bright. There was no need for a lantern. When they arrived, he stopped the wagon. He looked at her. She sat very still in the seat, waiting for Joel to come around to give her a hand down.

However, Joel remained seated. "Miss Bryant," he began.

She turned to look at him, her eyes questioning. "Yes?"

"I miss my wife very much."

"I know."

Joel continued. "Before my wife passed away, she told me that I must marry again soon for the children's sake. She said that it had been revealed to her that her children would be in as good of hands as if she were here herself. I saw you in the window tonight with the children—"

Joel stopped to take a breath. An owl hooted, and he noticed the sound of water in a nearby brook. Joel knew this was a strange proposal, but there didn't seem a better way to go about it. "Now that Annie is gone, I believe that you are the perfect mother for my children and the best woman for me to marry. What are your feelings?"

Miss Bryant's voice sounded very formal. "Mr. Johnson, your wife was my precious friend. I loved her. I know how you loved her. I love your children. However, there are two things we need to discuss. First, do you think it possible that you will love me someday?"

Joel closed his eyes for a moment. Miss Bryant sat beside him, statue quiet save the slight rise and fall of her chest as she breathed. His voice was gentle as he spoke. "Yes. I believe it is not only possible but certain."

She turned to him. "Then secondly, you should consider the reasons why I might not be the best choice for you."

"What reasons? My children love you. You are an excellent housekeeper with a strong testimony of the restored gospel."

"First of all, I am too excellent a housekeeper. I cannot rest if things are not in order. Sometimes, this is a weakness. Second, as far as the gospel is concerned, I don't think dancing is a sin. I learned numerous steps when I was young."

Joel smiled, his first natural smile since Annie's death. Miss Bryant was a curious young woman. "It will be interesting to see if you can keep my children in order while you teach them to dance. That is, if you accept my proposal."

"I do," Susan said.

Joel climbed out of the wagon. He took her hand to help her down and held it as he walked her to the door. He kissed her lightly on her forehead. "Thank you, Susan."

"You're welcome, Brother Johnson."

\* \* \*

Three days later, on Tuesday morning, dressed in their Sunday best, Joel, Susan, and the children took the wagon to Ramus, where they would meet up with the rest of the family to caravan together to Nauvoo. It was Joel and Susan's wedding day.

As they waited outside of Julia's house, all was not well in the back of the wagon. Nephi poked Susie, who cried. Sixtus cuffed Nephi to get him to stop. Seth tugged hard on Sariah's braid, causing Sariah to cry out. Joel looked sternly at his children. "You had better behave or Miss Bryant won't want to marry me and be your new mother."

"I don't want a new mother," Sariah said, her eyes filling with tears.

Susie cried harder.

"I want Mama," Nephi wailed.

"Stop it," Sixtus hissed.

Susan stood up and turned around. "Would one of you like to come sit with Papa and me?" Nephi shook his head, moving closer to Sariah. However, Susie reached out her arms. Sixtus handed her up to Susan. Then Sixtus took Seth, and Sariah hugged Nephi. The children quieted as Susan explained, "I will never take the place of your mother. She is yours forever, and she loves you even if she cannot be with you now. But if we try, we can be a happy family."

When Julia and the others came out and climbed into a separate wagon, Joel's family was ready to continue the journey.

Once in Nauvoo, they traveled to Sniders' Hotel, where Almon and Julianne waited. Almon performed the ceremony that united Joel and Susan. Tears filled Joel's and Susan's eyes—tears of sorrow because Annie was gone and tears of gladness because they were no longer alone. After

Joel kissed Susan, Almon and Julianne hugged them both. Julia took the children by the hand and led them up to congratulate their father and stepmother.

# 16

*All glory to our God!*
*His house we soon will rear;*
*He'll make it his abode,*
*And to his Saints draw near, . . .*

Joel Hills Johnson

Kirtland, Ohio. January 1841

MELISSA LEBARON COULDN'T BELIEVE WHAT she was reading as she stared at the copy of the Nauvoo *Times and Seasons*. It didn't make any sense. Red circles appeared on her cheeks. She stared at the October marriage announcements: "In this town by Pres't Joseph Smith Jr., Mr. Ben Johnson married to Miss Harriet Snider."

"I can't believe this," she moaned as her brother David looked over her shoulder.

"Believe what?" Naomi, her older sister, asked from the rocking chair where she was nursing the baby.

"That some girls actually get married to their suitors," David teased.

Melissa ignored him and pointed at the article. "That Benjamin Johnson is married. He went to Canada to continue his mission." She read Naomi the announcement.

"It must be a different Ben," Naomi commented. "He left in September, and the wedding was in October. He wouldn't have had time to go to Canada and then Nauvoo."

Melissa shook her head. "Sister Babbitt has mentioned a family named Snider and their daughter, Harriet. They know each other."

"Maybe he changed his mind and never went to Canada," David mused.

Melissa stood up and put on her new winter cape. "I'll go find out. David, get the sleigh ready."

"Yes, ma'am." David bowed deeply. "Where're we going?"

"To Father Johnson's. I'll pack him some supper. We'll take the newspaper with us and ask him about the wedding."

"But Father Johnson is intemperate," Naomi cautioned. "Don't go uninvited. It isn't wise."

David grinned as he put on his coat. "It's less wise for Melissa to continue thinking about a married man."

Melissa ignored them both as she ladled pork stew into a bowl and wrapped a loaf of bread in a cloth to take with her.

\* \* \*

It turned bitter cold as the sun sank in the sky. Ezekiel went inside and sipped brandy in front of the fire. A short time later, there was a knock at the door. He opened it to Melissa and David LeBaron. They looked like they were cut out of the same cloth—both tall, fair, and bright-eyed.

"Father Johnson," Melissa said with a smile, "I've brought you some supper. And I have a question to ask you."

"Then come in and sit by the fire," Ezekiel said as he took the food. After setting the food on the table, he refilled his glass of brandy and rejoined them.

"I just saw an announcement about a marriage in the Nauvoo *Times and Seasons.*" She handed the newspaper to Ezekiel. "Is this your son?"

Ezekiel read the article as the brandy warmed him and loosened his tongue. He chuckled. "This wasn't Ben's wedding. It was Joe's. Don Carlos Smith got them mixed up again." The hilarity of it struck Ezekiel. Reading the confused look on the LeBarons' faces, he explained. "I've a son named Joe and a David too. Years back, David and Carlos were friends. When Carlos came over, he'd get Ben and Joe mixed up. The boys played on it, purposely confusing him. Joe'd say he was Ben and vice versa. If my David were alive, he'd be laughing at this, laughing at Joe and Ben, laughing at Carlos's mistake. Unless Don Carlos got it wrong on purpose and the joke's on my boys."

Ezekiel laughed until he had tears in his eyes, until he noticed that young David LeBaron's laughter was forced, until he noticed that Melissa

LeBaron watched him with a look of piqued interest in her blue eyes—like she was figuring it all out, like she was a duchess straight out of England. Ezekiel's mirth died on his lips, filling the room with silence.

Then, like a pebble rippling the pool of quiet, Melissa stood and curtsied. "Mr. Johnson, thank you. We wish Joseph and Harriet happiness. We won't disturb you further."

"Thank you for supper," Ezekiel returned as the LeBarons walked to the door. They left without remembering to take the newspaper with them. Setting his brandy aside, Ezekiel picked it up. A newspaper article by Joseph Smith, the Prophet caught his eye.

*Under the provisions of our magna carta, The Nauvoo Charter, let ALL those who appreciate the blessings of the gospel, and realize the importance of obeying the commandments of heaven, remove to our city. The temple of the Lord is in the process of erection here. The Nauvoo Legion embraces all our military power, and the University of Nauvoo will enable us to teach our children wisdom, to instruct them in all knowledge and learning. We hope that those days of gloom and darkness have gone by. This gathering together of all the Saints must take place. Unite with us in the great work of these last days, and share in the tribulation, that you may ultimately share in the glory and triumph.*

Joseph's face was before Ezekiel's mind, majestic and bright with energy. But the shadow that fell from Joseph's light was Ezekiel's despair. It was completely over. Julia's prophet had spoken. The word *all* etched like fire into Ezekiel's mind. *All* of his children had raised their hands at the dinner table that long-ago day when he had asked if they believed in Mormonism. *All.* Julianne and Almon would not come back. Julia would not allow Esther to come. Not with a university in Nauvoo. He was alone.

\* \* \*

*Cincinnati, Ohio*

A light snow fell in Newport. Julianne walked with her cousin Caroline Hirst as they approached the Ohio River that separated Newport, Kentucky, from Cincinnati, Ohio. She and Almon would be in Cincinnati for three more months while Almon attended the school of law and became a licensed attorney. Though she missed Kirtland, she enjoyed becoming reacquainted with her cousin and extended family.

Born the same year, Julianne and Caroline had many things in common. Both were married, thirty-three years old, and childless. Both were spending the winter with relatives. Caroline and her husband, James, lived in Indiana but were staying in Newport with Caroline's mother, Rhoda Hills. Almon and Julianne were staying in Cincinnati in Aunt Nancy Taft's boarding house. The ease of their friendship at times reminded Julianne of being with Annie. Julianne hugged Caroline before boarding the boat that would ferry her across the river. "Will you and James join us tonight?" Julianne asked.

"Of course." Caroline grinned. "Tell Almon we'll bring him a cake and some locofoco matches so we can argue all night."

Julianne smiled as she boarded, thinking of Caroline's comment about the matches. Whigs referred to radical Democrats like Almon as "Locofocos," a type of match that could be relighted over and over again. The nickname originated in New York in 1836 on an evening when opponents had tried to stop the radical Democrats from taking over the party by turning off the gas lights before a vote. But the radical Democrats had used locofoco matches to light candles, and the meeting had continued.

Julianne stood on the deck and held the railing, snow settling on her dark hair and navy shawl. She thought about how much she and Almon enjoyed Caroline and James. The Hirsts were a handsome couple; both husband and wife were large boned, sharp minded, and good-natured. They were Methodists, abolitionists, and Whigs. Because they were set in their religious views, Almon had given up trying to convert them to Mormonism. However, he had not given up trying to change them from Whig to Democrat. To retaliate, the Hirsts called Almon their own Locofoco.

Warmth filled Julianne as her thoughts shifted. The name fit Almon—locofoco. He was like a match relighting the fire inside of her again and again.

\* \* \*

At suppertime, Almon strode into the boarding house with a frown on his face. He had a bundle of papers under one arm and a satchel over his shoulder, and he forced a smile and firmly shook the hand of Elias Woodberry, the powerfully built free black man who worked for Nancy Taft, Julianne's aunt.

"How was school today, Mister Babbitt?" Elias asked. "Don't look glum. You're one day closer to finishing!"

Almon shrugged. "But when I'm finished, I'll only have my license to practice law in Ohio. To get a license for Illinois, I need the signature of an Illinois Supreme Court Justice. Now how will I get that?"

Elias grinned. "You'll find a way, Mister Babbitt. You can count on that."

Aunt Nancy strode up to Almon, her navy dress and white apron swaying with her ample figure. She kissed him on the cheek and called him *nephew*. "Your wife is in your room waiting. Supper will be ready in a half hour."

"You spoil us," Almon said, forcing another smile.

"After what you went through in Missouri, you could use a little spoiling," Nancy returned.

Almon thanked Nancy and went to his room. Julianne left her knitting and greeted him with a kiss. But he could not return it. When he shut the door, he dropped his satchel and papers on the table.

"What's happened?" Julianne asked.

"I don't know where to begin." Almon paced the room, pent-up anger darkening his eyes and tightening his fists. Julianne sat down and waited, perched on the edge of her chair, worry in her eyes. Almon began. "Remember how I sent a letter to William Law a month ago outlining the financial opportunities in Kirtland?"

Julianne nodded.

"This morning before class, I pick a letter up from the post office. It's from William, saying that he is not coming to Kirtland. Short, precise, to the point. No explanation other than he discussed it with Joseph. Fine. It's William's choice. Then on the way home from school I stop by Brother Bennett's place to see if I'm preaching on Sunday. He tells me that someone else will deliver the sermon and hands me a copy of the Prophet's most recent revelation. Tells me I need to read it right away."

Almon's hands rifled through the papers on the table. "Listen to this! 'Let my servant William Law not take his family unto the eastern lands, even unto Kirtland.'"

"Then William is supposed to stay in Nauvoo," Julianne said. "He made the correct choice."

"I knew you would say that," Almon snapped. "That's not all." He continued reading the revelation. "'And with my servant Almon Babbitt, there are many things with which I am not pleased; behold, he aspireth to establish his counsel instead of the counsel which I have ordained, even the Presidency of my Church, and he setteth up a golden calf for the worship of my people.' What on earth! He's talking about me trying to convince William to come to Kirtland. I was commanded to build up Kirtland! William has money that would be beneficial. Of course, I want him to come. I'm not burying my talents but trying to multiply them as the Lord commanded. And here I am, chastened, embarrassed in front of the whole Church. Is this God? Or is it Joseph?"

Almon stopped walking and stared at Julianne, the hurt, anger, and tension in him palpable. She did not say anything, just focused on him with those sweet eyes that never looked away. Almon stood still for a long moment. Then he quipped, "The Lord and Joseph should be saying, 'Well done thou good and faithful servant.'"

Julianne reached her hand out and touched his. "He has. He will."

Almon's voice was lower, but the anger and hurt were still there. "In Kirtland, when the Safety Society fell, I never said anything to Joseph. But inwardly, I opposed it. I'm a locofoco Democrat. I believe in specie, in coin, not paper money. That's why I'm buying up Joseph's paper debts in Kirtland with real money. Doesn't he understand that? I'm doing this to help him. Now I own his debts. I could call them due. I could hurt him."

"But you won't," Julianne said, her eyes not straying.

"Why not? I am accused of building a golden calf. I might as well build one."

"Because you *are* the Lord's good and faithful servant. And because you know that Joseph is His Prophet."

The pain in Almon's voice brought tears to Julianne's eyes as Almon continued. "If this revelation came from God, why couldn't Joseph come to me privately? Now, how can I go back to Kirtland and take the keys of leadership from Oliver Granger? Who will follow me? I'm not even allowed to preach here this Sunday. After this revelation, the people will lose confidence in me. Yet I am commanded to build up Kirtland. What am I to do?"

Julianne stood up and put her arms around his waist. "You'll find a way. You are a locofoco, a match with a power to kindle fire again and again. Don't use this power to destroy what God has built; use it to ignite candles and torches, to cast light in darkness."

Almon buried his head in her shoulder. "Juli, Kirtland is home. Nauvoo is not. Will what I'm building, what I want, turn to dust?"

She wrapped her arms more tightly around him and laid her head on his chest. "You sent a message to me in Missouri when we were separated, when my heart was broken. You said that Zion is not lost. That Zion is where I am. Home is not Far West or Nauvoo or even Kirtland. Home is where you are. Where we are."

\* \* \*

Later that evening, the Hirsts arrived at the Babbitts' room with an apple cake that Caroline had made. Almon welcomed them enthusiastically, intent upon putting his anger and hurt on the shelf for the evening. After cake and drinks were handed out, the couples settled around the fire.

"My friend, what shall we debate about tonight?" James asked cheerily.

"You choose," Almon said.

"Me? Why this honor?"

"Because you are now my favorite Whig!"

"And who have I the honor of surpassing?" James asked after taking a bite of cake.

"An Irishman named William Law."

"An Irish Whig? Really? The world is full of surprises."

"An Irish Whig with money," Almon rejoined. "Poor fellow. No wonder he is misled. 'Tis easier for a camel to go through the eye of a needle than for a rich man to join the correct political party." James laughed so hard he nearly spit out his cake.

Caroline chuckled. "Julianne, your husband uses scriptures to his own ends."

"A habit I have attempted to rid him of."

"Speaking of using religion for one's own end," James commented as he pulled a newspaper article out of the pocket of his jacket. "I have a subject to debate tonight. This was reprinted in the Cincinnati paper. It's an editorial from a newspaper in Warsaw." He looked at Almon. "What do you know about Thomas Sharp, the editor?"

Almon answered nonchalantly. "Sharp is a young lawyer who started the paper in November. Announced that his newspaper is nonpartisan with Whig leanings. Nonpartisan, ha! With Whig leanings! It reeks of Whigism. Then again, Whigs are not known for their honesty—you, my friend, exempted."

"Hmm." Caroline eyed Almon. "Lawyers are not known for their honesty either—you, our friend, exempted."

Almon laughed. "You are as wise a lady as my Julianne."

Conversation lagged for a few moments as the men finished the cake and Julianne refilled their glasses. Then James stretched out his legs and continued. "Now for this article by Mr. Sharp. It's about Joseph Smith's call for the Mormons to gather in Nauvoo. He claims that the Mormon leaders are using religion for their own political ends. Listen to this: 'What may be the result is impossible to divine. But now that their members are concentrating, they begin to assume, at least in this state, a political and moral importance possessed by no other.'"

Almon found it more difficult to maintain his lighthearted mood. "Those types of claims began the Missouri difficulties. The old citizens feared our political power because most of us were Yankees and against slavery. But slavery is not an issue in Illinois. And there are both Whigs and Democrats among the Mormons. The presidency of the Church does not dictate a man's vote."

"But if your Prophet tells his people who he is voting for . . ." James raised the question.

Caroline followed it up. "Then wouldn't nearly every man follow him and vote the same?"

Almon thought of Joseph's openness. He wasn't a man to measure every word or to keep his views to himself. And when a revelation came, Joseph published it, no matter whom it hurt. "Our Prophet is not a politico," Almon reiterated. Then he shook his head and admitted, "But what you suggest could happen."

"If Sharp's arrow strikes the bull's eye, this could turn your neighbors against you," James said. "Be careful, my friends. This editorial is something to fear."

Julianne spoke up. "James and Caroline, we have experienced things you have not. We know that Mormonism is the restored gospel of Jesus Christ. This requires us to move forward with trust in God, not fear."

"We respect your beliefs," Caroline said.

Almon looked at his wife and his friends, the pressure and disappointment of the day pushing at him as memories of Missouri crowded in from all sides. False cheer was no longer an option. "It is more than belief," he said. "It is knowledge. Though I wish at this moment that I did not know for a fact that Mormonism is true."

*\*\*\**

*Nauvoo, Illinois. April 6, 1841*

Emotions welled within Julia. The cornerstones of another temple were about to be laid for the third time in the latter days. Hope filled her. She believed that things would be different this time; that they would not have to leave this house of God. The Prophet's optimism had been contagious the last few months. He thrilled at the hopes that lay before the Saints: the friendship of the Illinois public, the liberal charter, and the progress and potential of Nauvoo the beautiful. His optimism radiated energy as limitless as the God he knew. Joseph was the sun giving life to the seedling that had blossomed into a city.

Julia breathed in the fresh air. Delcena, Almera, Mary, and Esther stood close to her as they joined the other ladies just outside the foundation. The gentlemen who were not in the Legion filed in behind them. The crowd thronged, forming an opening as the choir and band moved into the center.

Artillery fire announced the arrival of Brigadier Generals Wilson Law and Don Carlos Smith. Sitting tall on their mounts, they cantered to the front of their brigades that totaled fourteen companies and over a thousand men. Julia shaded her eyes to see the spectacular sight more clearly. A cannon discharged in honor of Major General Bennett's arrival. Riding a spirited bay, Bennett galloped around the crowd, his dark eyes and arching eyebrows as fierce as the swish of his sword. As one, the Legion moved in time and ringed the assemblage.

"What do you think of General Bennett?" Mary whispered.

"He must be a good man," Julia said quietly. "The Prophet trusts him."

"He's done so much for our people," Delcena added. "We can thank him for the city's charter. And he's Joseph's right hand in building Nauvoo. This Legion is already the greatest military force in the state. Look, there's the Prophet now."

Lieutenant General Joseph Smith rode up on his black horse and saluted the officers. The Prophet wore full military uniform: a general's coat, pantaloons, boots, epaulets, and hat. His horse's neck arched proudly, and its coat glistened in the sunlight.

"Charlie is the most splendid fellow," Mary commented under her breath.

"Who's Charlie?" Esther asked aghast. "What about your *Dear Wilson?*"

Mary laughed. "Charlie is Brother Joseph's mount. Ben became acquainted with Charlie in Far West and told me about him."

"Poor George, playing second fiddle to a horse," Esther teased.

"Shh," Julia whispered as a hush fell over the crowd. Joseph dismounted and walked with his guard and field officers to the center of the foundation. The other generals and their staffs followed. Then a group of ladies, led by Emma Smith and Eliza Snow, presented the Prophet with a beautiful silk national flag. Joseph received it respectfully and unfurled it in the breeze. Tears filled Julia's eyes as she watched the United States flag fly high, her prophet and general embracing the country that had mercilessly driven, persecuted, and imprisoned him.

Following Sidney Rigdon's address, the first stone, the temple's southeast corner, was moved into place. Joseph raised his voice in prayer. "The principal cornerstone is now duly laid in honor of the Great God, and may it there remain until the whole fabric is complete, and may the same be accomplished speedily, that the Saints may have a place to worship God and the Son of Man have where to lay his head."

President Rigdon continued the prayer. "May the persons employed in the erection of this house be preserved from all harm while engaged in its construction, till the whole is completed, in the name of the Father and of the Son and of the Holy Ghost. Even so. Amen."

\*\*\*

Following the service, Esther walked with her mother and sisters through the streets of Nauvoo. Mary was all smiles and nearly skipping as she pointed out every new house and tree. Esther knew why Mary was so happy. Her sister was thinking about George Wilson, who had found them after the ceremony and invited Mary to meet him for dinner later in the evening.

Esther wondered if Mary's romance made Almera feel sad. She glanced over at Almera, who walked with her arm in their mother's, her long-lashed eyes often staring ahead but not really seeing what was around her. Almera had become so quiet. She didn't laugh, dance, or complain like Esther remembered. Esther wished Almera would tell her all that had happened with Sam. It felt strange and uncomfortable, the way everyone just went on with life, never mentioning Sam, like he had never existed.

Delcena suddenly stopped and, touching Esther's arm, pointed to a field. "That's where the University of Nauvoo will be built. Brother Joseph brought a group of us here last Saturday. How grand it will be! There will be an academy for girls too. Brother Joseph wants everyone to learn."

"It will be a wonderful place," Julia added, focusing on Esther. "A blessing to all of the young people who attend."

Esther tossed her head, fully aware of what her mother and Delcena were getting at. They wanted her to change her mind, to stay in Nauvoo rather than go back to Kirtland. "I'm sure it will be a fine university. But Kirtland has an excellent Young Ladies' Academy right now," Esther said in an effort to set them straight. "When Juli and Almon come next week, I'm going back with them—just like we've already planned. I won't be changing my mind."

"Are you sure?" Delcena pressed. "If you stay, you could move to Nauvoo with me and attend school here."

"No, thank you," Esther said, thinking that if she did that, she would have to help with Delcena's children every free moment. "I'm going to Kirtland," she added with finality. "Mother gave me permission a long time ago, and Papa is expecting me."

"But Papa isn't easy," Mary commented. "I stayed with him when I was your age. It was so hard."

"Esther could live with Julianne and Almon," Almera broke in quickly, almost urgently. "They have a big house."

"You see?" Esther said. "It will be perfect."

Almera turned to Esther. "But you'll need to visit Papa often. He can be hard, but he is very dear."

"I'll take him supper every day," Esther said emphatically. "That's why I'm going. To be near Papa. And to learn new things and to meet new people."

A smile broke out on Almera's face, and she had a light in her eyes. "Papa will be so glad." She put her arm around Esther's shoulders. "And you will love the LeBaron family. I've written them and told them you're coming. Melissa is looking forward to meeting you."

Esther put her arm around Almera's waist and leaned against her older sister as they walked. Warmth spread through her. Almera understood that she needed to see Papa again, that she needed an adventure all her own. Esther was fourteen years old; it was time to live in a big house and be done with hardship—at least for a while.

Then her mother sighed. "I won't insist you stay," Julia said. "But, Esther, things have changed since I gave you permission to go to Kirtland.

The Prophet has told all the Saints to come here. I think that eventually Julianne and Almon will move here too. I want you to pray about it and reconsider."

"I've already prayed about it, Mother. I'm going to Kirtland."

\* \* \*

*Early May 1841. Nauvoo, Illinois*

Joe and Harriet greeted Julianne and Almon warmly when they met them at the landing. "Did you get your law licenses?" Joe asked Almon as he helped heft the trunk.

"For Ohio. But I need one more signature to practice in Illinois," Almon said cheerfully. He glanced at Harriet. "It looks like married life is treating the two of you well."

"It's full of wonders," Joe said. Harriet blushed. She was five months pregnant.

"No one told us you were expecting a little one," Julianne exclaimed as she hugged Harriet, trying to hide the catch in her voice.

"We decided to make it a surprise," Joe remarked as he put his arm around his sister. He and Harriet were both sensitive to Julianne's longing for a child.

"When's the baby due?" Julianne asked.

"In September," Harriet said then added, "if all goes well."

Julianne took Harriet's hand. "I wish I could be here for the birth, but we'll be back in Kirtland. What a sweet baby you and Joe will have."

A few minutes later, Joe and Almon lifted the trunks into the back of the buggy. The ladies sat in the second seat. When they were on their way, Joe mentioned that Almon's friend, old Judge Adams from Springfield, was visiting Nauvoo with Judge Douglas.

"Do you mean Stephen A. Douglas of the Illinois Supreme Court?" Almon asked.

Joe nodded. "They're renting a room at Sniders' Hotel. Harriet helped her mother serve them breakfast this morning."

"What a stroke of luck!" Almon said exuberantly. "I need his signature on my Illinois law license."

Julianne smiled. "It might be providence—a blessing rather than luck."

Almon turned around to grin at his wife. "A lucky blessing!" Then he went on, addressing Joe. "I didn't know Adams and Douglas were well acquainted. But it makes sense. Adams is a wealthy old general and staunch Democrat. And Douglas is a wealthy young politician and a staunch Democrat."

Harriet spoke up. "They became friends at the Springfield lodge. They're both Freemasons."

"Really?" Almon's interest was piqued. "How do you know?"

Harriet answered simply, "Papa told me."

Joe urged the horses into a trot. Almon said with a grin, "Joe, since we're both Democrats, you should come with me to pay a visit to Mr. Douglas this afternoon. It never hurts to rub shoulders with the powerful."

Joe laughed. "All right. But the Laws mentioned that they hoped you would visit them this afternoon."

Almon shrugged. "I'll leave William to his afternoon nap. May the Whigs rest in peace."

* * *

An hour later, Stephen A. Douglas shook Joe's and Almon's hands as Judge Adams introduced them. Almon seemed completely at ease, but Joe felt self-conscious. Douglas seemed familiar—the short legs, large head, and booming voice. Then Joe remembered. Over three years ago, on a winter day while he waited in a Springfield store, destitute and nearly hopeless, Joe had overheard a debate in the back of the store. He had been drawn to the young lawyers—to the short man named Stephen with a giant's voice and the lanky fellow named Abraham, who laughed as they argued around a roaring fire.

"Mr. Douglas," Almon said, drawing Joe back to the present. "I've taken the necessary courses and have brought with me the required papers to obtain my license to practice law in Illinois. Would you be so kind as to sign my license?"

Douglas smiled charmingly. "Are you a Democrat?"

Almon nodded. "As thoroughly as I am a Mormon."

Stephen A. Douglas laughed. His voice was vibrant. "We need lawyers like you in Illinois. Hand me the paper, and my signature is yours."

"Thank you," Almon said as he pulled out the license. With no further ado and a flourish of his pen, Douglas signed it.

"Congratulations, Brother Almon," Judge Adams said. The elderly man's eyes, deep-set amid the wrinkles of age, were warm and proud, almost as if Almon were his own son.

Then Douglas took out his pocket watch and looked at it briefly. "Now, gentlemen, I will leave you. I'm scheduled to meet with General Smith and General Bennett in fifteen minutes. They've asked me to examine the Nauvoo Charter and Legislative Acts as they relate to the Nauvoo Legion." Douglas addressed Almon. "Mr. Babbitt, if you come to Springfield, pay me a visit. I'm curious about you. Judge Adams has told me that you answered his questions on Mormonism, which led to his baptism."

James Adams' eyes twinkled. "Stephen, I suggest Mr. Babbitt go with you to see General Smith. On the way, he could preach to you."

Almon quickly replied, "Though I wish I could go, I have only a day before my journey to Ohio. I've promised my wife I'll take her to Ramus to see her family."

"It's just as well." Douglas laughed. "Like I've told James many times, I'm a politician and *never* mix church and state."

"My dear boy," Judge Adams replied, smiling paternally at the supreme court justice, "*never* is a very long time."

Stephen Douglas bid the men farewell as he left the room. As Joe glanced at the refined, wealthy, fatherly Judge Adams, he felt a pang of longing for his own father, with his rough hands, his plain-spoken honesty, and his unfettered love.

*  *  *

Almon turned to follow Joe out the door. He knew Julianne and Harriet were waiting for them in the hotel parlor, anxious to be on their way to Ramus. Still stinging from the reprimand in the revelation, Almon was glad to be leaving Nauvoo. With his law license secure, he had little desire to see the Prophet. Then suddenly, Almon felt Judge Adams' hand on his forearm, detaining him. "Brother Almon, a word with you privately?"

"Of course," Almon said as he turned around. Joe graciously shut the door, leaving Almon alone with the judge. Adams invited Almon to take a seat. Almon forced a smile and sat down. James Adams was a former general and an experienced judge, the Prophet's wealthy benefactor and a Freemason. He brimmed with benevolence and fatherly advice.

Adams smiled kindly at Almon. "Son, will you be meeting with Brother Joseph before you go back to Kirtland?"

Almon shook his head. "No, sir. As I mentioned earlier, I've promised to take my wife to Ramus tonight. We'll spend tomorrow there. We leave for Kirtland with her youngest sister early the following morning."

The judge was thoughtful for a moment. Almon shifted uncomfortably in his chair, knowing Judge Adams was aware of the chastisement in the revelation. He would bet money that was what Adams planned to discuss.

Judge Adams cleared his throat. "Seven months ago, in the October conference, you were called to be the stake president in Kirtland. But you have not been back to Kirtland since then, and, therefore, I assume you have not been sustained by the members there."

Almon's heart went cold. Was Judge Adams aware of something he was not? Almon had left Cincinnati before the local Church leaders had received minutes from the April general conference. Changes could have been made. It was possible that someone else had been called in Almon's place. Almon forced his voice to remain calm. He could wear the mask as well as any man. "That's correct. I went directly to Cincinnati from here. Was a change made in the April conference that I'm unaware of?"

The judge shook his head. "No, my dear, young friend. But Brother Joseph and I have discussed your calling and the recent revelation regarding your standing before the Lord. The Prophet wants you to know that he loves you as a brother. Nauvoo is to be built up, and you should not hinder that. The Lord requires that the ordinance of baptism for the dead only take place within the font inside the walls of the Nauvoo Temple once it has been completed. It is necessary that the Saints gather here for their redemption and the redemption of their dead. These ordinances cannot take place in the Kirtland Temple."

Almon did not answer. Kirtland was a gift from God. Judge Adams had never been there; he did not understand.

Adams went on. "On the other hand, you are called, even commanded, to return to Kirtland to be the presiding authority. Can you support both of these commandments of the Lord? Can you support His prophet?"

Almon sat silently for a moment. He no longer smiled. That was the question. Could he still support Joseph after the chastisement? Where was the line between the Prophet's personal feelings and revelation from God? And what about his own personal revelation, that feeling he had that Kirtland was a land of promise? Judge Adams did not lower his gaze but looked intently at Almon.

Almon swallowed. "Yes," he said. "I continue to support Brother Joseph. But in the aftermath of the chastisement, it is possible that the Kirtland Saints will not support me. Brother Granger has long been critical of my judgment."

The judge nodded knowingly. "Joseph intends to write to Brother Granger and encourage him to cooperate with you. Brother Almon, remember that the Lord loves those whom He chastens. You are beloved of the Lord and a gentleman with many gifts. I have no doubt that you will be sustained by the Kirtland Saints."

# 17

*On Zion's hill thy people meet,*
*O Lord, in thy great name,*
*To bow the knee, to worship thee,*
*And thy protection claim.*

Joel Hills Johnson

*Kirtland, Ohio*

ESTHER ABRUPTLY CLOSED THE BOOK Julianne had given her before the journey. She wiggled impatiently—tired of the feel of the steamboat churning through the water, sick of the taste of hard cheese, and disgusted with the smell of men chewing and spitting tobacco. To make matters worse, she was thoroughly bored with *The Girl's Own Book*, which was annoyingly cheerful and full of advice, games, puzzles, and fairy tales. Actually, the games would be all right if there were friends to play them with. Yet, what had Julianne been thinking when she purchased it? It was meant for little girls, not young ladies in their fifteenth year.

Julianne, who sat beside her writing letters, turned to Esther. "Do you want to sing? Or rhyme together?"

Esther shook her head. "No, thank you."

"Don't you like the book?" Julianne asked.

Esther shrugged. She didn't want to hurt Julianne's feelings. "There are some funny forfeits, like requiring the loser to laugh in one corner, cry in another, and sing in the third."

"What about the fourth corner?"

"The players come up with their own idea."

Julianne smiled. "Be thinking. We'll have a party after you're settled. We arrive in Fairport tomorrow. Then the next day, you'll see Papa."

Esther nodded. She had been so excited about coming, but now she felt afraid. It had been nearly three years. She had been a little girl when they'd left. Would Papa feel like a stranger? Would he even recognize her? Would Julianne and Almon get tired of her and wish she hadn't come? Would she make friends? Esther shivered. She had been so certain about coming that she had gone against her mother's advice. Would she be sorry?

"When we get to Kirtland," Esther blurted. "I want to go to your house first so I can wash my hair and thoroughly brush it out. Then we can go to Papa's and tell him we're here. I want Papa to see me looking my best."

"All right," Julianne replied. Then Esther was silent as she stared out across Lake Erie. The water turned crimson as the sun set. She thought about her younger brother Amos. He had gone to the dock to see them off and hugged his sisters tightly. Then Esther had noticed the tears in Julianne's eyes. "What's wrong?" she had asked after Amos left.

"He's lost weight. He still suffers from sciatic rheumatism."

"He's stronger than you think," Esther had snapped.

Julianne stood up, interrupting Esther's thoughts. Julianne rolled her shoulders back, stretching them. "Let's go to bed early. Then when we wake up, we'll be nearly to Fairport." Esther picked up the book and followed Julianne.

Ten minutes later, Esther pulled her blanket to her chin and closed her eyes. She listened as Julianne sang a hymn. Then Julianne settled in the bunk next to her. "Almon will be along soon," Julianne commented. "After he finishes preaching."

Sometimes Almon's preaching worried Esther. What if a Missourian were among the passengers, just waiting to grab them while asleep and throw them overboard? Esther closed her eyes, imagining a place without mobs and tears, where diseases were healed with a touch and a prayer, where her father watched over her and a young man smiled at her, where it was never cold or lonely.

\* \* \*

Ezekiel went to the tavern in the late afternoon. He ordered a mug of brandy and sat down at a table while he waited for his supper. He was early today, but in the next hour, others would join him—men with their own stories, their own wads of tobacco and drinks in their hands, their own bloodshot eyes as they laughed and cursed at what pained them.

Ezekiel sipped his drink. It was the third week in May. He hadn't heard from Julianne for months. He cursed under his breath. She wasn't likely to come back. It would be better to forget he had a family, a wife and little ones whom he had not seen for three years. He had done it as a youth, had left his mother without turning back. But he had stayed away until it was too late, until she had forgotten him. When he finally went to find her, she was gone without a trace. What did that scripture in the Bible say? That a mother would not forget her sucking child anymore than God would forget about His people? Well, he had observed both situations—it was simply a godless world. He took another sip.

The boy who served the drinks tapped Ezekiel on the shoulder. "Mr. Johnson, some folks are outside asking for you."

Ezekiel left his drink on the table. He stood up and walked to the door. It maddened him the way his heart beat, hope trying to rear up inside. It was probably a complaining customer. Then he saw Julianne, with a young lady standing beside her, nearly as tall as her, with a nose like his own. Her dark hair was straight and long, brushed out and as shiny as satin. He stared at her, and she smiled tentatively—the smooth young skin, the chiseled features, the eyes brown and beautiful—little Esther's eyes.

"Esther," he said. "Baby girl." All the toughness in him evaporated like frost in sunlight. He held out his arms.

"Papa," she cried out and ran toward him. He gathered her to him, and she knew that he was crying—the tears of a grizzled old carpenter.

"Don't cry, Papa," she begged, hugging him as tightly as she could. "I'm here. It will be all right."

But he couldn't stop. A foolish old man crying like a child while his baby girl comforted him. "You came back," he said.

Now Esther was crying too. "I won't leave you, Papa. I won't ever leave you again."

\* \* \*

*Saturday, May 22, 1841. Kirtland, Ohio*

Just a few days after their arrival, Julianne sat with Esther in the Kirtland Temple as more than two hundred people gathered for stake conference.

She looked up at Almon on the stand—his straight shoulders, combed-back hair, green eyes focused and friendly. He looked very handsome and confident in his new suit. Yet last night, he had paced in the parlor, worrying, the ashes of bitterness still warm over the revelation's reproof. The primary business of the conference was to see if the people would sustain Almon and the counselors he had chosen.

The conference began. Amos Babcock, the elders quorum president, stood and explained that President Almon Babbitt, who had been called as stake president in last October's general conference, was back and was presiding over this stake conference. After the song and prayer, Almon took the stand. "Brothers and sisters," he said, diving in, "the business of this conference is the reorganization of the Kirtland Stake of Zion. Therefore, I resign from the office of president of this stake, that the conference might express its full right and choose its own officers by common consent."

Julianne shivered. She knew why Almon had resigned. Oliver Granger, the former stake president, had not moved from Kirtland as he had originally planned. Yet she wished Almon had simply called his counselors and requested a vote of consent. Following that opening statement, Almon went on to read several lengthy acts incorporating the Church in Kirtland, together with a code of bylaws. These were accepted and adopted unanimously. Then Almon instructed the conference to adjourn for an hour.

Perplexed, Julianne walked outside with Esther. The sun was warm and bright. Melissa and David LeBaron joined them. Julianne introduced Esther.

"I'm very pleased to meet you." Melissa smiled. "I hope you enjoy the academy."

Esther nodded. "I'm sure I will. I've heard you're one of the teachers."

"Both a teacher and a student," Melissa said wistfully. "Depending on the subject at hand."

"Are you teaching any subjects this summer?"

"No. But I'm taking a culinary class," Melissa said. "They have a new cookbook written by a Philadelphia lady. You ought to take it with me!"

Esther nodded brightly. "I'd love to. I'll be cooking for my father, and wouldn't he be surprised if I brought him fancy things."

David interrupted, his blue eyes twinkling. "But you shouldn't give all the fancy things to your good father. Save a few morsels for your friends."

Esther eyed him with a pretended pout. "But I'm new here and haven't any friends."

"That was a moment ago," David said. "Aren't we now friends?"

Esther beamed delightedly, a tease in her eyes. "But friendship is like planting a seed. It requires kind acts, like watering and sunshine, before it blooms."

David laughed. "Let the watering and sunshine begin."

Esther giggled delightedly and held out her hand to David. He took it and kissed it.

Julianne smiled tentatively. "It looks like conference is to start again. Esther, we'd better head back in. Melissa and David, it's always good to see you."

As Julianne walked back into the temple, she thought of how she was now living with two gregarious, mercurial temperaments—both Almon's and Esther's. Would she be able to properly rein Esther in? David LeBaron seemed much too old for her baby sister.

Conference reconvened. After the song and prayer, Brother William W. Phelps stood and said a few words. Then he nominated Almon W. Babbitt as president of the Kirtland Stake of Zion. However, before Elder Phelps called for a vote, Almon stood up and tapped him on the shoulder. Elder Phelps moved aside. Almon's face was slightly redder than usual as he gripped the pulpit with his hands. His eyes unmistakably filled with tears. Julianne's heart reached out to him. This wasn't like Almon. What was he going to say?

"Brothers and sisters," he began, "I decline the nomination." There was a murmur in the crowd. Almon went on. "As some of you know, I have made mistakes and was chastened in a revelation from God. I cannot accept this call unless I know beyond doubt that you are still able to work beside me, to hold up my arms as we move this great work forward."

Elder Phelps put his arm around Almon and asked if it would be all right to open the floor for discussion in light of his feelings. Almon nodded and took his seat. One person after another arose and expressed their love and support for Elder Babbitt. Forty minutes passed. Then Elder Phelps once again nominated Almon Babbitt as stake president. This time, Almon accepted the nomination, and the vote was unanimous.

Once again at the pulpit, Almon emotionally thanked the Saints for their support and said that with the Lord's help, he would serve them.

The meeting continued. Almon nominated Lester Brooks and Zebedee Coltrin as his counselors. The voting was unanimous. Then he delivered a discourse on baptism for the dead from 1 Peter 4:6. He explained how the doctrine was compatible with the mercy of God and the grand council in heaven. It was the power of salvation as revealed to the latter-day Prophet, Joseph Smith Jr. By the time he finished speaking, there were few dry eyes in the congregation.

Julianne looked up at her husband, her darling boy, and her stake president. A baby fussed near her. Julianne swallowed as tears burned her eyes. If only she could fill Almon's house with children. *Please, Heavenly Father,* her heart cried out. *Let this one desire be Thy will.*

\* \* \*

*Saturday, June 5, 1841. Nauvoo, Illinois*

In the early evening, Delcena walked quickly toward the Law's store on Water Street. Little Susan had been coughing and needed medicine before the Sabbath. Don Carlos Smith stepped out of the store as she approached.

"Hello, Carlos. How are you?" Delcena asked. Ever since his friendship with her brother David, Delcena had felt tenderly toward the Prophet's youngest brother. She wasn't alone; Don Carlos was beloved of the Saints.

"Sister Delcena." Don Carlos nodded a greeting before taking out a handkerchief and coughing into it. He looked pale. A short distance away, the wide Mississippi gleamed, winding like red molten lava as the sun set.

"You aren't well," Delcena said as threads of worry wove around her heart. "Rest more. Agnes told me you work too hard."

Don Carlos paused for a moment, as if he had something to say but didn't know how to say it. Then he began. "Thank you for your concern. But it's Joseph's life that hangs in the balance tonight. He's been arrested. We just received word. Please pray for him."

Delcena's stomach twisted. "What happened?"

"He went to Quincy to see Hyrum and Brother Law off on their mission." There was an edge to Don Carlos's voice as he continued. "Afterward, Joseph visited Governor Carlin. The governor welcomed him, acting very hospitable. Then after Joseph left, Carlin put together a posse with an officer from Missouri. They arrested him at Heberlin's Hotel. Missouri is trying to extradite Joseph to face the old charges."

Delcena's voice shook. "We can't let them take him."

Don Carlos spoke quickly. "I know. Thanks to God, Stephen A. Douglas is in Quincy. Last we heard, Joseph was on his way to see him to try to get a writ of habeas corpus. In ten minutes, men will leave Nauvoo in a skiff. If they have to, they'll intercept and rescue Joseph. Would to God that I was well enough to go with them!"

"It's difficult, Carlos," Delcena said, "sitting back while those you love are in danger—and simply sending prayers. But sometimes it's the right thing."

Don Carlos nodded and briefly touched her shoulder, as if he knew she was thinking about Lyman, about how he hadn't sat back when Joseph was in danger, about how it had cost him his life. Delcena numbly walked into the store. The possibility of Joseph dying in Missouri staggered her. Since Lyman's death, the Prophet and Emma had visited her household every week. Brother Joseph comforted, advised, and nurtured her children. If Joseph was sent to Missouri and died, the entire Church would mourn. But it would be even worse for her little ones. They had already lost their father.

\* \* \*

*Wednesday, June 9, 1841. Monmouth, Illinois*

Joe sat in the back of the courtroom with his father-in-law, John Snider. His foot tapped nervously as he waited for the court to convene and listened to the murmuring around him. This crowd was not friendly.

Joe's mind went over details of the past week. The Prophet had been arrested five days ago near Quincy. After Joseph had obtained a writ of habeas corpus, Stephen A. Douglas scheduled a hearing the following week in Monmouth, Warren County. On the way to Monmouth, the Prophet had spent a night in Nauvoo with his arresting officers. After witnessing this, John Snider had ridden to Ramus with the news. He had asked Joe to ride to Monmouth with him.

Now they sat in the hot and humid courtroom, crowded with over one hundred fifty people. Some stood in the aisles. When Joseph filed in with the officers, many in the crowd jumped out of their seats and craned their necks. Others shouldered and pushed to get a look at the infamous Joe Smith. There were catcalls of "False prophet," "Military saints" and "Send Joe back to Missouri." Judge Douglas looked at the sheriff. "Keep these spectators back, away from the prisoner." The crowd continued to surge as the sheriff did nothing. Judge Douglas spoke louder. "Sir, I hereby fine you ten dollars for not attending to your duty."

"I've told a constable to do it," the sheriff quipped.

"Clerk, add ten dollars more to that fine!" Douglas roared. Finding defiance expensive, the sheriff held his rifle horizontally across his chest and urged back the crowd.

Joe took a deep breath. Despite his short frame, Stephen A. Douglas was a giant among men. Joe tried to believe that everything would be all right. In Missouri, the judges had never been friendly, but it was different here in Illinois. Joe listened carefully throughout the hearing. A drunken Missouri lawyer did his best to convict Joseph. However, he had to temporarily leave the courtroom to throw up. Joseph's attorneys skillfully presented their case, stating that Joseph was unlawfully held in custody and that the indictment in Missouri was obtained by fraud, bribery, and duress. In the end, Douglas dismissed the case on a technicality, and Joseph was allowed to go free.

After having dinner with the Prophet and their friends, Joe and his father-in-law began the long ride home. They planned to travel until midnight then camp by the road, returning to Ramus the following day. As they rode, the moon rose, hanging three-quarters full in the sky. An animal howled. Hours passed, and gradually, even the crickets stilled. Joe's eyes became accustomed to the darkness as the black and gray world gained dimension. John Snider broke the silence. "I don't understand how this happened."

Joe sighed. "It doesn't surprise me that Missouri's governor came after Joseph. Letting him alone would be admitting guilt."

John went on. "It's not that. It's the reaction of the Illinois citizens. Less than a year ago, the entire state bent over backwards to befriend us. But the crowd today was hostile. It was like being in Missouri all over again. Why?"

"Bad press," Joe remarked dismally. He thought about how freedom of the press was a two-edged blade: one side protecting the rights of man, the other allowing falsehood bannered as truth. "Have you followed Thomas Sharp, the editor of the *Warsaw Signal*?"

John shook his head. "No, son. With all the work, it's all I can do to read the scriptures and the *Times and Seasons*."

Joe wondered if his father-in-law was indirectly criticizing him for not reading his scriptures as regularly as he ought. Harriet, in contrast, was fastidious and studied her Bible and Book of Mormon daily. Joe dismissed the thought and explained further. "The *Signal* is a Whig paper. Last month, Sharp wrote an angry editorial about Judge Douglas, a Democrat, appointing John Bennett, another power-hungry Democrat, as chancery in Hancock County. Then he wrote that the Mormons have control of the elections and that his paper utterly opposes the concentration of political power in the hands of a leader of a religious party."

"But Joseph doesn't tell us how to vote. I suppose Sharp sent the lie to Whig papers all over the country," John remarked.

Joe nodded. "It gets worse. Brother Joseph wrote a letter to Sharp, terminating his subscription and calling the paper 'contemptible.' In the following issue, Sharp reprinted the letter, ridiculed Joseph, and attacked the Nauvoo Legion, saying that we are 'fighting saints,' not 'praying saints.'"

John did not respond. His head bent forward, and his body slumped like he was very tired. The somber silence chilled the warm night. "Are you all right?" Joe asked.

"I don't see how we can live through another Missouri," John stated.

\* \* \*

*October 1841. Kirtland, Ohio*

"Ben, why are *you* here?" Esther squealed as she opened the door and flung her arms around her older brother's neck. She had not seen him for two years. Flour covered her apron and hands.

Weary and travel worn, Ben staggered to keep his balance. "I'm home from my mission." He hugged his little sister and asked, "What are *you* doing here? And where are Juli and Almon?"

"I live here now," Esther replied. "Almon and Julianne are gone so much that I'm practically the lady of the house. Right now they're taking food to some poor families who've just arrived in Kirtland. Does Papa know you're back?"

"Not yet."

"Ben, you're letting flies in." Esther pulled Benjamin inside and closed the door behind him. "Then we'll surprise Papa tonight. I'll take you with me when I bring him supper. You look tired."

Benjamin took a deep breath. "I am. And thirsty too."

Esther marched Benjamin down the hall and into a bedroom. After fluffing the feather pillow, she insisted he lie down while she get him some water. When Esther came back, he took a long drink. After setting the cup on the bureau, Esther sat down on the edge of the bed. "Before you fall asleep, take one minute and tell me where you've been and how many you've baptized."

Benjamin lay back on the pillow. It had been a difficult week, and exhaustion pressed upon him, but he appeased her. "I've been in Indiana, Canada, New York, and Pennsylvania. I've baptized over thirty people."

"Then why do you look sad? Are you just tired?" Esther peered down at him, her brown eyes intent and perceptive.

Benjamin swallowed, wondering if he ought to tell her the truth. Esther continued. "Please tell me what's wrong. Mama always thought I was too young to understand, but imagining bad things is worse than knowing the truth."

Benjamin sighed. His voice was soft and low as he explained. "About a year ago, I fell in love with a girl in Erie County, Pennsylvania. She loved me back, and we promised ourselves to each other. She wanted to be baptized, but her uncle, who she lived with, was against it. I left and continued my mission. But before coming here, I went back to see her and asked once more if she would be baptized. If she would, I told her I would bring her to Kirtland with me and marry her. But she refused to rebel against her uncle, though she said she loved me. I left her forever."

"That is the saddest story," Esther said. She was quiet for a moment but did not leave the room. Then she asked seriously, "Ben, how many girls have you loved in your life?"

"Three."

"What were their names?"

"Zina Huntington, Lucinda Morgan . . . " Benjamin paused briefly. "And the girl I just told you about: Matilda Jane Warren."

Esther's brow furrowed. "Oh, Ben, I'm so sorry for you. Three times having your heart broken. I wish I could do something."

Benjamin sank deeper into the pillow, wishing he hadn't said anything about his sad romances to his little sister. "Esther, I'm very tired. Let's not talk of it anymore."

Esther reached for his hand. "I know it is painful, but I just have one more thing to tell you. I have met the love of my life. Please try to be happy for me."

Benjamin could not keep his eyes open and found focusing on what she was saying very taxing. "Oh," he managed.

"I'll tell you his name if you promise not to tell Julianne or Papa."

Benjamin nodded as his eyes closed.

"David LeBaron," Esther whispered. "And, Ben, I'm quite sure that he is in love with me as well. He comes over often with his sister. He even held my hand once when we went outside together to pick apples. But he's five years older than me."

Esther looked carefully to see Benjamin's reaction, but her brother was already snoring.

* * *

Benjamin awakened to voices in the kitchen. "Your meat pies look perfect," a lady said. Her voice sounded familiar, but Benjamin couldn't place it. He arose from bed, took a comb from his bundle, and swept it through his hair.

Prior to being detected, Benjamin peered into the kitchen. Esther picked up a whisk and handed it to a blue-eyed young man. Then she put her hand over his and showed him how to move the whisk in a bowl full of cream. Esther giggled as the cream spilled over the side. Another young lady had her back to the door as she took pies out of the oven. Benjamin cleared his throat. The young lady turned around. Esther and the young man looked up.

"Ben, you're awake," Esther chimed as she took her hand off of the young man's. "These are my friends, Melissa and David LeBaron. Julianne and Almon came home and are gone again. They said to tell you they're very happy you're back."

David stopped whipping the cream. He put down the whisk and held his hand out to Benjamin. "Brother Johnson, you already know Melissa. But I was out of town when you were here before. It's nice to finally meet you."

"And you," Benjamin replied as he formally shook his hand.

Esther spoke up brightly. "Melissa and I are taking a culinary class at the academy. We practice almost every day. This is a dessert called 'the floating island.' It is a blob of stiff jelly set in the middle of sweet cream. Things are working out perfectly here in Kirtland. Melissa and I cook. David samples everything to make sure it is delectable. Julianne is glad not to *have* to cook every night, and Almon and Papa are delighted to eat new dishes. And you shall be glad to be here for Thanksgiving!"

"I shall," Benjamin replied with a smile. The young man smiled at Esther as if he were delighted with her chatter. Benjamin tried to recall something he had heard about David LeBaron.

Melissa set the pies down and stepped closer to Benjamin. He saw that her sky-blue dress matched her eyes. She stood straight-shouldered and queenly, with lovely, smooth skin. She smiled and curtsied as pink circles rose in her cheeks. "Brother Johnson, it's nice to see you again."

"It's my pleasure," Benjamin returned.

Later that evening, after the LeBarons had gone home, Esther and Benjamin left to take dinner to Ezekiel. As soon as they were alone in the buggy, Esther turned to Benjamin. "What did you think?" she asked.

"Of what?" Benjamin questioned.

Esther snorted softly. "Of David, my beau."

"Your beau?" Benjamin asked, mystified.

"I told you before you fell asleep. You promised you wouldn't say anything to Julianne or Papa. Don't you remember?"

Benjamin took a deep breath. "Esther, you're only fourteen. David is considerably older. You're far too young to have a beau."

Esther dismissed the chide. "The Prophet was fourteen when he had his First Vision. Come on, Ben, what do you think about David? Don't you think he is nice and very handsome? His father left him a big inheritance, but that's not why I love him."

Benjamin eyed Esther. "I refuse to think about him because you are too young to imagine that you're in love."

Esther humphed and turned silent. Benjamin changed the subject. "But I must admit that his sister is lovely."

Esther punched Benjamin in the arm. "Well, I shall tell Melissa to stay clear of a fellow who has loved three girls but who doesn't have the heart to understand his own sister."

\* \* \*

*A week later. Kirtland, Ohio*

Julianne awakened before dawn, following a fitful night. Yesterday in the temple, at the fall conference, Almon had given a discourse. A portion of the discourse troubled her deeply. Almon had talked about Kirtland's role in the gathering in the last days. He had spoken of it as a place of refuge from the storm, a stake in Zion that would grow in beauty and prosperity. While Nauvoo was rightfully the Church headquarters and gathering place, Kirtland, like a younger sister, healthier and lovelier than the elder, waited to come of age. How blessed were the Saints in Kirtland to be able to wait with her and build her up.

After that comment, Julianne had difficulty concentrating on the remainder of Almon's sermon. At least a third of those in attendance were converts who had left all to gather with the Saints. They had stopped in Kirtland on their way to Nauvoo. They felt Almon's warmth and concern. While some squirmed, knowing that Almon's counsel was not in line with the Prophet's, others looked up at her handsome and eloquent husband, their weary, grateful eyes taking in his every word. *Perhaps we have no farther to go. Perhaps we are home.* Julianne knew there would be discussion and argument regarding Almon's comments. What troubled her most was that she would be among those dissenting.

Later that night when they lay in bed, Julianne had tried to talk with Almon about it, reminding him of the Prophet's clear directive calling the faithful to gather to Nauvoo. He had become defensive. "I did not tell anyone that they should not go to Nauvoo!"

Julianne had not given up so easily. "You made Kirtland sound like the Garden of Eden. Your words will convince many to stay. Don't you see? It wasn't right. We were called to Kirtland, but most of the congregation was not. The Prophet wants them to gather in Nauvoo."

Almon's arms, which had been wrapped around her, had turned rigid, his words tense. "Don't tell me what is right and what is wrong. The converts are hungry and tired. I will not send them to a swamp-ridden city, where many of them will die of malaria—like Annie. I will not preach for them to hurry to Nauvoo while we grow rich, when they can prosper here and live."

Julianne's eyes had burned. "But, Almon, the Lord has called them to Nauvoo. He has promised that those who go there will be blessed."

"I won't discuss this anymore," Almon had said and rolled over. She had shivered, cold without Almon's arms around her. Sleep had eluded her as she thought about the merchandizing store they had opened two months ago. They had stocked it on credit, and the business was thriving. Almon was thrilled. He had told her that within six months, they would pay back their loans and be wealthy enough to purchase a law library. He would become as big a man as Judge Adams and William Law and as helpful to the Prophet and Church. But one fact haunted Julianne—that Almon's dreams and their current prosperity depended on the Saints remaining in Kirtland, a direct contradiction to a commandment of God.

\* \* \*

"Ben, come walk with me," Almon invited after supper. Benjamin glanced at Julianne, who was taking a load of dishes into the kitchen. She had been uncharacteristically quiet all day. Esther was away, spending the evening with their father.

"Perhaps Juli would like to go with us," Benjamin suggested.

"No. Just the two of us this time," Almon said quietly. "I've been so busy that we've scarcely had time to talk." Then he called out, "Darling, Ben and I are going on a walk. You don't mind, do you?"

"Of course not," Julianne called back.

The two left the house and walked briskly. The evening was cool and inviting. The temple rose into the sky; the trees were brilliant with color.

Almon swept his arm out. "I don't love any place so much as Kirtland."

Benjamin looked toward the flats, toward the hill where his brothers and sisters were buried. "I feel the past when I'm here. So many memories."

"The future is here too," Almon said. "I've been meaning to ask you what you thought of my discourse at conference yesterday."

Benjamin hesitated for a moment then said, "I liked what you said about the poor being our most important item of business, that without charity, our professions are vain, our teachings are vain, our religion is vain. That pure religion and undefiled before God is to visit the fatherless and widows in their affliction."

Almon smiled. "Helping the poor is my first priority. Speaking of priorities, it's good to know that you were able to listen to my discourse with Miss LeBaron next to you."

Not quite ready to discuss Melissa LeBaron, Benjamin turned the tide back to Almon's discourse. "By the way, I thought the announcement about the *Olive Leaf* publication interesting. However, you told me that Church funds are low with so many poor converts coming to Kirtland."

"The bishops' storehouse will continue to help the poor. The elders quorum will solicit separate donations for the *Olive Leaf*."

Benjamin glanced at Almon. "But aren't all additional donations supposed to be sent to Nauvoo for the temple fund?"

"Though the Nauvoo Temple is a priority, so is missionary work," Almon replied cheerfully. "The *Olive Leaf* can spread the gospel farther and faster through the medium of mail than any orator at the pulpit."

"I suppose," Benjamin said, unconvinced. Yet Almon was the stake president. Benjamin decided to change the subject. "How do you like the merchandizing business? I thought you were set on practicing law."

Almon grinned. "I wanted to discuss that with you. If you marry Miss LeBaron, *the heiress*, I could sell my store to you and set up a law practice with the proceeds. You would have two blessings in one."

"You seem to be hurrying my blessings."

"Come, Ben." Almon put his arm on Benjamin's shoulders. "You suffered a great deal in Missouri. And you cared for the sick in Kirtland's Camp and Nauvoo. Isn't it time for your happiness? Perhaps Miss LeBaron is a blessing from the Lord. Setting the money aside, she's a beautiful young lady of culture and refinement and a good Latter-day Saint. She is worthy of you and you of her."

Benjamin studied the maple tree up ahead, so brilliant in the lowering sun that it nearly looked like it was on fire. Yet in a matter of weeks, it would be bare. Although very attracted to Melissa, he could not forget the other women he had loved, the fire inside of him that had left him with nothing.

Almon broke Benjamin's silence. "Tell me truthfully, Ben. What are your feelings for Melissa LeBaron?"

Benjamin turned to his friend. "I believe I could love her, but other girls have professed their love then left me alone."

Almon laughed. "Ben, my boy, every man ought to have his heart broken at least once. But I'd bet my entire fortune that Miss LeBaron will not break yours."

Benjamin couldn't help but grin. "For a shot at your entire fortune, I'll give it a try."

\* \* \*

After putting the kitchen in order, Julianne sat on the parlor sofa in front of the hearth with her legs curled beneath her. She and Almon had kissed when he'd left this morning and when he'd returned in the evening—just like they did every day. Yet she could still feel the distance between them. How long would they both continue to act as if their conversation last night had never occurred?

Then Julianne took out the letter from Almera that Elder Barnes had dropped by that afternoon on his way east. She had been the only one home and had not told Almon or her siblings about it. It was just that she wanted to read it alone first. Julianne broke the seal and became immersed in Almera's round, flowing script.

*Dearest Sister,*

*I hope this letter finds you well. We received word from Benjamin a few weeks ago saying that he's going to Kirtland after his mission. Hopefully he is there with you now. Tell Papa and Benja how much I love them. I'll never forget what they did for me. Almon too—he's a blessing to us all. Tell Esther I love her and hope that she is happy, healthy, and taking good care of Father.*

*Juli, I'm so grateful to be here. I'm surrounded by Mama and the family. I feared that I might never have so much goodness again in this life. You mentioned in your last letter that I might want to marry again someday. I don't think so. For now, I am content to worship with the Saints, to listen to the Prophet, and to freely associate with beloved family and friends. I have Coattails too—my little friend. Thank Almon again for letting him travel with us.*

*We are well here, except for Amos, who continues to suffer from pain and weakness in his hips and legs. Mother worries about him constantly. Mary and George Wilson are fervently in love. Our George is courting a Southern belle named Marie Johnston. George writes her love poems that he hides from us.*

*Then there is Will. When not working, he is entertaining Amos. He often takes him to Nauvoo to watch the Legion drill. Will looks forward to the day when he is allowed to join the Legion.*

*We have two more nieces. Nancy Maria was born to Joel and Susan on August second. Our dear eldest sister now has a namesake. Then on September twenty-fourth, Mary Julia was born to Joe and Harriet, named after both her grandmothers. Joe teased Harriet, saying that our side of the family will only call her Julia, while Harriet's side forever will call her Mary. The poor little thing will be the center of a feud. However, after a lively discussion, we all settled on calling her Marge.*

*Now I must pen the news that I fear will grieve you. Perhaps you have already heard. Don Carlos Smith died from malarial fever on August seventh. All of Nauvoo mourned. To get through the funeral, I imagined Carlos embracing our brother David in heaven. I hope this news doesn't weigh you and Almon down too much. We are so fortunate to have the hope of eternal life. My beloved sister, I miss you and yearn for the day when we'll see each other again.*

*Your loving sister and friend,*
*Almera*

Julianne held the letter close as she looked into the fire. She thought of the new babies born to her brothers' wives and of her own empty womb. She closed her eyes, picturing David and Don Carlos together in heaven, both handsome and tall, brimming with life. Then she thought of Agnes, Carlos's wife, and her three little girls. She thought of the distance between herself and Almon. As a tear crept down her cheek, she did not know if she grieved for the dead or for the living.

# 18

*Again I lived those happy hours,*
*And roamed with thee 'mid springing flowers*
*When your kind word, or fond embrace,*
*For cares or sorrow left no place,*
*And all was joy.*

Benjamin Franklin Johnson

*November 1841. Kirtland, Ohio*

ALMON TOOK THE LETTER FROM Hyrum Smith back after allowing Julianne and Benjamin to read it. He read it once more as a tidal wave of fury and helplessness rose within him. He had been disfellowshipped again, but that was not the full force of the storm. All the faithful would leave Kirtland. He would be broken up in business before his debts were paid. He was ruined at the hands of the leadership of the Church he loved and served.

> *To the Saints in Kirtland,*
> *All the Saints that dwell in that land are commanded to come away, for this is "Thus saith the Lord"; therefore pay out no moneys, nor properties for houses, nor lands in that country, for if you do, you will lose them. And as to the design of the leading members as to the printing press, this is not according to the will of God; for they have neglected the house of the Lord in Nauvoo, the baptismal font, wherein their dead may be redeemed, where the key of knowledge may be turned, and the mysteries of God unfolded, upon which their*

*salvation and the salvation of the world and the redemption of their dead depend for "thus saith the Lord." If we are not diligent in this, the Church shall be rejected and their dead also. Therefore, dear brethren, any proceedings of the Saints otherwise shall not prosper; therefore, tarry not, but come forth unto this place from all the world, until it is filled up and polished and sanctified according to my word; therefore your doings and your organizations and designs in printing, or any of your counsels, are not of me, saith the Lord. Even so, amen.*

Julianne sat down in a chair. Benjamin broke the silence as Almon crumpled the letter in his hand. "What are you going to do?"

"What am I going to do? I'm ruined. What can I do but turn my heel against Joseph and Hyrum? Call due all the debts I've bought up for them. That would pay for some of my losses, maybe allow me to buy a small law library in Kirtland, free from them forever!"

"Please, Almon," Julianne reached out her arms, begging. "Don't talk like this."

"Talk!" Almon's anger crescendoed. "Don't you understand? Joseph and Hyrum have ruined us. They have stolen our prosperity and our home. Do you think I will sit by idly and allow that to happen?"

Julianne began to weep. Almon shouted, "Quit your tears and bear this with me!"

"I cannot—bear you." Julianne hurriedly left the room, crying.

Almon turned to Benjamin, shouting, "Go! Comfort my wife! Will I lose her too? The entire family?"

"No," Benjamin roared. "Don't you understand? You'll never lose us. Julianne loves you. I love you. We all love you. Don't do this to yourself!"

Benjamin's outburst stunned Almon. With fists clenched, he strode across the room and pushed the letter into Benjamin's hand as if it were a hot coal. "Take this," he said. "Tell Brother Phelps to read it at the meeting tomorrow. I won't be there." Then Almon turned and strode out into the night without a coat, slamming the door behind him.

\* \* \*

Almon walked for hours in the dark, freezing drizzle. He walked around the temple, past the small house he and Julianne had lived in when they had a son. He had buried his baby boy in that yard. Tears mingled with the rain as he stared at the small gravestone. Then he walked to the dark brickyard, where he had worked side by side with the men he loved, the men who were now dead. He turned and ran toward the Kirtland Flats, past the sawmill, schoolhouse, and orchard to the two-story house where Julianne's family had lived. No candlelight winked in the windows, no gray steam rose from the roof. Had the new residents left for the season? Almon climbed the sloping hill where David's and Seth's bodies lay. The rain stung his bare cheeks and hands.

"David! Seth! Lyman! Don Carlos!" he shouted into the wind. "We burned bricks together! Here! In Kirtland! David, you wielded that scythe to save my life! Seth! I dragged you into that river so that cholera would not kill you. I brought you back here! Here! To Kirtland! Lyman! We beheld the fire of the temple dedication! And you sang in tongues! Here! And Don Carlos." Almon moaned. "My friend Carlos. The river scourge killed you. We were boys together! I watched you become a high priest. I watched you lay the cornerstones of this temple. But you lied to me! You all died and left me alone. And Carlos, your brothers ruined me. Every one of you made me believe Mormon boys stick together! No more!" Almon bowed his head, his tears falling in the night.

Time passed. Almon did not know if it was thirty minutes or two hours. He only knew the dark rain had turned to snow, covering the graves. Then a shout rose above the wind. "Who's up there?" He saw the shape of a gun pointed at him; it was blacker than the night or the figure that held it. He knew the voice and the gun.

"It's Almon Babbitt," he shouted back.

The gun lowered, and the man trudged up the hill. "Son, what in hades are you doing here on a night like this?"

Almon shivered. "Talking to the dead."

Ezekiel stripped off his coat and put it around Almon's shoulders.

"You'll freeze," Almon said.

"If you die from exposure, my daughter will be a widow," Ezekiel returned. "At least I have a hat on."

Soaked from the rain and snow, the edges of Ezekiel's hat had begun to freeze. On any other night, Almon would have laughed. "How did you know I was here?" he asked.

"If I knew it was you, I wouldn't have nearly shot you. I just dropped Esther off at your house and decided to stop here before going to Mentor. Sometimes I come when no one else would be fool enough to go out in the weather. I talk to my children. I didn't think any other man was fool enough to do the same thing."

"We are such fools; you'd think we were blood relations," Almon said.

Ezekiel snorted at the irony then said gently, "Come on, son. My buggy's down the hill. I'll take you home."

Fifteen minutes later, when Almon walked in the door, he saw Julianne cuddled up on the chair near the hearth, where embers continued to glow. Tearstains glistened on her cheeks. Almon gently touched her shoulder. She opened her eyes and reached both arms up to him. He bent down, cradling her in his arms.

"You're so cold," she whispered as she clung to him. He held her tightly until they both stopped shaking.

\* \* \*

In the wee hours of the morning, Almon lay asleep beside Julianne. He dreamed that he was young again, back in the Kirtland brickyard, piling green wood into ovens. But he couldn't keep the fires stoked; each brick he touched crumbled. Where were his friends? They ought to be helping. He suddenly realized they were dead. When he was about to weep with despair, they came in view, approaching him—David, Seth, Lyman, and Don Carlos. *It's finished here*, they said. *Go westward to the temple of the Lord, where blessings await the living and the dead, where Mormon boys stand together, wielding the priesthood of God forever.* Almon opened his hands to explain, to debate, to make them understand that Kirtland had a temple.

He awakened with a jerk.

"Are you all right?" Julianne whispered.

Almon nodded and stared at his hands, open and empty above the bed covers. Would he follow his friends? Or would he be the Mormon boy without the strength to stick with them?

\* \* \*

Esther knew it wasn't right to peek through keyholes, but she needed to know what was going on. She hesitated. Benjamin had shut the door so he could be alone with Melissa in the parlor. Their voices were too low to hear. Esther crouched down and peeked through anyway. They were sitting very close together on the sofa. Esther stood back up. This wasn't helping any.

She thought about last night. It had been past ten when Papa had brought her back to Kirtland. Even through the howling wind, she had been warm cuddled against him in the carriage. When she arrived, Julianne and Benjamin were talking in the parlor, but they stopped when she entered the room. Esther knew Julianne had been crying.

Julianne had simply said that she and Almon had argued, but she was sure everything would turn out all right. It was time for bed now. Benjamin had read a passage in the Bible, and they had said a prayer together. Julianne had taken out her knitting and said she was going to sit up and wait for Almon. When Esther had offered to sit up with her, Julianne had insisted she go to bed. Benjamin had even had the gall to command her like she was a child. Esther had relented because she didn't want to make a scene and be sent back to Nauvoo. She hadn't forgotten the lesson learned when Joe was schoolmaster.

Then this morning Almon and Julianne had not gone to the meeting with Benjamin and her. Before the meeting began, Benjamin had whispered something to Brother Phelps and handed him a wrinkled piece of paper. He had read it from the pulpit. The paper was a letter from Hyrum Smith, and it commanded all the Saints in Kirtland, in the name of the Lord, to go to Nauvoo. Esther had immediately looked across the hall at the LeBarons. David had smiled at her then looked down. Hard resolve had filled Esther. She didn't care if Julianne and Almon moved back to Nauvoo. She would stay in Kirtland as long as her papa and David LeBaron were here.

Suddenly an idea came to Esther, and she squatted back down to the keyhole. Instead of peeking through the keyhole, she put her ear to it. She heard Melissa's radiant voice. "Of course I will go to Nauvoo in the spring." Esther turned quickly and looked. Benjamin put his arm around Melissa and kissed her.

\*\*\*

Esther pulled her coat on and snuck out the back door. The sun was bright, but there was snow on the ground. She ran all the way to the LeBarons'. David's seven-year-old niece, Harriet, was playing outside. Harriet joyfully ran up to Esther and hugged her. Esther embraced the little girl. "Is David home?"

"Yes, but not Melissa," Harriet chatted. "But you can come in my house anyway."

"I-I can't come in today," Esther said. "But would you see if David would come out here and talk with me?" Harriet nodded and ran toward the house.

A moment later, David came out in his shirtsleeves, oblivious to the cold air. His blond hair shone in the bright, chill sunlight, and his olive skin reminded Esther of summer more than winter. He was so beautiful that Esther wished she could just kiss him. David grinned and jogged over to her. "How's the prettiest girl in Kirtland?" he asked.

"Worried because of the announcement in conference," Esther said.

"What's Brother Almon going to do?" David asked as his smile faded. "Naomi and James are worried that he feels hurt. The Saints here think the world of him. Will he go to Nauvoo?"

Esther shrugged miserably. She didn't want to tell David that Almon and Julianne still saw her as a child and hadn't discussed anything with her. Only David and Melissa treated her as if she were grown-up and equal to them. "I don't know. He and Julianne went on a sleigh ride and still aren't home. Melissa is with Benjamin right now. They're in the parlor. Melissa said that she is going to Nauvoo in the spring. Benjamin is going too. I know my mother's going to send for me. What will you do?" Esther felt tears spring to her eyes. She blinked hard.

David took her hand. "I'll go to Nauvoo because the Lord commanded it. And we will see each other there. I promise." David took hold of her other hand too. "Why are you sad? Perhaps your mother won't be as strict as your brother. I would like to sit on a sofa with you in front of a warm fire."

Esther wiped her tears and held David's hands tightly. "Because my father is here, and I promised him I would never leave him again. What am I to do?"

David leaned close and kissed Esther's cheek. "Talk to your father. Try to get him to come to Nauvoo too."

\* \* \*

*December 25, 1841. Kirtland, Ohio*

Melissa arrived at the Babbitts' at five o'clock on Christmas morning. It was dark outside, and her breath steamed in the cold air. Esther answered her soft knock and pulled her inside, hugging her warmly. Esther was a dark-eyed beauty—intelligent, spirited, expressive, and sweet-natured, all rolled into one. No wonder David was determined to wait until she grew up to marry. Melissa smelled the pine wreaths hung in the hallways and parlor. The entryway was cold, but there was light coming from the kitchen where the hearth blazed.

"Is Benjamin back?" Melissa whispered, knowing that her fiancé had spent the night at his father's.

Esther shook her head. "No. Fortunately. It's terrible luck for the bride to see the groom before the ceremony on their wedding day. Are you nervous?"

"A little," Melissa admitted. Her cheeks were pink with excitement. "But Naomi is worse. She woke up an hour ago to make more trifles. She thinks a hundred people will come."

"Juli too. She was up late making rolls and preparing sweetmeats. Where are the roses?"

"David's waiting in the carriage with them."

"You brought David? I'll help him carry them in while you put warm water in the vases," Esther exclaimed as she quickly ran out the front door. Melissa shook her head. Keeping Esther and David apart was like keeping bees from honey.

"Are you sure this will work?" Esther asked when the three were in the kitchen and the vases were ready.

Melissa nodded. "Yes. I read about it and preserved one rose last year. Naomi and I decided to do sixty this year so we'd have a house full of roses at Christmas."

"Every drawer in the house had a box of roses in it last summer. It kept the drawers from stinking," David added.

"It kept *David's* drawers from stinking," Melissa corrected.

Esther giggled.

A few minutes later, at the table, Melissa unwrapped the first rose from its paper cocoon-like case. Esther watched carefully. David, of course, was watching Esther. Melissa explained, "Now that the rose is exposed to air, the trick is to handle it as little as possible and get it into the water as quickly as possible."

"Don't you need to take the sealing wax off the end of the stem?" Esther asked as Melissa put the bud in one of the six vases of warm water.

"No, you have to leave it on. I don't know why. Let's get the others into the water."

Esther looked doubtful as they unwrapped the sixty roses. When they were finished, she blurted, "These just look like old buds that were picked ages ago, before they had the chance to bloom. Melissa, do you seriously want these at your wedding?"

Melissa smiled. "Just wait a couple of hours, and they'll open up and smell and look wonderful."

David put his arm around Esther. "Oh ye of little faith."

Then the group heard a noise at the front door. "It's Ben!" Esther moaned. "He's seen your buggy. Melissa, hide in the pantry! David and I will distract him while you run out the back door."

Suppressing a giggle, Melissa went into the pantry and pulled the door closed, leaving just a crack to look out. Esther grabbed David's hand and pulled him into the parlor, where she sat down on the couch with him and put his arm around her shoulder.

Benjamin walked in, puzzled. "Is Melissa here?"

"Hello, Ben," Esther exclaimed loudly, drawing Benjamin's attention as dawn light crept in through the parlor window. "Of course she isn't here. You can't see her before the wedding. It would spoil everything!" As Benjamin walked into the parlor, Melissa left the pantry and deftly tiptoed down the hall. But before going out the back door, she stood in the dark hallway and listened to Benjamin confront her brother. "David, what are you doing here alone with Esther so early in the morning on my wedding day?"

David answered sheepishly, "Melissa asked me to bring the roses. They have to sit a few hours before they bloom. Esther was kind enough to help me put them in the vases."

"That's hardly a fellow's job. Esther, you should have awakened Julianne to help."

"Oh, Ben, Juli has enough to do today," Esther retorted.

All was quiet for an instant before David added, "Well the job's done, so I'd best be going. Merry Christmas, Esther. Ben, we'll be brothers in a few hours."

Benjamin's voice sounded more relaxed as he returned, "Wish Melissa a good morning from me, and tell her that I can scarcely wait for this afternoon." Then Benjamin turned to Esther. "And you, little sister, are not a rose. You have more to do than sit on the sofa and wait until you bloom."

"She's already bloomed," David added and was out the door before Benjamin could respond.

\* \* \*

Ezekiel sat in the front row between Esther and Julianne as he watched Almon perform the marriage of Benjamin and Melissa. There were white roses in vases throughout the house. How could that be in the middle of winter? The room was crowded with over a hundred people. Benjamin stood handsome and tall, filling Ezekiel with pride. Furthermore, he had always liked Melissa—lovely and queenly with her own spirit. Her father had died a long time ago. Yesterday, she had asked him if she could call him *Father* now. He had told her that a man couldn't have too many daughters.

After the ceremony, Ezekiel stood back from the festivities, keeping his eye on Benjamin and Melissa. They were so beautiful, dancing together. Then the single people went into the kitchen while Benjamin and Melissa went into the parlor to mingle with the married couples. David LeBaron left the single group with Esther on his arm. They said Benjamin and Melissa still belonged to the singles, as they were only wed for a matter of hours. The married couples opposed. A lighthearted tug-of-war ensued with Benjamin as the rope. The single group took hold of one of Benjamin's arms and the married group the other. There was a great deal of laughter until Melissa insisted it stop before her husband was pulled speechless. Then both parties clapped and cheered, demanding the bride and groom kiss. During the kiss, Ezekiel saw David LeBaron steal a quick kiss from Esther.

Then there was a tap on Ezekiel's shoulder. "Merry Christmas, Zeke," Almon said, handing him a glass of cider.

"Merry Christmas, son," Ezekiel returned.

"To the happy couple," Almon said as he lifted his glass. Ezekiel raised his drink, and the glasses chimed together. "Do you think Mother Johnson would approve of Miss LeBaron?" Almon asked.

Ezekiel took a deep breath. "Yes, Julia would approve."

Almon raised his glass once more. "Then to better days," Almon said.

"To better days," Ezekiel repeated.

\* \* \*

*January 1842. Kirtland, Ohio*

"Almon," Benjamin said as he went into the Babbitts' kitchen and found Almon at the table surrounded by ledgers, notes, and receipts.

"What is it?" Almon asked as he continued to look down and scrawl figures on one of the ledgers.

Benjamin plunged in. "Melissa and I have rented a carriage and are leaving Monday to go to Rochester to obtain her inheritance. We hope you and Julianne will agree to come with us."

Almon looked up. "Why would a couple like you want companions? This is a wedding trip."

Benjamin grinned encouragingly. "Because you and Juli are so amiable that the trip would be more enjoyable."

There was an ironic twist to Almon's smile when he responded. "Come, Ben. You are now a young man with means, and I'm a floundering fellow who is closing up business. There won't be much left when I'm through unless I call the Prophet's notes due. Which could cost me my membership in the Church and my marriage. I don't enjoy my own company right now and doubt anyone else will."

Benjamin swallowed, his smile fading. "I have a proposal. Next season, when Melissa and I join the Saints, we're going to settle in Ramus near Mother. I recently received a letter from Joe. The town is growing fast. They are in great need of a merchandizing store. I don't have the knowledge of goods or know-how to organize and run a business. If I supply the capital, would you consider being my business partner? That is, if you decide to leave Kirtland and reconcile with Brother Joseph."

Almon's head cocked as he looked at Benjamin. "You are determined to save my soul, aren't you?"

Benjamin smiled. "Yes. If it's possible."

Almon's green eyes softened. "And this is the boy I taught how to preach. That I taught how to debate. You've grown up well, my friend. Ben, tell me more about what you're thinking."

Benjamin grinned and pressed both hands into the table. "This is how I see it. In the spring, I will take Melissa, Julianne, Esther, and our belongings overland to Ramus, while you go by water to Cincinnati and St. Louis to buy the goods we need to start business. While you're in Cincinnati, buy books for a law library; I'll go in half. "

"Why would you want do to that? Are you interested in the law?"

"Somewhat. And Melissa insists that we don't put all our eggs in one basket."

Almon sat quietly for a moment. He closed his eyes. When he opened them, he looked hard at Benjamin. "You are more than a younger brother to me. You are my friend and confidant. I would advise you not to make any decisions just because of me. Make sure they are good for you and Melissa. Think about why you are offering so much."

Benjamin's answer came forthwith. "I'm offering this because you are the smartest man I know, and I need your help. I trust you as an elder brother. Years ago, here in Kirtland, you taught me two things: to base decisions on what matters most and that Mormon boys stick together."

Almon swallowed. He tightened his jaw to keep it from quivering. "There will be many details to work out."

"We'll discus them on the way to Rochester. Will you come?" Benjamin asked once more.

Almon nodded. "Yes, Ben. We'll come."

\* \* \*

*January 12, 1842*

"Papa!" Esther exclaimed as she burst into her father's house early Wednesday morning. Windblown, with her cheeks flushed and dark hair falling out of her bun, she exclaimed, "Papa, where are you? Do you know what today is?"

Ezekiel came out of the bedroom, yawning and disheveled. "Of course I know. You are fifteen today."

"And you are sixty-nine. It's our birthday!" Esther responded.

Ezekiel did not mention that it was also his and Julia's forty-first anniversary.

"It is," Ezekiel nodded as tears welled up in Esther's eyes. "Sweetheart, what's wrong? You aren't worried about your papa growin' old, are you?"

"Of course," Esther said and stomped her foot. "That's not all of it. Ben, Julianne, and Almon are all moving to Ramus. They said that I have to go with them. What are we going to do?" Esther put her arms around his neck and buried her head in his chest. He patted her back, treasuring her closeness, the fact that she loved him so much. He would carry it with him for the rest of his life. "Darlin', I knew this would happen. It was only a matter of time."

Esther threw her head back and looked at him. Wiping her tears with her sleeve, her brown eyes filled with fire. "Papa, are you going to give me up that easy? When I worked so hard to get here? When I promised I would never leave you?"

Ezekiel was taken aback. Did she really intend to stay here with him? He thought of Almera and what her life had been like in Kirtland. He would not saddle Esther to an old man. He looked directly in her eyes.

"You can't stay here. You belong with the Mormons in Illinois, with your mother and your young man."

Esther stepped back and looked at him squarely. "I made a promise. You always taught us not to go back on our promises. I will not go. I won't go unless you come too."

Ezekiel stared at his daughter. She was as stubborn as Julia and him put together. No wonder she was born on their wedding anniversary. She was young; she couldn't understand what it would be like for him—living so close to Julia but no longer having her for his own.

But that wasn't all of it. He would be near Joseph Smith and his people, vacillating between anger and respect, bitterness and love. He would never forget how Joseph had visited him after his son David died, had held Ezekiel in his arms when Ezekiel was half drunk and had wept with him. But he would also never forget how David had died from overwork on the temple and Seth because he went with Zion's Camp. His sons had died and Julia had left him because of Joseph's church.

"Sweetheart, it would be hard for me, being around your mother and the Mormons. Feeling like I'm never good enough."

"Isn't it harder being away from everyone?" Esther countered. "But it's your decision, Papa. I won't go though. I really won't go if you don't. And no one can make me."

Ezekiel looked into his daughter's eyes. She might throw tirades. She might be miserable, mourning for her beau. But she was his girl, born on his birthday. She had given her word and wasn't about to back down. He said gruffly. "I'll think on it. But know this, I won't have you stay here all alone with me, missing out on your life."

Esther plopped down on a chair, smoothed her skirt, and made herself comfortable. "I'll sit right here while you think on it, until you tell me one way or the other."

Dumbfounded, Ezekiel sat down across the room from her. Did young David LeBaron know what he was in for? Esther ought to understand that he had a business here, a means of living. Yet it meant little compared to his family. Only a weak man would follow a headstrong wife from one Mormon settlement to the next though. His wife? How could he even call her that when they had been separated for seven years? But their children and grandchildren were his still. He was almost seventy years old. Didn't he have the right to live near them before he died? Ezekiel cleared his throat. "I'll go."

Esther squealed in triumph and ran to him, kneeling at his feet. "Oh, Papa! I knew you would! This is the best birthday present in the world."

"No," he said as he stroked her hair. "You were the best birthday present in the world."

# 19

*The smile of love's a beam of light*
*That lifts the soul on high;*
*A heartfelt token of delight*
*That softens every sign.*

Joel Hills Johnson

*February 7, 1842. Ramus, Illinois*

JULIA SAT BETWEEN AMOS AND Almera. About thirty additional guests gathered in Joel and Susan's parlor. Joel stood in the front of the room by a window, ready to officiate in the marriage of his sister Mary Johnson and George Wilson. A hush fell over the gathering. Mary walked to the front of the room, with Joe escorting her.

Outside, dark clouds crowded the dreary sky, but Mary's hair hung in shiny blonde ringlets down her back. Her high cheekbones shone pink with excitement. She wore a white dress, high-collared, with a white silk bodice and a full skirt. She had sewn it with Julia and Almera's help. Smiling at Julia, Mary's brown eyes filled with tenderness and gratitude.

The ceremony passed quickly. George, with his native shyness, held Mary's hand gently. After they were pronounced man and wife, he kissed her quickly. Afterward, the guests crowded around the couple to congratulate them. When it was Julia's turn, she held her beautiful daughter close. "I am so happy for you," she whispered.

"Me too, Mama," Mary replied.

Then Julia embraced her new son-in-law, noticing how warm and loving his eyes looked.

A moment later, Amos touched Julia's arm. "Mother, I need to go home." Even through the fabric of her sleeve, Julia felt the heat in Amos's hand. The fever had returned, worse this time. There were shadows of exhaustion under her youngest son's eyes. He ate little and seemed more spirit and less body with each passing day.

"Of course," Julia said. "Sit down for a moment while I tell your sisters." Julia went into the kitchen, where Almera, Mary Ann, Susan, and Delcena were putting out the refreshments. She quickly explained that Amos wasn't feeling well.

Julia donned her cloak. With Amos slumped against her, shivering and limping, they walked the short distance to her house. He had recently turned thirteen but was still her little boy, her baby. She feared that he would not be with her long. The fever came and went, worse each time. The sciatic rheumatism crippled him.

When they were home, she helped Amos to bed. He looked at her, his eyes very serious. "When I die someday, will I be able to run again?"

"Yes, when we are resurrected, our spirits will once again be tabernacled in bodies, like the Angel Moroni. You will be able to run without pain or weariness."

Amos nodded. "What about before the resurrection, when I am a spirit?"

"Brother Joseph teaches that spirits are as beautiful as flaming fire," Julia said.

"Then I believe I shall be able to fly," Amos whispered.

While Amos slept, Julia added wood to the kitchen fire. Afterward, she sat at the desk and took a recent letter from Kirtland out of the drawer. She reread Julianne and Esther's words describing Benjamin's wedding and the roses his bride, Melissa, had preserved and put in water. The roses had opened up and filled the house with the smell of summer. Julia scarcely remembered Melissa LeBaron from the Kirtland days and wondered if Benjamin's bride would bring him happiness. Then she read again the last line of Julianne's letter, where Julianne said that they would move to Ramus in the spring. Next to those words, Esther had scribbled, *and Father is coming with us.*

Julia took out a pen and paper. She wrote her daughters, describing Mary's wedding and saying that Amos was very ill. Setting the pen down, she felt inexplicably tired. Would Amos still be alive when they received the letter? Would Ezekiel see his youngest again?

\* \* \*

*April 28, 1842. Nauvoo, Illinois*

After feeding her children lunch, Delcena took out the thick black syrupy medicine and poured a spoonful. Three-year-old Susan sat perched on the counter. "Not like it!" she squealed and sealed her small hand tightly over her mouth. Delcena considered her options. She could pry Susan's hand off her mouth or plug her nose to force her mouth open.

"Are you ready to go?" Delcena's sister-in-law Cornelia called from the adjacent room, where she waited with Lyman's mother, Asenath Sherman. The meeting of the Female Relief Society of Nauvoo was scheduled to begin in twenty minutes.

"Almost," Delcena called back anxiously. "If Susan would just take her medicine."

Asenath came into the kitchen to help.

With tears in her brown eyes and her hand still covering her mouth, Susan reached an arm out to her grandmother.

"Oh, my poor baby girl," Asenath crooned as she picked Susan up from the tabletop. She hugged her as she sat down in a kitchen chair. "Darling, give Grandmother a kiss." Susan shook her head, not moving her hand, then wiggled out of Asenath's lap and ran into the back of the house. Asenath chuckled. "Delcena, she's too smart for us. But she looks like she's getting better."

"She is," Delcena agreed. "But she's still supposed to take the medicine three times a day."

"I doubt one missed dose will hurt."

Delcena sighed. "If she gets away with it now, it will be impossible later."

"Losing one battle does not mean the war is lost," Asenath remarked encouragingly. "We'll outsmart her. I'll come at bedtime and help you give her the medicine."

Cornelia stuck her head in the kitchen. "Hurry, or we'll be late. I just checked on the children. They're fine."

Ten minutes later, at the meeting, Delcena listened attentively as the Prophet Joseph spoke. He described blessings and gifts of the priesthood which would be bestowed on women as they led virtuous lives and kept the commandments. But then he said that he would not long have opportunities to instruct the ladies, that the Church would not have him long. A lump formed in Delcena's throat, and her recurring fear surfaced. They needed Brother Joseph; surely the Lord would not take him.

Joseph continued confidently, almost as if the previous statement was of little importance. He spoke of delivering the keys of the priesthood to the Church and explained that the faithful members of the Relief Society should receive them in connection with their husbands. "And now I turn the key in your behalf in the name of the Lord," the Prophet declared. "This Society shall rejoice, and knowledge and intelligence shall flow down from this time henceforth; this is the beginning of better days to the poor and needy who shall be made to rejoice and pour forth blessings on your heads." The meaning of the Prophet's words filled Delcena. Whether the time was short or long, the time with Brother Joseph was a time to rejoice.

Following the meeting, Cornelia and Asenath decided to walk to the store on Water Street to buy cloth. Not wanting to leave the children alone any longer, Delcena declined the invitation to go with them. As she walked, the late afternoon sun lingered in the sky.

She had not walked far when Mayor John Bennett fell in step beside her. "Good afternoon, Widow Sherman," he greeted. His restless dark eyes darted up and down the street. Seeing no one near, he placed his hand on her arm, detaining her. He smiled and added, "I noticed you walking out of the Relief Society meeting this afternoon. I would like to speak with you alone and tell you about other teachings of the Prophet."

With his hand on her arm, Delcena felt uncomfortable. She had heard a strange rumor a few days ago about Mayor Bennett. Sister Miller, a young widow, had come over to her house very distraught. A man, whom Sister Miller would not name, had approached her. The man had claimed that General Bennett taught him that illicit relationships between men and women outside of marriage were allowed by God. Delcena then told Sister Miller that the man must have lied and wanted to take advantage of her. She suggested Sister Miller tell the Prophet or a member of the high council immediately.

But had the man been lying? Suddenly something felt wrong, terribly wrong. Delcena took a step away from General Bennett. "Sir, my little girl is sick. I need to get home and attend to her." With a pounding heart, she walked away quickly, without waiting for a reply or looking back. Fortunately, Bennett did not follow her. Why did his words make her feel so afraid?

When she arrived at home, the children demanded her attention. They had been drawing in the dirt with sticks and wanted to show her their pictures. Susan coughed and whined. Albey claimed to be starving. Delcena picked Susan up and told the children to wash up for supper.

An hour later, after they had eaten, there was a knock at the door. John Bennett's secretive comments entered Delcena's mind, and she felt momentarily worried. Then she remembered Asenath promising to come over to help give Susan her medicine. With Susan whining and tugging on her skirt, Delcena made her way to the door and opened it. Brother Joseph stood on the porch. He held a bag in his hands. "Sister Delcena," he said, "I saw Sister Asenath at the store. She has been detained." Then he looked down at Susan and reached his arm out. "So I've come to speak with little Susan myself."

Susan stopped whining and reached up for Brother Joseph. He scooped her up with one hand. Albey, from the kitchen doorway, shouted to the others that Brother Joseph had come. Within seconds, all of Delcena's children were gathered on the porch around the Prophet. Delcena noticed how dirty her boys' feet and knees were.

The Prophet sat down on the porch bench with Susan on his lap. "Now children," the Prophet said, "someday I will bring a surprise for each of you, but tonight I only have one for little Susan because she is youngest and she is sick. Do you understand?"

The children nodded.

Joseph opened a bag and showed Susan a lovely little bowl, decorated with the alphabet. The Prophet went on. "Susan, I've brought this for you and want to give it to you. Do you like it?"

Susan nodded and reached for it. Joseph held it out of reach. "But I'm only allowed to give it to you if you take your medicine. Will you please?"

Susan nodded emphatically.

"Bet she won't," six-year-old Seth declared.

Alvira hushed him.

Delcena hurried into the kitchen and came back with a spoonful of the dark liquid. Susan opened her mouth, swallowed it, and smiled.

"Good girl! Will you take your medicine every day?" Joseph asked. Susan nodded. Joseph placed the dish in her hands and kissed her forehead.

"Brother Joseph, if I don't take my medicine, will you come over with a pony?" ten-year-old Albey asked with a glint in his eye.

"Albey, don't you dare," Joseph said, laughing heartily. Alvira put her hands on her hips and said that she would take lobelia for a new dress, and Mary offered to drink poison if Brother Joseph brought her a lamb.

"If you ask for things, Brother Joseph might not visit again," Delcena warned.

"Not visit the smartest, wittiest youngsters I've yet encountered? Never." Joseph chuckled.

"Now it's time for these witty children to get ready for bed," Delcena said. She asked Alvira and Mary to take the little ones inside to wash while Albey fed the animals.

The Prophet offered to help Albey, but Delcena interrupted. "Brother Joseph, could I speak with you for a moment?"

"Of course," Joseph said.

As the daylight dimmed, Delcena told the Prophet about her encounter with John Bennett and the rumor she had heard the previous week.

Deep concern filled Joseph's eyes. "What you heard was not a rumor. John Bennett's iniquities have come to my attention. His lies and sins have hurt many in Nauvoo. When confronted, he begged me not to expose him publicly and I believed he was repentant. I forgave him and prayed for his salvation. But alas, he did not repent. Soon the high council will meet, and a court will be convened. I'm sorry that you were exposed to this."

"I'm sorry too. For all of Nauvoo," Delcena managed.

Joseph took a deep breath. "Sister Delcena, I have resolved to look forward, not backward. The Lord has revealed to me the ordinance of celestial marriage. It is a holy priesthood ordinance performed in the temple, where a man and wife can be sealed together, enabling them to enter the highest degree of the celestial kingdom and have eternal life as husband and wife. When the time comes, I will stand as proxy, and you will be sealed to Lyman for time and all eternity."

Delcena felt tears burn her eyes. Was John Bennett's fall part of Satan's plan to hinder this holy ordinance?

The Prophet continued. "You will be blessed with comfort, joy, and the assurance that you will be with Lyman and your posterity forever."

\* \* \*

*Mid-June 1842. Ramus, Illinois*

In the late afternoon, weary from the long journey, Ezekiel drove the buggy toward the hamlet called Ramus. Trees as full as clouds billowed on the side of the road. Decorated with Queen Anne's Lace, the waist-high grass swayed in the breeze. Esther sat next to him. Benjamin led the way in the covered wagon, with Julianne and Melissa behind him, driving the span of horses that pulled the Babbitts' family carriage.

Esther excitedly pointed out landmarks. "There's Crooked Creek, where I reeled in Amos's fish. There's the hill where Mary Ann slipped and tore her dress."

Ezekiel nodded as he stared ahead, unable to concentrate on anything but the fact that Julia would be expecting them. Four days ago when they had arrived in Springfield to rest their teams, some Mormons Benjamin knew had been leaving. The men offered to stop in Ramus on their way to Nauvoo to tell Benjamin's family that the company would arrive in time for supper on Saturday night.

* * *

An hour later, they arrived at Julia's. People flocked out the door. Ezekiel hesitated a moment in the buggy, but Benjamin leapt out of the wagon seat, grabbed Melissa, and ran toward the crowd. Ezekiel watched Julia hug Melissa, her new daughter-in-law. Julia wore a light summer dress and a white apron. Her gray hair was pulled back in a bun. She was still lovely.

"Come on, Papa," Esther encouraged.

Ezekiel slowly climbed out of the buggy. It had now been four years since Julia had left, since he had seen most of his children. Joe made it to him first—his dear son, thinner than Ezekiel remembered and with lines of manhood on his brow.

Joe hugged him tightly. He had tears in his eyes when he said, "Pa, this is Harriet."

Ezekiel embraced her then touched the cheek of the blue-eyed baby girl.

An instant later, Mary stood in front of him, smiling as she introduced her husband, George Wilson. Ezekiel shook Wilson's hand. Then he hugged Mary, her cheeks apple red—like Nancy's used to be.

His son George shook his hand. "Hello, Pa." They were nearly the same height. It felt like looking back in time. George was so similar to the young man Ezekiel had been—the high cheekbones, the square jaw, and the deep-set eyes. "It's good to see you, son. It's been too long."

"Much too long, Pa. I'm glad you're back," George said.

"Where's Will and Amos?"

"I'm here, Pa." A young man walked up. Ezekiel might not have recognized him on the street. At eighteen years old, Will stood six feet tall and was handsome. He had wavy, slicked-back hair, and his eyes were shaped like Julia's but restless and ready—a young man's eyes.

Esther's cry broke into his thoughts. "Papa!" She cried and ran to him, sobbing. "Mama just told me. Amos is gone."

Will stepped back as Esther buried her head in her father's chest. With his arm around Esther, Ezekiel looked across the yard at Julia. Her jaw quivered. This should be a joyful homecoming, surrounded by children and grandchildren. But it was not. His chest ached, the pain deep and raw. "When? What happened?"

She took a step toward him, and he felt her grief. She spoke, her eyes as expressive, her voice as caring as the day he'd met her. "He died on May ninth at four in the afternoon," she said. "It was raining outside. The fever took his life. He never forgot about you. The day before his passing, he said, 'Tell Pa I'll be waiting.'" Her shoulders were straight, but she shook uncontrollably. Benjamin walked to her and put his arm around her. Julia leaned into him.

Ezekiel felt rage welling up in him, a scream of agony that he could not release. Bright and loveable Amos had been their darling. But Julia had taken Amos away when only nine years old. Ezekiel would never hear his voice or touch him again or see how much he had grown in the last four years.

Julia reached out her hand to him. "I prayed that he would live until you came home. But he was in pain, and God mercifully took him."

"Mercifully?" Ezekiel repeated, unable to keep the bitterness out of his voice. Then he saw the hurt in Julia's eyes, and he remembered the drunken rage that had enveloped him at Seth's death, how he had injured Julia, whom he loved most in the world. He had left her the next day so it would never happen again. But still, anger reared up within his chest. Shaking, he clenched his jaw. With every ounce of strength he possessed, Ezekiel dammed his emotions, dammed them against the rising tide, against Julia, against Joseph Smith, against the Church that bore the name of Christ and the title Mormon. But there was a price. The dark well of pain tore a hole in his soul.

The door of the house opened, and Almera and the orphan girl, Mary Ann Hale, came out. Almera looked from her father to her mother, her eyes soft and sad like she understood. She said quietly, "Supper is on the table; please come in and eat."

With his arm around Esther, Ezekiel followed his family into Julia's house. After supper, he rode into Carthage and rented a room at the tavern. He sat at a table and ordered enough drink to survive.

\*\*\*

*Cincinnati, Ohio*

Franklin Hills, a large, loose-muscled, cheerful man, sat down across from Almon at a table in Aunt Nancy's boardinghouse. An old friend of Almon's, Frank was Julianne's cousin and Caroline Hirst's brother. Almon had stopped in Cincinnati on his way to Nauvoo to buy merchandise and books. Frank had come to see Almon before he left the next day for Nauvoo. Almon put down the newspaper he had just unfolded and warmly shook Frank's hand. "It's good to see you!"

Frank grinned. "Likewise. I remember when we met ten years ago and the law school would have nothing to do with you, a poor Mormon boy. Now, here you are, a licensed attorney putting together his own law library."

"I'll hang out my shingle," Almon smiled. "We'll see if anyone knocks on my door."

Frank laughed. "I know you. You'll do more than that. You'll run for office and win. On a Democratic ticket, of course." Frank glanced at the newspaper on the table. "So why do you have a Whig newspaper? In honor of James and Caroline?"

"Ah, I wish the Hirsts were still here. I enjoyed our debates. But that's not the reason. A Mormon friend gave the paper to me earlier today. There's an article reprinted from the *Quincy Whig* about the attempted assassination of Lilburn Boggs."

"The former Missouri governor?"

Almon's voice hardened. "Yes. The man who ordered the extermination of my people."

"Who tried to kill him?"

Almon shook his head. "Probably a political rival. Boggs was in a dirty race for the Senate seat. But I haven't read the article yet. I was about to when you came."

Frank pushed his chair back. "Well, get on with it. I smell roast duck. I'll go chat with Aunt Nancy and see how dinner is coming. You can fill me in while we eat."

While Frank was gone, Almon read about the rainy night of May sixth when Boggs was reading the newspaper in his home in Independence. Someone fired through the window. The buckshot hit him in the back of the head, but he survived. The article continued, quoting John Bennett, a former intimate of Joseph Smith who had broken with him. Bennett claimed that Joseph Smith had given Porter Rockwell fifty dollars and a new carriage to take to Independence. It was a known fact that Rockwell was in Missouri when the deed was done.

Frank brought plates of roast duck and boiled potatoes. "What did you find out?" Frank sat down and took a bite.

Almon responded. "The paper hints of a conspiracy involving Joseph Smith. Missouri could try to extradite him again."

"Could he be guilty?"

Almon shook his head. "I don't think so. The Joseph I know was never a killer."

"Will you represent him?"

"If they take him to Missouri, he's beyond my reach. But I'll study the Nauvoo Charter and laws involving writs of habeas corpus on the boat." Almon fiddled a moment with his fork then added, "I don't know. Joseph and I have our own differences right now. He may not trust my advice, and I may not feel inclined to give it."

"It sounds like you're talking about an imperfect man, not a prophet."

"This prophet never claimed to be more than a man."

"But you still believe he's a prophet?"

Almon nodded. "A prophet, nonetheless."

\* \* \*

Benjamin arrived in Nauvoo late Friday afternoon after the long ride from Ramus. He stopped briefly at the Sniders' to refresh himself before continuing on to the Prophet's home on the banks of the Mississippi. Though a warm, pleasant day, billowing clouds gathered over the wide river. Benjamin felt a bit nervous. Almon would arrive in Nauvoo within the month, but Benjamin needed to talk with Brother Joseph before he came.

As he rode through the city, he marveled at the improvement—the swamps had been drained, fruit trees and brick homes dotted the streets. Benjamin had left Nauvoo a poor, sickly young man. Other Saints had been worse off, some living in tents and dying of malaria. Now he was back, a successful missionary with a lovely wife and the means to set up a business. It appeared that the Lord had blessed Nauvoo as much as He had blessed Benjamin.

He knocked on the Smiths' door. Joseph answered it, looking unusually tired. However, his eyes brightened when he saw Benjamin. He embraced him warmly. "Come sit with me, Bennie, and tell me how you are and what's on your mind."

In the Smiths' sitting room, Benjamin opened up completely, describing Almon's hurt and frustration. He talked about Almon's business dealings in Kirtland. Benjamin explained the notes that Almon had bought up, the debts against Joseph and the Church. Almon had done this to protect the Church; however, after his recent losses, he had been tempted to call them due. Yet Almon was a good man. Because of Benjamin and Julianne's urging, Almon was on his way to Nauvoo. Benjamin paused for a moment. This was the first time he had spoken with Joseph as one man to another, expressing his own opinions on sensitive matters.

"Brother Joseph," Benjamin pled, "this has been a time of testing for Brother Babbitt. But with your arm around him, I believe he will remain true."

Joseph focused on Benjamin, his blue eyes soft with understanding. "I too love Brother Almon, and he is capable of great good. Bennie, bring him to me as soon as he arrives. The troubles shall all be bridged over, and Brother Almon shall have no reason to complain."

At the conclusion of their talk, Joseph embraced Benjamin once more, expressing that he loved Benjamin all the more for his honesty and for his concern for Almon.

\* \* \*

Benjamin spent the night with Delcena and her children. Little Susan's eyes looked so much like Lyman's that it astounded him. Outside in the cool evening while Delcena put her littlest ones to bed, he pulled sticks with Albey. Near them, Alvira and Mary, Delcena's oldest girls, played a game of graces by using knitting needles to throw and catch an embroidery hoop. They'd talked Benjamin into trying it and laughed when he'd blundered.

Delcena came outside and watched them for a moment. Stray hairs from her bun fell around her face. She scooted her three oldest to bed and asked Benjamin to sit with her on the porch for a moment.

They sat side by side as the darkness deepened. Some stars gained brightness, while others were occluded by ghostlike clouds. Benjamin thought about the terrible days after Lyman's death when he had moved Delcena to Quincy. Yet the sister next to him sat peacefully on the bench, and he sensed the depth of her strength.

"Ben," Delcena broke the quiet. "Did Brother Joseph talk with you about John Bennett?"

"No." Benjamin shook his head. "We only spoke of Almon. I feel certain that Brother Joseph will help him."

"I'm so glad," Delcena said. "I hope Julianne comes to visit soon." Then she looked up at the quarter moon as she returned to her original topic. "John Bennett has been excommunicated from the Church. He resigned as mayor and general of the Nauvoo Legion. Yesterday, he was also expelled from the Masons."

Benjamin turned to her quickly, almost in disbelief. "What has he done?"

Delcena swallowed. "Tomorrow morning the Prophet will speak openly about it in a meeting near the temple. Will you come with me?"

\* \* \*

The following morning, over a thousand Saints gathered. Joseph stood at the outdoor pulpit. Delcena placed her hand on Benjamin's arm to steady herself as the Prophet spoke with plainness about John Bennett.

He spoke of Bennett lying to women and men, teaching them that promiscuous intercourse between the sexes was a doctrine believed in by the Latter-day Saints. He spoke of the innocent and virtuous being deceived. He spoke of adultery. Then he told of John Bennett drinking poison because he was so full of shame. Fortunately, he was discovered and the antidote administered. Yet John Bennett had not ceased his abominable conduct. He had been excommunicated from the Church and left Nauvoo in disgrace. Joseph had been informed that he threatened to join the Missourians in their effort to destroy Joseph and the Church. But Joseph hoped and prayed that John Bennett would stop and no longer injure those who had befriended him.

*Alone no longer, can I roam,*
*My heart is with the pure and brave.*
*With thee and thine I'll find my home,*
*Myself and all my kin to save.*

Joel Hills Johnson

*Saturday, June 25, 1842. Nauvoo, Illinois*

BENJAMIN SLEPT LATE, AWAKENING A half hour after the sun had risen. Almon had arrived two days ago with a large stock of merchandise. Yesterday they had worked late into the night, unloading the goods into a rented building. Their store would open Monday morning.

Benjamin lay in bed for a moment, smelling butter biscuits and hearing Melissa and Almera chatting in the kitchen. Almera now lived with them in this large rented house that was once a tavern. He and Melissa would take in boarders as soon as they furnished the six bedrooms. Then Benjamin heard a door open and Almon's voice mingle with Melissa's and Almera's. Benjamin arose and dressed quickly then knelt down and prayed earnestly for guidance. After breakfast, Benjamin and Almon would ride to Nauvoo. They would meet with the Prophet in the afternoon. Only after their meeting would Benjamin know for sure that everything would be all right.

\* \* \*

The sun shone high in the sky when Almon and Benjamin arrived in Nauvoo an hour earlier than anticipated. Almon suggested that they ride to the temple grounds and view the progress before meeting with the Prophet. Once there, the men dismounted and tied their horses. The stone walls rose nearly five feet high. There was a deep well on the east side of the temple. Young, middle-aged, and elderly men worked steadily, with sweat on their brows, using a single crane to hoist heavy stones. Almon's mind went back to the dedication of the Kirtland Temple, when the heavens had opened. Would the heavens open when this temple was completed?

They talked with the workmen for a few minutes. While Benjamin continued talking with William Huntington, Almon went inside the walls. Near the east end, rising from the basement floor, a temporary clapboard building was roofed and walled off, forming a single, separate room. A dozen people waited on benches outside this makeshift structure with pieces of paper in their hands. A middle-aged man came out of the room dripping wet. Brigham Young followed him. He shook the man's hand and embraced him then walked over to Almon. "Welcome back to Nauvoo. That brother was baptized for his father," Brigham explained. "Come inside with me. Now that a font has been dedicated, this is the only place on earth where baptisms for the dead can be performed."

Almon followed Brigham into the room. A temporary baptismal font made of pine, with steps next to it, stood seven feet high and measured about twelve by sixteen feet in width. Twelve carved oxen projected from the base. Brigham climbed the steps and spoke briefly to the elder in the font waiting to perform the next baptism. Brigham climbed down and nodded to a young lady dressed in a simple white frock, with her long, brown hair tightly braided and bound at the base of her neck.

Before climbing the steps into the font, the young lady glanced at a frail, old woman in a cripple's chair. The young woman smiled, and the old woman nodded as tears coursed down her cheeks. Almon's heart went out to the woman. She was obviously too frail to perform the ordinance herself. He approached her and asked, "Would you like to see the baptism? Would you allow me to carry you up the steps?"

"Yes. Please," she responded, her lips trembling. Gently, Almon lifted her and carried her up the steps, her body limp, her bones sharp and brittle in his arms, her weight not more than a child's. He held her by the edge of the font as she wept during the ordinance. Then he carried her down the stairs and settled her in her chair. With Brigham's help, the men carried the woman in her chair out of the baptismal room.

"Sister, was the baptism in behalf of your mother?" Almon asked.

Sunlight bathed her elderly features. "No, for my only child, Lydia. She was sixteen when she died. My neighbor was baptized for her. When she smiled at me, I almost saw my Lydia in her eyes."

A moment later, Benjamin walked up. He smiled at the old woman and spoke to Almon. "We need to leave. Our appointment with Brother Joseph is in twenty minutes."

Almon nodded and shook the woman's hands. "It's a pleasure to meet you, sister."

"God bless you, Brother Babbitt."

His head tilted, surprised. "How do you know my name?"

"You spoke at conference about two years past. On the day I was baptized."

\* \* \*

Ten minutes later, Almon knocked briskly on the Smith's door, determined to face the situation head on. Regardless of Benjamin's assurance, he had no idea how the meeting would go. Though hidden behind a façade of confidence, his heart beat as if his very life were at stake.

Joseph answered the door dressed in his full military uniform—white breeches, high riding boots, and dark dress jacket bright with gold brocade and epaulets. His sword leaned against the wall as if he had just put it there. His wavy, fair hair fell back neatly away from his forehead.

The Prophet's attire shocked Almon. Joseph looked regal and imposing, very different from the homespun man Almon was accustomed to. Yet Joseph acted as if nothing were out of the ordinary. He smiled broadly. "Brother Almon, welcome! Come in." Reaching out, he shook Almon's hand.

"If you have another appointment, we can come back later," Almon responded. Then he added, "Unless you have dressed up like this in honor of our visit."

Joseph laughed and turned to greet Benjamin warmly. Then he explained, "I've just finished sitting for a drawing to be put on the lithograph of the map of Nauvoo. Come wait in my office for a moment while I change."

When Joseph came back, Almon had already taken the notes and papers out of his satchel and placed them in a neat pile on Joseph's desk. They chatted for a few minutes about friends and family. Then the tide of the conversation turned to business matters in Kirtland. Almon said he had honestly tried to build up Kirtland in righteousness. He explained the debt he had incurred due to his business closing and the fact that he had personally purchased notes the Church and Joseph owed to outsiders.

Joseph looked at the notes and figures, asking a few questions that Almon expounded on. The Prophet talked for a moment about the gathering in Nauvoo and the importance of the temple. "Within its walls, God's people will make covenants and receive an endowment beyond what was received in the house of the Lord in Kirtland," Joseph explained. "The revealed ordinances that take place in this temple will be a blessing to the living and the dead. It is the fulcrum of Nauvoo, the great necessity of the Saints in these latter days, and the reason for the gathering."

Almon swallowed. He loved the Kirtland Temple. But he had felt the blessings of heaven in the old woman's eyes today. He looked squarely at the Prophet and admitted that he had erred in his counsel to the Kirtland Saints.

Then the Prophet was silent for a moment while he looked down at his own hands folded on the desk, as if he were considering or praying. He raised his head and looked at Benjamin first and then focused on Almon. He said directly, "Brother Almon, let us not disagree. Here is Brother Benjamin. You have complete confidence in him and so have I. I suggest we leave all our differences to him. Let him decide what to do as far as our business dealings. Oh, I would have us be good friends forevermore."

Joseph reached out his hand. *Good friends forevermore.* The words bored into Almon. He suddenly knew exactly what the old woman had experienced earlier in the temple. He could almost see David, Carlos, Lyman, and Seth in the Prophet's blue eyes. Brother Joseph offered him hope and brotherhood, regardless of past differences, an eternal friendship beyond the veil of death.

Almon would not sit by any fireside in his beloved Kirtland again, yet this man had the power to take one's heart and thaw coldness with a word and touch. Almon nodded and reached out his hand to Joseph. "I too trust Benjamin implicitly, and I agree. Let us be good friends forevermore."

"Thank you, Brother Almon," Joseph said, his eyes showing his gladness. Then he turned to Benjamin and handed him the pile of papers. "Bennie, do what you believe is best between Brother Babbitt and me. It's right for you to remain in Ramus. I hereby appoint you as trustee or agent for the Church property there. I also give you power of attorney to use my name in buying, selling, and deeding property in Ramus. Brother Babbitt will help you with any needed legal proceedings."

When Joseph turned back to Almon, the lines of his brow deepened. He took a deep breath, and his shoulders sagged as if he were suddenly tired. "In this perilous time, I thank God for your friendship. You know that John Bennett has lost his positions and been excommunicated. I received word that he has been asked by the editor of the *Sangamo Journal* and other newspapers to expose me. He is angry, and I fear his accusations against me could hurt us all. He has already suggested that I was involved in Boggs' shooting. These developments, combined with Thomas Sharp's anti-Mormon paper, trouble me. I have some friends, especially among the Democrats, but I fear they will abandon me and that the Missouri atrocities could happen here. I-I had hoped we would enjoy peace."

Almon swallowed—his were not the only dreams that had been crushed. "How can I help?"

"I need time, Brother Almon—time to finish the temple and do all those things the Lord has commanded me. Do not wait to become involved in political matters. You can influence others. Joseph Duncan is the Whig candidate for governor. He is running on anti-Mormon issues and the repeal of the Nauvoo Charter. If he wins, all is lost. Get to know Thomas Ford, the Democratic candidate. Judge Adams tells me your family has a connection with him through Widow Forquer of Springfield, his late brother's wife. James Adams and perhaps Stephen Douglas will help you politically. Do everything you can to counteract Bennett's accusations. Talk to Thomas Ford and every man you know. You are a persuasive man, and people's hearts are drawn to you like John the Beloved of old. Live in Ramus if you choose, but come to Nauvoo often, for I will be in need of your counsel."

"I will," Almon said.

Then Joseph turned to Benjamin. "Bennie, I thought of something else that would interest you. My favorite horse, Charlie, is getting old. So I've bought another horse. He's a big bay fellow I'm in the process of breaking. Stop by and see him."

"What's his name?"

Joseph grinned. "Joe Duncan, after our political rival."

Almon laughed. "Perhaps we will soon break both Duncans."

On the ride home, Almon's heart beat quickly. He knew it was time for forgiveness. It was time for Mormon boys to stick together, to fire political bricks and build a spiritual temple. He could hardly wait to get home and tell Julianne that all was well.

\* \* \*

*A month later. Carthage, Illinois*

"Almon, you need to stop." Ezekiel took a drink in the Carthage tavern as he stared across the table at his son-in-law. A few minutes ago, Almon had walked in and ordered something to eat. Ezekiel had called Almon over to his table.

"Stop what?" Almon asked.

"The affidavits you're taking from place to place that say Bennett is a villain. Not a man outside Nauvoo believes you."

Almon responded, "You're wrong. Thomas Ford, the Democratic candidate for governor, believes me. Last week in Springfield, Ford told me John Bennett is a debauched and unprincipled character."

"Ford wants the Mormon votes."

"Ford's his own man. He's calling for a revision of the Nauvoo Charter. He's not Joseph's puppet."

"Maybe I don't know Ford, but I know the men in this tavern. They believe Joseph is a womanizer and a murderer. They're afraid of the Legion."

Almon turned the tables. "What are you doing, Zeke? Just sitting here and listening to it? Joseph's in hiding because Governor Carlin will send him to Missouri to stand trial for an attempted murder he didn't have anything to do with. You don't believe Joseph is a prophet, but you know what kind of man he is. Do you ever stand up and tell this rabble that he's not a killer, that he's a good man?"

Ezekiel's words came out defensive and bitter. "Keep your voice down. What can I do? Tell them about my Mormon wife who left me? My children who are dead? I keep my mouth shut and tell you the buzz of the countryside. Let Joseph know, if you think it will help him."

Almon's face grew tense. "Did you read the last thing Bennett wrote? That the citizens of Illinois should destroy the Mormons with arms, rush the reptile before it has grown powerful enough to sting them to the death."

Ezekiel's head ached. Almon talked too loud. He whispered stringently, "I know what Bennett said. I know what he is. But I don't want you to get hurt, to ruin your chances of running for office in Hancock County. And I don't want any of the Mormons hurt, least of all my family. I do know Joseph. Joseph lives on a bed of coals. And there's always someone willing to light the match."

Almon stood up to leave. "Just make sure you vote for Thomas Ford."

\* \* \*

*Saturday, August 6, 1842. Montrose, Iowa*

The morning dawned hot and humid. Almon had arrived in Nauvoo the previous day. With Joseph and a group of brethren, he crossed the river into Montrose. Almon stood next to Anson Call as the group gathered in the shade of a schoolhouse. There was a barrel of ice water under the bowery. Joseph took a drink of icy water. With the tumbler still in his hand, he looked on the brethren gathered around him. He spoke a moment about the Missouri persecutions and how they had followed him here.

Then Joseph's countenance changed, his features gaining an unearthly brightness as he seemed to see something far away. His voice rose strong and clear. "The Saints shall go to the Rocky Mountains; and this water tastes much like that of the crystal streams that are running from the snow-capped mountains." Joseph pointed to the men around him. "There are some here who shall do a great work in that land. There is Anson Call; he shall go forth and shall assist in building up cities from one end of the country to the other, and others of you shall perform as great a work as has been done by man so that the nations of the earth shall be astonished, and many of them will be gathered in that land and assist in building cities and temples, and Israel shall be made to rejoice. But, oh, the scenes the people will pass through, the apostasy that will take place before my brethren reach that land! But the priesthood shall prevail over its enemies, triumph over the devil, and be established upon the earth, never more to be thrown down. Remember these things, and treasure them up. Amen."

\* \* \*

*Wednesday December 28, 1842. Ramus, Illinois*

It was past ten o'clock, and the night was bitter cold, with a full moon and clear, bright stars. Julianne shivered beneath her cloak as she drove the buggy home. She had left Benjamin's house a few moments previous, after her mother, Esther, and Mary Ann had arrived. She felt slightly guilty for leaving, knowing that Melissa continued to pace around the house, nine months pregnant, enduring hard contractions every thirty minutes or so. Nonetheless, Melissa's water had not yet broken and this could go on for hours. Almon had promised to come home tonight after an absence of two weeks.

She was anxious to see her husband and hear the news. Joseph had been in hiding much of the summer and fall due to Governor Carlin's support of the Missouri order demanding Joseph's arrest for the attempted murder of Lilburn Boggs. However, now that Thomas Ford was elected the new governor of Illinois, there was hope that the Prophet would be exonerated. Almon had spent the past two weeks taking letters back and forth between the governor and the Prophet.

When she arrived at home, the windows were warm with hearthlight. Almon's saddle horse whinnied to the mare pulling Julianne's buggy. In an instant, Almon came out the front door, his breath steamy in the freezing air. "Where were you?" he asked.

"At Benjamin's. Melissa's in labor. She's doing fine. The baby will come tonight or tomorrow."

Almon nodded and unhitched the horse without comment. Julianne knew he grew weary of hearing about the births of other men's children. "Go in and get warm," he suggested as he led the mare to the pasture. After caring for the horse, he joined Julianne in the sitting room. They snuggled on the sofa with the quilt around them both.

"Your hands are freezing," he said, placing her hands between his.

"Not for long." She smiled at him. "You are always so warm." Then she changed the subject. "Tell me the news."

Almon began. "The governor sent Joseph a letter saying that the Supreme Court was unanimous in their opinion that the requisition from Missouri was illegal; however, Ford did not think it wise to override the former governor's decision. Instead, he suggested Joseph go to Springfield, where his case will be heard in the courts. Joseph left yesterday."

Julianne's heart sank. "Oh no."

Almon took a deep breath. "It should be all right. Ford promised him safety and that justice would be served."

"Can Ford be trusted?"

"Ford tries to uphold the law, but who knows what his true motives are. However, I'm comfortable with Joseph's decision. James Adams assured me that he knows the courts in Springfield and is certain Joseph will be let off. He wrote to Joseph as well, calling him 'son' and encouraging Joseph to come before the court in Springfield for a discharge under habeas corpus."

"If that happens, it will be over. Joseph will be free of Missouri."

"Yes," Almon said, holding her close. "As long as the vigilante wolves stay at bay. I pray they are frightened by the Legion's fire."

As they watched the hearth flame dance, Julianne wondered if she should tell Almon her secret. If only she were positive. If she were wrong, not even the warmth of a hearth fire could chase away the wolves of her disappointment.

\* \* \*

The next morning dawned frigid. Almon and Julianne arrived at Benjamin's shortly after breakfast. Outside, Benjamin dragged a span of wood toward the house. "I've a new son," he called out, beaming. "Born after midnight. Benjamin Franklin Johnson Jr. Melissa is doing well."

"Congratulations," Julianne and Almon responded in unison.

"How is Joseph?" Benjamin asked as Almon hefted an additional armload of wood.

"I'll tell you inside, where it's warm," Almon returned.

Julianne smiled warmly at her brother as they neared the house. "Benja, you'll be a wonderful father! But it looks like you're trying to heat all of Illinois." Julianne pointed at the thick smoke piling out of all four chimneys.

Benjamin grinned. "Couldn't have my baby boy arriving to a cold house, now could I?"

Inside the spacious parlor, Ezekiel held the tiny baby in a large, comfortable chair. Esther perched on the arm of the chair with one of her hands on her father's shoulder and the other index finger inside the newborn's tiny fist. Julianne immediately hugged her father and admired the baby. She pulled up a chair close to them. Will and George sat in two additional armchairs and stretched their legs in front of the fire. At Benjamin's request, Almon relayed the information about the Prophet and the court in Springfield. Almon glanced at Ezekiel, who focused on the infant as if he wasn't listening.

Seconds after Almon finished, Julia, Almera, and Mary Ann entered the room and said Melissa was sleeping soundly. Julia took a seat across the room from Ezekiel. They did not make eye contact. Julia asked Almon to tell her everything that had happened to the Prophet.

Almon was halfway finished with another recital of the contents of Ford's letter when Julianne suddenly stood up. "It's hot in here. I'll be right back." She gulped and ran out the front door. Cold air whooshed in as it slammed behind her.

Almon stared after her then glanced at the family. Julia and Almera looked at the door but didn't seem overly concerned.

"Hmm," Esther said nonchalantly. "I've seen this before."

"Isn't anyone concerned about my wife's welfare?" Almon asked, annoyed. Didn't they realize how difficult it was for her, watching her siblings bear child after child? Were they all too wrapped up with the new baby and the Prophet to care? No wonder she needed to get out of the house.

"That's your job, boy," Ezekiel grumped loudly. "Quit talking and tend to your wife."

Almon put his coat on and grabbed Julianne's cloak. She was a short distance away from the house. She wiped her mouth and turned toward him. Steam rose from the vomit in the snow. "You're sick," Almon exclaimed. "Let's get you home." He hurried to her and wrapped the cloak around her shoulders.

Then he almost lost his balance as Julianne hugged him around his waist, nearly dancing on the icy lawn as she laughed and cried at the same time. "Darling boy," she exclaimed. "I've been sick like this for the past two days. I've wanted to be sick like this for a very long time."

Suddenly realizing what she meant, Almon picked her up and swung her around in his arms. Fortunately, she did not vomit again. Tears came to his eyes. His wife was with child. Julianne's family, even Ezekiel, with the new baby in his arms, stood on the front porch and cheered.

## 21

*True friendship is a treasure*
*And of the greatest worth*
*And gives the sweetest pleasure*
*Of any gem on earth.*

Joel Hills Johnson

*Saturday, March 11, 1843. Ramus, Illinois*

"Why, if it isn't her Royal Highness Miss Esther Johnson and Miss Mary Ann Hale, the adopted princess," sixteen-year-old Jeremiah Morse teased. The large young man with heavy features and a quick tongue caught up with the girls and fell in file beside Esther. "Where are you going in such a hurry?"

Esther turned to him. "To have lunch at Benjamin's. The Prophet just arrived. Tonight there will be popcorn and a stick pull at the store. Brother Joseph wants to challenge your older brother Justus because he's champion here."

"Brother Joseph will lose," Jeremiah said. When Esther raised her eyebrows, he added, "So Brother Joseph is staying with the royal family again. And, Esther, have you heard from LeBaron lately? Is it the name that attracts you? Mistress *LeBaroness?*"

"Don't you have something else to do?" Esther asked. At one time, she had been friends with Jeremiah, but now he purposely annoyed her. Last fall, he had made the mistake of trying to kiss her at a corn husking party—even though Mary Ann had warned him not to. On that occasion, Esther had told him in no uncertain terms that her beau, David LeBaron, would soon be arriving in Nauvoo. But David still wasn't here.

The sarcastic edge in Jeremiah's voice deepened as he turned to Mary Ann. "Miss Hale, how do you like living with royalty?"

Mary Ann looked down. Esther's cheeks grew hot. How could he make fun of Mary Ann? With her pale eyes, wispy hair, and soft voice, she would not hurt a fly. Didn't Jeremiah realize she had lost her parents and still grieved for them? Or did he just not care? "Ignore him," Esther said as she walked faster.

"Ignore me?" Jeremiah wedged between the girls, putting an arm around each of their shoulders. "Everyone in town knows the Johnsons are royalty. That's why they call you The Royal Family."

"That's ridiculous," Esther remarked, pulling away.

"Come on, Esther, think about it. This place is swarming with Johnsons. Your brother Joel Johnson is stake president. Benjamin Johnson owns the store. The Prophet always stays with him when he comes. Joseph Johnson is schoolmaster, postmaster, and town clerk. He's a rising politician and even wrote the town charter and changed the name to Macedonia."

"Almon is the politician, not Joe," Esther informed him.

"I almost forgot! The Democrat's favorite Macedonian, Almon Babbitt, is a Johnson too," Jeremiah exclaimed. "He even knows Thomas Ford. People are just tired of it."

"Come on, Mary Ann," Esther said, taking her hand and quickly walking away. "He's not worth listening to."

"I forgot to mention, rumor is that while the queen reigns in the Johnson Kingdom," Jeremiah called out after them, "the disgraced king lives on the edge of town in exile. Brandy is his friend."

Rage flooded Esther. She let go of Mary Ann's hand, and her fists knotted. She stopped in her tracks, shaking with the urge to attack Jeremiah. Mary Ann placed her hand on Esther's arm. "Keep walking. He really isn't worth it. You said so yourself."

\*\*\*

Benjamin stood in the dining room, holding his baby boy while Almera and Melissa set the silverware and plates on the table. The Prophet was in his room washing up. Esther burst in, with Mary Ann at her heels. Every bit of Esther seethed with anger. "What's wrong?" Benjamin asked.

"Everyone in town is making fun of us, calling us the Royal Family," she burst out with angry tears in her eyes.

"Why would they do that?" Benjamin asked. "We've done nothing but build up this town."

"Jealousy," Mary Ann said simply.

Esther continued. "It's because there're so many of us, and we own businesses. And because the Prophet stays at your house. It makes me so mad."

Almera turned to Esther. "But we can't worry about what others say. We have to do our best and turn the other cheek. If they call us the Royal Family, then let it be."

The Prophet walked in, having heard much of the conversation. He smiled and sat down at the table. "The townspeople are correct. You are a royal family. It is and should be a reality."

Esther swallowed. "But they make fun of Papa. They call him the disgraced king in exile. Because of his drinking."

"Then they go too far," Benjamin said, his eyes darkening.

The Prophet looked at Benjamin, Almera, and Esther. "I know your father. Better days will come for him. He shall yet be a great man and stand at the head of a kingdom."

Later that night, during the stick pulling contest, Brother Joseph pulled up Justus Morse with one hand. Esther eyed Jeremiah, then with her hand resting on her father's arm, she cheered triumphantly.

\* \* \*

*Sunday, March 12, 1842. Macedonia, Illinois*

The following morning, Julia gathered with her family and the Saints in the new meetinghouse, where the Prophet would speak to the congregation. Joel and Susan occupied the pew in front of her. Joel held Susan's hand, with the children on either side of them. Outwardly, they seemed fine, but Julia knew they grieved inside. Susan and Joel had lost their baby girl a few months ago. The baby's death had affected Melissa. Regardless of Benjamin's wishes, she kept their baby at home, out of cold weather and away from crowds.

Just before the opening prayer, Julia looked around. George and Mary were not there. Mary was in the seventh month of a difficult pregnancy. Julia had visited her yesterday evening during the stick pull. Mary had looked frail as she lay in bed with a miserable cold. Julia had made Mary broth and thought of how small Mary looked for seven months along. Julianne, at four months, was already as large.

After the opening prayer and hymn, the Prophet stood at the podium. He opened his Bible and explained that he would speak on the scripture in the fourteenth chapter of John. "In my Father's house are many mansions," he began.

As Julia listened to the discourse, she found herself wondering if Joseph was preparing the Saints for the revealed doctrine that Delcena had talked to her about last week. The Prophet had told Delcena of sacred ordinances that would take place in the temple, endowing Saints with power and sealing husbands and wives together for eternity, a prerequisite to entering the highest degree of the celestial kingdom—the most holy mansion prepared by the Father. Delcena's eyes had shone when she'd said that Lyman, though he was dead, could be sealed to her forever.

Although Julia longed to rejoice in this doctrine, it cast a shadow over her heart. She saw Ezekiel quite often because Esther not only invited him to family events but dragged him to them. Though Julia would never tell Esther, it was difficult for her. At times, she could tell Ezekiel had been drinking; often, he scoffed at the Church, and always, he would scarcely look at her. Still aching from the look he shot at her when he learned of Amos's death, she felt his bitterness like a tangible force. This knowledge, that he blamed her for their children's deaths and his shattered life, wounded her. She could not escape the memory of who Ezekiel had been or what they had shared. Each time she saw him, the weight of broken dreams was more difficult to carry. And now she had lost even more, the highest degree of heaven.

\*\*\*

When the meeting concluded, George Wilson was waiting outside the door of the meetinghouse for Julia. "Mother Johnson," he said with panic in his eyes. "Mary worsens. She has a sinking cold and is having contractions. I fear we'll lose both her and the baby. Do you think Brother Joseph will come bless her?"

Julia nodded. "Yes. Go ask him. I'll go to Mary." Julia set off immediately, afraid to take the time to tell anyone she was leaving. She hurried. It was a short distance to Mary's. When she was nearly there, the Prophet and George caught up to her, striding quickly over icy puddles.

Inside the house, Julia saw the pain in Mary's eyes. Joseph knelt by her bed. He placed his hands on Mary's head and, in the name of the Lord, blessed her that she would live and bear a son. Then, while George sat with Mary, the Prophet helped Julia prepare a poultice for Mary's chest. Ten minutes later, when Julia and the Prophet were again at the bedside, Mary looked up at them. "George and I have settled on a name for our son. He shall be called David Johnson Wilson."

"He will be a great man," the Prophet said. "Like his namesake."

A short time later while Mary slept, the Prophet asked Julia to walk back to Benjamin's house with him, assuring her that Mary would be all right. On the way, Joseph talked about David, Seth, Nancy, and Susan, about the day they first met in Kirtland and became neighbors. Julia thought about how Joseph was like a son to her.

They passed Benjamin's store, and Joseph asked if she would sit with him for a moment on the bench outside, in spite of the cold. It was the Sabbath, and the street was empty. After they sat, Joseph talked with Julia about the temple and about the covenants of Abraham, Isaac, and Jacob. He taught her of the endowment and of the sealing power of celestial marriage.

With a heart full of emotion, Julia explained to the Prophet that Delcena had already told her of these blessings. Then she could not stop her tears.

"Mother Johnson, what is it?" Joseph asked.

"Ezekiel is lost to God and bitter toward me. The fullness of these blessings will not be ours. I don't see a way to enter the highest degree of the celestial kingdom, that mansion my heart yearns for."

Joseph responded, "No righteous woman will be held back because her husband is not worthy." He spoke again of Abraham and explained in more detail the law of celestial marriage. His brother Hyrum could be sealed for time and eternity to both Jerusha, although she had died, and Mary Fielding, his wife now. Joseph went on. "Already, men like John Bennett have misunderstood and perverted this holy doctrine. Only one man on earth holds all the keys of the priesthood and can bind on earth what is bound in heaven. For a short time longer, I am that man. Dear Mother Julia, the Lord directs me to comfort you and to tell you that if you choose, you may enter into this holy covenant with a righteous priesthood bearer."

Julia's heart pounded. She would not be held back; she could partake of all the blessings of the temple and of eternal life. Yet doubt clung to her. What of Ezekiel? Years ago, they had broken each other's hearts. Even so, they were bound together—because of their children, because of the love that had been, the love she could not forget. "Brother Joseph, if I choose to break my marriage tie to Ezekiel and be sealed to someone else . . . If circumstances changed by some miracle, is it possible that what is bound can also be loosed?"

Joseph looked deep into her eyes. "Yes. The apostolic power is to bind in heaven what is bound on earth and to loose in heaven what is loosed on earth. But these are the powers of eternity and cannot be trifled with."

Tears filled Julia's eyes. "I would go forward. I would be sealed to someone who holds the holy priesthood."

The Prophet nodded. "Our Father in Heaven will guide you." Then the Prophet laid his hands on Julia's head and blessed her, promising that, because of her faithfulness, the priesthood would remain with her posterity forever. "None of your children will leave the Church. Not a jewel in your crown will be lost."

\* \* \*

*Monday, March 13, 1843. Macedonia, Illinois*

The temperature had dropped, and the mercury read three degrees below zero at sunrise. Even with the fires burning in Benjamin's house, there was ice in every basin. After breakfast, Joseph went to the store with him, and the morning passed pleasantly. Visitors stopped by, and the Prophet talked, played games, and matched couplets in rhyme. William Wall, the most expert wrestler in Macedonia, challenged him to a match. Joseph threw him. At noon, Julia brought lunch and the happy news that Mary was doing better. In the afternoon, Joseph preached to a large congregation. Almon was sustained as the presiding elder. When the meeting concluded, Joseph told those gathered to bring their children back at seven that evening, for he desired to bless them.

\* \* \*

Parents brought their children forward. Joseph's fervency and love filled the room as he pulled down the powers of heaven. Joel and Susan wept as the Prophet blessed Sixtus, Sariah, Nephi, Susie, and little Seth. Then Joseph blessed Mary Julia, Harriet and Joe's little girl. The blessings continued. In the candlelight, tears shone on the Prophet's cheeks as his hands rested on the children's heads. Joseph rebuked the influences that sought to destroy their precious souls. He strove with all the faith and spirit within him to seal upon them the blessings that would secure their lives upon the earth. After blessing nineteen children, Joseph, pale and drained of strength, turned and asked Brother Brigham to bless the remaining eight.

A short time later, on the way home with Benjamin, the Prophet closed his eyes. "Bennie," he explained, "I saw that Lucifer would exert his influence to destroy the children. Virtue, the spirit of life, went out of me into the children, leaving me weak."

"Rest my friend," Benjamin said, deeply moved. When they arrived, the Prophet seemed a little better. Inside the house, Melissa rocked the baby near the parlor hearth. She had not taken him to the meeting because the night was so cold. Disappointment filled Benjamin because his firstborn had not been blessed. He turned to Melissa. "We have lost much by our babe not being at the meeting tonight."

Joseph took off his coat. "You shall lose nothing. I will bless him too." With Melissa holding the sleeping infant, Joseph laid his hands on the baby's head and pronounced a beautiful blessing. Afterward, Melissa left the room to nurse the baby.

Joseph sat back heavily in a big chair before the fire and exclaimed almost as if Benjamin were not there, "Oh, I am so tired—so tired that I often long for my day of rest. This life has held so much tribulation for me. From a boy, I have been persecuted by my enemies, and now my friends again join with them to hate and persecute me. Why should I not wish for my time of rest?"

The weight of Joseph's words stunned Benjamin. "Oh, Joseph! How could you think of leaving us?"

Joseph looked at him kindly. "Bennie, if I were on the other side of the veil, I could do many times more for my friends than I can do while I am with them here."

A few minutes later, Benjamin and the Prophet parted for the night. Benjamin laid awake in bed as Melissa cradled their tiny son against her. He could not sleep, for Joseph's words rang in his mind and the dark iron of sorrow filled his soul. The next day, the Prophet rode back to Nauvoo in a snowstorm.

*And may we to our trust prove true,*
*The law of God still keep in view;*
*That with our crowns in worlds above,*
*We'll meet in endless joy and love . . .*

Benjamin Franklin Johnson

Late March 1843. Macedonia, Illinois

ESTHER THOUGHT IT THE CHILLIEST March of her entire life. In the midafternoon, she and Mary Ann sat close to the fire, stitching shirts to donate to temple workmen. Above the crackle of the flames, Esther heard voices outside. Her fingers stilled. It was her brothers, Will and George, who had spent the week in Nauvoo working on the temple.

A moment later, Will stuck his head in the doorway. "Esther, come here for a moment. We need help with the horses."

"I'm busy, and it's cold out."

"Come on, or you'll be sorry." Will grinned.

"I'll be sorry?" Esther repeated, her curiosity piqued. She looked over at Mary Ann.

"Go," Mary Ann encouraged.

Once outside, Esther gathered her cloak tightly around her to ward off the wind. "Come to the stable. George has a surprise," Will said as he led his horse. Esther followed him. Inside the barn, George stood next to a different horse, a pretty black mare with deep, kind eyes. "Is Maria here? Did she get a new horse?" Esther asked enthusiastically. Maria Johnston was George's girl. Once in a while, she came back with George after he worked in Nauvoo. Esther loved her Southern drawl. Was she hiding somewhere? Having her come would be a nice surprise.

"Maria couldn't come this time," George said. "Her mother is ill."

"I'm sorry." Esther stroked the mare's neck then frowned. "Then whose horse is this?"

A voice spoke from behind Esther. "Yours."

Esther whirled around. David LeBaron stepped out of the shadows. She squealed with joy and ran to him. He held her close, kissing her in spite of her brothers' presence. Will whistled, but George frowned.

"Your letter said you wouldn't get here until May," Esther exclaimed.

"I hurried to surprise you." He laughed. "I missed your birthday in January, so I brought your present. How do you like her?" He held Esther's hand as they stepped close to the horse. "Her shiny black coat made me think of your hair."

Esther beamed and kissed the mare on the nose. "I hereby christen you Joy." Then she turned to David. "We will have fun riding together, Joy and I."

"What about me?"

"I suppose you can come along. And, David, I'm sixteen now, old enough to be courted."

David laughed. "I've been counting the days."

"But not old enough to marry," George commented.

Esther beamed. "Brothers! They are all the same. But George is right. Papa said I have to be at least seventeen to marry."

"Why, that's just around the corner." David kissed Esther again.

Later that night, after David had left to sleep at Benjamin's, George and Will cornered Esther in the parlor, sitting down on either side of her.

Will began. "David told us that he truly wants to marry you someday. So don't fun around with him."

"I'm not," Esther said defensively. "I want to marry him with all of my heart."

George cut in. "Go slowly. Make sure he is the right one."

"I am sure," Esther said confidently. "I love him. George, do you love Maria?"

"I wasn't certain for a time. But now I am."

"Then why don't you marry her?"

"I plan to. When the time is right."

"Oh, time! You can't wait on time, for it won't wait on you," Esther exclaimed.

George tensed. "Marriage is a big step, Esther. That's what I'm trying to get across to you."

Esther turned to Will, looking like a marionette rotating her head from one brother to the other. "What about you, Will? Have you ever been in love?"

"Never. But when I meet the right girl, I'll know it for certain. And I'll marry her quick as a wink. No waiting on time for me."

Esther smiled mischievously. "If she wants you."

Will stood up and flexed his muscles. "Who wouldn't want me?"

Esther burst out laughing.

George stood up to leave. Will asked him where he was going. "To bed," George replied. "You two wear me out."

\* \* \*

*Sunday, April 2, 1843*

It was four-thirty in the afternoon. Benjamin, driving his family carriage, dropped Julia off at her house following the afternoon meeting. The Prophet, who was again visiting Macedonia, remained in the carriage and went on to Benjamin's home with Melissa, Almera, William Clayton, and Orson Hyde. Julia had promised to make gingerbread nuts, one of the Prophet's favorite treats, and bring them to supper in an hour.

After alighting from the carriage, Julia stepped carefully across the yard, holding her skirt up to keep it from getting muddy. Her younger children were taking a pleasure ride in the buggy but would be back in time to take her to Benjamin's for supper. It continued to snow—large, wet flakes that melted as soon as they hit the ground. Julia reached up to open the door as a snowflake fell on her navy sleeve, and she saw in the second before it melted the details of its intricate pattern.

"Julia." Ezekiel's voice startled her as she walked inside. He stood uncomfortably in the entryway. His eyes were bloodshot, but his voice was steady. He had been drinking, but he was not drunk. "I didn't mean to frighten you. Just didn't want passersby staring at me." She could not tell him that it wasn't his voice that frightened her. She was frightened by how normal it felt for a sharp instant—him calling her by name inside her home.

"Why are you here?" she asked, though she thought she knew the answer. A few days ago she had sent him a letter explaining that she had taken the steps to make their separation final.

His voice was flat, empty as a hollow shell. "Why did you send me that paper? We already live separately. I leave you alone."

"We-we have been separated for so long. It's time we are free to go on with our own lives."

"Free? You no longer love me? Do you love another man?"

"No," Julia answered honestly.

His words came out loudly. "I know you well and there *is* more to this. I was already without hope. I left you alone. Why do this now? Why pour vinegar into a wound? That is not like you."

Julia looked at him. "You don't understand."

"Explain it anyway. Give me that last courtesy."

"I cannot," Julia said. She could not tell him that soon she would be sealed to another for eternity although she would continue to live singly with her children. Ezekiel would not understand the meaning of the temple and of the priesthood. Was her inability to speak because it was casting pearls before swine or because it would destroy a pearl that was already scarred beyond recognition? Julia did not know.

"I loved you," Ezekiel said between gritted teeth. He cursed the Mormon Church. "I loved you forevermore."

The bitter irony of his words sank into Julia. Her hands shook, and her eyes filled with tears. "Go, Zeke. Leave me."

He stared at her for a moment; his mouth opened and closed tight over something she would never hear. He turned and slammed the door behind him.

\* \* \*

That night in the evening meeting, a group of Saints gathered in Benjamin's large parlor. As William Clayton wrote down the Prophet's words, Julia listened with her whole soul. ". . . but they reside in the presence of God, on a globe like a sea of glass and fire, where all things for their glory are manifest—past, present, and future, and are continually before the Lord."

Then Julia understood. The souls of those who had lived on the earth, the angels on the sea of glass and fire, saw the purpose of God, Jehovah's work for their glory—past, present, and future. And she prayed that Ezekiel would be on that globe one day, that place of glass and fire, and that he would see his glory and know that his soul was continually before the Lord, even if she were not there to see it with him.

\* \* \*

*May 1843. Macedonia, Illinois*

Six weeks passed before the Prophet and William Clayton came again to Macedonia. On that day, Melissa cooked beefsteak pie and sugared carrots for supper. They spent the evening singing and matching couplets in rhyme. When it was time to retire, Joseph asked Benjamin and Melissa to remain in the parlor with him and Brother Clayton. A light breeze from the window broke the heat, and the candle's flame occasionally wavered. Melissa held their sleeping baby in her arms.

Joseph, sitting next to Brother Clayton, turned to Benjamin and Melissa, who were across from him on a couch. "I would like to marry you according to the law of the Lord."

Benjamin remarked lightheartedly, "I shall not marry my wife again unless she courts me! For I did it all the first time."

"Brother Benjamin, this is not a matter of levity; I am in earnest," Joseph gently chided. His blue eyes were serious and full of faith as he explained. "The new and everlasting covenant of marriage has been revealed to me. Soon it will only take place in the house of the Lord. But you are one of the chosen who is to receive this blessing even now." The Prophet continued, instructing them on the meaning and nature of the priesthood. Then he put his hand on William Clayton's knee. William picked up his pen and paper and wrote Joseph's words:

> *Except a man and his wife enter into an everlasting covenant and be married for eternity while in this probation, by the power and authority of the holy priesthood, they will cease to increase when they die; that is, they will not have any children after the resurrection. But those who are married by the power and authority of the priesthood in this life and continue without committing sin against the Holy Ghost will continue to increase and have children in the celestial glory.*
>
> *In the celestial glory, there are three heavens or degrees; and in order to obtain the highest, a man must enter into this order of the priesthood, [meaning the new and everlasting covenant of marriage]; and if he does not, he cannot obtain it. He may enter into the other, but that is the end of his kingdom; he cannot have an increase.*

Then the Prophet Joseph sealed Benjamin and Melissa for time and all eternity with the holy sealing keys he held.

\*\*\*

The following afternoon, Joseph, William Clayton, Benjamin, and Melissa dined at the Babbitts' home. Tired from her pregnancy, Julianne was glad when she and Melissa had the supper on the table. She sat down heavily in a chair, feeling twice as big and three times as clumsy as during her first pregnancy.

The Prophet thanked Julianne and then asked, "How is your sister, Mary? Has she safely delivered her son, David Johnson Wilson?"

Julianne smiled. "Yes, just a week ago. The Wilsons are all doing well."

The Prophet nodded, his look contemplative. "I remember the infant's namesake, your brother David. It feels like a long time ago. I was away when he died. How the news grieved me. I feel as if that was our first loss as a people."

"It felt like our first loss as a family," Julianne said.

"Yet the Lord has been with us," Joseph added.

Ten minutes later, while they were eating, Joseph turned to Almon. "Have you prepared the legislative speech we talked about against the repeal of the Nauvoo Charter? John Bennett is constantly pressuring our lawmakers."

Almon nodded. "Of course. Here's a small portion." Almon threw his shoulders back and orated. Julianne let out a quick breath, hoping that no one else realized he was imitating Sidney Rigdon. "Be just then, regard the principles of equal rights and deal out to the citizens of every portion of our state evenhanded justice, forget not your duties in the madness of prejudice."

Joseph chuckled and had a knowing twinkle in his eye. "I like it very much."

Almon grinned then went on more seriously. "Joking aside, I have nearly finished it and will be glad for you to review it. Also, I leave in July for Cincinnati to take the refresher course in law that we spoke of. I will find out the best ways to aid you in your legal entanglements."

"Thank you, Brother Almon," Joseph said. Then he looked at Julianne with a slight crease in his brow. He turned back to Almon. "I regret the need for you to leave Sister Julianne at a time like this."

Julianne smiled brightly. "Brother Joseph, last time I traveled with Almon in this condition, we had a most interesting experience. This time I am happy to stay home with my mother and sisters."

Joseph smiled warmly. "Sister, you will be blessed beyond measure for this sacrifice."

\*\*\*

*June 30, 1843. Nauvoo, Illinois*

Almon rode hard to Nauvoo. Word had reached him that, due to the feverish accusations of John Bennett and Lilburn Boggs, Thomas Ford had been pressured into signing a writ for Joseph's arrest on the old Missouri treason charge. The rest of the news was even worse. Joseph had been kidnapped when he was two hundred miles north of Nauvoo visiting relatives of Emma. The arresting officers were Harmon Wilson from Carthage and Joseph Reynolds, an old mobocrat from Jackson County, Missouri.

When Almon arrived in Nauvoo, he found a crowd gathered in the grove near the temple. Astounded and overjoyed, he watched as Joseph, free again, took the stand and described his ordeal. Apparently, Joseph's captors had made the mistake of abusing Joseph by driving their pistols repeatedly into his sides, badly bruising him and taking him captive without due process. Brothers William Clayton and Stephen Markham had arrived in time to arouse the fair-minded authorities who interceded. With the help of Whig lawyer Cyrus Walker, Joseph had been taken to Nauvoo, where the city charter had the power to try writs of habeas corpus. Of course, Joseph was released.

After the speech, Almon saw his friend William Law, now second counselor in the First Presidency. Almon walked up to him and grinned. "I can't believe it. Joseph has escaped again! He's like a cat with nine lives."

William did not smile but returned, "It was because of Cyrus Walker. If he hadn't issued the writ of habeas corpus, Joseph would be in Missouri. Mr. Walker asked Joseph for his vote in return for his legal services. Joseph agreed."

Almon chewed on this. "I might have done the same thing if I were kidnapped and about to be dragged to Missouri." Almon scratched his head. "No, even then I wouldn't vote for a Whig!" William did not seem amused. Almon continued. "Come, William, Joseph is free. You ought to be happy about this, and I ought to be murmuring. The Whigs will gain a vote."

William responded vehemently. "I heard the conversation. Joseph knows that Walker expects the whole Mormon vote. A Prophet should not use his ecclesiastical power in political or business affairs."

Almon looked carefully at William. He knew his friend had been deeply frustrated when Joseph had spoken out months ago, suggesting immigrants buy Church-owned lots to help with the Church's debt. Since then, William had not been able to sell his land. William continued. "If Walker doesn't win, every Whig in Hancock County will be after Joseph's blood."

"Except for one," Almon said, looking carefully at William.

"Of course," William said, "except for me."

\* \* \*

*Saturday, July 1, 1843. Carthage, Illinois*

Ezekiel heard the ruckus in the street. He had been drinking more heavily during the summer, telling himself that he had been separated from Julia for a long time and this was nothing more. Some of the time, he believed it.

With a drink in his hand, he walked out of the tavern. Two men stood on a box on the street corner, surrounded by a large crowd. Ezekiel recognized one from the tavern—Constable Wilson from Carthage. The other introduced himself as Sheriff Reynolds of Jackson County, Missouri.

The constable held up a paper. "Ladies and gentlemen, do you see this?" he shouted. "It's a writ for the arrest and extradition of Joe Smith, who committed treason in Missouri. It's signed by Governor Ford himself. We arrested him, but he was allowed a trial at Nauvoo and has been released. The Nauvoo City Charter defies the laws of our great nation!"

There were shouts from the crowd.

Reynolds took the stand, holding up another paper. "Here is a petition asking Governor Ford for a posse to retake Smith, dead or alive. Sign it, my friends! I knew Smith in Missouri. He is the worst of fiends! We arrested him in Dixon County, where he viciously lied to the citizens there, convincing them we were the aggressors. Such is his devilish power! The constable and I were forced to Nauvoo at gunpoint. His fearsome Legion took our arms. He mocked us, forcing us to sit with him at his table as if we were his infernal friends."

Suddenly, Ezekiel burst out laughing. There was no one else on earth like Joseph who would take his enemies into his home and serve them his wife's cooking. But Ezekiel no longer had a wife. He shouted, not caring who heard, "So old Joe gave you food instead of a bullet. Sounds like the worst of fiends to me!"

Someone laughed. There was a moment of silence, as if the entire crowd was wondering what Ezekiel had meant. Was Ezekiel Johnson friend or foe? Then the rabble continued with shouts to stop Smith's demagoguery, to repeal the Nauvoo Charter, and to round up a posse. Far down the street, Ezekiel spotted Almon and an elderly gentleman slip from the crowd, enter a buggy, and turn down the road toward Nauvoo.

* * *

*Two days later. Macedonia, Illinois*

Almon arrived home late at night. He went into the bedroom, where Julianne slept. He had spent the past couple of days with Judge Adams—first to see the lay of the land in Carthage and then to try to minimize the damage back in Nauvoo. He had done as much as he could to help Joseph. A remonstrance against the Carthage proceedings had been put together and delivered. A petition to the governor, praying that he not issue anymore writs, had been signed by the citizens of Nauvoo and sent to Springfield.

In two days, Almon would leave for Cincinnati to study the law once more, to find out if there was anything else that could be done to protect Joseph. But at this moment, crickets sang and moonlight streamed through the window onto Julianne's form. She was hope and joy, the clean tenderness of a summer night, all he had dreamed of as a child. She embodied the teachings of Christ and made life worth living.

He took off his boots and climbed into bed beside her. She snuggled into him. He felt his child move within her. This time she would not go with him to Cincinnati. Each night in his prayers he told God to take care of his Julianne and their unborn child, laying his petition before the King of Heaven, explaining that his service was, and would always be, a thank you for that gift.

# 23

*Thy holy cause I will defend,*
*And all thy sorrows, joys and care,*
*Shall be my own, till life shall end,*
*With thee eternal lives to share.*

Joel Hills Johnson

*Tuesday, August 15, 1843. Macedonia, Illinois*

JULIANNE WINCED FROM THE PAIN of the contraction, Delcena's steady hands on her abdomen. Then another came. Delcena's hands were as light as a butterfly as the pressure within Julianne's body wrung her like laundry pushed through the rollers. Sweat poured from her. Her mother bathed her brow. Julianne's fists squeezed tight, and she was not conscious of the imprints of her own nails.

"You're almost there. Push, now!" Delcena commanded. Julianne pushed for Almon, for herself, for all the joy and pain that was and is.

"You did it, darling! She's a girl."

Her mother's words were like music. Julianne reached out to her baby girl, her own Ann Caroline! But then Julianne screamed as another contraction as hard and terrible as the last gripped her.

Delcena was calm. She had told Julianne this might happen. But Julianne had not believed that such a wonderful thing would be reality.

"Another baby is coming. I see the head," Delcena announced. "Push, Juli. Again. Again."

The rhythm of pain seized her until her son was born. Don Carlos Babbitt let out a lusty scream, as if he were enraged at the indignity of birth.

Julianne's head melted back into the pillows. Her son was born. Her sister and mother wept. Were they remembering Delcena's first son, the twin who did not live? Or were they weeping with joy for Julianne, whose empty arms were now full?

\* \* \*

*Cincinnati, Ohio*

Dining alone at Aunt Nancy's boardinghouse, Almon opened the letter from his brother-in-law Joe. The script was flowing and friendly, and the news hit him like shooting stars. *Your family is here in the room with me as I write,* the letter said. *It has grown considerably since you left—you have both a new son and a new daughter. Julianne is feeding your little girl, Ann Caroline, who is bald as a peeled apple. My wife holds your son, Don Carlos. He has a tuft of black hair in infancy and hopefully will retain it in old age. Your wife is chiding me and says to tell you that they are both perfect and she is in good health. She will add a note to this letter as soon as the twins finish nursing, which may never occur. They both have ferocious appetites.* Almon skipped to the second page and found Julianne's neat script. *God bless you, my darling boy. My joy would be overflowing if you were here. I can scarcely wait for the day when you come home and meet your little ones. The delivery went well with Mother and Delcena by my side. Delcena had told me for many months that she believed we would have twins. She laughs now because I did not believe her. Don Carlos is hungry again so I must appease him. All three of us are well and strong. I long for your return. Only you know how much I love you. Your devoted wife, Julianne Babbitt.*

With the letter in his hand, Almon stood up and announced the news to Aunt Nancy. She called for drinks for the whole house. White laborers and free blacks, Irish and German, men, women, and children of different denominations cheered and toasted the arrival of the Babbitt twins.

\* \* \*

It wasn't until after dinner that Almon realized he hadn't finished reading Joe's letter. Sitting in his room on his bed, Almon unfolded it once more. The second paragraph told the results of the recent election in Hancock County. Mr. Hoge, the Democrat, had won. Joe, who was nearly as locofoco as Almon, applauded the results—at least from a political standpoint. However, the Whigs were up in arms, and Thomas Sharp spun virulent articles in the *Warsaw Signal* that said they no longer had to rely on Bennett's or Boggs' testimonies; they now had their own proof of Joe Smith's tyranny.

Then Joe had copied some of the phrases from the Prophet's speech the day before the election. It was the only way to explain how the tables had turned on Cyrus Walker, the Whig candidate. *I am not come to tell you how to vote today,* Joseph had said. *Every man should stand on his own merits. As for Mr. Walker, he is the Whig candidate and a high-minded man who helped me. He's my friend, and I'll vote for him. However, Brother Hyrum tells me this morning that he has had a testimony to the effect it would be better for the people to vote for Hoge; and I never knew Hyrum to say he had a revelation and it failed.*

Almon stared at the letter, almost in disbelief. The Democrats had taken the election. The whole countryside knew Joseph had promised his vote to Walker. Almon realized how furious William Law would be now. He could not even imagine what Thomas Sharp and the anti-Mormon party would do. Almon took a deep breath. He thought about Julianne and his little ones. He thought about the trouble the Prophet was in. It was time to go home.

\* \* \*

*Friday, October 6, 1843. Nauvoo, Illinois*

The morning dawned cloudy and threatening as the brethren gathered near the temple for a special conference. Distant lightning pierced the sky, and thunder clapped as Almon arrived and walked up to the wooden platform. He would be saying the opening prayer. The First Presidency and Hyrum Smith, the Patriarch, had already arrived. Palpable tension pulsed between Joseph and his counselors, Sidney Rigdon and William Law. Their handshakes were formal, not warm. Almon knew William could scarcely keep in check his animosity over Joseph's political and business decisions. Additionally, he questioned Joseph's recent revelations. In turn, Joseph feared that Sidney Rigdon, his other counselor, had turned against him.

Conference convened. After the opening hymn, Almon stepped up to the podium and said the opening prayer. He thanked the Lord for His abundant blessings, the progress on the temple, and the revelations from heaven. Then he begged for peace among the Saints and protection from their enemies.

After Almon's prayer, Joseph took the stand, explaining that the first item of business was the case of Sidney Rigdon. Joseph explained that due to circumstances, he believed that Elder Rigdon was no longer fit to be his counselor unless those difficulties could be removed. However, he desired Elder Rigdon's salvation and wanted him to retain a place among the Saints.

Joseph outlined his case. John Bennett had written a letter to Sidney Rigdon and Orson Pratt, asking for their aid in his war against Joseph. Orson had immediately taken the letter to Joseph, but Sidney had waited. In addition, Sidney had neglected to give Joseph a letter from Esquire Butterfield, which was for Joseph's benefit. Finally, Porter Rockwell's mother said that Rigdon had written to Missouri's governor, telling him that Joseph was going to Dixon and to arrest him there.

Sidney Rigdon took the stand, pleading his case. He claimed that he had never written John Bennett and only received one communication, which he had handed over to President Smith. He had been ill when Butterfield's letter had come, causing it to be accidentally set aside. He had never corresponded with Governor Carlin or been a traitor to the Prophet of God. The wind increased, and rain fell in torrents. Conference was adjourned until the weather permitted.

On Sunday morning, the rain had stopped, though dark clouds still layered the sky. Conference convened at ten o'clock. Sidney Rigdon continued his plea, tearfully appealing to Joseph as he spoke of their past friendship, association, and suffering. He was willing to resign his place, though with sorrowful and indescribable feelings.

Joseph arose and again explained the supposed treacherous correspondence between Elder Rigdon and Governor Carlin. "This causes me deep concern. I was arrested in Dixon and nearly kidnapped. Someone I was close to told the Missourians exactly where I was. Elder Rigdon may be speaking the truth, but I don't know for certain," Joseph said. "A counselor needs to be trusted fully. I desire Elder Rigdon's friendship and membership in the Church, but I cannot accept him as my counselor."

To Almon, it seemed that there was only circumstantial evidence against Rigdon, nothing that could be proven in a court of law. Hyrum, moved by Sidney's tears, stood and spoke of mercy, especially in regard to their aged companion and fellow-servant in truth and righteousness.

Almon voiced his support of Hyrum's opinion. William Law also gave his opinion in Rigdon's behalf. On a motion by William Marks, and seconded by Hyrum, the conference voted that Elder Rigdon be permitted to retain his station as counselor in the First Presidency.

The wind picked up. Conference was adjourned for one hour. Elder Rigdon left the stand. Joseph stood and turned to Hyrum, William, and Almon. His eyes were deeply concerned, and he took a deep, tired breath. "You have put him on my shoulders again. But you must carry him, for I cannot."

\* \* \*

The following day when conference reconvened, Almon felt Joseph's grief as the Prophet spoke about James Adams, who had recently passed away. Almon thought about his own association with the elderly gentleman. He would miss him. However, Joseph's loss ran deeper—James Adams had protected, cheered, and blessed Joseph as if he were his own son.

"Brother Adams has gone to open a more effectual door for the dead," Joseph said, the power and pathos of his voice touching the congregation. "The spirits of the just are exalted to a greater and more glorious work; hence they are blessed in their departure to the world of spirits. Enveloped in flaming fire, they are not far from us and understand our thoughts, feelings, and motions and are often pained therewith. Hasten the work in the temple, renew your exertions to forward all the work of the last days, and walk before the Lord in soberness and righteousness."

After his discourse, the Prophet closed the conference with prayer, pronouncing his blessings on his beloved people. The prayer touched Almon deeply, and he realized once again that he loved Joseph as a prophet and as a friend. He knew Joseph's weaknesses and did not expect him to perform beyond human frailty. He looked over at William Law. His friend's face was emotionless, an unreadable mask.

\* \* \*

*Late March 1844. Nauvoo, Illinois*

Outside, it was a dull, cloudy day. Almon and Benjamin entered the Red Brick Store on Water Street and climbed up the steps to the assembly room. Both men had been in Nauvoo for much of the past three months and had been attending meetings. The Prophet had given the faithful little rest. Once, Almon overheard another man lament to Orson Pratt about this. Orson had smiled, a little tiredly, and responded, "When I asked Joseph this same question, he answered, 'The Spirit urges me.'" Today, only those invited would attend. Sidney Rigdon and William Law were not among them.

Yet the assembly room was crowded with chairs. Nine of the Twelve and their wives were already sitting in the front rows near Joseph, who stood. Almon, Benjamin, and other faithful brothers and sisters filled in the remaining seats. A few minutes later, Joseph seemed somewhat melancholy in spirits as he opened the meeting, yet he smiled at those assembled and spoke of how he loved his friends. Then the Prophet and Hyrum performed the ordinance of the washing of feet. Almon sat very still, his active green eyes focusing steadily on the Prophet, who wiped his feet clean, his heart experiencing the same holiness he had experienced in the Kirtland Temple. Joseph moved on. Almon saw the tears on Benjamin's cheeks as the Prophet washed his feet. Almon closed his eyes, wondering if it would have made a difference if William Law were here to witness the Prophet's humility. But William could not be here, for his anger would hinder the spirit of the meeting. Almon prayed that William would realize that he was wrong, that Joseph was not a fallen prophet.

Following this ordinance, Joseph explained that he and Hyrum would now conduct every ordinance of the Holy Priesthood according to the pattern that had been shown him in vision. These ordinances took the remainder of the morning. Afterward, Joseph sealed upon the heads of the Twelve all of the keys and powers that God had bestowed upon him.

In the afternoon, Joseph stood for three hours as he taught the assemblage the doctrines of the kingdom. It was nearly early candlelight. The Prophet's face shone like amber. His words seared into Almon's mind. The Prophet looked at the Twelve in particular and said, "The Lord bids me hasten the work in which we are engaged. Some important scene is near; it may be that my enemies will kill me, and if they should, and the keys and power that rest upon me are not imparted to you, they would be lost from the earth. Upon the shoulders of the Twelve must the responsibility of leading this Church henceforth rest. Thus can this power and these keys be perpetuated in the earth. Should any of you be killed, you can lay your hands upon others and fill up the quorum. Brethren, you may have many storms to pass through, and sore trials await you. Should you have to walk right into danger and the very jaws of death, fear no evil; Jesus Christ has died for you."

Then Joseph became animated, all weariness swept away like dust in a storm. His blue eyes shone like gems as he threw back the collar of his coat and said, "I roll the burden and responsibility of leading this Church from my shoulders to yours. Now round up your shoulders and stand under it like men, for the Lord is going to let me rest awhile."

However, Joseph did not rest; he rejoiced. He sprang into the air, shaking and shouting for joy as he clapped his hands. "Hallelujah, hallelujah, I am clear of the responsibility of the kingdom from this time forth! I have done that which the Lord commanded me. I have set up His kingdom that will never be thrown down. It will never be given to another people."

\* \* \*

*April 4, 1844. Macedonia, Illinois*

Ezekiel's ten-month-old grandson, David Wilson, took hold of Ezekiel's knee and used it to stand. His eyes were a golden brown, and he was blond like Mary. Ezekiel tapped the baby's nose and smiled at him. David grinned and plopped down to the floor. Nearby, Mary combed and arranged Esther's hair.

It was Esther's wedding day, and she was full of life as she chatted. "Did you know that George told me to get married on the fourteenth with him and Maria? They thought we should save everyone the trouble of two weddings. But I couldn't bear to share mine with another bride. And it has all worked out. It is finally a lovely, warm day. Almon is finally back from Nauvoo and can marry us. And Papa will give me away."

When Mary had finished, Esther stood and twirled. She wore the dress Melissa had married Benjamin in, white with brocade and lace. Her hair was pulled on top of her head and cascaded down in dark ringlets. "Papa, do you think I'm a pretty bride? If you say 'pretty is as pretty does' like Mama, I shall scream."

Ezekiel chuckled and shook his head at his daughter. "You are a beautiful bride."

Esther's nose wrinkled when she grinned. "And you look handsome in your suit, Papa. It looks brand new. I suppose you've only worn it five times—at your daughters' weddings. Wait—just four times. You weren't at Mary's wedding."

"Six times," Ezekiel corrected. "I was at Ben's wedding, and I went to church once."

Mary suddenly laughed. "I remember, Papa. You were cleaning Betsy, then you stopped and put on your suit. You joined us for the meeting."

Ezekiel's eyes met Mary's. "You were just a little blonde thing, running wild with the animals whenever your Mama would let you. You've changed since then."

"I have," Mary said, putting her hand on his shoulder for a moment. "But you've stayed the same, Papa."

Ezekiel wasn't sure if he wanted to know what Mary meant by that.

While Esther admired herself in a looking glass, Ezekiel watched little David reach his arms out for his mother. Mary picked up her son and kissed him. He was a quiet, affectionate baby. Mary's hair was darker than it had been when she was little and her cheeks more pallid. Her sweet brown eyes looked tired today. She had been ill much of the winter.

"Mary, don't you wish Papa could have given you away?" Esther called out.

Mary smiled rather wistfully and said, "Oh yes. But we rarely get all we wish for."

"I know that," Esther said, hugging Ezekiel. "Papa, I wish you would move to Nauvoo with David and me."

"Perhaps when I'm too old to take care of myself," Ezekiel said, holding her close.

"Perhaps when you are too old to drink anymore," Esther replied with a bright smile as she kissed Ezekiel on the cheek.

\* \* \*

*Monday, April 15, 1844. Nauvoo, Illinois*

Almon paused outside of the Law's home. His thoughts roved—just a few years ago, he'd stood beside William, who was full of faith, as they witnessed the wedding of Almon's brother-in-law Joe. But yesterday, at George and Maria's wedding, Almon had felt the loss of his old friend, knowing how far away William was and how painful the Prophet's assignment would be.

Almon took a deep breath, remembering the long-ago days when he was a young missionary in Canada. William Law had been his prize convert. But now, things could not be more different. William had been dropped from the First Presidency in January and was virulently preaching that Joseph was a fallen prophet. His excommunication trial was scheduled in three days. Joseph had asked Almon to attempt reconciliation.

Almon knocked on the door. William's wife, Jane, opened it. The strain in her eyes was visible, but she seemed a bit relieved when she saw it was him. Almon took off his hat and held it in his hands. "Is William home?"

"Just a moment," Jane said, excusing herself. When she came back, she said William would see Almon in the study. Almon found him there, sitting behind a large oak desk, writing in his diary. Almon reached out his hand. William shook it and invited him to sit down. "How are you, my friend?" Almon questioned.

William ran his fingers through his receding hair. "Almon, I have been turned upside down by all of this. It's been horrible for Jane. How are you and your wife? Your children?"

"We are all well," Almon said. Then he was quiet for an instant; the friendly small talk threw him off track. His heart ached.

William broke the silence between them. "Did the mayor send you?"

Almon shrugged slightly. It was *the mayor* now . . . no longer *Joseph*. "Joseph knows I came. He wants you back in the fold as much as I do."

"What fold? The fold of hypocrites?"

Almon held his tongue for once in his life, knowing that being defensive with William was pointless.

"Can you tell me in all honesty that you think what he did to Cyrus Walker was justified?" William asked.

"It was understandable," Almon said. "But no. It was not justifiable."

"It was base trickery! Under the guise of *Hyrum's* revelation! They should not meddle with politics."

"No, they should not. But it is not entirely their fault. Politicians meddle with them. William, I understand how you feel."

William let out a quick breath. "Then join me. Did you hear Smith's discourse at conference?"

Almon nodded. Joseph had spoken in response to the death of Elder King Follett. He had talked about the dead, about the character of God, about the meaning of creation, and about how exaltation involved becoming a god like our Father in Heaven.

William slapped his hand down on the desk. "Those were some of the most blasphemous doctrines ever preached on this earth—a council of gods! A multiplicity of gods! That our God wrought out His salvation in the flesh the same as you and me. This is blasphemy, not Christianity!"

Almon bristled. "On that point, I could not disagree with you more. In his letter to the Philippians, Paul states that 'being in the form of God, thought it not robbery to be equal with God.' William, could we open the scriptures together as we used to?"

"No." William's face reddened in frustration. "We were like schoolboys then. I am a Christian man and will not squabble over interpretations. And to think that I testified against John Bennett for Joseph Smith's sake. Now I know that Bennett's allegations are not lies."

"Bennett is lecherous and a base liar. You know that!"

"So is Smith! And a fallen prophet too," William snapped. "I will never waver when Satan's doctrines stare me in the face. If Joseph does not repent, he will be stopped. He will be exposed."

Almon's heart beat quickly. He knew how explosive the countryside was. Whigs and mobocrats wanted nothing more than to drive out the Mormons and kill Joseph. "I plead with you not to break open hell. Don't put your own salvation in jeopardy."

William jumped to his feet. "Don't speak to me about *my* salvation!"

Almon matched his movement. The men stared at each other. The taut anger, the clenched fists, the furious energy in William's eyes nearly broke Almon's heart. William must have seen it, for he bit back his rage. He sat down at his desk and looked up at Almon. "I know you are an honest man. Old friends ought not to come to blows. Leave me."

\* \* \*

*May 27, 1844. Macedonia and Carthage, Illinois*

Joe was winded when he rode into Macedonia. He had spent the past several days in Nauvoo. He needed to get a message from Almon to Julianne. When he arrived at the Babbitts' house, the buggy was gone. Knowing that she often took lunch to their father, he decided to stop there first. Ezekiel was sitting on the porch with his gun, Betsy, when Joe arrived.

"What's the news?" Ezekiel asked.

"Almon's on his way to Carthage with Joseph and a company of two dozen men."

Ezekiel cursed. "Joseph Jackson bragged in the tavern that when Joseph comes to Carthage to answer the perjury writ against him, he'll never leave alive."

Joe paled. "Almon advised him. He thought it would be better for Joseph to go to the circuit court and request to have the indictments against him investigated before there's a warrant for his arrest."

Ezekiel shouldered Betsy and headed for the stable.

"Pa, where are you going?" Joe asked.

"To warn my fool son-in-law!"

"Wait, I'll go with you."

Ezekiel eyed Joe's horse. "Nope. Your horse is tired, and I only have one sound mount. I'm not waiting."

\* \* \*

Ezekiel rode hard to the courthouse. Joseph Jackson stood on a green, watching both the courthouse and Hamilton's Hotel. Ezekiel spotted Almon striding briskly between the hotel and courthouse. Ezekiel galloped up to him. "Jackson has sworn to kill Joseph, and he's waiting."

"We know," Almon said. "Charles Foster warned us when we arrived."

"I thought Foster hated Joseph too."

"Not enough to want blood on his hands."

"What are you waiting for? Get Joseph on the road back to Nauvoo. I'll keep an eye on Jackson."

"Right now Joseph's safe in his hotel room. We're still trying to get his trial brought forward so he doesn't have to come back to Carthage. But the prosecution says their material witness is absent. I just informed Joseph. I'm going back to talk with the judge one more time. If we can't get him in court within the next hour, our boys will take him safely back to Nauvoo. We know better than to have him here at nightfall."

Ezekiel nodded. "I'll stay out here and watch your back. Are you going home tonight?"

"I hope so," Almon said.

The courthouse shade cooled the moisture on Ezekiel's brow as he waited, watching Jackson, his finger close to Betsy's trigger. Jackson watched the hotel and courthouse, oblivious to Ezekiel's presence. Twenty minutes later, Almon came out of the courthouse. He motioned for Ezekiel to wait then headed to the hotel. A short time later, Ezekiel watched as men saddled and harnessed the horses. Then Joseph came out and mounted Joe Duncan. Porter Rockwell shadowed his every move, remaining between the Prophet and his enemy's line of fire.

After the entourage rode off, Almon walked over to Ezekiel. "They've put the trial off until the next term. Joseph'll be home by nine tonight."

"Would you have been fool enough to ride back home alone?" Ezekiel questioned as they mounted their horses.

Almon took a tired breath. "Yes. But I'm glad you're here."

Ezekiel eyed him. "I figure us fools better stick together."

\* \* \*

As Almon rode back to Macedonia with Ezekiel, the late afternoon sky grew heavy with thick clouds. It had been a taxing two weeks in Nauvoo. In addition to filing charges, the apostates, with William at their head, had purchased a press and distributed the prospectus of a newspaper called *The Nauvoo Expositor*. The first issue was scheduled to be published in eleven days, on June seventh. When that happened, there was no telling what would come next.

As if reading his mind, Ezekiel suddenly asked, "What does Joseph think about that paper coming out? What's it called? *The Nauvoo Exposition?*"

"Expositor," Almon corrected without comment.

"That's the one."

"He's going to wait and see. If it's libelous and damaging enough to incite mob violence, he may encourage the city council to act. He will not allow a paper that will lead to another Missouri war."

Ezekiel glanced at Almon. "Our Constitution guarantees freedom of press."

"That's true. But there are limits. Other presses in the United States have been destroyed with no legal repercussions. Take the Latter-day Saint press in Independence, Missouri. It was destroyed even though it attacked no one. In the *Expositor* case, there is a legal leg to stand on. Blackstone, an English legal authority, in volume 2, page 4, states that a libelous paper is illegal and can be termed a nuisance and stopped. The Nauvoo Charter allows the city council to pass ordinances. They could pass an ordinance on libel and remove the press."

"You mean destroy it? You don't think that would trigger the mobs?"

"Of course it could. And it could be deemed illegal. Man decides what is legal and what is not. Like you said, our Constitution guarantees the freedom of the press. They could arrest Joseph and the entire city council. I'm certain that it would mean a repeal of the Charter. Joseph is caught between two rocks squeezing the life out of him. The thing he fears most is a repeat of Missouri. All of us fear it."

"What are you going to do now?" Ezekiel shouted over the thunder that clapped in the sky just as it started raining.

"Go home to my wife and children."

\*\*\*

*June 16, 1844. Nauvoo, Illinois*

Rain drummed on the rooftop. With a violent jerk, Delcena awoke from a nightmare. Recent events had triggered the dream. The first issue of the *Nauvoo Expositor* had been released ten days ago. It seethed with the apostates' fury and called upon all citizens in Hancock County to stop Joseph Smith's abuses. Afraid that the newspaper would incite the mobs to attack Nauvoo, Joseph and the city council had declared it a nuisance and had it destroyed. Then the countryside had exploded in wrath. Constable Bettisworth from Carthage had come to arrest the Prophet, but Joseph had been released by the Nauvoo Municipal Court. Bettisworth had cursed and shouted, promising to be back. Delcena had dreamed of Bettisworth coming with an army, but the man he'd dragged away was Lyman, and the army had jeered at her, the teeth of each man razor sharp.

Wakefulness brought no relief. The nightmare mirrored Nauvoo's jagged reality. She could not get the words in the *Warsaw Signal* out of her mind. Thomas Sharp called for violence: "We have no time for comment, every man will make his own. Let it be made with powder and ball!!!"

Trying desperately to push back her fear and exhaustion, Delcena arose from bed. The Prophet was scheduled to preach in the grove east of the temple in two hours. She knew Joseph would be there despite the rain, despite the ache in his lungs and chest when preaching over the sound of a storm. He would be there because he loved his people, because he might not have the opportunity to preach to them again.

Numbly, she awakened Albey. Her twelve-year-old, hair awry, went out to milk. Delcena ate cold oatmeal, allowing the others to sleep in. She hadn't the energy to get the little ones up, and her teenage girls, Alvira and Mary, needed the rest. When Albey came in, Delcena was dressed and had a small tarpaulin in her hand. Alvira stood in the bedroom doorway, sleepy eyed. Albey placed the pail of milk on the counter and said, "I'll come with you."

"Me too." Alvira walked into the kitchen. Delcena nodded, grateful for their companionship.

A short time later, Delcena sat with Albey and Alvira on each side of her, huddled together with the tarpaulin over them. The grove was full of Saints. With the backdrop of the unfinished temple, Joseph stood in front of them, his hair flat and darker in the rain. He looked so strong, his shoulders straight, the rain dripping from him.

His voice rose above the weather, almost as though he were oblivious to the downpour, as he bore testimony. "I have always declared God to be a distinct personage, Jesus Christ a separate and distinct personage from God the Father, and that the Holy Ghost is a distinct personage and a Spirit: and these three constitute three distinct personages and three Gods." Joseph's voice penetrated Delcena's soul. "So long as men are under the laws of God, they have no fears. When men open their lips against these truths, they do not injure me, but they injure themselves. I want to see truth in all its bearings and hug it to my bosom. I believe all that God ever revealed." Joseph continued, speaking of his vision, of glory upon glory—one glory of the sun, another glory of the moon, and another of the stars. "Every man who reigns in celestial glory is a god to his dominions." He spoke of the priesthood and of the new dispensation. He spoke of all the truth the world possessed and independent revelation. He spoke of those who relied only on man. "When the floods come and the winds blow, their foundations will be found to be sand, and their whole fabric will crumble to dust."

The rain increased, falling in torrents, blurring the temple, the Prophet, the world. Alvira hid her face in her mother's shoulder. Albey tried to see through the storm. Joseph the Prophet shouted above it all. "God will bear me off triumphant. I wish I could go on."

It seemed that it couldn't rain harder, yet it did. The Prophet turned and left the stand. Delcena could not see twelve inches in front of her. Alvira and Albey huddled against her, clutching the thin tarpaulin as rain pounded around them. When would the deluge stop? Delcena wept for Joseph, the teacher who opened the eyes of the blind, the man who sheltered her children with love, and the Prophet who yearned to stay with his people and finish their temple. She tasted the salt of her own tears mixed with the fresh fury of rain as she wept with the Saints in their shining and shattering world.

# 24

*In their warfare, hard and lonely,*
*They did fight without a fear;*
*Sealed at last their testimony*
*With their blood, in Carthage, where*
*They were martyred.*
*They a martyr's crown shall wear.*
*Crown them then! The Saints are crying;*
*They a glorious work have done.*
*And the heav'nly hosts replying,*
*With the Savior they are one*
*Crown them gladly;*
*Crown them, Father, through thy Son!*

Joel Hills Johnson

*Wednesday, June 19, 1844. Carthage, Illinois*

EZEKIEL ANSWERED THE KNOCK AT the door. Hard lines creased Almon's face. As commander of the Ramus Company of the Nauvoo Legion, Almon was dressed in uniform. The company had been on alert for the past two days. A meeting in Warsaw had called for the death of Church leaders and the expulsion of the Mormons. In Nauvoo, the Legion had been activated and martial law enforced. High water made it difficult to get messages back and forth between Macedonia and Nauvoo. Each day, Almon met with Ezekiel to get news from the tavern. Carthage and Warsaw vigilantes were armed and organized, setting up blockades and preparing for war against Joe Smith and the Mormons.

"We finally have orders from Nauvoo," Almon said as he handed Ezekiel a paper. Ezekiel scanned the note from Joseph Smith, ordering the company to come immediately to Nauvoo to help defend the people there.

Ezekiel swore bitterly. There were companies of armed vigilantes between Macedonia and Nauvoo. And if by some miracle the men made it to Nauvoo, who would be here to protect the women and children? Yet Delcena and Esther lived in Nauvoo—the mobs' first target.

"It will be worse than Haun's Mill," Almon said bitterly. "Our boys slaughtered on their way and Macedonia ravaged."

"It's an order from your lieutenant general," Ezekiel spit out the words. With honor and duty at stake, what choice did Almon have? He was a captain in the Legion. Ezekiel picked up Betsy and made sure she was loaded. "I'll hide in the brush along the Carthage Road. If a force tries to enter the city, they'll hear from me."

"No man can single-handedly hold off a mob," Almon returned. "I care more about innocent lives than orders!" Almon turned and left the house.

Ezekiel followed him. "You're talking about mutiny?"

Almon spun around, his jaw protruding defiantly and his eyes desperate. "Can you think of another option?"

\* \* \*

In the town square, Almon marshaled the men into line. George Wilson, Benjamin, and Will were among them. Joe, who was not a member of the Legion, walked over to Ezekiel. Almon wished he could get a message to Governor Ford to find out if troops had been called out to protect the Mormons. But there wasn't time. Besides, those troops might not be any more inclined to obey the governor's orders than Almon was to obey his prophet-general today. But there was a difference. Almon's mutiny was to save lives, not take them. Additionally, the high water complicated the situation. Joseph might not be completely aware of the danger.

Almon hesitated. Was he really prepared to openly disobey an order? Then he saw his nephew Sixtus among the men—sweet faced and large boned—just fifteen years old and barefoot. Sixtus grew too fast for Joel to keep him in boots. Almon looked into the faces of the other young men. Numerous others were barefoot too. Some he didn't know well, but they each had a story and a life that needed saving.

Almon cleared his throat and read the order. Thick silence surrounded him. Then Almon raised his voice loud. "I believe this move foolish.

Because of high water for the past four days, General Smith may not know there are armed troops between here and Nauvoo. If any of you go, you will not get to Nauvoo alive. I will not lead you to destruction."

The elderly John Smith shook his head and stepped forward. "I disagree with Captain Babbitt. Any man who goes at the call of the Prophet shall go and return safely, and not a hair of his head shall be lost; and I bless all of you in the name of the Lord." The majority of the men agreed with John Smith. Almon resigned his command. Uriah H. Yager, second in command, took charge of the company. He told the men to go home and eat then be prepared to march at sunset. They would travel under the protection of night.

Almon watched as Ezekiel embraced his sons and grandson. He might be a bitter old man, but he was proud. He would send his boys into war with his blessing. However, Almon did not change his mind. He was not going. If Macedonia was attacked, he would crouch in brush at the side of the road with his father-in-law, where he would shoot the leaders of the mob one by one before he would let them near his wife and babies.

\* \* \*

Benjamin was reminded of the Missouri days, marching through the prairie in the mud, rain, and darkness. Most of the men walked silently, ignoring feet torn by rocks and sticks. Sixtus marched between Will and Benjamin, his breathing loud and scared.

Yager commanded his men to halt and then extinguished his lantern. Far ahead in the darkness, two flags flew, blood-red in color, visible in the enemy's torchlight. It was a company, double their size, with a position in the north wood near the road.

"We'll pass by stealth," Captain Yager whispered. "One man at a time, silently, in the deep shadow on the opposite side of the road, leaving ten feet between each man."

When Benjamin's turn came, he squinted his eyes and stared ahead, knowing he was in rifle range as he crept along with Sixtus ten feet behind him and Will behind Sixtus. Benjamin knew how to control panic. The days as a prisoner in Missouri had taught him. Back then, Benjamin had prayed for the Lord to let him live until he had a son to bear his name. That prayer had been answered. He prayed for Sixtus, a brave, big boy like he had been, and for Will, his younger brother. When the three were out of rifle range, they gripped arms and waited in silence for the rest of the company. Several shots were fired at the last two men, but the shots whizzed past their heads.

\* \* \*

The Ramus Company from Macedonia arrived in Nauvoo at dawn. Joseph met them; the sky had cleared, and the red, new sun rose behind the emerging temple. When Joseph embraced Benjamin, his tired face opened into a smile. "Ben, we have passed through dark water, you and I, but we will come forth triumphant and friends through all eternity."

"We will, Joseph," Benjamin said, fighting the tightness in his throat, the burning of his eyes.

Joseph shook Will's hand. "God bless you, my friend."

Then he looked at Sixtus and smiled as he shook his hand. "Sixtus, remember the cocks? I would still rather chop wood than fight any day. Yet sometimes we have to stand up as men."

Joseph glanced down at Sixtus's bruised and bare feet. He moved through the rest of the company, greeting and embracing the men, while noticing how many of them were without shoes. "Quartermaster," Joseph called out. "Furnish these men with shoes."

\* \* \*

*Friday and Saturday, June 21 and 22, 1844*

It was eleven in the morning when Almon returned home. He had left earlier that morning to gather information. Julianne nursed Don Carlos in the rocking chair. Little Annie crawled around the room, sometimes stopping and chewing on the edge of the braided rug. Julianne thought of how Almon had worked in a frenzy for the past two days, poring through books from his law library, scribbling notes, writing letters, and finding couriers to deliver them. When he wasn't busy, he paced. Her father had stopped by twice to tell Almon what he had seen and heard in Carthage.

"There's bread pudding to eat," Julianne said.

Almon brought a bowl of pudding out into the parlor and sat down to eat. Annie crawled over to him and pulled herself up on his pant leg. She had brown eyes and dark hair that curled at the nape of her neck. Almon helped her stand, kissed her cheek, and gave her a bite of pudding. Then he looked at Julianne. "Governor Ford just arrived in Carthage. I'm going to see him."

Don Carlos felt Julianne's tension and stopped nursing. "You can't," Julianne begged. "Papa said that hundreds of armed men are there. They won't be friendly to the man who defended Joseph Smith a month ago."

Almon walked over and put a hand on her shoulder. "It will be all right. Ford respects me as a fellow Democrat. He believes in the rule of law. I'll offer my services. Maybe I can help negotiate a truce. Besides, the militia wasn't here in May. Most of the vigilantes don't know me."

"The apostates are there. They know you," Julianne warned.

"William and Wilson are the apostates. They were our friends."

"Oh, Almon, they hate us now."

"No, they hate the Smiths, not us."

"Surely Joseph has sent someone from Nauvoo to talk with the governor."

"But Joseph did not send me. Thus, I might be the only person able to help him. I talked with your brother Joe this morning. He's coming with me. He's met Ford before. I don't know when we'll be back. If the governor has a message for Joseph, I'll ride straight to Nauvoo to deliver it."

Julianne blinked back her tears. She wanted to tell Almon that this was bigger than him, that they were only leaves on a mighty tree. They had not the power to bend the branches. But Almon had not rested since he had disobeyed the Legion's orders. He had to go.

\* \* \*

It was near sundown when Joe and Almon arrived at Hamilton's Hotel in Carthage. Joe's heart skipped a beat when he saw nearly fifteen hundred armed men milling around the town square where they had set up camp. After he and Almon unhitched their horses, they shouldered their way through the crowd, largely unnoticed.

Once in the hotel, Almon immediately explained that he was Lawyer Babbitt and requested a meeting with the governor. A few minutes later, Joe and Almon were ushered into Ford's room. The governor, usually handsome and at ease, had hollows beneath his eyes.

He shook Almon's hand. "Lawyer Babbitt, why have you come?"

"To offer my services in settling this difficulty," Almon responded.

Governor Ford glanced out the window. "I gladly accept your services. Yesterday I was awakened to the report that the Mormons had already burned, destroyed, and murdered innocents. I sent out an edict for every man able to bear arms to come to Carthage for the protecting of the country. Now I find these claims to be false. However, I have an army on hand, many who want to kill the Mormon leaders and drive the rest from

Illinois. Additional companies are arriving hourly, swelling this so-called military. I don't know how long I will be able to control them.

"Joseph and Hyrum Smith can no longer avoid arrest, or the county will go up in flames. In my opinion, they broke the law when they destroyed that press. But this is a matter for courts, not mobs. If I write a letter explaining the danger to their people and promising my protection, do you think they will submit?"

"Perhaps. What about the other members of the city council and the officers who destroyed the press? There are writs against them too."

"The others should not come at this time," the governor said. "It will be difficult enough to protect the Smiths. But I pledge my protection with my honor. If they are arrested, I will be able to disband these troops and stop others on their way. The Smiths will be charged with riot and the case bound over for next term. They could return to Nauvoo for a time. We will let the courts settle this without bloodshed."

Almon nodded. "Sir, I would be honored to carry your message to General Smith."

Ford called for pen and paper. He finished writing the dispatch then said, "Lawyer Babbitt, if the Smiths submit, I request you to continue in the state's employ. You understand both parties from the inside; I do not."

"I am your willing servant," Almon said with a slight bow. A few minutes later, Governor Ford gave Almon the dispatch for Joseph.

As quickly as possible, Almon and Joe hitched the horse to the buggy and started across the side of the public square. A shout arose in the crowd, and within moments their buggy was surrounded by a mob of angry and violent men, swearing and threatening them with knives and guns. The horse reared.

"Babbitt," a man shouted. "Give me that letter!"

"I cannot. It's a dispatch from the governor. I am under his employ." Almon sat up straight in defiance.

"A dead man is employed by no one!" someone shouted. "That letter is for Joe Smith."

"It has the governor's seal. He wants justice."

"Justice!" a shout rang out. "There will be no justice until Joe is dead and the Mormons are driven from the state of Illinois." Shouts of "shoot 'em," and "kill 'em" filled the air.

Terrified and angry, Joe felt his heart pounding. He said loudly, "We are innocent, law-abiding citizens doing our duty! This is base religious persecution."

"You are Mormon fiends! Better dead than alive!"

Sheriff Backenstoes crowded his way through the mob and climbed into the carriage with Joe and Almon. "These men are employed by the governor," he shouted. The mob hissed and laughed mockingly, calling Backenstoes a Jack Mormon.

Then Joe saw Governor Ford press his way through the mob, his shoulders straight and his face grim and set. He too climbed into the open buggy and stood tall. It took several minutes, but the uproar toned down so he could be heard. "I am the governor of the state of Illinois and your chief commander!" he shouted. "Each of you is ordered to his quarters immediately. These men are to pass freely to and from this city. Any who disobey will be under immediate arrest!"

The mob parted around Joe and Almon. "I will protect the Smiths," Ford said under his breath as he climbed out of the buggy.

The crowd opened as Almon urged the horse forward. Muffled threats followed them: "You will never reach Nauvoo alive with your dispatch. Not over our dead bodies or yours."

Darkness approached, and the sky thickened with clouds. A light rain began to fall. Almon drove the buggy three miles out of Carthage at a moderate gait. Then Almon put the whip to the horse's rump, and they traveled as fast as they could toward the open prairie. Once on the prairie, darkness enveloped them and the rain increased.

The buggy tipped and almost overturned. "If we don't light the lanterns, these ditches and sloughs will be the death of us." Almon grimaced as he stopped the horse.

"We can't risk a light," Joe said. "I'll get out and feel the way while you drive."

As Joe walked with the horse, his mind wandered. Before the trip, he had honestly not believed that men in Carthage would try to kill him. Except for the rain beating on his shoulders, the night felt surreal. Would he have come had he known? What kind of rage made one man destroy another? These were the sort of experiences his brothers had, not himself. Seth had marched with Zion's Camp. Benjamin had gone to the Missouri front. But Joe ought to be studying the stars, not traversing the prairie with desperadoes after him. However, there were no stars out tonight.

Suddenly, Joe startled at the thundering footfalls of a troop of horsemen heading from Carthage to Nauvoo. Almon halted the horse. Joe sprang to the horse's head and stroked him while holding his mouth to keep him from neighing. The troop went on.

"If we make it to Nauvoo alive, I'll buy you supper," Almon whispered. "It's my turn to walk." Taking turns, Almon and Joe crept their way throughout the night, through the constant rain, with nothing to eat.

When daylight came, the rain had ceased. They neared the east boundary of Joseph's farm, where the mud was knee deep. They unhitched the horse, leaving the buggy. While wading through a slough, the exhausted horse staggered and fell into the deep mud.

"Let's leave him in that field," Almon said, nodding to the west.

"If we can get the poor fellow there," Joe added. Using ropes, the men heaved the horse from both sides until the animal staggered to its feet. They opened the fence and left the horse. Covered in mud and too weary to speak, they trudged four miles until they came to a creek. Almon looked at Joe, and a trace of his old smile crossed his features. "We can't go into civilized society looking like this." Wedging the dispatch in the branches of a tree, he lay down in the water and rolled in it, washing himself and his clothing. Utterly exhausted, Joe lay down in the creek and joined Almon. The difficulty was finding the strength to get up. Ten minutes later, they came to Sniders' Hotel, having walked over thirty miles that night.

When Mary Snider opened the door, she gasped when she saw the condition of her son-in-law and Almon Babbitt. Joe staggered and fell to the floor. Eddie and John carried him to a bed. Nearly insensible from exhaustion, Joe saw Almon looking down at him. "Rest, my friend," Almon said. "I'll be back after I get this dispatch to the Prophet. I'll buy you supper tonight."

\* \* \*

*Sunday and Monday, June 23 and 24, 1844*

On Sunday morning, Almon awoke with a start in his room in Sniders' Hotel. He had slept past dawn. Someone knocked briskly on the door. Almon jerked out of bed, wincing at his aching limbs. Yesterday, he had given Ford's message to Joseph, who had promised to inform Almon when he had made a decision. Pulling on a clean shirt the Sniders had provided, Almon hurried to answer the knock. Eddie Snider told him Emma Smith was in the sitting room waiting for him.

A few minutes later, Almon sat on a chair across from Emma. Visibly pregnant and neatly groomed, she couldn't help how her brown eyes betrayed how depleted she felt. However, she spoke directly. "Joseph is across the river in hiding. He plans to appeal to Washington and escape to the Rocky Mountains. Do you believe Governor Ford can protect Joseph and Hyrum?"

Almon took a deep breath. "Governor Ford risked his own life to protect Brother Johnson and me. With his honor at stake, he will try his utmost. But only God knows if he can keep that promise."

"How long would they be in Carthage?"

"A day or two at the most. Joseph and Hyrum would appear before court on a charge of riot. The case would be bound over for the next term, and they would each pay five hundred dollars in bail. Then Governor Ford would escort them back to Nauvoo. But there are hundreds of armed men in Carthage who . . ." Almon stopped when Emma's face paled and a stifled cry escaped her. She already knew what the mob planned.

"And if they don't go to Carthage?" Emma asked.

"The governor said they will be hunted as fugitives, and he does not think he could stop the mob from attacking Nauvoo. He fears the loss of hundreds of innocent lives."

"Thank you for explaining this to me," Emma said. She turned to leave.

"Where are you going?" Almon questioned.

"To write Joseph a letter," Emma responded. Her posture was perfect as she walked out the door. Almon could only imagine the sheer effort and strength it took.

\* \* \*

That evening another messenger came to the hotel. Still very weak, Joe shuffled to the door while Almon slept. Joe read the note: *To Messrs. Babbitt and Johnson. General Smith and his brother have returned to the city. They will leave for Carthage tomorrow morning to deliver themselves up under promise of protection from the governor and trusting that all troops shall be disbanded and sent home. General Smith wishes you to wait until next morning to bear him company.*

To bear the Prophet company. Joe sat down heavily. Tears pricked his eyes as he thought of Simon of Cyrene, who had carried the Savior's cross. As the cruel cross bore down on his body, had Simon realized the honor it was? Joe knelt down and prayed for the strength and courage to bear Joseph and Hyrum Smith, those great and good men, company on their trail to Carthage.

\* \* \*

At six in the morning, Almon got the horse and buggy ready. In his weak condition, Joe had difficulty climbing into the seat. "Perhaps you should stay here. I don't mind," Almon said.

Joe shook his head. "Joseph requested us to bear him company. I will do it."

A short time later, when Joseph, Hyrum, and the other men on horseback were ready, they headed east. Joseph paused when they came to the temple. He gazed at the building rising to the sky then looked back at the city and remarked with tears in his eyes, "This is the loveliest place and the best people under the heavens; little do they know the trials that await them."

The rest of the journey passed quietly. Joe struggled to sit upright in the buggy. Shortly before ten in the morning, four miles west of Carthage, a man named Captain Dunn met them with his militia of sixty mounted soldiers.

"Brethren, be not alarmed," Joseph said calmly. "They can do nothing worse than kill the body." Almon looked at the pistol on the seat between Joe and him but did not reach for it.

The captain approached Joseph and said he had an order from Governor Ford requiring the relinquishment of the arms of the Nauvoo Legion. Joseph immediately countersigned the order. After further discussion, it was agreed that Joseph and Hyrum would briefly return to Nauvoo with Captain Dunn and his men so the relinquishment of arms would occur peacefully. When that was accomplished, Dunn and his militia would escort the Smith brothers back to Carthage. Dunn pledged their safety with his own life as forfeit. The militia raised their hands in agreement. Joseph and Hyrum complied.

Almon and Joe climbed out of the buggy and walked toward Joseph. The other men from Nauvoo dismounted. Joseph turned to his friends. "I am going like a lamb to the slaughter, but I am calm as a summer's morning. I have a conscience void of offense toward God and toward all men. If they take my life, I shall die an innocent man."

Joe and Almon embraced Joseph and Hyrum and told them farewell. Then they watched as the Prophet and patriarch rode away with Captain Dunn and his militia.

\* \* \*

*Wednesday, June 26, 1844*

In the evening, somber with worry, Julianne sat on the bed feeding Ann Caroline while Don Carlos slept next to her. Almon was packing his personal items in a satchel, preparing to leave for Carthage early in the morning. Almon paused and looked at her. "I don't like leaving you alone."

Julianne's eyes pricked. "You are the one who will be in danger."

"I'll take one pistol. You keep the other one handy."

Julianne looked away from Almon, exhausted from the fearful and aching farewells. Ann Caroline closed her brown eyes. Julianne lay down and curled up between her babies. They slept so peacefully, oblivious to the cruelty and violence so close to them. Yesterday, the governor had sent word to Almon that Joseph was now charged with treason. The governor realized it was a spurious charge issued to keep Joseph in Carthage, but he claimed that he could do nothing as an executive. Since it would have to go through the courts, he requested Almon to come to Carthage as one of his legal advisors.

Julianne didn't understand all of the procedures, why the riot charge was bound over for the next term, or why Joseph had not yet appeared before the court on the treason charge. She only knew that Joseph and Hyrum were still in Carthage in grave danger. And Almon was going into the fury with them, hoping to legally get them back to Nauvoo before it was too late.

"Don't worry about me," Almon said as he walked over and sat down on the edge of the bed. He stroked her hair. "I have the governor's protection."

*But so do Joseph and Hyrum*, was the only thought that crossed her mind.

\* \* \*

A moment passed as Almon sat on the bed looking at his wife and children—his beautiful ones. It was nearly dark outside. There was a knock at the front door. Almon felt Julianne tense. They feared each message. Would this be the one saying Joseph had been killed? Without a word, Almon went to answer it. The young courier looked no more than sixteen years old as he handed Almon the letter. "Mr. Oliver Cowdery requests that you personally deliver this letter to General Joseph Smith."

Almon's forehead creased as he thanked the courier and closed the door. He sat down heavily at the table, thinking. After leaving the Church, Oliver and his brother had set up a law practice in Illinois. Oliver must be following Joseph's plight. But how did Oliver know that Almon was going to Carthage tomorrow? Did he know that Governor Ford had asked for his assistance? He went back into the bedroom with the letter in his hand. Julianne's eyes were wide. He placed it in his satchel and explained what it was. She took a deep breath and closed her eyes. Almon lay down with his family, exhausted, even though it was not yet eight o'clock.

Then another knock. When would it end? Again Almon answered it. It was John Smith. The elderly man looked haggard. He explained that he had just visited his nephews in Carthage Jail. He hesitated for a moment, as if he weren't sure about the propriety of the rest of his message. Was it distrust? Almon knew John had bristled at his refusal to march the Ramus Company to Nauvoo. Then John Smith said, "Joseph asked that you come to assist him as an attorney at his expected trial tomorrow for treason."

Almon took a deep breath. "You came too late. I'm already engaged on the other side." John Smith turned and walked out the door without another word. Almon knew he should go after him and explain that he was already working with the governor, not the apostates. He was working to get Joseph out of Carthage, but he could not be Joseph's lawyer while he was engaged by the governor. Almon walked to the doorway, but John Smith was already in his buggy with the whip on his horse, as if he couldn't get away fast enough. Almon let out a breath. He would see Joseph and Hyrum tomorrow and explain. He went into the bedroom where Julianne waited.

\* \* \*

*Thursday, June 27, 1844. Macedonia, Illinois*

Ezekiel was at Almon's house shortly after dawn.

"Any news from Carthage?" Almon asked as he prepared to leave.

Ezekiel looked at him grimly. "Word is that Ford's riding to Nauvoo today with the militia—says he's going to talk with the citizens. The soldiers from Warsaw and Carthage are planning to mutiny. They intend to sack and burn Nauvoo."

"I'll inform the governor," Almon said.

"Esther and Delcena are in Nauvoo." Ezekiel gripped Almon's shoulder. "Joseph and Hyrum gave themselves up to stop women and children from being massacred. This better not happen."

Almon met his eyes. "Not on my watch."

\* \* \*

*Midmorning*

A light rain fell. Almon was admitted into Ford's presence, and he told him of the mutinous troops.

Governor Ford hardly looked at Almon. "My militia officers have already informed me that some of the companies plan to destroy Nauvoo. Thus, I disbanded the military and sent the men home. I'll travel with a small, trusted force. Do you think the Mormons will harm those who have left Smith's church? The Laws, Fosters, and Higbees fear for the lives of their friends in Nauvoo."

"Most of the Mormons are peaceloving. I doubt they will be harmed. But there are always the wild cards, the unpredictable few."

"The few? Are you certain? I'm going to talk sense to your people and explain to them the crime of destroying the *Expositor*. Also, martial law should not have been imposed. They ought to be praying saints, not military saints. The torch has already been lit in Carthage and Warsaw. One misstep and the city will be ashes, with extermination immediately following. But never by my orders! I do not want innocent women and children to die. I will aid them if I can."

"What about Joseph and Hyrum? Who will protect them if you are gone?" Almon pled.

"I will leave an adequate guard. I do not believe the citizens so cruel as to harm them. And the Carthage Grays have given their oath to obey me."

"The citizens are not so cruel? What are you saying? A moment ago, you said you feared extermination!"

"Lawyer Babbitt, I am doing the best I can to save lives. I have left an order giving you leave to visit General Smith if you desire. You are dismissed."

Almon stood outside the courthouse as Governor Ford left Carthage with Captain Dunn and his men. His mind spun. What were Ford's motives? Was there a conspiracy? Had he agreed to let the mob kill Joseph and Hyrum in return for the lives of the citizens of Nauvoo? Were Joseph's premonitions prophecy? Was he a lamb to be slaughtered? Recoiling at the thought, Almon felt the letter in the pocket of his overcoat. He ran the short distance to Carthage Jail, ignoring the men watching him with their fingers on triggers. When he was almost there, Dan Jones strode up to him. "Joseph wants to see you," Jones said.

"And I him. I'll go directly."

"You Mormons better get out of town if you value your lives," a nearby soldier warned.

"Get the horses and wait here," Almon whispered to Jones. Then he walked up to the guard standing outside the jail. Almon gave his name and handed over his pistol. The guard nodded and led him up the stairs and into the prisoners' room. Almon thanked God they were not being held in the iron cage. There was a bed, a mattress, and a writing table. Light came in through the window. Joseph, who was sitting on the bed, stood up and shook Almon's hand. Almon sat down on the bed next to Joseph. A somber quiet filled the room. "So, Brother Almon," Joseph said, "do you have any advice for me?"

Almon tried to smile. "Yes, but first I've brought a letter for you from Oliver Cowdery."

"Oliver?" Joseph's voice was wistful, questioning. "At this hour? Be so kind as to read it to me."

Almon read the letter aloud. It was friendly and contained legal advice. There was a reference to their past friendship. For a fleeting moment, the hint of a smile entered Joseph's eyes. After the letter was read, they discussed Joseph and Hyrum's defense. Almon explained that he couldn't legally defend Joseph because he had been engaged by the governor. However, he advised Joseph to immediately send for Mr. O. H. Browning of Quincy. Although not a Mormon, he was a brilliant lawyer and would serve him well.

Joseph immediately wrote the letter. He handed it to Almon. "Give this letter to Dan Jones, who waits outside. Tell him to take it to Quincy in all speed. Then go home and remember me to the dear Saints in Macedonia."

Joseph embraced Almon. For a fleeting instant, Almon felt the beat of the Prophet's heart and the weight of a six-shooter in his pocket. "Defend yourself," Almon whispered. "Ford will be back late tonight, and all will be well."

Once outside the jail, Almon quickly found Dan Jones, who stood with their horses. He handed him the letter. "Take this to Quincy forthwith," Almon whispered.

A guard whirled around and shouted to the mob, "Old Joe has sent a letter to raise the Nauvoo Legion to come and rescue him!" The mob gathered round, screaming for the letter and threatening Jones.

"This is a dispatch written at Governor Ford's request." Almon shouted out the distraction. Jones swung on his horse and galloped off at full speed. A shout rang out to waylay him. In the chaos, Almon mounted his own horse and sped away in the opposite direction.

\* \* \*

Almon galloped hard back to Macedonia. He couldn't ride fast enough. A defense for Joseph wheeled through his mind. If Joseph could only live through the night until Ford returned. What were the odds that he would live? The Legion ought to be out thundering toward Carthage. They were strong. They could rule the day! But what of civil war? What of houses burning and women raped and children bayoneted? What of the gospel of Jesus Christ? Where was God in all of this?

When night came, his body lay exhausted next to Julianne, but his mind would not stop firing, like small bolts of lightning crisscrossing through his brain. Nightmares swirled around him. The gun in Joseph's pocket. A city in ashes. The bloody, broken bodies of his friends. Another pounding at the door. Was it real or part of his dreams?

Almon lit a candle and picked up his pistol. He opened the door. A courier from Hamilton Hotel stood before him in the wane moonlight. "A dispatch for you, sir."

Almon knew what it contained before he read the words: *Joseph and Hyrum are dead. John Taylor is wounded. I am well. The deed was done by a band of 100 to 200 men with blackened faces. The citizens here are afraid of the Mormons attacking them. I promise them no! Willard Richards.*

Almon spun around at the sound of footsteps. Julianne stood in the doorway, her face shadowed by darkness. Almon dropped the letter as he stumbled forward. She ran to him, grabbing him by the shoulders as he doubled over. "Joseph and Hyrum are dead," Almon sobbed brokenly. "This has been the hardest day of my life."

\* \* \*

Almon left at dawn the next morning while Julianne fed the babies. Other lives did not stop with the Prophet's death. He first went to Joel's and asked Nephi to run to each of the Johnson households to tell them to gather at Benjamin's house in a half hour. Then he handed the dispatch to Joel. The muscles in Joel's face quivered as he read the letter aloud. Then he fell to his knees and prayed. Weeping, Susan gathered the children and joined him.

John Smith must have also received the same dispatch, for Almon heard weeping as he passed his house. At Benjamin's, the family sat in chairs in the parlor. Their faces were pale in the thin morning light. The windows were open. Almon read the dispatch one last time.

What are the bounds of grief? Almera wept with her arms folded and her head bowed, rocking back and forth.

"They gave themselves up. 'Calm as a summer's morning?'" Joe cried out with a torn sob.

Tears crept down Will's face. George and Maria wept openly. Mary's hand flew to her mouth as her husband clutched her to him. Little David whimpered.

Holding the baby and crying, Melissa reached out her hand to Benjamin, but he seemed not to feel her touch. Dazed with grief, he stood up. He roared with indescribable anguish, "Oh, God, what will thy orphan Church and people do now?"

Julia ran to Benjamin and wrapped her arms around him. She wept while Benjamin groaned and groaned, the burning grief in his soul searing away healing tears.

\* \* \*

Ezekiel walked past Benjamin's house, the sound of weeping through open windows raging in his ears. With Esther married in Nauvoo, none of his children looked to him for comfort. The Smith brothers were dead. Why? He ought to laugh bitterly at the absurdity of it all—Joseph's life headed toward Armageddon. He had warned Julia.

But Joseph could have called out his Legion. He could have rained down blood and fire on Illinois. But he had not. Instead, he had turned himself in. He had turned the filthy mob away from Nauvoo, away from Esther and Delcena.

"*Why?*" Ezekiel roared as his arms flung open. Granite rage burned in his heart. Why did the innocent die? Seth and David died because they followed Joseph! Nancy, Susan, and Amos were dead too. But never on purpose. Never in cold blood.

Where was the treachery that Thomas Sharp shouted from the rooftops in the *Warsaw Signal*, rallying murderers? Where? Ezekiel knew the answer. It lay in the power of Joseph's soul—like Zeus, he wielded a lightning rod, searing hypocritical belief, holding the rod out for all to grab hold—that destructive, life-giving rod of Joseph's vision of God.

Thomas Ford had promised the Smiths protection and had turned his back, shattering the rule of law in the state of Illinois. Joseph, whose visions had stolen Ezekiel's family's hearts. Joseph, who wept when Ezekiel's children had died, who testified that he knew God and that Ezekiel's children lived beyond the grave. Joseph, a rough-hewn boy like Ezekiel's own. He was as dead as Ezekiel's marriage to Julia. Ezekiel ground his teeth as silent, bitter tears fell from his eyes.

\*\*\*

*Thursday, August 8, 1844*

At ten in the morning, thousands of Saints gathered in the grove. Sidney Rigdon stood on a wagon rather than the preaching stand in order to avoid the strong wind. Benjamin sat with the council of fifty. Almon was at his side.

Sidney's voice rose with the wind as he expounded his claims. He told of a revelation he received in Pittsburgh on the day of Joseph's death. It was not an open revelation but a continuation of what he and Joseph had received years past. He was to hasten back to Nauvoo to be the guardian of the Church. He was called to be a spokesman to Joseph and was commanded to continue speaking for Joseph through revelation. His duty was to build up the Church to Joseph.

Regardless of his oratory skill, Sidney's words rang hollow in Benjamin's ears. The past month had gone by in a daze, with grief too bitter for tears. He had not gone to the Mansion House to view Joseph and Hyrum's bodies. The thought of seeing their cold, mutilated flesh sickened him. He wanted to remember them as they were in life. But Joseph was gone. As Benjamin sat listening to Sidney, lines of grief and pain deepened in his face, like clay cracking in summer's hot, relentless wind. The entire congregation was silent, weighed down by sorrow.

In the early afternoon, Brigham Young arose and stood on the preaching stand. His hair blew back in the wind. He called for the attention of all. "This congregation makes me think of the days of King Benjamin, the multitude being so great that all could not hear. We will do the best we can. For the first time in my life, without a prophet at our head, do I step forth to act in my calling in connection with the Quorum of the Twelve Apostles, as apostles of Jesus Christ unto this generation—apostles whom God has called by revelation through the Prophet Joseph, who are ordained and anointed to bear off the keys of the kingdom of God in all the world. This people have hitherto walked by sight and not by faith. You have had the Prophet in your midst."

Benjamin jumped to his feet as Brigham Young continued to speak. He pivoted to look at him straight on. It was not Brigham's image or voice before him. He saw Joseph—Joseph's image, his clothing, his countenance, the whistle in his voice—all of it, Joseph! Beloved Joseph, glorified and speaking in Brigham's place. The vision receded. Many in the congregation stood, riveted as they listened to Brigham Young, some seeing, some hearing, some feeling the mantle of Joseph fall upon him.

Joseph's words to the Twelve rang again in Benjamin's mind. *I give unto you all the keys and powers bestowed upon me, and I say unto you, round up your shoulders and bear off this kingdom.*

Then other words, private thoughts to a dear friend, filled Benjamin. *Bennie, if I am on the other side of the veil, I can do many more things for my friends than I can do here.* Benjamin's tears finally came, coursing down his cheeks like the healing water of baptism. How glad he was to have been Joseph's friend!

"God bless you all," Brother Brigham said before sitting down.

The rushing wind seemed to fill the congregation with renewed hope. Tears shone in many's eyes. Through the power of the Holy Ghost, they knew who would lead them. They were not forsaken. They were not alone.

# 25

*The gold was once my father's watch
That made the little band
'Twas made and lettered to be worn
Upon my Mother's hand*

George Washington Johnson

*Monday, February 9, 1846. Nauvoo, Illinois*

THE AFTERNOON SUN SHONE COLD and dim through the clouds while Benjamin ran from the Mansion House to the temple. Yesterday, eleven hundred Saints had been endowed in the house of the Lord, but today smoke curled from the temple's roof. Benjamin arrived at the same time as Brigham Young. The black smoke turned to white steam. Almon, David LeBaron, and other brethren were on the deck roof, waving their buckets as they shouted "Hosannah!" The fire, caused by a stovepipe in the upper room overheating, had been put out. A few shingles had been lost, but the temple was saved.

Brigham strode up to Benjamin. "I was at the river helping George A. Smith put his wagons and teams on the flatboat when I saw the smoke. Yet it was out of my power to get here in time to help put out the fire."

"Many of the brethren responded quickly," Benjamin remarked. "I heard your wagons are packed. When will you cross the river?"

"Within the week," Brigham said. "What's your condition? Are you and your company ready to go?"

Benjamin shook his head. "Not yet. The rumors of bodies buried under the Mansion House stables slowed us down. But we are making wagons again."

"You have faithfully fulfilled your assignment at the Mansion House. Now you need to leave as soon as possible for Sugar Creek and go west with the first group. I've asked Brother Boswick to help you obtain an outfit."

Benjamin swallowed, thinking of Brother Joseph, Sister Emma, and the Mansion House. After the Prophet's death, he and Melissa had been called by the Twelve to come to Nauvoo and be the caretakers of the Mansion. They had come, losing a small fortune on the sale of their Macedonia property. They had spent everything that remained in keeping Joseph's house in good repair and entertaining military officials and notables, such as Stephen A. Douglas and James Arlington Bennet. Recently, the basement of the Mansion House stables had been turned into a wagon-building shop in preparation for the exodus to the Rocky Mountains. The mob spirit was so volatile that the noise and activity in the basement caused suspicion, and rumors started circulating about Mormons murdering people and burying their bodies beneath the stable.

Almon and David joined Benjamin and Brigham, where they gazed at the temple. "Thank you, brethren," Brigham said, shaking their hands.

"All's well that ends well," Almon said, his face smudged with soot.

Brigham looked hard at Almon, as if he were seeing beyond the moment. "Brother Babbitt, you will remain in Nauvoo for a time while many of us go to establish a home in the Rocky Mountains. I have seen the place in vision, and there will be other temples. But you have a mission here. You've been elected to the legislature. The council has made you trustee in charge of the sale of Church properties. Yesterday, the Twelve met in the attic of the temple. We knelt around the altar and prayed that the Most High would enable us to completely finish the temple, that He would preserve this building as a monument to Brother Joseph. But we must leave this week. This sacred trust is now in your hands. May the Lord bless you."

"It will be finished by April," Almon said solemnly. "I promise you that. And though he is no longer with us, I promise Brother Joseph as well."

\* \* \*

Later that night, Benjamin held Melissa close as he told her what Brigham had said, that they should leave as soon as possible. There was a knock at the front door. Benjamin left Melissa and opened it. Ezekiel came in quickly, his face grim. He was breathing hard. Something was wrong.

"Pa, what's happened?" Benjamin questioned. He waited for his father to speak as he focused on Ezekiel's face in the firelight, at the dear, hardened features. A day would soon come when he wouldn't see his father again.

"You have to leave," Ezekiel said.

"I know. I talked to Brigham today. I'll have an outfit this week. I'll send you word before I go."

"That's not soon enough. I've been to Carthage. The cursed lies about Mormons murdering and burying the dead at the Mansion stables run rampant through the countryside. There's a posse forming. Ben, they have a warrant for your arrest! Go to the river tonight and stay with friends. Cross when you can. Almon, David, and Will will pack your wagons and help Melissa and the children join you at Sugar Creek. It's arranged."

Benjamin nodded as tears burned his eyes. He enfolded his father in his arms. "God bless and keep you, Pa."

\* \* \*

*Two months later. April 1846. Macedonia, Illinois*

"Grandpa!"

It was nearly midnight. Ezekiel jumped out of bed and ran outside. Joel's son, seventeen-year-old Sixtus, banged on the door. He was sweating profusely despite the cold weather. He doubled over, shaking violently, and tried to catch his breath as Ezekiel helped him inside. "What happened? Is anyone hurt?"

Sixtus shook his head. "No. It was Levi Williams! He came to the house with a hundred mobbers."

Ezekiel knew Levi Williams. He was a colonel from Warsaw and a drinking man. Long ago, Ezekiel had met him in the Carthage Tavern. He had seen him last when he took Sixtus to watch the trial of Joseph and Hyrum's murderers. Williams had been one of the accused. Despite the evidence against him, Williams was acquitted. It sickened Ezekiel. By fall of 1845, Williams had been busy again, burning out Mormons in outlying communities. Most of Ezekiel's family had moved to Nauvoo. Now Benjamin was safely out of Illinois, in the Mormon Camp headed west. But Joel and Susan had moved back near Macedonia and Carthage to the old sawmill on Crooked Creek. It was the only way Joel could earn the money to go west. Ezekiel had stayed in Macedonia. He wasn't Mormon and had nothing to fear.

"Where's your Pa?" Ezekiel asked Sixtus.

"He and Susan are in Nauvoo. The younger ones and me were home. Williams said to tell Pa that if he didn't leave immediately, they'd come back and kill us all. Sariah is shaking so bad. Seth and Susie are crying. Nephi is standing by the door with the rifle. He won't put it down."

"I'll go back with you," Ezekiel said as he picked up Betsy off the mantel. "No one will hurt your family tonight."

He rode with Sixtus back to Crooked Creek in the darkness, seething with anger. Now that Levi Williams had gotten away with murder once, he thought no one could stop him.

\* \* \*

*May 31, 1846. Macedonia, Illinois*

The rising sun shone bright overhead. Ezekiel helped Joel heft the final barrel of flour and attach it to the side of the wagon. "Pa, are you sure you want to stay here?" Joel questioned. "You'd be safer in Nauvoo with Esther and David."

Ezekiel snorted softly. "The mobbers aren't after an old, mean non-Mormon. Esther keeps begging me to move in with her, but then she threatens to dump my brandy."

As they kept loading the wagon, Ezekiel thought about Joel and his family. After the mob had threatened the children, Joel hadn't left immediately. Then the first of May, at two in the morning, Joel and Susan had awakened to horsehooves and shouts. They had stood at the door in their bedclothes, holding hands, squinting into torchlight as a hundred men with guns, swords, and dirks had asked them if they were preparing to leave. Joel told them he was. "If you aren't gone before June first, you're a dead man." After that, Joel had moved his family into Ezekiel's home for safety. He had traded his property for some undeveloped land in Knox County without a house or cabin on it.

An hour later, the wagon was ready. Ezekiel hugged Joel, Susan, and the children. He sipped from a flask of brandy, his gray eyes shaded by his old hat as he watched them roll away.

\* \* \*

That night, shortly after midnight, Ezekiel awakened to the sound of gunfire. With a throbbing head, he stumbled to his feet.

"Joel Johnson!" a voice thundered. "It's June first, the last day of your life."

Enraged, Ezekiel flung the door open. He looked straight at Levi Williams and smelled the liquor on his breath. Behind and around him were about one hundred fifty men. "My son's gone. He left this morning."

Levi smirked. "Smart man. We warned him to get out of Hancock County."

Ezekiel eyed him. "Levi, are you gonna be Thomas Sharp's errand boy your entire life?" In his newspaper, Sharp continued to call for violence.

Williams laughed. "Zeke, you gonna be a Jack Mormon all your life?"

"Get out of here!" Ezekiel cursed. He turned to go in the house and slam the door but stopped when he felt the point of a bayonet in his back.

"We're not waiting through summer for the rest of the Mormons to leave Nauvoo," Williams threatened, the bayonet quivering in his hand. "The deadline has passed. Warn your kin if you see them again in the flesh." Williams withdrew the bayonet. "And, Zeke, an old man isn't safe alone in a ghost town."

\*\*\*

That night Ezekiel lay with Betsy by his side. Most of the Mormons had already left Illinois, and the rest were trying to get away. Yet the vigilantes refused to rest. Levi Williams's threats echoed in his mind. Ezekiel was not afraid for himself, but he feared for his family. Benjamin was safe from the mob. George was in Tennessee with his wife's family. Joel was on his way to Knox County. But the rest were in Nauvoo. Did they understand the danger? They said they would eventually go west, but Joe was running a drugstore. Will was courting a new resident, a quaint little Quaker girl named Jane Brown. Almera had married Reuben Barton and was about to deliver her first child. Delcena taught school. Almon was the Church's trustee. Esther and David were caretakers of the temple.

The Mormon temple—that was the reason the old citizens didn't believe they would really leave Nauvoo for good. While families built wagons and purchased oxen, they had continued with increased energy to finish the temple—Joseph's dream and the symbol of their faith. Almon had spoken at its dedication on April first. Their temple stood grand and majestic on the hill, a constant reminder of the former power of the City Beautiful.

Ezekiel stared into the darkness. Julia lived in Nauvoo too. Regardless of the years that separated them, she haunted his dreams. In a small brick house near the temple, she cared for their grandson, three-year-old David Wilson. A year ago, Ezekiel's blonde-haired Mary had died giving birth.

Within six months, the newborn had died. Grief stricken, George Wilson had left little David in Julia's care and joined the Mormon Battalion.

Ezekiel had seen Julia a month ago at a dinner at Esther's. Her shoulders had been less straight, as if age finally weighed upon her. Yet, how tender and protective she had been of little David. Ezekiel knew that look and that touch. David was Julia's shining gem, her precious gift after so much loss. Did she know that when Ezekiel looked at little David, he felt like he stared at a looking glass back in time, when his mother had held his hand as they'd looked into a mirror, on the day she had married Jonathon King?

Ezekiel ought to leave this place, to move in with Esther to protect them. Esther had begged him to stop drinking, had implored him to try to believe in God. Ezekiel thought of the rank smell of liquor on Levi Williams's breath and the look of violence in his eyes. Full moonlight shone through the window. His mind went back to another moonlit night sixty-one years ago. As a fourteen-year-old boy, he had plowed a fallow field at night in hopes of going to the circus the next day. Instead, he had received harsh words and a beating from his stepfather. *Pray, boy, for forgiveness. Perhaps God will forgive an illegitimate child.* He remembered Isaac Chapel's words on the day he ran away from home: *Zeke, you've learned all the wrong things about God.*

Ezekiel arose from bed. He had thought long and deep since Joseph's death. If he tried to pray, it would not be to the God of men who beat children and murdered innocents. It would be to the God Joseph called Father, whose glory was to make men like Himself. If there was one thing he had learned from Joseph, it was the meaning of will, the fact that some things were worth any price. With grim determination and the strange request that Joseph's God give him strength, Ezekiel took his crate of brandy out in the yard and poured out every bottle. Tomorrow, he would go to Nauvoo and move into Esther's house. He would watch and wait with his wits about him. He would protect the jewels in Julia's crown—his own precious ones.

* * *

*Summer 1846. Outside the city of Nauvoo*

Near the Parley Street entrance to the city, Ezekiel stood behind a tree, watching the mob approach. They planned to invade the city. When they drew close, Ezekiel stepped out from the cover of the tree and cocked both barrels at Levi Williams, shouting, "Halt! Hands up!"

Taken by surprise, Williams halted his company. Ezekiel's voice rang out in the still evening, addressing all of the men. Ezekiel cursed, saying he didn't care about his own life. "I'm an old man without a home of my own and few friends. But you will cross over my dead body before you enter this city tonight. If you do not about-face this instant and march out of the city limits, I will pull the trigger and blow the head off your captain."

"Colonel, tomorrow is another day," a redheaded Irishman called out.

"You're right, Major McAuley," Williams said and ordered his men to about-face.

When the company was out of sight, Ezekiel turned around and walked swiftly to his horse. He galloped to LaHarpe Road, the second entrance to the city. An hour passed, and the shadows of the same mob-militia again came into view. Ezekiel hid in the brush. When they neared, Ezekiel exploded, "I will shoot you on sight if you say one word. Turn around!"

In silence as thick as hate, the militia obeyed. They returned to their camp at Golden Point, six miles south of Nauvoo. Instead of attacking the people, they decided to lay siege to Nauvoo, not allowing anyone to leave the city, except by ferry to Iowa. Two weeks later, eight men who were harvesting wheat outside Nauvoo were surrounded by McAuley and eighty armed men. They were forced to kneel down in a ditch and were beaten.

\* \* \*

"Papa, you have to leave," Esther begged in tears. It was almost dark. Sixtus and Nephi had arrived before dawn that morning, having traveled all night to avoid the regulators. They brought the news that an old friend of Joel's from Carthage had sent a warning. Williams and McAuley planned to come after Ezekiel.

"Grandpa, Pa told us not to come back without you," Sixtus said.

"I'm sorry for you, Grandpa," Nephi added. "There's eight of us in a one-room hut. But at least you won't be killed."

Ezekiel took a heavy breath. He didn't want to leave his girl, not when he had finally quit drinking. Staying the winter in a one-room hut with eight people did not sound comfortable. Ezekiel looked at Esther's husband, David LeBaron, who hadn't said a word during the conversation. "Son, what do you think?"

David's jaw was tense, but his eyes were steady. "Almon hasn't heard of any legal proceedings against you. We think Levi Williams was embarrassed that an old man turned his militia around. I think Joel's right. They'll seek vigilante justice."

Esther knelt down in front of Ezekiel, taking his strong, wrinkled hands in hers as she looked up at him with her brown eyes filled with tears. "Papa, I beg you." He had seen that look before, in Julia's eyes when he had first met her. *Sir, if by wishing or praying I could bring back your family, I would.*

Esther was a gift to him, like little David was to Julia, the embodiment of hope. The reminder of what had been—the golden thread of his old age that whispered the possibility of a loving God. A thought filled his mind. If he were alone with Esther when the vigilantes came, what would happen to her?

Ezekiel stood up. "I'll go get my things."

Esther leapt up and threw her arms around his neck. "Stay with Joel for the winter, Papa, then come back to me. Surely they will have forgotten about you by then."

\* \* \*

## 1847

Time passed. Word came that Joe and Harriet had left Nauvoo to go west, but George and Maria had returned to the city. The winter came and went—long, cold, crowded days with Joel and his family. They battled illness, stress, and poverty. Ezekiel tended to the sick, chopped wood, played checkers with the children, and listened to the Bible and Book of Mormon read by candlelight. He often thought about the future, the secret world of death that lay before him. Was there a chance that Joseph was correct, that there was more than nothingness?

Winter turned to spring. Joel was still too poor to head west. Ezekiel sowed, with his son and grandsons, ten acres of corn and twenty of wheat. Joel fell ill again, and Ezekiel helped Sixtus and Nephi gather in the harvest. It was more fruitful than expected, especially considering the dryness of the season. Then, when Joel was on his feet again, Ezekiel announced that he was heading back to Nauvoo. Joel sent Sixtus with him.

\* \* \*

Sixtus and Ezekiel were nearly to Parley Street when the mob surrounded them. Levi Williams ordered the two to dismount and lay down their weapons. A man laughed. "Colonel Williams, this day has been a long time in coming. But come it has at last."

Sixtus's heart pounded, afraid and furious at the same time. He glanced at his grandfather, but Ezekiel was staring straight at Levi Williams. "I'll do what you say without a fight if you give your word not to touch the boy."

Williams cocked his head and grinned maliciously. "We give you our word. Watching may teach him a thing or two."

Sixtus shook with rage and fear as he was forced to sit on the ground with guns trained on him. "Don't move, Sixtus," his grandfather ordered. "Not until this is over. I need your word!"

Breathing hard and fast, Sixtus nodded. He stared at his grandfather as the mobbers stripped off Ezekiel's shirt and tied him to a wagon wheel. Tears ran down Sixtus's face as the mobbers of Warsaw and Carthage, some of the same men who had killed the Prophet, beat his seventy-four-year-old grandpa with hickory goads until blood streamed from his body and he slumped into the wagon wheel, unconscious.

* * *

Memory crept into consciousness—the lash falling on his back, the perpetrators unaware that they couldn't hurt him anymore, that though his body jerked, it was as if someone had wrapped their arms around him, bearing the blows, uncloaking His existence. *I was wounded for your transgressions, I was bruised for your iniquities; and with my stripes you are healed.*

Then pain again while Sixtus carried him. Sixtus covered in his grandfather's blood. George and Will laying their hands on his head. The shine of his gold watch as George took it out of his crumpled shirt. Esther, Almera, Julianne, and Delcena taking turns at his bedside, bathing his wounds, giving him cups of warm broth to sip, crying and holding his hand. How was it that he had not believed in God when angels attended him?

* * *

*January 12, 1848*

Julia sat by Ezekiel's side, watching him. He was unconscious. His breathing was labored. Infection from his wounds was spreading through his body like poison. She knew he might not live through the day. Julia took a deep, shaky breath. Joel had written her a week before Ezekiel came back. *Father has changed. He no longer partakes of strong drink. He has grown patient. He desires to return to Nauvoo. I pray that the mobbers have forgotten him.*

But they had not forgotten—even though they had won the battle of Nauvoo, even though they had desecrated the temple, even though a year had passed. They had still felt the need to crush one old man. And for Julia, they had stolen her chance to know the man Joel had written about.

Julia's eyes stung as she realized she was wrong. She did know him. She remembered Ezekiel standing before her on the first day they'd met, so handsome that she could hardly look at him, with such passion and pain in his eyes. She remembered his tenderness on their wedding day—how he'd lit a hundred candles in her soul. She knew his kindness and love for their children. It was the bitter, angry man she did not know.

Julia reached into her pocket and took out the gold chain Ezekiel had given her nineteen years ago today, on the same day she had given him his watch. She had not worn it for a long time and had brought it today to give to Esther, to comfort her. Julia lifted it up and put it around her own neck. She prayed that Ezekiel would open his eyes and be with her this day. She turned at the sound of the door opening. Esther came into the room with bowls of roses.

\* \* \*

Ezekiel awoke from the dream, the layers of light enveloping him. The light faded. His vision blurred then cleared. He knew where he was—Joseph's Mansion House, where Esther and David now boarded. There was a fire in the hearth. Snow fell beyond the lace curtains that lined the window. The room smelled like summer roses.

"Ezekiel?" It was Julia's voice. For a moment, he felt her soft hand on his forehead. Had she been the light in his dream? "Esther, he's waking up," Julia said and was gone.

"Papa." Esther held his hand now, her tears falling on his fingertips. "I prayed you would be with us today. I waited to get out the roses I preserved last summer. They were going to be Christmas roses, but instead, they're birthday roses. Can you smell them, Papa? It's our birthday today."

Ezekiel nodded and squeezed her hand. Did she know that they weren't only birthday roses? They were also anniversary roses. "Where did your mama go?" he whispered to his baby girl.

"I'm back, Zeke, with some of our children." Julia was in the room once again. Behind her stood Delcena, Almera, Julianne, George, and Will. One by one, his children came forward, smiling and crying as they kissed him and told him they loved him.

Ezekiel focused on Julia again, the dark beauty of her eyes, the best part of his life. "How many years ago?" he whispered.

"Forty-seven," she answered and placed her hand on his cheek.

"My twenty-eighth birthday. Our wedding day."

"A blessed day," Julia said. She was crying.

"The best day," Ezekiel managed. Julia kissed his forehead as her tears fell. She wore the chain he had given her nineteen years ago. It brushed against him. He coughed and tried to sit up. There was one more thing to do. Julia put a pillow behind his head then a sponge to his mouth to wet his lips and quench his thirst.

"My gold watch?"

"I'll get it, Papa," George said. He took it from a drawer and put it in Ezekiel's hand. Ezekiel closed his fingers around it. Then he found the strength to lift his arm and hand it back to George. "Take this and have a ring made for your mother."

"I will, Papa," George promised.

Ezekiel's tongue felt thick, but the words came as he looked at Julia. "Is there still regret between us?"

"No, dearest Zeke," Julia said, taking his hand and putting it to her lips. "You are the choice of my heart."

Ezekiel swallowed. "I love you forevermore."

As Julia wept silently, Ezekiel closed his eyes to rest.

Julianne, with her arms around Almera and Delcena, sang the words of Psalm 126, "The Lord hath done great things for us; whereof we are glad. They that sow in tears shall reap in joy. He that goeth forth and weepeth, bearing precious seed, shall doubtless come again with rejoicing, bringing his sheaves with him."

\* \* \*

*Authors' note*

Ezekiel died around midnight on January 12, 1848, on his seventy-fifth birthday, Esther's twenty-first birthday, and the forty-seventh anniversary of his marriage to Julia. Milas E. Johnson, George's son and Ezekiel's grandson, did Ezekiel's temple work on March 19, 1879. By permission of the First Presidency of the Church, Julia and his children were sealed to him. As the Prophet Joseph foresaw, Ezekiel stands at the head of his kingdom.

# Authors' Note

It is difficult to find the words to express our feelings as we bring this series to a close. We have decided to write this final letter, not just to our readers but to those we have written about.

> Dear Johnson family,
>
> Your voices have whispered within our hearts these past eight years, taking us down many different paths to your destination of faith and courage. We felt your closeness as we sat in the Palmyra Temple, as we walked through the Pomfret woods on a fall day, as we stood on the mound of Adam-ondi-Ahman overlooking the green and lovely valley, as we stared at the wind-swept grassland where Far West once lay, as we touched Annie's gravestone in Webster, Illinois, and as tears filled our eyes at Carthage. You are more than names on a family tree; you are our friends.
>
> David, Seth, Susan, Nancy, and Amos, we will never forget your goodness and your sacrifice. Telling others of you was one of the reasons we started this project in the first place. You did not leave progeny, but you left your example. Imagining your lives and contributions has touched us in a myriad of ways. You live on.
>
> Mary, you also died so young. You left your husband and little son. Young David thrived and gave you a progeny of faith. Your brother Benjamin wrote that you were the most angelic of womankind. The candle of your soul burns on brightly.
>
> Esther, thank you for emerging in this novel, unforeseen, and almost unimagined. You took on a life of your own, and

how we enjoyed getting to know you! You were a joy to your father, and you are a light to your numerous posterity.

George and William, because of editorial constraints, we could not write as much about you as we would have liked. You were young when your parents separated, yet you grew to become men of great integrity as you followed the Prophet of God. You raised large and faithful families. We honor you.

Joseph Ellis, you made us laugh. You touched us with your intelligence, creativity, kindness and love for life. Thank you for lightening our load with the memory of your happy, bright soul. Your children, nieces, and nephews wrote of their delight in knowing you.

Dear Almera, how we longed to comfort you, to know that you found happiness. You endured so much loss. You suffered at the hands of one husband, and another husband left the Church. As a single mother, you traveled to Utah and nurtured your daughters. You were sealed to the Prophet Joseph and have reason to rejoice.

Lyman and Delcena, Annie and Joel, we wept when we imagined your separation and loss. It was so hard writing of your children's grief. But as the Prophet Joseph taught, God does not see things as we do; He sees eternity. You taught us the definition of a celestial family. Your children held to the iron rod, and your descendants call you blessed.

Julianne, we pray that we have written of Almon as you would have wanted us to, that those who read this volume will know how he loved and was loved, that his contributions ought to be sung out with praise rather than drowned with criticism. Thank you for the sweetness of your life and the hope you instilled within us each step of the way.

Benjamin, our great-great grandfather. You are our fabled ancestor, the one we heard stories about as little girls, the hero of our childhood. Thank you for writing your life story, for sharing the details of your adventures, your feelings, and the passions of your heart. Thank you for your faithfulness and love. We hope our efforts will cause you to live on in the hearts of many.

Dear Julia, thank you for starting us on this journey. How excited we were when we first learned about you in Nauvoo. How you shone in the souls of your children! How you endure in our hearts! You are a beloved and beautiful wife and mother. You are the example we treasure in our lives. These books are a monument to you, a queen forevermore.

Ezekiel, your voice speaks to each of us in this imperfect world as we fall, stagger, and stand again. Like you, we are weak in some things and iron strong in others. Yours is the legacy of every father and husband who loves his family, of every hero who offers his life for others. Truly, there is no greater love. Your roots run deep. Thank you from our hearts.

And Joseph the Prophet, how blessed we feel to have come to know you on this journey with the Johnson family—to love you and honor you as they did. Through the depth of our research, we learned of your faults and your brilliance. We cried when we read of how you longed to preach to the people of Nauvoo one more time, when you had to leave your beloved family and ride away to Carthage. We marveled at the strength of your will, the depth of your love, and your vision of eternity. You were like a bolt of lightning in our Heavenly Father's hand, a prophet of God. Good and evil were spoken of you then, just as they are spoken of you now. We hope that our voices resound with your goodness.

Finally, thank you to our readers, for your encouragement and kindness. We know there are human flaws in our telling of this story. Thank you for your patience with our imaginings. We would like to have told more than we were able to. Please know that sharing this journey with you has been one of the wonders and joys of our lives.

With love,
Marcie and Kerri

# NOTES

## CHAPTER 1

The Winters, Burdick, LeBaron, and Holman families were living in Kirtland. They most likely interacted with Ezekiel and Almera, although it is fictional that Ezekiel was hired by the Winters or Holmans at this time. The LeBarons, Holmans, and Johnsons, who later became connected through marriage, most likely became acquainted in Kirtland.

Lyman Sherman and Almon Babbitt are fictionally placed in the same hotel General John B. Clark was staying in. However, the scene when Clark addressed the firing squad and bestowed upon them the "honor" of shooting the Mormon leaders at eight o'clock Monday morning (November 12, 1838) is fact. Twenty-two-year-old Mormon Jedediah M. Grant, who recorded his response, overheard and challenged the legality of shooting the Prophet. Clark did send a courier to inquire concerning military law (LaMar C. Berrett and Max H. Parkin, eds. *Sacred Places, Missouri*, 245).

It is not exactly known all that Almon did in Richmond. Traveling to inform Doniphan is fictional; however, it is fact that he carried letters from the prisoners to their families in Far West during this period (Omer Whitman and James L. Varner, *Neither Saint Nor Scoundrel*, 27). Joseph's letter to Emma from Richmond Jail, November 12, 1838, does state that Bro. Babbitt was waiting to carry the letters. Almon went to Fort Leavenworth after he delivered the letters.

Lyman did travel to Richmond and most likely Liberty during this period on a "mission" to see the Prophet Joseph (Benjamin F. Johnson, *My Life's Review [MLR]*, 43).

## CHAPTER 2

It had been "deemed best" that Julia, the younger children, and Joel and his family remain in Springfield, Illinois, where they settled for a time. Benjamin had decided to continue on "to the front, where I could again see and hear the Prophet"(*MLR*, 26). The family in Springfield was most likely anxious for news of his safety, along with the welfare of the Shermans and Babbitts. That following winter, George wrote, "There was much sickness. My mother and myself were very near dying with Typhoid Fever" (*Autobiography of George W. Johnson [GWJ]*, 3). Both brothers reported the death of Samuel Hale and his wife, leaving a ten-year-old daughter, Mary Ann, whom Julia adopted and whom remained a part of the family throughout her life, eventually marrying Benjamin (*GWJ*, 3; *MLR*, 26).

Sarah Melissa Holman was born November 18, 1838 (*MLR*, 359). Naomi's husband, James, was in Missouri at the time of the birth of this daughter. Almera's role in the birth of Sarah Melissa is fictional.

The escalating volatile relationship between Sam and Almera is based upon family records of her brief marriage in Kirtland. Although never named by the Johnson family, Benjamin wrote that she "had married a man in no way worthy of her" (*MLR*, 59). Ezekiel's feelings, concern, and protection of Almera are not documented but are consistent with the love and commitment he had for his children.

## CHAPTER 3

It is not known that Lyman Sherman witnessed the Prophet arriving in Liberty. Lyman Littlefield's (a Mormon who worked there) description is used in Sherman's thoughts as the Prophet exits the wagon and politely greets the crowd (Berrett, 221).

Although it is not known that Lyman Sherman stayed in the Kingsley's barn, Samuel Kingsley and his wife, Olive, did live directly across the street from the jail and tried to provide help to the prisoners. Littlefield's memoir, as found in *Sacred Places, Missouri*, provides this insight:

> Just across the street, directly opposite the jail lived a family of Latter-day Saints, who were full of sympathy for their imprisoned brethren. This family befriended them in the only way within their power. Having heard it whispered that their food was not,

at all times, of a very good quality, they, as often as convenient, and when safe to do so, found means to pass to them through the prison grates (which could be reached by a person standing upon the ground from the outside), various articles of food, such as cakes, pies, etc., which they themselves prepared. This had to be done very cautiously, under the cover of night. (Berrett, 223)

Although the scene of Lyman singing outside the window as Joseph slept with his small son is fictional, Emma did bring Joseph III to the jail, and he remembered staying overnight with his father ("The Memoirs of President Joseph Smith (1832–1914)," *The Saints' Herald*, November 6, 1934).

In the Missouri High Council minutes on December 13, 1838, it is noted that Lyman Sherman attended and was voted to take the place of Newell Knight "until he returns" (Cannon and Cook, *Far West Record*, 223). The individuals who were present and what they said is consistent with the notes of the meeting (221–223).

Joseph Smith Jr. instructed the Twelve while in Liberty Jail to call George A. Smith and Lyman Sherman to take the places of Orson Hyde and Thomas B. Marsh as apostles in the Council of the Twelve (Orson F. Whitney, *Life of Heber C. Kimball*, 250). Heber C. Kimball stated he accompanied Brigham Young in early February to visit Joseph in Liberty Jail. He wrote, "When we left there Lyman Sherman was somewhat unwell. In a few days after our return he died. We did not notify him of his appointment" (Orson F. Whitney, 251).

Heber C. Kimball performed the marriage of Lyman Sherman's "baby" daughter Susan to James Henry Martineau on January 18, 1857. Martineau remembers of that day:

> The snow was almost three feet deep. When Br. Kimball took the paper on which was written our names, he read Susan's name and said—Are you the daughter of Lyman R. Sherman! Now I look at you, I see you have his eyes exactly—and his hair. He was a good man—Joseph's right hand man. He was a most beautiful singer, especially in singing in tongues—the finest I ever saw. He died a martyr to the Gospel, and will receive a Martyr's crown. I was much rejoiced to hear Br. Kimball say this, for it shows to me that a truly good man will never be forgotten, in time, nor in

eternity. (Donald G. Godfrey and Rebecca S. Martineau-McCarty, eds., *An Uncommon Pioneer, Journals of James Henry Martineau 1828–1918*, 62)

There is some question of the exact death date of Lyman Sherman. A family group record in the Family Search Ancestral File lists his death date as January 27, 1839. Heber C. Kimball's record indicates that it may have been in early February, and Benjamin F. Johnson stated that when he heard of Lyman's death, "about the first of March," he left Fort Leavenworth for Far West to help Delcena (*MLR,* 45).

CHAPTER 4

In January 1839, Joel "removed" his family "to Carthage the county seat of Hancock County, Illinois, . . . near Crooked Creek" and rented "an old vacant store" (Joel Hills Johnson (JHJ), "A Voice from the Mountains," 23–24). He began to preach in the community, taught, and baptized the Ute Perkins family, who had settled the Crooked Creek area in 1826 (Susan Sessions Rugh, *Our Common Country,* 32–38). Joel organized the first group of Mormons in the Crooked Creek Branch on April 17, 1839, and was called to preside (Rugh, 33; *JHJ*, 23). Carthage Jail was being constructed in 1839. Family stories indicate that because of Joel's expertise in shingle making, he worked on the roof of the newly constructed jail. In July 1840, Ute Perkins, two of his sons, and a local farmer sold the Church two hundred eighty-five acres of land to establish a town named Ramus (Rugh, 32–38).

Joel possibly recommended the area around Commerce in Hancock County for gathering the displaced Mormons as they were fleeing from the extermination order in Missouri. He stated, "I had not been here long before Sidney Rigdon, Bishop Partridge and others who had fled from Far West . . . and on hearing that I was in Carthage bent their course thither and made my house a stopping place until they could find a suitable location for the Saints" (JHJ, 24).

Benjamin's experiences traveling to and working in Fort Leavenworth, as portrayed in this chapter, are found in *My Life's Review* (42–45). "Great was this change for us; whereas we had been so long hungry, cold, weary and persecuted, here we found every real comfort of living with safety, and good wages, and it seemed in the kindly spirit of the officers, and the advantages offered, that the Lord had opened our way and led us there" (44). Benjamin also described in detail his wrestle with Orkey, the "good-natured German." Ben's adventure crossing the river when leaving Fort Leavenworth is inspired by the following story:

> As I had the promise of being carried over [the river] I stepped in the canoe, when six others came in also, which with the baggage was likely to sink the canoe. The ferryman told us it was dangerous and some had better get out, but no one would do so. And when the canoe was still her rim was not more than one inch above the water. It was fearful and almost hairs-breadth escape, sculling through the masses of floating ice. But we landed safely. (*MLR*, 45–46)

Almon's direction and feelings of protection for Ben were fictionally included to portray how painful Lyman's death was for the Johnson family. Shortly after returning to Far West, Ben and Almon attempted to see the Prophet but "could not . . . or learn anything satisfactory about the prisoners." They traveled to Richmond to retrieve their arms, including Benjamin's gun, which was "said to be the most valuable rifle in all upper Missouri" (*MLR*, 46).

In March, Benjamin "was ordained an Elder under the hands of apostle Heber C. Kimball" and called "to go with him the coming season on a mission to England" (*MLR*, 47).

## CHAPTER 5

In Springfield, Illinois, Joseph Ellis Johnson, "the Yankee Schoolmaster," taught sixty students "through the winter with much satisfaction and success" (Rufus Johnson, *JEJ Trail to Sundown*, 64).

Almon and Benjamin were able to obtain "an outfit" and prepared to leave Missouri with Julianne, Delcena, and her children. Although their circumstances traveling to Illinois are fictionalized, they are based on the conditions and experiences recorded by other Saints. The incident with the rude woman is loosely based on actual experiences of the Butler and Smoot families. They were treated rudely and, at one time, stopped at a home to warm themselves and the woman would not speak to them but went into another room while they crowded around the fire (William G. Hartley, *My Best for the Kingdom*, 89). Amanda Barnes Smith (her husband and son were murdered at Haun's Mill) described, "I started for

Illinois . . . without money, (mob all the way), drove my own team, slept out of doors. I have five small children; we suffered hunger, fatigue and cold; for what? For our religion, where, in a boasted land of liberty, 'deny your faith or die,' was the cry" (*HC* III:325).

Of the journey, Benjamin wrote, "About the last of March we left Far West to recross the Mississippi and find a home elsewhere as best we might. Roads were bad, with storms and cold weather, but we safely crossed the river at Quincy to meet many of our people and to find that citizens of Quincy and of Illinois were showing great kindness to the persecuted Saints" (*MLR*, 47).

Delcena did stay in Quincy; Benjamin said she was determined to remain there until "the next gathering place" was announced (*MLR*, 47). Delcena's relationship with the Eells family is fictional to portray the extent to which the individuals in Quincy helped the Saints as they escaped Missouri. However, Dr. Richard Eells, his wife, Jane, and their two adopted children were an actual family in Quincy whose house stands today as a nationally recognized Underground Railroad Site (George M. Irwin, "The Dr. Richard Eells House," *A City of Refuge*, edited by Susan Easton Black and Richard E. Bennett, 261–273). Lyman's mother, Arsenath Sherman, may have also provided support for Delcena at this time.

## CHAPTER 6

The Latter-day Saints began to seek redress for their losses in Missouri with the federal government. A great deal of effort by the Prophet Joseph Smith, with more than 800 petitions for redress by the membership of the Church, focused on requesting aide from President Van Buren and Congress. In late 1839 and early 1840, Smith traveled to meet with the President of the United States in the White House. Neither Congress nor the President of the United States offered to represent the Mormons in their cause. In fact, even though President Van Buren sympathized, he said, "Gentlemen, your cause is just, but I can do nothing for you. If I take up for you I shall lose the vote of Missouri" (*HC* III: 80; Richard L. Bushman, *Rough Stone Rolling*, 391–394; Glen M. Leonard, *Nauvoo, A Place of Peace*, 275–277).

Julia Hills Johnson wrote a letter to her sister Diadamia dated March 13, 1839, from Springfield, Illinois. She described the loss of Nancy, Seth, David, and Susan. "They were all taken from us within four years.

How shall, How can I express my feelings? 'But the Lord giveth and the Lord taketh away and blessed be the name of the Lord.'" She continued by pleading with Diadamia. "Study the scriptures the prophecies and then you will learn that the Lord in the last days will bring forth His work, His strange work, His act, His strange act, that truth shall spring out of the earth and righteousness shall look down from Heaven. That Zion will be builded, the Saints gathered.... Therefore, I will close by begging you to inquire into the truth of these things. Ask the Lord in sincerity to show you the right way" (Judy H. Cluff and Franklin K. Gibson, *Johnson Gems*, 23).

The letter to Ezekiel is fictional, as is the stress portrayed in Joe and Esther's relationship.

## CHAPTER 7

Emma Smith and her children occupied a room in the Cleveland home in Quincy. In the memoirs of Joseph III, he wrote that the Dimick Huntington family lived close by.

> One of the homes nearest to the Cleveland residence was a small one on the top of a gently rising hill. It was occupied by Dimick Huntington, his wife, and children.... I think Fannie was the oldest of the children and Allen next in age. He must have been two or three years older than I, for he was allowed to take his father's rifle and go out into the pasture and brush to look for rabbits.... We used to form quite a little band of players, ranging the farm at will. (Mary Audentia Smith Anderson, ed., "Memoirs of Joseph Smith, III," *Saint's Herald*, November 6, 1934)

He continued writing that his mother, Emma, did not feel that the Huntington boy, with his rifle, was a safe companion for her children and punished Joseph III several times until he obeyed her (*Memoirs of Joseph Smith, III*).

Joseph Smith arrived in Quincy and was reunited with Emma on April 22, 1839, after six months. Joseph Smith wrote, "I arrived in Quincy, Illinois, amidst the congratulations of my friends, and the embraces of my family, whom I found as well as could be expected, considering what they had been called to endure" (*HC* III:327). Dimick

Huntington was the first man to see Joseph. Albey's fictional witness of the poor, cloaked beggar is taken from Dimick Huntington's statement:

> I Dimick Huntington saw Joseph land from the Quincy ferry boat about 8 oc. in morning. He was drest in an old pair of boots full of holes, pants torn, tucked inside of boots, blue cloak with collar turned up, wide brim black hat, rim soped down, not been shaved for some time, looked pale & haggard. I Dimick rode down at the request of Emma to enquire the news if any, from the west. When I got with-in about 16 ft. of him he raised his head. I exclaimed My God is it you Bro. Joes. He raised his hand & stopped me saying Hush, Hush. He then asked where is my family. I told him they were 4 miles east at Judge Clevelands in a room. . . . On arriving at the house where his family was Emma knew him as he was dismounting from his horse. She met him half way to the gate. Joseph not knowing the universal friendly feelings that existed in Quincy, was fearful he might be arrested again. (Dimick B. Huntington statement, cited in Baugh, "We Took Our Change of Venue to the State of Illinois": Gallatin Hearing & the Escape of Joseph Smith and the Prisoners from Missouri. *Mormon Historical Studies*, Spring 2001)

Joseph and Emma's visit to Delcena's home was imagined. However, Joseph did help and support Delcena. When Benjamin visited Nauvoo, he found Delcena in "his [Joseph's] care, and that he provided for [her] comfort" (BFJ letter to George S. Gibbs, 1903). Delcena did stay in Quincy and then moved to Nauvoo, not Ramus, where most of her family resided. Joseph III also remembered going to school with "Widow Sherman['s]" children (*Memoirs of Joseph Smith, III*). During the Nauvoo period, Joseph Smith became Delcena's "proxy" husband. This meant that Delcena was a plural wife to Joseph Smith for time (mortality) and Delcena was sealed to Lyman Sherman for eternity (*MLR*, 85).

## CHAPTER 8

James Adams was an influential Illinois lawyer residing in Springfield and a close friend to the Prophet Joseph Smith. B. H. Roberts wrote, "Judge Adams treated the Prophet with all the kindness of a father, and became a most staunch and reliable friend during the remaining years of his [Adams] life." Joseph often stayed at the home of "General Adams" when he traveled through Springfield (B. H. Roberts. *CHC* II:29). James Adams lived in Springfield at the time of his conversion, maintaining his home there and often visiting Nauvoo until his death in 1843. He served in the military (and was sometimes referred to as "General"), as an attorney, justice of the peace, and probate judge and unsuccessfully ran for governor of the state of Illinois. He was also influential in promoting the practice of Freemasonry in the LDS Church (Leonard, 314).

The interactions between Benjamin and the young widow, sister-in-law of Benjamin's employer Charles Lamb, are found in *My Life's Review*:

> While in Mr. Lamb's employ, associated with his family my vanity was at least a little flattered . . . by the partiality of a rich young widow who lived with and was sister to Mrs. Lamb. She was married very young, but had one child, and was the relict of Secretary of State [George Forquer], who had died the year previous. I had often to attend them in their carriage, the finest equipment in the city, and I could feel I was not indifferent to her." (48)

On May 4–6, the first general conference since the Prophet had returned from Liberty Jail was held near Quincy. On the first day of the conference, Almon was "appointed to a traveling committee to gather up and obtain all the libelous reports and publications which have been circulated against our church" (*HC* III:345). On May 5, during the second day of the meeting, he was called instead to go to Springfield to strengthen the Church there (*HC* III:346). It is most likely that Joseph received information, possibly from Almon himself, between the two meetings that facilitated the change of his assignment.

## CHAPTER 9

After school closed, Joe and Micham set out to claim land in Iowa (just across the river from Commerce). On the way, they visited Joel and Annie in Carthage and most likely stopped in Commerce (Nauvoo). Joe prepared medicines and nursed some of the people who had malaria. He later contracted the fever, and when Joel found out his younger brother was seriously ill, he crossed the river to Iowa and brought Joe to his home to be cared for (Rufus Johnson, 70).

Benjamin explained why he chose to end the relationship with Mrs. Forquer:

> Her little boy just commencing to talk, almost stole my heart whether his mother did or not. She was reputed very rich—a millionaire, and I felt very sure I could win her if I would, especially after I had ~~heard~~ overheard a conversation between her and her sister, who did not appear to favor her partiality for me.
>
> I pondered the matter prayerfully, and I could not but feel that to marry a woman with wealth would be to bind myself to the world, and would keep me from my mission, and if allured away from my calling in the gospel, then all the new and bright hopes that had waked within me would become a failure; and I felt it would be a sacrifice too great even for a lovely wife with inheritance of wealth. (*MLR*, 48–49)

It is not recorded that Joel was actually witness to the meeting of Joseph Smith, the Twelve, and some of the Seventies on July 2, 1839. The words in the text of the chapter are quoted from the meeting as recorded by the Prophet Joseph. Many of those present were about to depart on their mission "to Europe, and the nations of the earth, and the islands of the sea" (*HC* III:382).

Although, medication—quinine—was limited at this time, it is fictional that Ezekiel sent quinine to Nauvoo.

## CHAPTER 10

Joe returned to Springfield when he was well enough to travel. He described the joyful reunion with his mother, "who embraced me with tears of joy, this having been the longest absence from her presence that I ever suffered. O! how I had missed her! Under her watchful care I soon became convalescent" (Rufus Johnson, 70). It is not known exactly when he moved to the Sniders', but he went within the time frame of this chapter and began a courtship with Harriet. "Between the daughter and myself an acquaintance soon sprang up . . . and nothing intervened to hinder our often meeting and reunion. When sick, her lavishing and tender care won upon my sympathies and we were mutually betrothed" (71).

Benjamin chose to go back to Nauvoo, arriving just three days after "Mother Huntington died." The Huntingtons contracted malaria in late June, and Mother Huntington died on July 8, 1839 (Bradley and Howard, *4 Zinas*, 104).

Benjamin remained friends throughout his life with Zina Huntington, a "mutual attachment . . . with hopes [in Far West], which although not realized in full did not hinder our being ever the warmest and truest of friends" (*MLR*, 47).

Benjamin's experiences in nursing the sick, working with the physicians Wiley and Pendleton, contracting the illness, watching for the Robison girls, becoming engaged to Lucinda Morgan, being asked by the Prophet Joseph to nurse him, and then going with him to heal the sick are written in *My Life's Review* (49–51). In Ben's final words about this time of sickness and healings, he testified, "The Prophet then visited . . . places full of the power of God, healing the sick, as has been heretofore written in his life, all of which with many other things I know to be true, for I was with him as a younger brother and companion much of the time" (51). Other details of these miraculous healings are found in *HC* IV:4–5.

## CHAPTER 11

The opening scene of the playful writing contest in Joe's schoolroom is fictional but based on an album book (1839–1846) of Joseph Ellis Johnson. Nancy Carroll, Nancy Ann Vance, and Sylvia Carter did attend school in Springfield, and their poems are factual. Rufus Johnson stated that Harriet had "inscribed two long poems . . . 'Forgive and Forget' and 'Where Is She?' but does not include the words" (Rufus Johnson, 64–67). The verses for these two poems were not written by Harriet but created by the author in this chapter for the purpose of strengthening the romance between Harriet and Joe.

In *Times and Seasons*, John P. Green described the meeting on Monday, September 9, 1839, in Kirtland, Ohio, when Oliver Granger had addressed the members of the Church still living there. Green said, "People listened with attention; the tears of many, and the deep anxiety manifested, bespoke the impressions making on many hearts" (*Times and Seasons 1*, no. 2, December 1839). The close of Granger's speech, as fictionally written in Chapter 11, included the actual counsel given by the Prophet in the previous conference on May 4, 1839: "To the brethren living in the Eastern States [the advice] is, for them to move to Kirtland and the vicinity there of, and settle that place as a Stake of Zion; provided they feel so inclined, in preference to their moving farther west" (*HC*

III:345). In that conference, Granger was instructed to go to Kirtland to oversee the general affairs of the Church there. Babbitt was sent to Springfield. This "advice" for those in Kirtland must have provided hope and security for the families who chose to stay.

Benjamin recorded that Julia and Mary wrote a letter to him saying they were ill and anxious for him to return to Springfield. Because the actual letter no longer exists, the text of the letter in the novel was fictionally created. Benjamin had been in Nauvoo for two months, had spent the money saved for his mission to England, had ruined his best clothing, and was feeling very "worn, sick, poor, and sad." The playful "scuffle" with the Prophet, Ben's weakness and tender emotions, and the comforting blessing that "an Angel should go with me and protect me" are recorded in *My Life's Review* (51). He did return home ill and moved in with the Sniders.

The details of Benjamin's illness at the Sniders' and his decision not to leave to England with Brigham Young and Wilford Woodruff are recorded in *My Life's Review* (52–53). Brigham Young and Heber C. Kimball, both ill and unfit to travel, arrived in Springfield on October 5, 1839, "where they were kindly treated and nursed" (*HC* IV:11). Benjamin explained that "when they saw how sick I was, and without money or suitable clothing they did not urge me to go but left it to my own faith and desire." He desired to go but "feared" and lacked the confidence, and because "they would feel me a burden I had not faith enough to start. They told me to take a mission east as soon as I was able, and this I was determined to do" (*MLR*, 52–53).

A letter from Elder Almon Babbitt did appear in the December 1839 issue of *Times and Seasons* and was written on October 18, 1839, in Pleasant Garden, Putnam Co., Indiana. It was written to D .C. Smith and E. Robinson. Babbitt reviewed his missionary experiences (which are included in this chapter) after leaving Springfield in September. He reported over thirty-three meetings and ten baptisms (five prior to arriving in Pleasant Garden and five in Pleasant Garden).

## CHAPTER 12

The Laws may have been traveling through Pleasant Garden on their way to Springfield just prior to Julianne and Almon's departure for Kirtland, thus making it possible (but not recorded) that they stopped to visit. In their fictional conversation, Almon's feelings of rebuilding Kirtland were reflected. "It is clear from Babbitt's continued insistence that Kirtland be developed, that this was his Zion; that he loved it in manifold ways, and that he believed everyone else should love it too" (Whitman & Varner, 31).

Joseph Smith did leave for Washington DC, traveling in a two-horse carriage on Tuesday, October 29, 1839, with Sidney Rigdon, Elias Higbee, and Orrin P. Rockwell to seek redress from the federal government for the "grievances of the Saints while in Missouri." They met William Law's company one mile from Springfield and, as reflected in the chapter, "put up with Brother John Snider" (*HC* IV:17). The Laws had known the Sniders in Canada.

December 3, 1839, a letter from the First Presidency and High Council in Nauvoo was printed in *Times and Seasons*, indicating a changing vision in gathering the Saints. They wrote to those who lived westward of Kirtland, as Almon read in the chapter: "Should any be so unwise as to move back there, without being first counseled so to do, their conduct will be highly disapprobated" (*HC* IV:45). Julianne's voice and understanding of the process of gathering to Nauvoo offers balance to Almon's focus on rebuilding Kirtland.

Although Joel's letter to his mother is fictional, his son Nephi remembered that Joel furnished lumber for the Carthage Jail. It is factual that Carthage Jail was under construction during the time that Joel lived in the area.

Almon supported the Equal Rights Party, or "Locofocos," a splinter group of the Democratic Party during the 1830s and 1840s. They valued trade and greater circulation of specie but opposed paper money, financial speculation, and state banks. Almon's collection of bank notes may have been related to his personal political leanings. Benjamin witnessed Babbitt's purchase of these notes (*MLR*, 76).

Four months after Young and Kimball left Springfield, Benjamin began to feel that he needed to leave on his mission. As reflected in the chapter, he struggled with confidence but found the courage and left with only a few items and the money his brother Joseph E. had given him (*MLR*, 53–55). In his own words, he described the following experience from his mission: "When the congregation came I opened the meeting as best I knew how and arose with my eyes shut and commenced to talk. The spirit to talk came upon me and I preached one hour and a half as I was told afterwards, with my eyes tight shut. . . . A number now came forward for baptism, and here I baptized my first convert" (*MLR*, 55).

Joel's conversation with Sixtus refers to the disappointing outcome of Joseph Smith's visit with President Van Buren in Washington D.C. (*HC* IV:80). Sixtus's story about the Prophet Joseph is found in the following: "While quite small we moved to Illinois. . . . One day while I was chopping wood, two cocks are fighting nearby. . . . Prophet Joseph Smith, came by, stopped to chat, took an ax and chopped the wood. When handing me the ax, he said, 'my boy, I would rather chop wood any day than fight'" (David E. Johnson, *Leaves from the Family Tree of Sixtus Ellis Johnson 1829–1916*, 143).

## CHAPTER 13

Benjamin determined to save Dr. Knights from killing "the young doctor" and "saw that something must be done to deter him." They left for Kirtland to join the Babbitts (*MLR*, 57–58). The story of Knights' fury and homicidal rage is based upon Benjamin's recollections, although some details of the story have been altered (55–58). Benjamin received a letter during this time from Lucinda, telling him she had married another man. Benjamin described his feelings, "Those who in early life have been too roughly awakened from a dream of happiness need not be told of the influence of such a disappointment upon an organization like mine. I concluded to go with the doctor . . . and was, with all my idols broken, ready for a start" (*MLR*, 59).

Even though the scene with Melissa LeBaron witnessing Almera's fall is fictional, it is possible, although not documented, that Benjamin met her in Kirtland before continuing on his mission to Canada. The fictional details of Almera's abusive marriage are loosely based upon information in Benjamin's record. "And so . . . visiting my father and my sister Almera, who had married a man in no way worthy of her (and who, when his wrongs were told me I went for, but he left quick, or I would have thrashed the earth with his bones)" (*MLR*, 60). Almera separated from her husband at this time and traveled to Nauvoo with the Babbitts.

## CHAPTER 14

The Johnson family settled in Ramus, located eight miles northeast of Carthage and twenty miles southeast of Nauvoo. It was an important settlement of the Church in Illinois. Joseph Smith visited Ramus often, and two of his sisters, Catherine and Sophronia, lived there.

Almon's reaction to and perspective of the problems in Kirtland during the spring and summer of 1840 are fictionalized but pieced together from historical records to provide possible reasons and an interpretation of the accusations, Church actions, and conflicting reports. Almon and Julianne occupied Joseph and Emma's home in Kirtland in 1841 (*MLR*, 76). It is not known when they moved in, but they were possibly living there in 1840.

Oliver Granger was trusted by the Prophet and was Babbitt's greatest critic during this transitional time. The accusations in the text are based upon a letter Granger wrote Joseph Smith on June 23, 1840 (Whitman and Varner, 32–33; *HC* IV:164–165).

In July, Joseph Smith replied to Oliver Granger. He expressed surprise that "a man having experience which Brother Babbitt has had, should take any steps whatever, calculated to destroy the confidence of the brethren" (*HC* IV:165). He continued in his concern that Elder Babbitt and other brethren wished "to reform the Church" and direct others to Kirtland "instead of to this place" and informed Granger that it was "resolved that fellowship should be withdrawn from Babbitt until he makes satisfaction for the course he has pursued." Granger did notify Almon of this and "demand[ed] his license" as directed by the letter (166–167).

Before finding out about the Church action, the Babbitts, Dr. Knights, and Benjamin traveled to Canada. Benjamin continued on his mission in Canada, and the others returned to Kirtland. After arriving, Almon learned he was disfellowshiped and immediately left for Nauvoo with Julianne, Almera, and Dr. Knights (*MLR*, 60). Almon faced the High Council in Nauvoo on September 5 and 6, which is documented in the *History of the Church*:

> Council adjourned till the 6th September, at 2 o'clock, when Council met according to adjournment, the evidences were all heard on the case pending, and the councilors closed on both sides. The parties spoke at length, after which, Joseph Smith withdrew the charge, and both parties were reconciled to each other, things being adjusted to their satisfaction. (IV:187–188)

Joseph not only withdrew the charges during Almon's time in Nauvoo but also called him as a high priest and involved him in multiple leadership opportunities (*HC* IV:206; Whitman & Varner, 33). The doctrine of baptism for the dead began to be practiced during this period (Leonard, 238).

Annie died on September 11, 1840, after struggling with fever and chills. Her dreams, words of comfort from the Lord, and counsel for Joel to take a new spouse are quoted almost word for word from her husband's autobiography (JHJ, 25). The verses at the end of the chapter are from two original poems Joel wrote about her (25–26).

## CHAPTER 15

Joseph Smith Sr. died in Nauvoo three days after Annie passed away. Although it is not recorded, it is probable that some of the Johnsons attended Smith's funeral. The words in this chapter spoken at his funeral by Elder Robert B. Thompson are taken from the speech in *History of the Church* (IV:191–197).

The trust the Nauvoo leadership had in Almon is accurately portrayed in this chapter. In general conference on Saturday, October 3, Almon was called as stake president in Kirtland and also directed to organize stakes between Nauvoo and Kirtland. He opened the Sunday meeting of October conference with prayer. On Monday morning, an article on the priesthood, composed by President Joseph Smith was read, "after which Elder Babbitt delivered an excellent discourse on the same subject, at considerable length" (*HC* IV:206).

The Prophet Joseph Smith married Joseph and Harriet on October 6, 1840, in Nauvoo. Family tradition suggests that it was the first marriage ceremony the Prophet performed in Nauvoo. However, there is no documentation of this. Wilson Law acted as "groomsman" for Joe, and William Law and John C. Bennett were also in attendance (Rufus Johnson, 72–73). Joe, Harriet, and Julianne did have a narrow escape from drowning the day after the wedding as represented in the chapter. The "passers by [who] came to their assistance" are not known; however, Anson Call lived in the area, and George Wilson provides fictional opportunity for interaction with Mary (Rufus Johnson, 73).

Susan and Joel were married on October 20, 1840, a little over a month after Annie died. Joel simply wrote, "I took to wife by marriage Miss Susan Bryant. . . . (She assisted in taking care of my former wife through her sickness)" (JHJ, 26). Almon Babbitt officiated in the wedding ceremony.

## CHAPTER 16

The mistake in the *Times and Seasons* regarding Joe and Harriet's marriage is factual: "In this town [Nauvoo] by Pres't Joseph Smith, Jr. Mr. Ben Johnson, married to Harriet Snider" (October 1840). Don Carlos Smith was an editor of the newspaper. The background information concerning

Nauvoo in this chapter is taken from "A Proclamation of the First Presidency of the Church to the Saints Scattered Abroad, Greeting" (*HC* IV:268–273), actually written January 15, 1841.

Although the date is not exactly known, Almon Babbitt did attend law school in Cincinnati (Whitman & Varner, 19, 206). Julia's siblings did live in the area. Nancy Taft (Julia's sister) was in Cincinnati, Ohio, and Joel Hills (older brother) and his family lived across the river in Newport, Kentucky. Although the scenes with Caroline Hirst and her husband are fictional, the information regarding their ages and that they resided in Indiana is accurate.

It is not known where Almon heard the revelation when he was chastised for having set up "a golden calf" (D&C 124:84), but it was given prior to his return to Kirtland as stake president. Benjamin provided insight into his response. "He felt hurt by the rebuke . . . and he was in great temptation to complain " (*MLR*, 76).

Discussion of Sharp's Whig newspaper, the *Warsaw Signal*, is found in Leonard's, *Nauvoo: A Place of Peace, A People of Promise*. He said, "Much of the public opposition to the Latter-day Saints in western Illinois grew out of the rhetoric created by politicians and the political press" (304). The accusation that Church leaders were using "moral power for political ends," in the fictional discussion between Hirst and Babbitt, are the actual words of an article written by Sharp in January 1841 (305).

The cornerstones of the Nauvoo Temple were laid on April 6, 1841, the "first day of the twelfth year of the Church of Jesus Christ of Latter-day Saints!" (*HC* IV: 326). The description of the Nauvoo Legion, the laying of the cornerstones, and general optimism are consistent with historical records (*HC* IV:326–330; Leonard, 112–119).

Judge Stephen Douglas, who later ran for president against Abraham Lincoln, "invested Babbitt with his Illinois license" (Whitman & Varner, 43). Although it is not known exactly when and how Douglas signed Almon's license, Judge Stephen Douglas did visit Nauvoo in the spring of 1841 (Leonard, 294–295).

Although the conversation with Judge Adams is fictional, Babbitt returned to Kirtland as stake president. The prophet wrote a letter to Oliver Granger on July 26, 1841: "I should be glad if you would cooperate with Elder Babbit [sic] and both lay your shoulders to the work, and if you do so I think you will be a blessing to the Church, and prosperity will Smile on you" (Whitman & Varner, 35).

## CHAPTER 17

Although Benjamin did record that Esther returned to Kirtland, the exact details of her journey back to Kirtland and reunion with her father are fictional (*MLR*, 72). Almon's appointment as stake president and his speech about baptism for the dead, as presented in the chapter, were taken from the minutes of the "general conference" in Kirtland on May 22, 1841 (Kirtland Elders Quorum Minutes).

Delcena and Don Carlos's meeting is fictional, but their conversation factually reflects Joseph Smith's travel to Quincy, the arrest at Heberlin's Hotel, Missouri's efforts to extradite him to face an old charge, and Stephen Douglas's assistance in freeing him (*HC* IV:364–365). The court case and Judge Douglas's fining the sheriff are as presented in the *History of the Church* (IV:366–369).

On Sunday, October 3, Almon did speak about "the gathering" (Kirtland Elders Quorum Minutes). However, the words of his speech were not included in the minutes but were fictionally created to be consistent to the general theme of Almon's desire to rebuild Kirtland.

Almon was prospering in Kirtland and "proposed that we [Benjamin and he] buy together a small law library" (*MLR*, 77).

Almera's letter to Julianne is fictional but tells the news of the family and of Don Carlos Smith's death, as recorded by the Prophet Joseph Smith (*HC* IV:393–399).

## CHAPTER 18

Hyrum's letter to the Saints in Kirtland, recorded in *The History of the Church* was written after he and Joseph received the minutes of the October 1841 Kirtland conference, which "constituted a company to establish a press in Kirtland, and publish a religious paper, entitled *The Olive Leaf*" (VI:443). Hyrum's letter stated that these pursuits were not of the Lord and called all to gather in Nauvoo (443). Details of Almon's reaction are based upon Benjamin Johnson's record: "Br. Babbitt now saw that he would be broken up in business. . . . He was in great temptation to complain, and to turn his heel upon the Prophet. . . . He had bought many notes and claims against the prophet or the Church, and with these be tempted to do a great wrong to himself, and such was my love for him that I felt to make any sacrifice to promote his love for the gospel and his fellowship in the Church" (*MLR*, 76–77).

Melissa and Benjamin were married Christmas Day by Almon in "the house in which the Prophet lived in Kirtland" (*MLR*, 76). He describes, "The only thing worthy of note, besides festivity and general mirth was the division of the company into separate rooms. The married people now claimed us now, which was disputed by the unmarried, who insisted, that as bride and groom we still belonged to them. Each party laid hold of me to make good their claim, and before they knew it they had pulled me speechless, and really came near killing me with their kindness. So we were at liberty to enjoy and be enjoyed by both as suited us best" (*MLR*, 76).

*The Girl's Own Book,* first published in 1834 by L. Maria Child, reviews and explains the preservation and care of roses in a section entitled "To Preserve Roses Till Christmas" (249). Although filling the house with white roses on the wedding day is fictional, the book was available to the young girls in Ohio and Illinois.

Ben and Almon did go into business together in Ramus. Although it is not factually known who had the idea of the business, Benjamin explained, "Br. Babbitt had bought a fine stock of merchandise with which to start business, and as the brea[k] at Kirtland had complicated him financially, and wishing to associate our business, by the power of attorney all transactions were in my name" (*MLR*, 81).

The scene where Ezekiel decides to move to Nauvoo on his birthday is fictional. However, he did leave Kirtland to travel and move to Illinois with Benjamin, Melissa, Julianne, and Esther.

## CHAPTER 19

Mary Ellen Johnson and George D. Wilson posted their intentions of marriage February 2, 1842, and were married on February 7, 1842 (Rolla V. Johnson, comp., *Johnson Pioneers of the West,* 112).

Delcena; her mother-in-law, Asenath Sherman; and her sisters-in-law, Cornelia and Electa were voted as members of the newly organized Relief Society in early April (Nauvoo Relief Society Minutes, 28) and most likely attended the meeting on April 28 and heard the Prophet instruct the sisters. "He [Joseph Smith] said . . . that he did not know as he should have many opportunities of teaching them—that they were going to be left to themselves—that they would not long have him to instruct them—that the church would not have his instruction long" (37).

At this time, there were incidents and accusations that John Bennett and others were preaching that "illicit sexual intercourse was acceptable [to the Lord] if kept secret," as suggested by Delcena in the fictional scene with John Bennett and her discussion with Joseph Smith (Bushman, 460). Although Delcena did not actually speak to Sister Miller, on May 20, 1842, Chancy L. Higbee was charged with having taught "the doctrine" to the widow Miller (Fred C. Collier, ed., *The Nauvoo High Council Minute Books*, 56) In the *Nauvoo High Council Minute Books*, on May 25, 1842, a charge was brought forth against Mrs. Catherine Warren for "unchaste and unvirtuous conduct with John C. Bennett and others . . . stating that they taught the doctrine that it was right to have free intercourse with women" (Collier, ed., 57–58). Bushman, in *Joseph Smith, Rough Stone Rolling* said, "It was a nightmare for Joseph to have his carefully regulated celestial marriages debased into a device for seducing the unsuspecting" (460).

The story of Joseph coming to give Susan her medicine is taken from an account written by Susan's husband, James Henry Martineau: "While Widow Sherman lived in Nauvoo, Joseph Smith came to see her, while Susan, her little daughter (my wife) was sick and bribed the child to take some medicine by promise of a plate with letters around the edge, as she sat upon his lap" (Donald G. Godfrey and Rebecca S. Martineau-Mccarty, ed. 559–560).

Benjamin wrote of Amos's death after his arrival in Ramus: "There had come another bereavement, another wave of sorrow for us all as a family. Our youngest brother, Amos P. who had always been delicate, and had suffered from sciatic rheumatism through nearly the whole period of my absense, had died but a few weeks previous to my return. He was bright and most loveable, and being the youngest was the darling of my poor mother whose loving heart had so often been made to bow to the sorrows of bereavement. He was born Jan. 15, 1829 and died May 9$^{th}$ 1842, in his fourteenth year" (*MLR*, 80).

Although the conversation of Frank Hills and Almon in Cincinnati is fictional, the information about the attempted murder of the Missouri governor Lilburn Boggs, including John Bennett's accusations against Joseph Smith, is accurate. Porter was in Independence to take his wife to her parents until she gave birth to their fourth baby at the time Boggs was shot. "If Rockwell was innocent, as the best evidence suggests, his efforts to care for the needs of his pregnant wife had put him in the wrong place at the wrong time" (Leonard, 280). Both Smith and Rockwell were charged with the attempted murder of Boggs.

Benjamin's conversation with the Prophet Joseph Smith about Almon is taken directly from his recollection and writing of the experience. Many of the conversation's words in the chapter are exactly as Benjamin recalled (*MLR*, 80–81).

On June 18, 1842, as recorded in Wilford Woodruff's journal, "Joseph Smith the Seer aroused and spoke his mind in great plainness concerning the iniquity, hypocrisy, wickedness and corruption of General John Cook Bennett" *(HC* V:34).

The content of the Prophet's speech in this chapter is taken from an address the Prophet Joseph wrote [possibly the same one he delivered a few days earlier] and published on Thursday, June 23, as recorded in the *History of the Church* (V:34–38).

CHAPTER 20

Almera lived with Benjamin and Melissa in Ramus. Benjamin and Almon met with the Prophet to resolve the Kirtland issue: "We found Br. Joseph in a happy mood and glad too see Br. Babbitt, and when business matters were brought forward relating to notes bought from outsiders against him or the church, br. Joseph said to him, 'Now, brother Almon, we will not disagree, for here is Br. Benjamin; you have all confidence in him and so have I; and now let us leave all our differences to him and stand by it, and be good friends forevermore,' to which Br. Babbitt agreed. All was settled at once." (*MLR*, 81).

Although Benjamin doesn't give a specific date, this meeting probably took place on June 25, 1842, when the Prophet Joseph Smith wrote, "Transacted business with . . . Mr. Babbitt, and sat for a drawing of my profile to be placed on a lithograph of the map of the city of Nauvoo" (*HC* IV:44). Joseph most likely was dressed in his uniform as Lieutenant General of the Nauvoo Legion, which is what he is wearing in the likeness printed on the early map of Nauvoo (Dean C. Jessee. *The Papers of Joseph Smith*, vol. 2, 391–392). The Prophet did ask Benjamin to act as "trustee or agent for the Church Property" in Ramus. "He [Joseph Smith] then made and executed to me a power of attorney to use his name in buying, selling, and deeding property; which power I held and acted upon fully until the day of his martyrdom" (*MLR*, 81).

The scene of Almon helping the elderly woman witness the proxy baptism is fictional. However, the ordinance of baptism for the dead was performed during this time at the temple, even though the temple was not yet completed. After the laying of the cornerstones in 1840, the most urgent need was to build a temporary font for proxy baptisms. Foundational walls were built near the east end of the basement level. A thirty-foot-deep well was sunk to provide water. Elijah Fordham made ornamental moldings and carved twelve oxen out of pine. When completed, Brigham Young dedicated it for use on November 8, 1841 (Leonard, 250–251).

It is fictional but possible that Almon collected affidavits concerning John Bennett, because the prophet organized "corps of missionaries going out to counteract John Bennett's charges and saw to the publication of affidavits attesting to Bennett's corruption" (Bushman, 475). Almon was involved in the political and legal issues of this tumultuous period and was most likely present for much of what happened (Whitman & Varner, 43).

Bennett wrote a series of articles about Joseph Smith's followers from July to September for the *Sangamo Journal* (Bushman, 462). Bennett claimed that the Mormons were fanatics, and as Bushman, in *Rough Stone Rolling*, explained, "fanatics always forced their beliefs on the rest of the world and exterminated anyone who resisted" (465). He called for "fellow citizens" to come together, destroy the Mormons, and "crush the reptile before it has grown powerful enough to sting them to death" (465).

The political backdrop, the attempt to extradite Joseph to Missouri, and the account of the court held in Springfield are historically accurate and come from several sources: *History of the Church*, *Rough Stone Rolling*, and *Nauvoo: A Place of Peace, A People of Promise*. Adams did refer to the Prophet as "Son" and reassured Joseph that he would be discharged in facing charges in Springfield (*HC* IV:206).

Although not recorded, it is possible that Almon was present for the "Rocky Mountain Prophecy." A number of brethren were present, but names were not given. Anson Call was the only one who reported the experience. Joseph's words in the chapter are not exact but are consistent with Anson's records (Gwen Marler Barney, *Anson Call and The Rocky Mountain Prophecy*, 99).

## CHAPTER 21

The name of the town of Ramus was changed to Macedonia in 1843 through the efforts of the Johnsons. Rufus Johnson wrote "that a charter for municipal government was obtained and that he [Joseph Ellis Johnson] assisted in getting it into operation. He was elected trustee for two successive years" and was postmaster and opened the first school. He also became the secretary to John Smith when he moved to Macedonia as Patriarch (Rufus Johnson, 73). The activities and involvement of the Johnsons in the town of Macedonia as represented in the chapter are fact.

Once Benjamin moved to Macedonia, "he [the Prophet] lodged in no house but mine, and I was proud of his partiality and took great delight in his society and friendship. When with us, there was no lack of amusement; for with jokes, games &, he was always ready to provoke merriment . . . matching couplets in rhyme" (*MLR*, 82). The Johnsons were called "The Royal Family" in Macedonia. "In Macedonia the Johnsons were quite numerous and influential and the envious dubbed us the 'Royal Family.' When Joseph heard of this <u>honor</u> conferred upon us by our neighbors, he said the [name] was and should be a reality; that we were a royal family; and he knowing the intemperance of my father said that he should yet be a great man and stand at the head of a kingdom" (*MLR*, 83).

The Prophet Joseph Smith arrived in Ramus/Macedonia on Saturday, March 11, and left in a snowstorm on Tuesday. He stayed with Benjamin during this time (*HC* V:302–303). Events recorded in *History of the Church*, *My Life's Review*, and other family records are reflected in the storyline as presented in this chapter. Joseph did preach Sunday morning, March 12, 1843, "taking for text $14^{th}$ chapter of John . . . and then stayed at Brother Benjamin F. Johnson's all night" (*HC* V:302–303).

The exact date of Mary's healing and Julia's blessing from the Prophet Joseph are not known, but both are recorded in family histories. The Prophet heard that Mary was "gravely ill" and not thought to live. He came and gave her a blessing, promising that she would bear a son (Rufus Johnson, 113). The blessing that Julia received from the Prophet was also recorded: "In blessing Julia he made a promise to her. . . . We have always understood that he promised that when she should receive her ultimate reward 'not one of her jewels in her crown would be missing'" (70).

Joseph's throwing William Wall in a wrestling match, appointing Almon Babbitt as presiding elder, and blessing nineteen of the twenty-seven children present are recorded in the *History of the Church* (V:303). "In the evening meeting [Monday, 13] twenty-seven children were blessed, nineteen of whom I blessed myself, with great fervency. Virtue went out of me, and my strength left me, when I gave up the meeting to the brethren." Joseph Smith explained, "The virtue here referred to is the spirit of life; and a man who exercises great faith in administering to the sick, blessing little children, or confirming, is liable to become weakened" (302–303).

It is likely that the Johnson children were blessed at this time. Benjamin's recollection of this day, the blessing of his own baby son that evening at home, his personal time with the Prophet, and the words

Joseph spoke to Benjamin about his weariness and working beyond the veil are quoted or paraphrased from Benjamin's memory (*MLR*, 86–87).

## CHAPTER 22

Benjamin recorded, "Sometimes when at my house I asked him [Joseph Smith] questions relating to past, present, and future; some of his answers were taken by Br. Wm. Clayton, who was then present with him, and are now recorded in the Doc. & Covenants" (*MLR*, 82). It is not recorded but is possible that Julia was in Benjamin's home also. He recalled that one evening "he [the Prophet Joseph] wished to marry us according to the Law of the Lord. I thought it was a joke, and I should not marry my wife again, unless she courted me, for I did it the first time. He chided my levity, told me he was in earnest . . . and [we] were sealed by the Holy Spirit of Promise" (*MLR*, 86).

This is also recorded in the *History of the Church*. The Prophet, along with others, left May 16, 1843, for Ramus at three thirty in the afternoon. Joseph said that he "went to Benjamin F. Johnson's with William Clayton to sleep. Before retiring, I gave Brother and Sister Johnson some instructions on the priesthood." He then put his "hand on the knee of William Clayton" and made remarks included in D&C 131:1–4. These remarks may have been the "instructions" given to Ben and Melissa as they were sealed, that "a man must enter into this order of the priesthood, [meaning the new and everlasting covenant of marriage]" to obtain "celestial glory" (*HC* V:391–392; Robert C. Fillerup, comp. *William Clayton Diaries*, 42).

The next day, it is recorded that the Prophet dined at the Babbitts' with William Clayton and the Johnsons (*William Clayton*, 43). The conversation during dinner is fictional but accurately represents some of the issues facing the Church, as well as Babbitt's plans and his relationship at this time with the Prophet.

Although not specifically mentioned in the text, during this time, Julia was sealed to John Smith, and Almera was sealed to the Prophet. However, records indicate that both women continued to live with the Johnson family.

Information concerning Missouri's attempt to arrest and capture Joseph, the individuals involved, the political players and climate, and general information of this period in Nauvoo is correct, as found in various historical records, including Leonard's *Nauvoo: A Place of Peace, A People of Promise*, Bushman's *Joseph Smith: Rough Stone Rolling*, and *The History of the Church*. Almon's conversation with William Law is fictional but is based on their relationship and presents background information on Law's eventual turn against the Prophet Joseph.

## CHAPTER 23

The role Joseph and Hyrum Smith played in the election between Cyrus Walker, a Whig, and Joseph Hoge, a Democrat, is factual and was a significant cause of the anti-Mormon sentiment in the area (Bushman, 508–509). Both candidates, Walker and Hoge, wanted the Mormon vote, and contrary to "most expert legal opinion," both supported the Nauvoo Charter, authorizing the municipal court to issue writs of habeas corpus. This resulted in freeing the Prophet from extradition to Missouri (508). Joseph pledged his vote to Walker but then in conference shared Hyrum's revelation to vote for Hoge, swaying the expected outcome. The block vote went to the Democrat, Hoge. That perceived betrayal incited the Whig press, especially Thomas Sharp, and "nothing was too extreme to be charged against the Mormons" (509).

The October 1843 general conference was postponed on Friday, the sixth due to bad weather. On Saturday, Almon opened the meetings with prayer. The Prophet Joseph Smith brought charges against his first counselor, Sidney Rigdon. Joseph worried about a Missouri kidnapping attempt and suspected Rigdon of betraying him (Bushman, 510–511). Rigdon denied his involvement, gave answer to every account, and tearfully pled his case. He won the sympathy of Hyrum Smith, Almon Babbitt, and others. However, Joseph continued to question Rigdon's "integrity and steadfastness" (*HC* VI:49).

The following Monday, October 9, at two o'clock, "conference re-assembled, and listened with profound attention to an impressive discourse from President Joseph Smith, commemorative of the decease of James Adams, Esq." (*HC* VI:50–52). Joseph Smith's words in this chapter are taken from the longer and more doctrinal speech given.

"The Last Charge," in March 1844, is detailed in Truman Madsen's research and talk "The Life and Teachings of the Prophet Joseph Smith." This meeting was the climax of many that had occurred in a three-month period. Benjamin described the meeting:

> At one of the last meetings . . . after all had been completed and the keys of power committed . . . [he] said that the Lord

had now accepted his labors and sacrifices, and did not require him longer to carry the responsibilities and burden and bearing of this kingdom, and turning to those around him, including the 12, he said "And in the name of the Lord Jesus Christ I now place it upon you my brethren of this council, and I shake my skirts clear of all responsibility from this time forth," springing from the floor and shaking his skirt at the same time. (*MLR*, 89)

Wilford Woodruff, fourth president of the Church, at age ninety, was given the opportunity to record on a Graphophone. In his short testimony of Joseph Smith, he discussed being present at this meeting. He described Joseph Smith: "He was clothed with a power I had never beheld in any man in the flesh, his face shone like amber. The majesty of the glory of God was upon him. . . . His charge is still ringing in my ears" (Truman G. Madsen, http://www.believeallthings.com/1026/wilford-woodruffs-testimony-video/).

Almon Babbitt visited William Law in April of 1844, "requesting a reconciliation" (Lyndon W. Cook, *William Law: Nauvoo Dissenter*, 67). Law was angry about certain doctrines, specifically the eternal progression of man toward godhood, celestial marriage, and plurality of wives. The conversation created by the authors is consistent with some of the reasons for Law's disaffection, as outlined by Cook (62).

Almon Babbitt was a lawyer representing the Prophet Joseph during this critical time. In the *History of the Church* (VI:405–415), it states that on Saturday, May 25, 1844, Marshal John P. Greene and Almon Babbitt informed Joseph that there were two indictments against him. Babbitt counseled with Hyrum Smith, Edward Hunter, and others. It was "concluded not to keep out of the way of the officers any longer" and to face the charges in Carthage. The two charges were of "false swearing (perjury)" and "polygamy." Almon was in Carthage with the Prophet on Monday, May 27, and was one of Joseph's presenting lawyers. Although it is not known that Ezekiel was there, it is factual that there were incidents and threats by Joseph H. Jackson and others as the group of Mormon men arrived in Carthage. Joseph safely left Carthage and traveled back to Nauvoo, as described in the chapter.

The information and issues presented concerning *The Expositor* through conversation between Almon and Ezekiel are found in several sources (*HC* IV:412; Bushman, 538–39; *CHC*, II:485).

The Prophet Joseph Smith gave his final sermon in a torrential rainstorm in the grove just east of the temple. Delcena's presence at this sermon, as far as we know, is fictional, although it is very possible that she was there (*HC* VI:473–479; Bushman, 543–544).

CHAPTER 24

In this chapter, facts and information have been gathered from a variety of sources to tell the personal story of the Johnson family during the week of the martyrdom of Joseph and Hyrum. The dates reflect the known timeline of the events of that week (*HC* IV:504–622; Leonard, 380–418; Rufus Johnson, 84–90; Whitman & Varner, 46–50). The confusion, fear, and upheaval for the Johnson family and all Latter-day Saints that week, climaxing in the Carthage Jail on June 27, 1844, are consistent with how they were presented in the sources.

The Ramus Company of the Nauvoo Legion was called to defend Nauvoo on June 19, 1844. Almon, as captain, refused to lead the company. John Smith promised that none would be injured. When the company arrived at daybreak, the Prophet directed the quartermaster to furnish the men with shoes (*HC* IV:515). Benjamin stated, "We started, and to avoid attack traveled all night across the prairie through mud, rain, and darkness, terrible to those who were there. The Prophet [came] out to greet us" (*MLR*, 91).

Almon failed to obey the call to Nauvoo but later put his life at great risk to travel to Carthage to aid the Prophet. He rode with Joe to receive a letter from Governor Ford. Joe recorded: "At the period of difficulties in Hancock county I was residing in Macedonia (once Ramus) in the eastern portion of the county where the late Almon W. Babbitt also resided. The next day after the arrival of Governor Ford in Carthage, Bro. A. W. Babbitt asked me to go with him to Carthage and see the governor and if possible learn something of his intentions" (Rufus Johnson, 85–88). The chapter is consistent with Joe's recollection of the danger in Carthage, where Joe and Almon "had expected death" but were delivered from the "infuriated mob as a miracle" (86). In the *History of the Church*, Joseph Smith recorded, "Almon W. Babbitt arrived from Carthage this morning, having come at the request of the Governor, who thought it not wisdom to have . . . others of the City Council go to Carthage" (VI:528).

Emma's request for Almon's insight into Governor Ford's intentions is fictional. However, the information presented in this vignette is accurate, as found in letters by Ford to the Mormon leaders. Ford stated in a letter written June 22, 1842, "I am anxious to keep the peace. A small indiscretion may bring on a war. . . . I fear the militia when assembled, would be beyond legal control. . . . If you, by refusing to submit, shall make it necessary to call out the militia, I have great fears that your city will be destroyed, and your people many of them exterminated" (*HC* VI:536).

In this same letter, Ford gave his "guarantee" for "the safety of all" coming from Nauvoo either "for trial or as witnesses for the accused" (537).

It is factual that Almon and Joe accompanied the Prophet as he left Nauvoo for Carthage the morning of June 24 (Rufus Johnson, 88). Joe wrote: "When Gen. Smith was ready, we accompanied him until arriving near Carthage." Captain Dunn met them with orders requesting the state arms, which were used by the Nauvoo Legion. Almon and Joe did not return to Nauvoo with the rest of the group, including Hyrum and Joseph. They said good-bye. "Adieus were hastily said and we parted there—the last parting with these good and great hearted men who gave their lives to save their friends" (88). The details of this morning as portrayed in this chapter are consistent with the *History of the Church* (VI:553–558). Later that night, escorted by Captain Dunn, the Smith brothers arrived in Carthage and checked into the Hamilton Hotel, surrendering early the following morning (559–561).

John Smith visited his nephews at Carthage Jail at five thirty the night of June 26 and was told to inform Almon Babbitt that Joseph wanted him to assist as his attorney "at the expected trial tomorrow" (*HC* VI:598). It is recorded that John delivered the message to Almon and received the reply, as quoted in the chapter, "You are too late. I am already engaged on the other side" (600).

Some historians have interpreted Almon's statement to mean that he became a traitor to the Prophet. However, that conclusion is inconsistent with Almon's actions during this time. In piecing together all of the available records, his actions demonstrate a continued desire for the welfare of the Prophet Joseph Smith. Whitman and Varner, in their biography of Babbitt, proposed that the "other side" meant that he was working with the governor, believing that he could affect the Smiths' safety more quickly and effectively. They explain:

> Babbitt more likely meant that he considered himself to be engaged in behalf of Joseph Smith from the side of the state

legal system. . . . Babbitt may have felt he had a legal obligation to Ford, and that he would be working through the governor's office to help the Prophet, rather than counseling Joseph on the law in Carthage and filing affidavits and depositions. . . . In further support of this view, on the day of his death, June 27, 1844, Joseph Smith again asked Almon Babbitt to come to the Carthage jail. This does not seem to be the action of one who considered his attorney to be at odds with him. (49)

Almon was with Joseph and Hyrum at eleven-thirty that morning, just hours before they died. He delivered and read a letter from Oliver Cowdery to the Prophet, and then the Prophet wrote a quick note to the well-known lawyer O. H. Browning, who had defended him previously (*HC* IV:368–369), to request his services again. "Babbitt, again at great personal risk from the unstable mobs surrounding the jail, walked outside and gave the letter to [Dan] Jones" (Whitman and Varner, 49). His actions that day were not ones of a traitor but of a brother and friend, risking his own life. His granddaughter wrote that he fell upon his knees sobbing when he was notified that Joseph and Hyrum were dead, saying it was the hardest day of his life.

The actual message Willard Richards sent from Carthage Jail to Governor Ford, General Dunham, Colonel Markham, and Emma Smith, informing them of the martyrdom, is used in this chapter (Leonard, 398). It is not known whether Almon directly received the message of the deaths from Richards the next day. In Macedonia, "a Scottish immigrant remembered: 'The people wept outloud. One could hear the sobs and crying from every quarter. They felt as though the hosts of hell were let loose'" (Rugh, 44).

Benjamin's "feelings of woe and unutterable sorrow" and the reason for not going to view the bodies or "look into their grave" are as written in *My Life's Review*. His overwhelming emotion was, "Oh, God! What will thy orphan church and people do now?" (91). He also witnessed President Young's transformation. "Pres. Young arose and spoke. I saw him arise, but as soon as he spoke I jumped upon my feet for in every possible degree it was Joseph's voice, and his person, in look, attitude, dress and appearance was Joseph himself, personified." Benjamin continued. "I knew for myself who was now the Leader of Israel" (93). Although Benjamin did not record the date, it is recorded, in addition to other details, in the *History of the Church* (VII:229, 232–236).

## CHAPTER 25

The exodus from Nauvoo began in early February 1846. Brigham Young recorded that on the same day George A. Smith's family crossed the river, February 9, 1846, "the roof of the Temple was discovered to be on fire.... I saw the flames from a distance, but it was out of my power to get there in time to do any good towards putting out the fire" (*HC* VII:581). He continued to explain that lines were formed and the fire, caused by an overheated stovepipe, "raged near half an hour" (581). When he arrived, "after the fire had been extinguished, the brethren gave a loud shout of Hosannah, while standing on the deck roof" (581). Benjamin, Almon, and David LeBaron's involvement is not recorded but is very possible.

The information concerning Benjamin, the rumors of murders in Nauvoo, and the need for him to quickly leave with the first group of Saints due to an arrest warrant are from his own account (*MLR*, 94–97). Benjamin wrote of a conversation with Brigham, saying that President Young "asked my condition and I told him all. He said I must go, and told Br. Hyrum Bostwick one of my company, a man of means, to help me to an outfit" (*MLR*, 95).

The Saints continued working to finish the temple. Brigham Young described the prayer of the Twelve on February 8, 1846, prior to leaving Nauvoo. "We knelt around the altar, and dedicated the building to the Most High. We asked his blessing upon our intended move to the west; also asked him to enable us some day to finish the Temple, and dedicate it to him, and we would leave it in his hands to do as he pleased; and to preserve the building as a monument to Joseph Smith" (*HC* 7:280). The conversation between Brigham Young and Almon about the temple is fictional; however, Almon was elected to the legislature and became one of the three trustees overseeing Church property. Furthermore, Almon was given the charge to prepare the Nauvoo Temple for the final dedication upon completion. On April 31, 1846, Almon spoke for ninety minutes at the public temple dedication of "the inspired design of the Nauvoo Temple and of a temple even more glorious to be built in the tops of the mountains" (Leonard, 589).

Levi Williams was the leader of the anti-Mormon vigilante mob. There is strong evidence that he, in conjunction with Thomas Sharp, planned the attack on Carthage Jail (Dallin H. Oaks and Marvin S. Hill, *Carthage Conspiracy: The Trial of the Accused Assassins of Joseph Smith*, 38). After the martyrdom, Williams and his mob traveled through the countryside, destroying property and threatening the lives of Mormons living in the outlying communities. Leonard stated, "Church members living in settlements away from Nauvoo felt the brunt of resurgence of vigilante action. . . . Over several weeks, bands of old settlers led by the Warsaw regulator Colonel Levi Williams torched two hundred homes and farm buildings, plus mills and grain stacks" (525).

The plot of the chapter is consistent with family records. Joel and Susan were gone when the mobs came and threatened their children. Although it is not known that Sixtus ran to his grandfather's home for help, it is known that his grandfather was not far away, living in Macedonia. The mobs also came in the middle of the night on May 1 and told Joel, "If I did not leave the county by the first of June that my life would be taken and my property destroyed" (JHJ, 34). Joel's family moved in with Ezekiel in Macedonia for a short time until they left on May 31. "The night after I left an armed mob surrounded the house where they supposed that I was and called for me, but I had gone the morning before and saved them the trouble of killing me as they had anticipated" (34). Assuming that the home he left from was Ezekiel's, there could have been a confrontation of the mobs with Ezekiel, as written in this chapter.

It is factual that there was a confrontation between Ezekiel and "a company of soldiers. . . . Ezekiel heard of treachery on the part of the mob, and his anger knew no bounds. He swore by all the powers of good and evil that those soldiers should not come into the city Nauvoo that night" (Rolla V. Johnson, 33). In *Nauvoo: A Place of Peace, A People of Promise*, it explains that in late June, "several hundred armed volunteers led by Levi Williams of Warsaw marched toward Nauvoo to demand an immediate surrender and evacuation." However, because of some resistance at this time "the vigilantes considered their options and dispersed to their homes" (Leonard, 600–601). Although Leonard did not state that Ezekiel was involved in this resistance, it is likely that the confrontation occurred around this time.

"Ezekiel became a marked man" (Johnson, 34). He did live with Joel in Knox County for safety. Ezekiel did, at some point, return to Nauvoo, where he was stopped and whipped. Sixtus's son David Ellis Johnson stated, "I have heard my father, (Sixtus Ellis Johnson, son of Joel) tell of his grandfather, Ezekiel Johnson. He was there when Ezekiel was whipped by the mob which caused his death. I heard father and President Wilford Woodruff talk about it when I was only ten years old, but it made such an impression on me that I asked father about it when I was grown. . . .

Brother Woodruff said to father, 'I know your grandfather was one of the first martyrs to the cause of Christ in this dispensation'" (35).

Benjamin, having already started west, was not present at the death of his father. Almon brought the news to him as he was traveling to Winter Quarters. Ben wrote, "But with this great grief there was much consolation, for during the last year of his life he had ceased to use ardent spirits, and realized the great wrong he had done himself and family by his opposition; he knew the Gospel was true and had asked for baptism" (*MLR*, 108).

Some family members wrote that Ezekiel died on January 12, 1848, while others stated that he died on January 13. One record explained this discrepancy, stating that Ezekiel died around midnight on the night of January 12. January 12 was Ezekiel and Esther's birthdays, as well as the anniversary of Ezekiel's wedding to Julia.

The information regarding Ezekiel's temple work was provided in the family compilation *The Johnson Pioneers of the West* (Chapter 1, "Ezekiel Johnson, Boyhood and Marriage," by Rolla V. Johnson, 35) and the website "New Family Search."

After spending a brief time in Winter Quarters, Benjamin and Joel, with their wives and children, traveled to the Salt Lake Valley in 1848 with the Willard Richards Company. Joe and his family fled Nauvoo after the Battle of Nauvoo but remained in Winter Quarters (Council Bluffs) for many years. Following Ezekiel's death, the remainder of the family in Nauvoo removed to Winter Quarters. The Babbitts and the George W. Johnson family arrived in the Salt Lake Valley in 1851. Almon became the representative and secretary for the Territory of Utah. Almon was killed in an Indian raid in 1856, near Council Bluffs, while traveling to Washington D.C. Julianne died the following year, also in Council Bluffs, while on a trip to gather information about Almon's death.

Mother Julia passed away at Council Bluffs in 1853 surrounded by many of her children. Delcena and her children Albey and Susan, as well as Esther and her family, left the following year for the Valley. Delcena's other children died at Winter Quarters in 1850. Delcena passed away in October 1854, a few months after her arrival in Salt Lake City. For an extended time, Joe and William lived in the Council Bluffs area, aiding Saints in their migration west. In 1861, Joe and William, with their families, made the trek to Utah in the Sixtus E. Johnson Company. Almera, whose husband, Reuben Barton, had left the Church, joined this company and migrated to the Salt Lake Valley with her three daughters. Ezekiel and Julia's children colonized numerous areas in Utah and Arizona and were civic and Church leaders. They remained faithful members of The Church of Jesus Christ of Latter-day Saints throughout their entire lives. Ezekiel and Julia have one of the largest progenies in the Church today. (Information taken from family and Church records.)

# SELECTED BIBLIOGRAPHY

Barney, Gwen Marler. *Anson Call and the Rocky Mountain Prophecy.* Salt Lake City, UT: Call Publishing, 2002.

Black, Susan Easton, and Richard E. Bennett. *A City of Refuge: Quincy, Illinois.* Riverton, Utah: Millennial Press, 2000.

Berrett, LaMar C., Keith W. Perkins, and Donald Q. Cannon, eds. *Sacred Places, Ohio and Illinois: A Comprehensive Guide to Early LDS Historical Sites,* vol. 3 . Salt Lake City, UT: Deseret Book, 2002.

Berrett, LaMar C., and Max H. Parkin, eds. *Sacred Places, Missouri: A Comprehensive Guide to Early LDS Historical Sites,* vol. 4. Salt Lake City, UT: Deseret Book, 2004.

Bushman, Richard Lyman. *Joseph Smith: Rough Stone Rolling.* New York: Alfred A. Knopf, 2005.

Cluff, Judy H., and Franklin K. Gibson, comp. *Johnson Gems, A Small Collection of Writings and Stories Related to Benjamin Franklin Johnson.* Mesa, Arizona, 1996.

Collier, Fred C. ed., *The Nauvoo High Council Minute Books.* Hannah, UT: Collier's Publishing, 2005.

Cook, Lyndon W. "William Law: Nauvoo Dissenter," *BYU Studies 22,* Winter 1982.

Gardner, Loni, comp. *Benjamin Franklin Johnson: A Royal Legacy.* Provo, UT: Benjamin Franklin Johnson Family Organization, printed by Brigham Young University, 2010.

Hartley, William G. *My Best for the Kingdom: History and Autobiography of John Lowe Butler, a Mormon Frontiersman.* Salt Lake City, UT: Aspen Books, 1993.

Huntington, Oliver B. *History of the Life of Oliver B. Huntington: Also His Travels and Troubles Written by Himself.* L. Tom Perry Special Collections, Harold B. Lee Library, Brigham Young University.

Jessee, Dean C. ed. *The Papers of Joseph Smith*, vol. 2. Salt Lake City, UT: Deseret Book, 1992

Johnson, Benjamin F. *My Life's Review, Autobiography of Benjamin Franklin Johnson.* Provo, UT: Grandin Book Company, 1997 and Benjamin F. Johnson Family Organization, 1999.

Johnson, David E. *Leaves from the Family Tree of Sixtus Ellis Johnson 1829–1916*, Church History Library, 1955.

Johnson, George Washington. *Diary of George W. Johnson.* L. Tom Perry Special Collections, Harold B. Lee Library, Brigham Young University.

———. *Jottings by the Way.* St. George, UT: C. E. Johnson, 1882.

Johnson, Joel H. "A Voice from the Mountains," 1881.

———. *Diary of Joel Hills Johnson.* L. Tom Perry Special Collections, Harold B. Lee Library, Brigham Young University.

Johnson, Joseph Ellis. *The Papers of Joseph Ellis Johnson.* Special collections department of University of Utah Libraries.

Johnson, Rolla V., comp. *The Johnson Pioneers from the West. Records and Histories of Ezekiel—Julia Hills Johnson.* Published by the Johnson family.

Johnson, Rufus D. *JEJ Trail to Sundown, Casadaga to Casa Grande, 1817–1882, The Story of a Pioneer: Joseph Ellis Johnson.* Salt Lake City, UT: Joseph Ellis Johnson Family Committee, printed by *Deseret News* Press, 1961.

LeBaron, E. Dale. *Benjamin Franklin Johnson: Friend to the Prophets.* Provo, UT: Grandin Book Company, 1997.

Leonard, Glen M. *Nauvoo: A Place of Peace, A People of Promise.* Salt Lake City, UT: Deseret Book and Provo, UT: Brigham Young University Press, 2002.

Madsen, Truman G. http://www.believeallthings.com/1026/wilford-woodruffs-testimony-video/

Martineau, James Henry. *An Uncommon Pioneer: The Journals of James Henry Martineau 1828–1918.* Edited by Donald G. Godfrey and Rebecca S. Martineau-Mccarty. Provo, UT: Religious Studies Center, Brigham Young University, 2008.

Oaks, Dallin H., and Marvin S. Hill. *Carthage Conspiracy: The Trail of the Accused Assassins of Joseph Smith.* Urbana and Chicago, Illinois: University of Illinois Press, 1979.

Roberts, B. H. *A Comprehensive History of The Church of Jesus Christ of Latter-day Saints, Century I.* 6 vols. Provo, UT: Brigham Young University Press, 1965.

Rugh, Susan Sessions. *Our Common Country, Family, Farming, Culture, and Community in the Nineteenth Century Midwest.* Bloomington & Indianapolis: Indiana University Press, 2001.

Smith, George Albert. *History of George Albert Smith.* L. Tom Perry Special Collections, Harold B. Lee Library, Brigham Young University.

Smith, Joseph. *History of The Church of Jesus Christ of Latter-day Saints.* 7 vols. Edited by B. H. Roberts, Salt Lake City, UT: Deseret Book, 1980.

Whitman, Omer (Greg), and James L. Varner. *Neither Saint Nor Scoundrel: Almon Whiting Babbitt—Territorial Secretary of Utah.* Baltimore: Publish America, 2009.

Whitney, Orson F. *Life of Heber C. Kimball.* Salt Lake City, UT: Kimball Family, 1888.

# ABOUT THE AUTHORS

MARCIE GALLACHER, A GRADUATE OF Brigham Young University, has written four previous novels: *Amaryllis Lilies, Fixed Stars, Whispers of Hope,* and *Homeward.* Her publication credits include an article in the *Ensign* and stories in the *New Era* and *Friend.* She resides in Wilton, California, with her husband, Gray. They have four children: teenagers Brett and Michelle, who live at home with them; Matt, who is living in Provo, Utah; and Jamie, who is married to Jordan Cline. Her greatest joy is the time spent with her family, including her parents, Tal and LaRae Huber. She is also passionate about her stubborn horse, Dobbin; her rambunctious golden retriever, Rusty; and her perfect cats, Lancelot and Midnight. Marcie hopes to be a grandma someday!

KERRI ROBINSON, ALSO A GRADUATE of Brigham Young University, is a licensed clinical social worker. She is currently working part-time as a psychotherapist. She has also published in this field of study, including an article in *Helping and Healing Our Families: Principles and Practices inspired by "The Family: A Proclamation to the World."* Researching and writing, being a grandma, and attending BYU football games are her present passions. She and her husband, Brent, who live in Alpine, Utah, became empty nesters this year and treasure the time they spend with their blended family: the Freemans—Josh and Sarah, Erik and Catherine, Mark and Amy, and Ryan, and Cassidy; and the Robinsons—Andrea and Brady Nord, and Tim, Scott, and Julianne. Kerri's number of grandchildren will double from four to eight this year!

Marcie and Kerri are sisters and have found tremendous joy in this journey together!

Visit their website at www.abannerisunfurled.com or e-mail them at marcie@abannerisunfurled.com or kerri@abannerisunfurled.com.